WOLF UNTAMED

PAIGE TYLER

Published by Sourcebooks Casablanca, and imprint of Sourcebooks
P.O. Box 4410, Naperville, Illinois 60567–4410
(630) 961-3900
sourcebooks.com

Printed and bound in Canada.
MBP 10 9 8 7 6 5 4 3 2 1

With special thanks to my extremely patient and understanding husband. Without your help and support, I couldn't have pursued my dream job of becoming a writer. You're my sounding board, my idea man, my critique partner, and the absolute best research assistant a girl could ask for. Love you!

PROLOGUE

Dallas, Texas, October 2012

Officer Diego Miguel Martinez strapped the breaching ram into place along the inside wall of the Dallas PD SWAT operations truck, then stepped out into the torrential downpour, cursing as what felt like a frigging bucketful of freezing-cold rain found its way down the back of his coat. As much as he despised the long raincoat that was part of his uniform, he really should have worn it tonight. Behind him, someone chuckled, and he turned to see Officer Hale Delancy regarding him with a grin, blue eyes twinkling with amusement.

"I'm not complaining about the help, but if you're out in this monsoon much longer, you're going to start sprouting gills." Tall and heavily muscled with dark blond hair, the SWAT cop unloaded the M4 carbine he held, dropping the magazine and taking out the round in the chamber. "They had you securing the perimeter for what, four hours?"

Diego laughed. "Actually, it was closer to five, but who's counting?"

Perimeter duty was what patrol cops with barely three years on the force like him did while officers like Hale—one of his best friends in the department—and the other members of the SWAT team got to kick in doors and save lives. Tonight, Diego had stood and watched from the outside as four members of the Dallas Police Department's most elite unit had gone up against a deadbeat husband who'd gotten high as a kite and barricaded himself in his house with his three children. The man had threatened to kill the kids if the police didn't bring him more drugs. Because, according to him, everyone knew the cops had a lot of drugs locked up in their evidence room.

After hours of unsuccessful negotiations with a suspect who was quickly coming unglued, Hale and his three teammates had entered the house. While Hale and his SWAT buddies were all huge, they'd moved so quickly and quietly in the total darkness surrounding the property that Diego had never even seen them. One second, the father had been shouting he was going to end them all, and the next, SWAT was bringing the children out of the house, along with their handcuffed druggie dad.

It had been awe-inspiring to see and enough to finally convince Diego that he wanted to get into SWAT. He'd been thinking about it ever since running into Hale months ago during another hostage situation at a bank. He knew getting past the physical assessment exam at the SWAT compound would be tough as hell, but when had he ever let a challenge hold him back?

"Though if we're being honest," Diego added as he shook Hale's hand, "I was soaked to the bone after the first thirty minutes. The rest was just for fun."

Hale winced as he stepped in the vehicle and locked his weapon into the rack mounted on the wall. "Sorry it took us so long. We wanted to give our negotiator a chance to talk the guy down and get him to come out without a fight. Didn't go that way in the end, though. But at least those kids are safe. That's the important thing."

Diego didn't know the SWAT team's negotiator very well. All he knew was the guy was as big and jacked as

Hale, and he must have the patience of a saint to do that job. While Diego appreciated the man's conflict-resolution skills, there was no way in hell he could ever be a negotiator. Talking a person on a three-day meth bender off a metaphorical ledge wasn't his thing. Kicking in doors and saving a bunch of kids, on the other hand? Let's just say that deal had his name written all over it.

"Don't worry about it," Diego said as Hale came back out of the truck. "I knew tonight was going to be miserable the moment I saw the weather report this morning. I'd rather get soaked standing out here helping you and your team rescue those kids than handing out tickets to a bunch of doofuses for urinating in public."

Hale laughed, falling into step beside Diego as he walked along the street toward his patrol car. "Ah, the trials and tribulations of a beat cop in North Division on a Friday night. Can't honestly say I miss that stuff. The clubs along Harry Hines Boulevard still generating lots of calls?"

Diego snorted at the mention of the seemingly endless nightclubs around the intersection of Northwest Highway and Harry Hines, and how much time he spent in them when he was on duty. "A dozen fights every weekend, along with almost that many stabbings and at least one shooting a month, just like clockwork."

"Sounds like nothing's changed since I worked that beat." Hale stopped beside Diego's patrol cruiser and turned to look at him, thumbs hooked in his tactical vest as he regarded him from beneath his ballistic helmet. "I know you like being on the streets, but when are you going to take my advice and apply for one of the department's special units? Any of them would take you in a heartbeat."

Hale had been on his case for months to advance his career, and the best way to do that was to get out of patrol. Diego had already decided to try out for one of the specialized units, although maybe not the one Hale thought.

"Actually, I'm thinking about showing up for the next SWAT assessment test." He shrugged. "I figure, why not take a chance. What's the worst that can happen?"

Hale snorted. "You mean other than embarrassing yourself? Nothing at all."

Diego couldn't help laughing at the good-natured ribbing. "Ha-ha."

"Seriously, though," Hale added. "You have as much chance as anyone in the department of making it onto the team. I mean, it's a small chance, but it's still a chance."

Diego opened his mouth to make a crack about it obviously not being that difficult to get on the SWAT team if Hale had been able to do it, but the dispatcher's voice coming over the radio on his belt interrupted him. "Charlie 204, we have a possible disturbance in the ten thousand block of Harry Hines."

Diego threw Hale a long-suffering look, then keyed his mic, letting dispatch know he was on his way as he opened his car door. "I'll see you around," he said to Hale. "Be safe out there, huh?"

"You, too. I'll make sure you're on the list for the SWAT assessment coming up in two weeks. Don't do anything to screw it up."

Diego gave him a wave, turned on his wipers, and then pulled away from the curb, flipping on his lights and hitting the gas. The ten thousand block of Harry Hines Blvd. was dead center in the area he and Hale had been talking about.

You'd think on a rainy-ass night like this, people would stay home where it was warm and dry, but no such luck. If anything, crappy weather seemed to bring the morons in droves.

Diego turned the heat up, hoping to dry out a little before he got there, but it didn't help. His wet clothes clung to him like a second skin. Damn, he really needed to start keeping a backup uniform in the car. Especially if he wasn't going to wear that stupid raincoat.

Wipers moving back and forth rhythmically across the windshield, he sped along the highway, grateful when other drivers moved out of the way for him. Even without sirens, he made it to Harry Hines in less than eight minutes. Slowing, he thumbed his mic as he scanned the sidewalk.

"This is Charlie 204. I'm in the area of that disturbance. Do you have the location of the reporting party or description of the suspects?"

"Negative, Charlie 204," the dispatcher said. "The reporting party called from Cue Two saying there was a fight of some kind in the parking lot. Nothing further."

"10–4."

Diego wished he could say that wasn't the norm, but in reality, he rarely knew what the hell was going on when he showed up at a scene. More often than not, that was the way it worked. He showed up, asked questions, trusted his instincts, and figured things out as best he could.

He pulled up into the parking lot of Cue Two and parked alongside the curb near the entrance, watching as a few people ran for their cars through the pouring rain. The lot was nearly full, even on a night like this. That said a ton about the place, part pool hall and part dance club. People obviously liked coming here. But with good food and half-price drink specials, who could blame them, right?

Diego cut the engine, then stepped out of his patrol car into a puddle that could have been mistaken for a small pond. He cursed under his breath as cold water found its way into his patrol shoes, making his feet wetter than they already were. More than a few people eyed him warily when he walked into the club, no doubt assuming he was there to put a crimp on their fun. Ignoring them, he stood there, rain dripping off his uniform to splash on the floor as he swept the crowded room, trying to figure out why he was there. Between the deafening music, clacking of billiard balls, and people shouting to be heard as they tried to have conversations with one another, it was frigging loud as hell, but nothing seemed out of place.

That was when he saw the bartender waving him over. Despite the uniform and badge, it still took him nearly a minute to shove his way through the crowd to reach her. Tall and reed thin, she had wild, curly red hair and tons of freckles.

"You the one who called Dallas PD?" he asked, shouting to be heard over the noise. "Some kind of fight?"

She nodded, continuing to mix some concoction involving five different kinds of alcohol that didn't look like they'd taste great combined together. But to each their own, he guessed.

"It wasn't really a fight. It was something I saw that made me uncomfortable," the bartender yelled back. "Three women were at the bar drinking for a while and got a little tipsy, so I helped them order an Uber. When they went over to the door to wait, two rough-looking dudes started hitting on them." She paused mid-story to deliver her collection of drinks to the waitress standing impatiently at the bar. "It was obvious they were trying to convince the girls to leave with them, and just as obvious the girls wanted nothing to do with them."

"So, what happened?" he nudged.

She sighed. "I'm not sure, and that's the part that worried me. I turned my head for a minute, and when I looked back again, the women were leaving. A few seconds later, the two men walked out."

Diego could think of half a dozen different ways the scenario the bartender had described might have played out. And most of them didn't end well.

"I'm telling you, a shiver ran down my spine as those men walked out." The bartender shook her head. "Anyway, I finished up what I was doing and ran outside to make sure the girls were okay. I didn't see them, but I saw those two guys running down Harry Hines away from the club area. I couldn't tell for sure if they were chasing anyone, but it felt like they were up to no good, you know?"

Diego frowned. Of all the scenarios he'd envisioned, the guys chasing the three women down the street wasn't one of them. If something like that happened on any other night, there would have been twenty calls into 911. But tonight? It was extremely possible no one saw anything because they were too busy trying to get out of the rain.

"Can you describe the two men?" he asked.

Normally, he would have written down what the bartender told him, but his notebook was probably as drenched as the rest of him, so he didn't bother. He could remember two guys with dark hair between five-ten and six feet wearing jeans and T-shirts.

Giving the bartender a nod, he headed outside to his patrol car, glancing in the direction she said the men ran. The only thing that way were strip malls and industrial buildings. If the women had gotten so spooked they'd decided to abandon the club before their Uber got there, why head someplace where there wouldn't be anyone to help if they needed it? Going to another club—or staying here—would have been much safer. Then again, people did strange things when they were scared.

Diego climbed in his vehicle and radioed dispatch, telling them what he had and that he was going to drive around and check out the area north of the club.

"Roger, Charlie 204. Sending additional units to your location."

"Copy that," he said.

The strip mall was filled with stores that had been empty of tenants for months. Everything looked fine from the front, but when he drove around to the back, he caught sight of an open door in the beam of his spotlight. Diego's gut tightened and the hairs on the back of his neck stood on end. He was out of his car the moment it rolled to a stop, updating dispatch even as he grabbed his flashlight and Glock.

He'd barely stepped foot outside when a woman's scream came from the building, piercing the night.

Shit.

He couldn't wait for backup. Not when someone's life was in danger.

Grip tight on his weapon, Diego slipped through the doorway, immediately taking cover behind a concrete support column. He moved the beam of his flashlight back and forth around the space ahead of him, but other than a lot of bare shelves and crushed cardboard boxes, there wasn't much to see. Then he caught sight of a doorway on the far side of the wide-open area and realized this store was connected to the one next to it. He cursed his luck. He'd hoped this strip mall was composed of individual units.

He cautiously made his way across the room, trying to see behind every support column, shelf, box, and dark corner all at the same time. That was damn near impossible to do on his own. Dammit, he should have waited for backup. Other units called out their location over the radio, but they were all a good distance away. He prayed one of them was a K9 team. What he wouldn't give to be able to see in the dark like one of his four legged coworkers. And being able to smell like a K9? Crap, that would be awesome.

He couldn't see in the dark—or sniff out bad guys—and he never would. But he was going to risk his life to find those girls anyway...if they were in here.

Diego stepped through the second doorway into the next store to find it even darker and more cluttered than the first. He was slowly weaving his way through the mess when he heard a gunshot immediately followed by a woman's scream.

Shit.

He thumbed the mic on his radio. "Shots fired. I repeat, shots fired."

Then he was moving, less concerned about checking every dark space and more concerned about getting to the woman. Running through one store after the other without thought to the fact that there might be a bad guy waiting to shoot him was reckless and stupid. But when someone was in trouble, helping them was the only thing his head would let him do. It was the way he was wired.

Diego let his instincts guide him as he worked his way through the confusing twists and turns of the shops, running all the way to the far end of the interconnected strip mall without seeing anyone.

Where the hell is she?

He turned to retrace his steps when he heard a soft whimper, so quiet he barely made it out over the thud of his own heart. Sure it came from somewhere to his left, he headed in that direction, keeping his flashlight and weapon pointed forward as he slipped around a metal storage rack.

Three dark-haired women huddled on the floor behind it, holding on to one another as tears ran down their faces. None of them could have been more than twenty-five years old, but the one in the middle looked a hell of a lot younger than that as she lay between them, blood soaking through the white blouse she wore and the yellow rain slicker she had on over that. In the glow of his flashlight, he could see she was in pain and pale as death. Crap, she was almost certainly bleeding out. Even as he watched, her eyes fluttered open and closed as she fought off her body's attempt to pass out.

He hurried over, dropping to a knee beside them. Still holding onto the flashlight, he reached out and gently pulled back the edge of the injured girl's raincoat to check the bullet wound in her stomach. Oh, shit, it looked bad. If she didn't get help soon, she was done for. Thumbing his radio, he requested EMS with air evac.

"Officer Martinez," he said, quickly introducing himself to the trio of women. "Where are the people who did this?"

The woman on the left shook her head, gray eyes darting left and right like a terrified rabbit. "We ran in here to get away from them, but they found us. They've been messing with us for the last ten minutes, saying all kinds of psycho stuff they were going to do to us."

"We tried to hide, but one of the guys found us," the other woman added. She had pink streaks in her straight hair and a diamond stud in her nose. "He didn't even say anything. He just walked up and shot Tina, then took off. Maybe they left when they heard you come in."

Diego hoped she was right, but his gut told him there was no chance the men had left. More likely, they were hiding somewhere, waiting to make their move. Hell, they might be close enough to hear him and the women talking. The smart thing to do would be to stay here and protect the women until backup arrived, but he knew if he did that, Tina would be dead.

Holstering his weapon, he handed the flashlight to the girl with the pink streaks in her hair, then leaned forward to scoop up Tina in his arms.

"Shh," he whispered when she groaned in pain. "I know this hurts like hell, but I have to get you out of here. You just have to hold on. Can you do that for me, Tina?"

She murmured something that might have been agreement, but he wasn't sure. Regardless, he headed back the way he'd come, the other two women close behind. He stopped at each doorway, poking his head out to make sure the coast was clear. After more than a few times of doing that, he started thinking maybe the girls were right about those guys bailing.

He was halfway across a store that must have once

carried ladies' fashions—at least judging by all the female mannequins eerily watching them—when he heard a crunching sound. He snapped his head around to see a man standing in the shadows.

Diego had a fraction of a second to shove the two women with him aside and twist his body around in an attempt to protect the girl in his arms before the sound of a large caliber handgun going off shattered the darkness. A bullet hit him in the back, and his vision went dark as pain engulfed him.

"Run!" he shouted even as another gunshot rang out and a red-hot lance of agony sliced across the top of his right shoulder inches from his spine. "Go…go…go!"

He was forced to stay behind the two women running and losing their collective minds in front of him. Tina screamed in his arms, the jostling too much for her, but there was nothing he could do to avoid it. They had to run, or they'd all die.

When the shadow of a man emerged out of the darkness ahead of him, Diego didn't pause to think. He simply tucked Tina closer to his body and lowered his shoulder, slamming into the guy at full speed. There was a grunt followed by a weapon going off, then all three girls were screaming.

Diego felt something stab through his stomach above his left hip, right below his tactical vest. When the pain showed up this time, there was no doubt in his mind that he was screwed.

He went down hard, Tina slipping from his arms to tumble across the floor. The fact that she didn't make a sound as she skidded across the linoleum and thudded into a pile of boxes worried him, but then the man he'd crashed into—a big, burly guy matching the bartender's description—pointed his gun in Diego's direction, and that situation sort of required all his attention. He had to stay alive long enough to get the women out of here.

Diego lunged forward, landing on the man and shoving the pistol in his hand aside as it went off again. Out the corner of his eye, he saw the two women whose names he still didn't know scramble to their feet and run. He only prayed they didn't run straight into the second guy.

A punch came his way and he ducked, letting the blow graze the side of his head instead of taking it straight in the face. The move was purely instinctive on his part. Just like it was instinct that had him throwing a punch of his own. Something crunched under his fist and the man let out a grunt of pain. Hoping that meant the guy was at least temporarily stunned, Diego reached for his own gun.

The flash of a blade glinted in the dim light coming from the street, and he twisted to the side, his weapon forgotten. The knife plunged deep into his right shoulder, bringing with it a whole hell of a lot of agony. Diego had never been shot before tonight—or stabbed—but he'd take a bullet over a blade any day. His shoulder was on frigging fire.

Diego rolled one way and then the other, managing to get the weapon dislodged from his shoulder and punching the man in the face again. He was able to keep the man's pistol away from him, but the knife came close to his throat more than once before he was able to get in a punch to the man's temple that took the fight right out of him.

As Diego pulled out his handcuffs, he realized he couldn't feel the rough metal under his fingers. In fact, he couldn't feel his legs either. Breathing seemed to suddenly be a lot more trouble than it was worth, too. And the pain spreading through his body was way worse than before.

That was probably really bad.

The guy he'd knocked unconscious was slowly coming to, but Diego somehow managed to get the gun and knife shoved away before cuffing him.

Diego started to clamber to his feet, intending to pick up Tina and get the hell out of there. Unfortunately, it was hard finding the energy to move, much less stand, so he knelt there on the floor, telling himself he would just take a second to catch his breath. But the seconds began to drag out, and even though Diego knew he had to get moving, if it wasn't for the sound of footsteps nearby, he probably would have stayed right where he was until help arrived.

He lifted his head, frowning when he saw it was darker inside the building than it had been before. Even so, he could still make out the shape of a man standing ten feet away, an automatic pointed in Diego's direction.

Diego reached for the Glock still holstered at his waist, but knew he'd never get it out in time, not with his reflexes slowed from the blood loss. Even when he got his right hand on the polymer grip of the weapon, he couldn't seem to pull it out. The slow smile spreading across the other man's face in the dim light told Diego he'd run out of time.

Then out of nowhere, a cardboard box flew through the darkness, slamming the asshole in the side of the head.

From the corner of his eye, Diego saw Tina slumped to the floor, all her energy exhausted in her effort to throw the box. It wasn't enough to rip the man's head off or anything close to that, but it distracted him enough for Diego to finally get his weapon out.

The man shoved the box aside with a curse and fired at Diego just as he pulled the trigger on the Glock. The guy fell to the floor even as a bullet slammed into Diego. Pain bloomed in the center of his chest and breathing became impossible, making Diego doubt his vest had been able to stop the round. But it must have, or he'd be dead.

Rolling painfully to his knees, Diego crawled toward Tina, terrified all of this was going to be for nothing. But when he slipped a hand under her shoulder and rolled her over, she let out a little groan and he released the breath he hadn't known he was holding.

"Let's get you out of here, okay?" he murmured.

Diego slowly picked Tina up and stumbled to his feet, only to promptly drop to a knee, his head spinning so fast, he thought he was going to pass out for sure. Gritting his teeth, he struggled to stand again, and this time, he stayed upright. He staggered toward the exit, ignoring the guy he'd left cuffed on the floor, murmuring the whole time to the girl in his arms, promising she'd be okay.

The trip through the shops, which had seemed rather short on the way in, had lengthened considerably. He was convinced he'd stumbled at least a hundred miles and still didn't seem close to getting out of there.

Diego didn't realize he'd fallen to his knees until he felt the grit of sharp rubble digging into his skin. He immediately tried to regain his feet, but instead, slid to the floor in a boneless heap. He twisted sideways at the last second, so his shoulder slammed into hard linoleum instead of Tina. She lay a few inches away, her hazel eyes fighting to stay open as his started to close.

"I'm so sorry," he whispered, the words little more than breath moving across his lips. "I know I promised, and I'm sorry."

Tina's eyes opened for a moment, and he thought he saw understanding and forgiveness there. Or maybe that was simply wishful thinking.

Diego fought the blackness, trying to reach for his radio mic so he could beg them to hurry and get to the girl before it was too late. But his arms were beyond numb and movement impossible. All he could do was lay there and watch Tina fade away.

It was so damn wrong.

Then, all at once, cops and paramedics were surrounding them. He closed his eyes, relieved. Tina would be okay.

"You still with me, Diego?" a deep voice asked.

Diego opened his eyes once again to see Hale leaning over him, concern written all over his face. For a moment, he wondered how the hell his friend was there. Then he stopped worrying about the meaningless shit and asked the only question that really mattered.

"The girl?"

Hale nodded, gripping Diego's hand and giving it a reassuring squeeze. "The paramedics just took her out. They're loading her on the helicopter right now. It will leave the second you're on it. You just have to hold on."

Then he was on a gurney and paramedics were shoving him full speed through the abandoned stores and out into the freezing rain. But no matter how fast they moved, Hale kept up with them, stuck right there at his side, holding Diego's hand in his.

"Just a little bit farther," Hale told him. "The bird is in

the empty lot across the street. We're going to wheel you straight there. Just hold on."

Black spots swirled above Diego, blurring out the glare of the streetlamps and flashlights around them. He swore he could hear his heart thudding in his chest and the sound it was making did nothing to convince him that it wanted to continue the effort.

"I don't think I can," he mumbled, his words slurring as something metallic and nasty filled his mouth and throat, making it difficult to breathe, much less talk. "Tell my family that it didn't hurt. That…it was quick."

That was a lie, of course. In reality, the pain in his chest felt like there was a living creature inside him, slowly digging its way out. But he didn't want his mom and dad or brother and sisters to know that. It would make what happened to him even harder on them.

Hale cursed, his eyes misty even as his lip curled in anger. "None of that shit," he growled. He frigging *growled*. And even though Diego knew it was nothing but a pain-driven delusion, he thought for a second his best friend's eyes were glowing vivid yellow-gold. "Don't even think you're getting out of that SWAT assessment this easy. You said you were going to do it, and you can guarantee I'm going to hold you to that promise. Now, suck it up and keep breathing until you get to the hospital. Or I'm telling your mom you gave up because you were afraid to face humiliation in front of me and the rest of the SWAT team."

Diego wasn't so sure his friend's speech was having the desired effect, but he supposed he couldn't blame the guy for trying. He would have done the same thing.

"Don't give up on me, Diego," Hale urged, his voice

barely audible over the thump of the helicopter blades that signaled they were getting close to the bird. "Don't give up on yourself. There are hundreds of people out there waiting for someone like you to help them out of whatever shit they've found themselves in. Thousands, maybe. You've spent years helping other people, but if you ever want to help another living soul, you're going to have to fight to stay alive. Fight like you've never fought before."

Diego let those thoughts roll around in his head as the paramedics lifted the gurney into the helicopter and the damn rain finally stopped hitting him. Outside, Hale was shouting at him to fight—for himself and all the people who'd depend on him in the future.

The doors of the helicopter slammed closed, shutting out whatever else Hale might have said. Then a paramedic was leaning over him with an IV bag and the bird was taking off. As he drifted off into the darkness of unconsciousness, Hale's words echoed in his head. His friend was right. Helping other people was his purpose for living. If he wanted to keep doing it, he was going to have to make it through this.

There was just one problem with that.

He wasn't sure he could.

CHAPTER 1

Dallas, Texas, Present Day

"Forget it, Diego. No way in hell am I letting you walk into that diner with some psycho in there."

Diego Martinez sighed, resisting the urge to point out to Senior Corporal Mike Taylor, his squad leader, SWAT officer in charge on this incident, fellow werewolf, and all-around good guy, that calling a suspect a "psycho" was considered politically incorrect. Even if, in this case, it was almost certainly correct.

"I know you're trying to protect me, but you have to let me do my job," Diego said, his attention focused on Mike while still keeping an eye on the video monitor of the retro-looking diner across the street. The one that should have been bustling with the usual 8:00 a.m. breakfast crowd on a weekday morning, but was instead surrounded by police vehicles, cut off from the rest of the world.

Mike scowled. Diego knew he wasn't a big fan of sending him into the situation blind, but with the shades in the diner down, the door barricaded with racks of dishes, and all phone connections cut after the brief conversation he had with the gunman that's exactly what they were. Which was why Diego needed to go in. Other than a bizarre request for a news crew with a live feed to the internet and all the networks, the armed man holding an unknown number of hostages hadn't said a word since.

"Look, we have a diner full of scared people, a gunman

who's either high on drugs or mentally unstable, and two cops who might be bleeding to death as we speak while we stand here arguing about whether I should be able to take a risk I'm paid to take," Diego said.

Mike muttered a curse. "Okay. But the second I think the situation is going sideways, we're coming in, so make sure you don't put yourself between the target and our entry points. Got it?"

"Yeah, I got it."

Diego knew the drill. He'd been a negotiator on the SWAT team for the past seven years—a job he'd never thought he'd do until Hale Delaney pointed out he had a knack for staying calm and talking people out of doing something stupid—and one thing he'd learned early on was don't be in the way when your teammates make an entrance. Getting shot might not kill a werewolf, but when your pack mates were doing the shooting, it was embarrassing as hell. And he hated being embarrassed. He hated getting shot, too, of course, but on a relative scale of discomfort, being ragged by his own buddies was right up there beside taking a bullet.

Pushing that thought aside, Diego stepped out of the operations vehicle to find Hale, Senior Corporal Trey Duncan, and Officer Connor Malone regarding him expectantly.

"Well?" Hale prompted. "Did you talk Mike into letting you go in?"

Diego nodded, walking over to one of the SWAT SUVs. Opening the back door, he started shedding his tactical gear, dumping everything on the back seat. Department-issued SIG Sauer .40 caliber, small-frame backup piece in the same caliber, vest with its protective ballistic plate, Taser, cuffs, radio—everything. People who took hostages tended to get upset when you walked into their territory wearing violent fashion accessories. And if the recent incidents the SWAT team had gone on were any indication, this guy would be even more pissed than normal.

"Am I the only one thinking this hostage situation looks a hell of a lot like the other calls we've been getting lately?" Connor asked. Big and tall with dark-blond hair and hazel eyes, the team's sniper had a definite surfer-dude vibe going on. He was originally from California so that made sense. "You know, the ones with the suspects acting strange AF."

Diego shrugged as he pulled the folding knife off his belt and tossed it on the table along with the other stuff. He'd been thinking the same thing. Yeah, being a SWAT team full of werewolves practically guaranteed more than their fair share of weird calls, but the ones they'd gone on in the past few weeks had been outside the norm, even for them. The calls had involved extremely volatile and violent suspects, most of whom refused to give up without a fight, and all of whom had no criminal record of any type. Hell, they came way closer to Boy Scouts than cold-blooded killers, yet in the end, they'd all been more than willing to commit murder.

Even more bizarre, none of the suspects he and his teammates had taken down could explain why they'd done what they had. Hell, they couldn't even remember doing it. Things had so gotten bad the Special Threat Assessment Team—aka STAT—a joint FBI-CIA supernatural task force very few people had heard of, had started sniffing around to see if there was something paranormal involved. Diego had worked with the group in Los Angeles a little while back, and he'd gladly take their help now. But so far, all they had was a bunch of whacked-out suspects with no connection to one another. So, STAT had backed off and was letting the SWAT team deal with the problem. Yeah, the feds were helpful like that.

"It doesn't matter if this is another one of those cases," Diego finally said. "That guy walked right into a crowded diner and shot two cops, then took the rest of the customers hostage. We don't need to understand why he did it. We just need to get him out."

Beside him, Trey's blue gaze strayed to the front of the diner, his usually serious face even more solemn. "I agree, but I'd feel a lot better about this if we could see through those windows."

"Agreed," Connor said. "I'll be on the roof across the street with my sniper rifle, but with the blinds pulled down like they are, there's not a whole lot I can do."

"I'm not sure I can do anything about the blinds, but I'll try," Diego told him. "Be ready to come in when I give the signal."

Diego wouldn't be wearing a radio, but with their enhanced hearing, his pack mates would be able to hear him give the code phrase if things went sideways.

"We'll be there," Hale promised before he and Trey walked over to stand by the cluster of patrol cars forming a semicircle in front of the diner.

"Be careful," Connor said, then turned to jog across the street.

Mike came out of the team's operations RV a moment later, giving Diego a nod as he moved over to join Hale and Trey.

Taking a deep breath, Diego slowly walked toward the front door of the diner, trying to appear confident without looking threatening. That was difficult to do when you were as broad and muscular as he was, not to mention wearing a dark-blue tactical uniform and combat boots. He did it anyway, just in case the bad guy was looking out the window.

Which he obviously was since the door opened before Diego even had a chance to knock.

A man peeked out the crack, regarding him suspiciously before his eyes darted around wildly like he was looking for something or someone behind Diego. "What do you want?"

"I'm Officer Martinez. We spoke on the phone earlier."

"I'm done talking to you. Go away!"

Fear and anger rolled off the man in equal measures, his gaze once more going this way and that. Like he was strung out on something. Diego inhaled, trying to figure out what drug it was. If the guy was using something like heroin, fentanyl, or PCP, Diego should be able to smell it, but he couldn't pick up anything. Maybe the guy was on something completely new.

"I would, but the camera crew you asked for is here," Diego said. "Before we can let them go in there, I need to make sure it's safe. The department's lawyers won't let civilians in if I can't assure their well-being."

He knew it was a long shot, but the one demand the guy had made before he hung up on Diego was that he wanted a news crew with a camera so he could tell everyone about the monsters. It might simply be the rantings of a madman, but the first rule of negotiating was to figure out what the suspect wanted and make them believe you could give it to them. If lying to the guy about the news crew was what it took to get inside, Diego was damn well going to do it.

The guy stared at him, eyes glassy and heart pounding like he'd run a marathon—or was scared to death.

"I'm not armed," Diego volunteered when the man didn't say anything. Lifting his hands, he slowly turned in a complete circle. "I just need to come in and make sure everyone is okay. Then we can go from there. How does that sound?"

The man continued to look suspicious, but after a few seconds, he nodded. "Okay. But you're the only one who can come in. No other cops."

Without waiting for an answer, the guy pushed away the rolling rack of dishes he'd put in front of the door. Unlocking it, he opened it wider, then stepped back, gun in his hands trained on Diego.

"Hurry up and get in here!" he ordered.

Diego stepped inside, pushing the door closed behind him.

"Lock it," the man said, motioning with the gun. "Then move the rack back in front."

Diego turned to lock the door, only to freeze when a scent completely out of left field hit him like a baseball bat. There was a young, newly turned male beta werewolf in the diner. Diego knew what kind of werewolf he was because every type of werewolf—alpha, beta, and omega—had a distinct scent. Another thing he could smell was fear, and this beta was so scared right then that he was on the edge of losing control.

Shit.

As he turned the lock, Diego looked directly at Connor, Trey, and Mike through the glass. "There's a new werewolf in here, and he's barely keeping it together," he whispered too softly for anyone in the diner to hear him, but loud enough for his pack mates to pick up everything he said.

"Say the word and we're there," Trey murmured.

Giving them an almost imperceptible nod, Diego rolled the plastic rack in front of the door. It wouldn't really slow his pack mates down when they came in, but if putting it back helped keep the gunman calm, Diego had no problem doing it.

When he turned around, Diego resisted the urge to look at the beta werewolf right away, instead focusing on the man who'd taken the diner hostage. Average height and in his midforties, he wore a silk suit and a pair of Italian leather loafers that were probably worth more combined than Diego's top-of-the-line large-screen TV. His blond hair was wild and unkempt, but Diego got a whiff of the styling gel in it and even that smelled expensive. The gold ring on the man's right hand was as pricey looking as everything else, with a crest on it that looked like it was from some kind of fancy Ivy League school.

Maybe this situation *was* like all the other calls he and his teammates had gone on lately.

Because nothing about the guy screamed that he was your everyday garden-variety hostage taker. Well, except for the desperate look in his eyes, sweat beading on his forehead, gun in his hand, slight smear of blood on his jaw, and all the terrified people in the diner. Then there were the two SIG Sauers stuffed in the guy's waistband. They were standard DPD issue exactly like the one Diego had left in the SUV, which meant the hostage taker had gotten them from the cops he'd shot. The table beside him was strewn with cell phones he'd obviously taken from the hostages.

Still keeping an eye on the man with the gun, Diego took a second to look around. Two waitresses, two cooks, and a younger guy who was probably the dishwasher cowered behind the counter while all of the other hostages—including the beta werewolf—were huddled on the far side of the diner, sitting on the floor.

The teen boy was kneeling beside one of the patrol officers who'd been shot, pressing a dishrag to the gunshot wound at the officer's shoulder. The teen's breathing was a little fast and his heart was thumping hard, but he was holding it together—for now. Diego remembered what it was like right after he'd turned, when the slightest bit of stress would have his fangs and claws ripping out all on their own—usually at the worst possible time.

This kid was a beta, though, which meant he was smaller, less aggressive, and not as prone to violent outbursts as Diego had been when he first became an alpha. Still, this was a tense situation. There was blood everywhere, a diner full of terrified people, an unhinged guy with a gun, and dozens of cops outside with more firepower. It could definitely push a new werewolf—even a beta—over the edge. Diego needed to get the kid out of here soon, before this situation became even messier than it already was. Because a teenager sprouting fangs and claws definitely wouldn't look good on the evening news.

A pretty woman with long, golden-brown hair and features so similar to the kid's that she had to be his mother was on the floor near the other cop, using a towel to stanch the blood seeping through his pant leg from a shot to the thigh. While the two cops didn't appear to be in immediate danger, getting them medical attention was still a priority. Diego gave them a nod, getting two back in return.

Diego glanced at the gunman to find him staring straight ahead, his eyes glazed over as he muttered to himself in a tone so low and fast, it was incomprehensible. It seemed like the guy was seconds from passing out, but Diego had dealt with enough unstable people to know even one sudden movement could change everything in a situation like this. So, he simply wouldn't do anything sudden—until he had to.

Instead, he turned his attention to the beta werewolf again. Before today, the youngest werewolf Diego had ever met was eighteen, but this kid couldn't be more than fifteen, sixteen at the most, and he couldn't help wondering how the boy had turned.

His gaze moved to the woman he assumed was the kid's mother. Even though she was focused on keeping pressure on the cop's wound, she kept glancing at the boy out of the corner of her eye. Did she know her son was a werewolf, or had he hidden the change from her?

The sudden urge to protect the young beta from both the gunman and possible exposure was unlike anything Diego had ever felt before. His gums tingled as his fangs threatened to come out, and he bit back a curse. Taking a deep, calming breath, he focused on the gunman to see the guy staring at him, eyes narrowing in suspicion, as if he'd never seen Diego before. In a flash, the man lifted the weapon and aimed it at him.

Diego stiffened. A werewolf could absorb a lot of punishment, but a bullet through the heart or head would end him just as fast as it would anyone else.

"You know, this would be a lot easier if I knew what to call you," he said calmly, ignoring the gun. "I'm Diego. What's your name?"

"Ken," the guy finally muttered after a long, tense delay.

Getting the guy to tell him his name was a good start, at least. Even if he kept the gun pointed at Diego.

"I know you don't want this situation getting any worse than it already is, Ken, so maybe you can lower your weapon. Then we can talk about why you took all these people hostage."

Ken looked at him like he was a million miles away, and Diego wondered if he'd even heard him. Hand shaking, he slowly lowered the gun, only to immediately jerk it back up. It was as if there was a fight going on inside the guy. Part of him wanted to put down the gun, while another part wanted to pull the trigger.

Just when it seemed like the guy was going to have a complete breakdown, his eyes abruptly cleared and he lowered the weapon.

"He makes people do things," Ken said softly, the words tortured, like it was a struggle to get them out.

"Are you saying someone forced you to come in here and take these people hostage?" Diego prompted.

Even though he'd asked the question softly, the words set Ken off anyway.

"You don't believe me!" he shouted. "Monsters are real, dammit. And I can prove it."

Backing away, Ken swept his weapon around the inside of the diner before finally pointing it straight at the kid. The beta werewolf's eyes went wide with fear. He looked like he was half a second from losing it.

Shit.

Diego lifted his hands in a placating gesture, desperate to get the guy's attention back on him. "Take it easy, Ken. I believe in monsters."

"No, you don't!" Ken swung his weapon in Diego's direction. "You don't believe me. No one does. Monsters are all around us. People don't realize it because they look just like the rest of us on the outside, but on the inside they're ugly and evil."

Diego opened his mouth to say something he hoped would calm Ken down before he totally went over the edge, but the guy cut him off before he could get a word out.

"You said there was someone here with a camera," Ken said, taking a step closer to Diego. "Get them in here. I can't hold on much longer, and the world needs to know about the monsters."

Diego was ready to dismiss the psychotic rant for what it was, but then Ken swung his weapon away from him, leveling it at the kid again with a look in his eyes that was unsettling as hell.

The answer hit him like a ton of bricks. *Shit.* Somehow, Ken had figured out the kid was a werewolf. Maybe he'd seen the claws and fangs, or the glowing eyes. Either way, Ken knew, and he intended to expose that fact to the world.

From the panicked expression on the boy's face, he knew it, too. Yellow glimmered in his eyes, a sure sign his body was trying to shift. It was a natural response when a person's inner wolf felt threatened.

Diego slowly moved until he was positioned in between Ken and the boy on the floor. "You have to know there's no way they're ever going to allow that camera crew in here while there are police officers bleeding to death. You're going to have to let the paramedics take them outside."

Out of the corner of his eye, Diego saw both cops shake their heads, indicating they wanted to stay. Because that's what good cops did—risked their lives for others. But Diego wanted to get everyone out of here alive, and it started with the two of them.

"Look, you're simply giving up two injured people," Diego pointed out when Ken hesitated. "You do that, and you get everything you want in return. You know you have to do this."

It felt like the whole room was holding its collective breath, waiting to see what the unbalanced man with the gun would do. A few feet away, the beautiful woman on the floor looked from her son to Ken, then finally fixed all her attention on Diego.

Her brown eyes were warm, like whiskey mixed with honey, and Diego would have enjoyed getting lost in them. Unfortunately, right now wasn't the time for that.

Sudden movement in Ken's direction had Diego snapping his head around to see the man squeezing his temples with both hands, like he was trying to make some kind of horrible pain go away. Grip tight on the gun, he smacked the butt of the weapon against his head several times, his eyes clenched closed in obvious agony, fresh sweat beading on his forehead. But when he opened his eyes a moment later, they were clearer and more aware than they'd been since Diego had first stepped into the diner.

"Get the cops out of here now," Ken said, breath coming in gasps as he continued to press his fists against his temples "Before he makes me stop you."

Diego had no idea who he was talking about, but he wasn't going to waste the opportunity while he tried to figure it out. Bringing paramedics in with gurneys would take too long, so he was going to have to improvise.

"You four," Diego said, pointing at two big guys and two younger women huddled close to the wall near the cops. "Help me get the two officers outside."

Diego could easily have picked up the injured cops himself, but this way, he'd be able to get the four hostages out with them. The kid moved the dish rack aside while his mom held open the door. Diego had every intention of shoving them out the door along with the others, but then Ken was there, his eyes looking positively vacant as he reached out and grabbed the kid's shoulder, dragging him back into the diner.

And Mom wasn't leaving without her kid.

"They stay here," Ken said, wrapping his arm tightly around the kid as he backed away from the door, the barrel of the automatic waving around wildly, threatening everyone in the place even as he glared at Diego. "I know what you were trying to do. You don't care about the truth, but I have to stop him. I can't let him get away with what he's done. Don't you see we're all just a bunch of puppets to him?"

The vein at Ken's temple throbbed, and he gripped the gun so tightly his knuckles were white. The people huddled in the back of the diner must have known things were going to get ugly in a minute because they visibly started to panic, more than a few of them eyeing the door like they were going to make a mad dash for the exit.

That would be suicide.

Tears filled Ken's eyes even as he lifted the gun and pressed it against the kid's head. Like he genuinely didn't want to kill the boy but couldn't stop himself.

The teen werewolf must have realized what was coming

because his eyes flashed yellow-gold and there was a hint of fangs visible as they extended in response to the fear rushing through his body.

Beside Diego, the kid's mom tensed, like she was going to jump on the man holding her son, regardless of the gun he was holding.

"It's getting hot in here, guys," Diego murmured, giving the signal to his teammates outside as he launched himself at Ken.

His muscles twisted and spasmed in a partial shift, his body becoming a blur as he moved. It went without saying that he was a lot faster than the boy's mom, even if she did look fit as hell.

Diego slammed into the kid and the gunman at the same time, taking them both to the floor just as his pack mates crashed through the front windows behind him. Diego ignored the hostages freaking out all around him and focused on separating Ken from the boy—and from his weapon.

The kid hit the linoleum floor and slid into the side of a nearby booth, while Ken bounced toward the kitchen, losing his grip on the Glock. Diego didn't need the weapon—he had plenty at the ends of his fingertips—but slashing up a man in the middle of a diner with people all around wouldn't be the best idea in the world. So, he went with discretion over valor and dove for the gun the other man had dropped.

A small growl slipped out from Diego's throat as he covered the distance to the weapon in one savage leap, then scooped up the auto and spun around to get a bead on Ken as the man recovered from his own tumble and came to a knee holding one of the SIG Sauers he'd taken from the patrol officers.

"Freeze!" Diego shouted, even as the man kept moving in a weird slow-and-mechanical fashion, like he was a frigging robot. "Dammit, Ken, don't lift that weapon any higher. I don't want to shoot you. It's over. Just drop it!"

Three red dots appeared unwavering in the center of Ken's chest as Trey, Hale, and Mike all ordered him to drop the weapon, too. Ken ignored them, locking eyes with Diego. The anguish in them was unlike anything Diego had ever seen before.

"Don't let him get away with this," Ken whispered, bringing the Glock the rest of the way up to his chin and pulling the trigger.

The moment the man in the expensive suit and Italian loafers walked into the diner, Bree Harlow was sure she recognized him. She couldn't remember where they'd met, but she was certain they had. In fact, she'd been so sure, she'd stopped in midconversation with her son, Brandon, to give him a smile and a wave. But before she could so much as lift her hand, the man had walked up to the table where the two police officers were sitting and shot them.

Without saying a single word.

Without even waiting for them to notice him.

He'd just...shot them.

Before Bree realized what was happening, she and Brandon were on the floor trying to stop the bleeding while the man in the suit was ranting and raving about monsters and voices in his head.

She'd taken Brandon out to breakfast this morning so

they could relax and hopefully talk. Bree knew her son was dealing with some stuff, and she desperately wanted to help. But between the nightmares that had him ripping up his sheets and the way his brown eyes flashed yellow whenever he got upset—which seemed to be all the time lately—she had no idea what to do.

Two months ago, Brandon had gotten shot simply because he was in the wrong place at the wrong time. She'd been terrified he was going to die, and it was a miracle he didn't. He hadn't been quite the same since, though. She thought at first it was because he was addicted to the pain meds the hospital had given him, but she didn't know of a prescription drug that had those side effects. That was when she started to worry he was taking some kind of designer drug. To cope with what had happened at the convenience store and everything else going on in his life right now.

But no matter how many times she'd tried to get her son to tell her what was wrong, he wouldn't. If anything, he became even more withdrawn. Bree thought having breakfast at the diner that made his favorite chocolate-chip pancakes might put him in a talkative mood, but then the guy with the gun had shown up, and keeping Brandon and those police officers alive had become the only thing that mattered to her.

Hope had flared bright when that big cop had walked in. Diego's presence commanded the room even though he was unarmed, and Bree had found herself believing there was nothing he couldn't do. When he convinced Ken to release the injured officers and four other people, she started thinking the whole thing would ultimately end okay.

Then Ken grabbed Brandon, and Bree watched in horror

as the humanity left the man's eyes and he'd lifted the gun to her son's head. Terror flashed yellow-gold in Brandon's eyes, tearing her heart out. He hadn't lived through the shooting at the convenience store to die here.

If her son died, she'd die, too.

Bree would have done anything she had to do to save Brandon's life—even putting herself between him and the gun—but it felt like she was buried in Jell-O, unable to close the distance between her and the man threatening her son, no matter how hard she tried.

All at once, a blur of movement caught her eye, then the SWAT cop was knocking Brandon and the guy with the gun to the floor. A split second later, three more cops were suddenly in the diner, smashing through the windows with a deafening crash. Screams of fear echoed around her as the other hostages freaked out, but the only thing she could focus on was her son—and getting to him.

She'd just reached Brandon when she heard Diego shouting for the guy with the gun to drop it. She grabbed her son to protect his body with her own, even as her gaze went to the scene playing out a few feet away. When Ken placed the gun under his chin, every instinct she had begged her to look away, but she couldn't, and the sight of him taking his own life was the most horrible thing she'd ever witnessed.

The overwhelming chaos in the diner disappeared, replaced by silence, and time seemed to slow as Ken slowly tumbled to the linoleum floor.

There was so much blood.

Bree had no idea if seconds—or hours—passed, but then she heard something so out of place with her surroundings that it immediately snapped her back to reality.

Growling.

Low, soft, pained...growling.

And it was coming from Brandon.

She looked down to find him gazing up at her with vivid-gold eyes, half-inch-long fangs visible over his bottom lip.

Bree had always considered herself to be a strong person. She'd gone through a lot in her life and dealt with it. But she couldn't ignore the obvious. The accumulated stress of this situation had been too much for her. She was having a mental breakdown. Because there was no way she was seeing what she thought she saw.

Suddenly, the SWAT cop was at her side, pulling Brandon up and talking to him in a slow, calm voice, telling him to relax and breathe, that everything was over and he was going to be okay at the same time he used his big body like a shield, keeping other people in the diner from seeing her son's face. His voice was the most soothing and calming sound she'd ever heard in her life, and even though he wasn't talking to her, she found herself breathing in time with his instructions—in through the nose, hold it for five seconds, and out through the mouth.

Bree watched in stunned fascination as the yellow glow slowly receded from her son's eyes and the fangs disappeared. All at once, his panicked breathing and frantic features relaxed, and she realized it was the first time in months he didn't seem tense.

There was a commotion behind her, and she glanced over her shoulder to see the other officers—dressed like Diego but with weapons and heavy-looking tactical gear strapped across their chests—quickly moving the rest of the hostages outside, herding them in such a way that they didn't have time to look at the body on the floor...or Brandon.

It was like they were all working together to keep anyone from seeing what was happening with her son. Like they all somehow knew something unexplainable was going on with him.

"There you go, kid." The SWAT cop's deep voice made her turn back around, and she saw him standing there with his hands on Brandon's shoulders. "Just a few more deep breaths and you'll be good to go."

Diego was right. A few seconds later, Brandon was fine, and Bree found herself wondering if everything she'd seen was a figment of her confused mind.

It could have been, right?

She felt a gentle hand on her arm and looked up into the warmest brown eyes she'd ever seen, a little overwhelmed by the concern she saw there. Diego didn't even know her, and yet he seemed genuinely worried.

"I think we should get out of here," he said, nodding toward Brandon. "This place is about to be crawling with cops, crime-scene techs, and general-purpose gawkers. I'd rather be somewhere else before they show up. We have a lot to talk about."

She was about to ask what he meant by that, but then it hit her. Everything she'd seen had been real. Diego had seen it, too. And now he wanted to talk about it. Because that's what cops did. They dug into stuff until they knew everything.

Bree's heart began to thump hard all over again as she realized the danger her son might be in now. What if Diego revealed what he'd seen? Brandon would be treated like a monster. From the look on Brandon's face, he realized the same thing and was on the verge of freaking out.

"Relax," the cop said softly, looking first at Brandon, then her. "I'm not a threat to your son. I promise."

Gaze locked with hers, Diego's eyes flared vivid yellow-gold. The color was only there for a second before it disappeared, but it was impossible to miss. Or mistake it for anything other than what she'd seen in her son's eyes. The cop looked at Brandon, earning a wide-eyed gasp. Bree had no idea what any of this meant, but it had to be a good sign…right?

"Like I said," Diego murmured. "We have a lot to talk about."

Bree nodded, her head spinning as she tried to understand what was going on. What was happening to her son, and how could a cop they'd just met know what it meant when she couldn't?

All rational thought was wiped out the moment the three of them stepped out of the diner. The parking lot and area around it looked like the circus had visited the zoo—and eaten too much sugar.

Cops and paramedics were everywhere, with at least twenty patrol cars parked on the street. There was a line of EMS vehicles behind them, and to the left was an RV with a SWAT logo painted on the side. At the end of the block, just behind the row of crime-scene tape, reporters and camera crews vied for space with crowds of onlookers trying to find the perfect spot to take pictures with their cell phones.

Which reminded her—her phone was still back on a table in the diner along with everyone else's. She wondered if the cops would give it back or need it for evidence.

Diego was leading her and Brandon toward the RV when

a tall officer intercepted them. His uniform was ripped and torn in a dozen locations, and while it was impossible to miss the blood running from myriad cuts he had, he didn't seem bothered by it.

"Sorry to interrupt, but Chief Leclair just showed up and she's demanding a sitrep," he said to Diego. "She wants to know how that guy in the diner ended up dead, and she wants you to tell her."

Diego sighed, nodding even though it was obvious he didn't want to go talk to his chief. While Bree desperately wanted to hear what Diego had to say, she also understood what it was like to deal with management types who wanted to have all the answers five minutes ago.

"We'll go," she said, her chest tightening at the look of panic on her son's face. "Maybe we can meet up with you later? So we can talk?"

Diego shook his head, motioning to a paramedic as the other SWAT cop headed for the RV.

"If you don't mind, I'd rather have a paramedic take a look at you and your son," Diego said. "I know you don't think it's necessary, but it would make me feel a lot better. By the time you're done, I should be finished with my chief. That way, we can have that talk sooner rather than later."

Bree didn't feel it was necessary to have a paramedic check her out, but Brandon was a different matter. He'd gone down hard when Diego had tackled the gunman. She wouldn't be surprised if her son had a concussion or even a cracked rib or two. So, she agreed with a nod.

"This is Trent Barnes," Diego said, introducing the tall, dark-haired paramedic who jogged over. "He'll take good care of you two until I can get back. I'll be as quick as I can."

Bree nodded again, surprised to realize she didn't care how long they had to wait. She tried to tell herself it was because they needed to talk about Brandon, but as Diego regarded her with those chocolate-brown eyes, she admitted there was something more to it than that. She didn't want to think about what that might be right now, but it was there all the same.

CHAPTER 2

Chief Shanette Leclair turned and pinned Diego with an impatient look the moment he stepped into the RV. Trey, Connor, Hale, and Mike, on the other hand, regarded him curiously. Probably wondering what was up with the young beta werewolf.

"Good of you to join us, Officer Martinez." Tall and slender with medium-brown skin and black hair swept back in a neat bun, the chief had a reputation for being tough, but fair. "When you didn't come back with Corporal Taylor, I was worried you were injured. I'm relieved to see you're simply slow."

Diego ignored the jab. While the new chief of police had only been on the job for a few months, it hadn't taken very long to figure out the woman only revealed her snarky side to those she respected. And damn, did she love to get sarcastic with her SWAT team.

Of course, the chief's special relationship with the SWAT team might also have had a lot to do with the fact that she had a thing for Mike. True, the chief of police had a right to be interested in the health and welfare of every single one of her officers, but a werewolf would have to be absolutely clueless not to pick up on the way the woman showed up at any incident involving Mike. Or the fact that her heart tended to race like mad until the moment she confirmed he was safe.

"Sorry it took me a while," Diego said, closing the door behind him. "I wanted to get a paramedic to check out two of the hostages."

"The boy and woman I saw you come out of the diner with?" The chief's hazel eyes filled with concern. "Corporal Taylor mentioned they'd risk their lives to help the two officers who'd been shot. Are they okay?"

"They're okay," he said. "The boy went down hard when I tackled the suspect, but something tells me he's tougher than he looks."

Leclair nodded. "That's good to hear. Now, maybe you can tell me what the hell happened in there. How did we go from a guy shooting two cops and taking a diner full of people hostage to him killing himself?"

Diego told the chief everything. Well, not the whole werewolf thing, of course. But he definitely emphasized Ken's bizarre behavior and how the guy had floated in and out of awareness throughout the situation.

"Those were his exact words before he shot himself—'Don't let him get away with this'?" Leclair frowned. "What does that even mean? Who was he referring to? Did someone make him do all this, including shooting himself in the head? Or was it some convoluted Freudian reference to his inner id?"

Diego crossed his arms over his chest. "I'd be lying if I said I knew the answer to any of those questions. All I can say for sure is that right there at the end, Ken didn't look like someone who wanted to take his own life—or anyone else's."

"What do you mean?" the chief asked.

He shrugged. "I'm not any kind of expert on the subject, and I'm certainly not a shrink, but as a negotiator, I've been in the horrible position of watching way too many people kill themselves. And in every one of those cases, right before the person went through with it, a moment of calm came over them. I've always assumed it had something to do with accepting what they were about to do. But when Ken killed himself, he was fighting tooth and nail against it."

The chief was silent as she considered that. Diego glanced at his teammates to see they looked as confused by his take on what had happened in there as she did. *Join the club.*

After a long moment, she sighed. "Okay, once we confirm his identity, I'll get our detectives working on trying to link this guy to any of the previous suspects."

The impromptu meeting ended shortly after that, and Diego took the opportunity to slip away while the chief chatted with Mike about attending a seminar on transformative management techniques the department would be putting on in a couple weeks.

Mike nodded like he was riveted by the idea. More like enthralled with Chief Leclair. "I think I've heard about that program. It sounds really interesting."

Diego exchanged looks with his other pack mates to see if they were hearing the same thing he was. The amusement on their faces confirmed it. He'd be damned. Mike was flirting with the chief over a management seminar.

Shaking his head, Diego opened the door. He smelled the young beta the moment he was outside the RV. Surprisingly, he also smelled the kid's mother just as easily. Actually, in some ways, her scent seemed even stronger. Diego let himself focus on her fragrance for a moment, picking out hints of strawberry, vanilla, and a distinctly feminine scent that seemed uniquely her own.

He crossed the street, following her scent while doing his

best not to dwell on why it was so tantalizing. She smelled amazing. That was as far as he cared to go at the moment.

Both scents led him to one of the many ambulances lined up outside the security perimeter. Heading around to the side door, he tapped on the metal doorframe as he stuck his head inside. The beta werewolf and his mom were sitting side by side on a gurney while Trent checked them out.

"What's the word, Trent?" Diego asked.

His buddy from Dallas Fire and Rescue looked over with a grin as he pulled a blood-pressure cuff off the kid's arm. "Bree is dealing with an elevated heart rate and her pressure is a bit high, but that's to be expected considering what she went through this morning."

Bree.

So, that was her name. It was beautiful. Just like the woman it belonged to. Diego had noticed how pretty she was when he'd first laid eyes on her in the diner, but now that he had time to appreciate her, it was impossible to miss how stunning she was. An angelic heart-shaped face, plump pink lips, and eyes the color of creamy milk chocolate. She was definitely something else.

Diego didn't realize he was standing there staring until he noticed Trent had been talking the whole time and he hadn't heard a single word.

"Brandon, on the other hand, is as fit as a horse," Trent said with a laugh. "In fact, he's got the pulse rate and blood pressure of an elite marathon runner. He's got some bumps and bruises from you tackling him, but by and large, it's like the stuff this morning didn't bother him at all."

Diego chuckled as he stepped into the tight confines of the ambulance. Even without three other people in here, these vehicles weren't meant for men his size. Hearing Trent go on about how healthy Brandon was after what happened wasn't a surprise. All werewolves were fit AF.

"Now that you've checked them over and made sure they're okay, do you mind if I borrow your ambulance for a few minutes?" he asked. "I need to talk to Bree and Brandon about a few things, and your ride is about the only privacy available in a five-block radius."

Trent nodded. "No problem. The rig is all yours until we catch a call."

Diego heard Bree's heart beat a little faster as Trent stepped outside and closed the door. Brandon's pulse kicked up a notch as well.

"Before I say anything else, I guess formal introductions are in order," he said, sitting on the fold-down seat across from them and holding out his hand. "Diego Martinez."

She leaned forward, clasping his big hand with her smaller one. Diego couldn't miss how soft her skin was or how badly he wanted to rub small circles on the back of it with his thumb.

"Bree Harlow," she said, and maybe it was his imagination, but she seemed to hold on to his hand for an extra second or two. "And this is my son, Brandon. You saved his life in that diner. Thank you for that."

Diego opened his mouth to tell her he was simply doing his job, but the look of true gratitude in her eyes stopped him.

"Brandon is my world, and you risked your life to keep him safe," she said softly. "If I live to be a thousand years old, I'll never be able to pay you back for that. I'm not sure how to try beyond saying thank you."

The heartfelt words tugged at Diego in a way he'd never felt before. It might be his job, but Brandon was her son. Saving Brandon's life wasn't just another day at the office. It had been a very big deal.

"You're welcome," he said.

His voice sounded huskier than normal, and he cleared his throat as he reached out to shake Brandon's hand. The kid had a firm grip.

"You said we have a lot to talk about?" Brandon said, sitting back. "Does that mean you can explain what happened to me in that diner? Because it's been happening to me for months."

Out of the corner of his eye, Diego saw Bree's eyes widen in surprise, then fill with pain. As though she hadn't known her son had been dealing with something like this for so long. Diego had never thought about what it must be like for a mother or father of someone going through the change. Then again, how often did a teenager have to deal with becoming a werewolf?

"How old are you, Brandon?"

Brandon seemed caught off guard by the question, but after a moment, he sat up straighter, squared his shoulders, and put on his I'm-older-than-I-look face.

"I'm fifteen," he said, pinning Diego with an expression that dared him to say anything. "I'll be sixteen in four months."

Diego resisted the urge to chuckle, even if his first instinct was to reach over and ruffle the kid's already tousled hair. He couldn't imagine being fifteen years old and dealing with claws and fangs. He'd been an adult when it happened to him, and even with Hale helping him through it, the whole werewolf thing still seriously messed with his head.

"Do you remember exactly when you realized there was something strange going on with you?" Diego asked, wondering if Brandon's change would follow the typical steps considering he was so young.

Brandon looked introspective for a moment. "I got shot about two months ago. It was right after that."

Diego wanted to ask how Brandon had gotten shot, but that was something they could talk about later.

"What kind of things started happening?" he prompted.

Brandon frowned. "I can smell things way better than I ever used to. And I keep having these weird dreams about running through the woods. They're so real it's like I'm really there, then when I wake up, there's blood in my mouth and my fingertips are bleeding."

The kid was quiet for a long time, and this time, Diego didn't rush him. He remembered dealing with those exact things and how much they'd scared him.

"I thought it was just my mind playing tricks on me, you know?" Brandon continued, his heart beating a little faster now. "But when I have the dreams now, I wake up and my bedsheets are all ripped up. It's really freaking me out."

Diego opened his mouth to tell him it was okay and that all of this was normal—at least in the beginning—but before he could say anything, the kid spoke again.

"The past week has been the worst," he said, his voice on the edge of panic. "My muscles twitch and spasm all the time, my bones hurt like hell, and my teeth come right out of my gums and get longer, then go back in again. Like in the diner earlier."

Brandon was breathing so fast he was on the verge of hyperventilating, and yellow swirled in his eyes. Diego reached out for him, knowing the teen was close to losing it right there in the back of the ambulance.

Bree got to her son first.

She enveloped his clasped hands in hers, squeezing them tight. That simple touch, along with a mother's loving proximity, seemed to be all Brandon needed. He calmed within seconds.

"Honey, why didn't you tell me about any of this?" she whispered, a mix of concern and disappointment on her face. "I've been worried about you for weeks, but every time I tried to get you to talk to me about it, you shut me out."

"I'm sorry, Mom." Brandon's voice was soft, his eyes full of chagrin and embarrassment as he looked at her. "I wanted to tell you so many times, but I didn't think you'd believe me. I didn't believe it myself, and it was happening right in front of me. I thought I was going crazy or something."

Bree blinked quickly, like she was fighting tears, then turned to look at Diego. "Can you tell me what's happening to my son?" she asked, her voice close to breaking. "I was sure this was some kind of drug addiction, but after hearing the things he's describing, it doesn't sound like any kind of drug I've ever heard of."

Brandon flushed, making Diego think Bree had touched on a separate issue they'd have to deal with. Later. After they got through the werewolf thing. That was going to be hard enough for these two to handle.

"Yeah, I know what's happening." Diego looked from mother to son and back again. "I know because I went through the same thing eight years ago. It was scary for me, too, but I promise it has nothing to do with drugs or insanity."

Brandon seemed to relax a little at that. His mother, on the other hand, seemed to tense up even more.

"While I know exactly what you're going through, it isn't going to make what I have to tell you any easier to understand. Mainly because it's complicated and hard to believe," Diego continued. "Your first instinct will be to tell me I'm crazy, then run out of here screaming and never look back, but I need you to trust me."

Bree's beautiful, dark eyes filled with alarm. "You're starting to really freak me out. Just tell me what's wrong with my son."

"There's nothing wrong with him," Diego said gently. "Your son is going through a change that started when he was shot. Everything he's experiencing—the claws and fangs, the ways his senses have gone haywire, the strange dreams, the muscle spasms—are simply his body adapting to its new abilities. It's his inner wolf coming out."

Bree stared at him in confusion. "I don't understand what you're saying. What new abilities? And what the hell do you mean by 'inner wolf'?"

Diego took a deep breath. Damn, he wished someone else from the Pack was here to explain this. Because he was already screwing it up.

"I know this is going to sound crazy, but your son is a werewolf."

Bree didn't say a word. Expression suddenly hard, she stood, yanking Brandon to his feet and starting for the door.

Diego caught her arm. "Bree, please. Remember when I said I needed you to trust me? Let me finish and all of this will make sense."

She glared at him. "How can you seriously expect me to listen to this? What you said isn't just insane. It's impossible!"

Diego cursed silently. Knowing it was probably the very worst way to handle this volatile situation, but not having a better idea, he leaned back and let his own inner wolf partially out. He allowed his eyes to change from deep, dark brown to vivid yellow-gold, upper and lower inch-long canines to slide out, and deadly looking claws to extend. He could have pushed it all the way, until his clothes fell off, thick fur covered every part of his body, and he grew a frigging tail.

But that might be a bit much for Bree and her son to deal with at the moment.

Turns out the fangs, claws, and glowing eyes were over the top as far as Bree was concerned. She let out a little scream and scrambled backward until she thumped against the far side of the vehicle. She probably would have fallen out the door if it had been open.

But at the same time his mother was freaking out, Brandon froze solid. Then a second later, he stepped closer, his expression equal parts relief and concern.

"This is real?" he asked. "This is why I grew fangs in the middle of the diner full of people? I'm turning into a monster?" His eyes went wide. "Crap! Is that why the guy in there was shouting about monsters? Did he know what I am? Was he going to tell the world about me?"

Diego let his body shift back, the corner of his mouth edging up. "That's the same thing I said when I went through my change, so I understand what's going through your head. You aren't turning into a monster, and that guy had no idea you're a werewolf. He was messed up, that's all. As far as what's going on with you, things are merely a little out of control right now. Your fangs came out in the diner because you were frigging scared. Once you gain control of your abilities, that won't happen to you anymore. I can help you gain that control, if you'll let me."

The inside of the ambulance fell silent, the sounds from outside the only thing filling the space. That was it. He'd made his pitch. Now, it was up to Brandon—and Bree—to accept his help or walk away.

Diego held his breath as Brandon turned to look questioningly at his mother. When Bree gave him a tremulous smile and nodded, it was as if a weight he hadn't even realized was there lifted from his shoulders. When had this kid become his responsibility?

"This is totally insane, but if you can help my son, I don't care how crazy it is," Bree said, stepping away from the wall and turning her gaze on him. "You saved our lives. That earns you the benefit of the doubt."

Diego was so relieved, he felt like laughing, but he restrained himself. Neither of them would appreciate him laughing at a serious moment like this.

"So," Brandon said, hope warring with worry on his face. "How does this work? Are there classes for something like this, or will this be more like an on-the-job thing?"

Diego opened his mouth only to close it again. Damn, he didn't have a flipping clue how to answer that question. But he knew someone who would.

"There are some people I'd like you to meet who will help you and your mom have a better understanding of what it means to be a werewolf," he said.

"Other people?" Bree said slowly. "You mean other werewolves?"

Brandon's heart thumped faster again. "There are other people like us in the world?"

Diego grinned. "Other werewolves? Yeah, you could say that."

When they stepped out of the ambulance, Bree's heart was thumping so fast she was sure it was about to jump out of her chest and run screaming across the street and down the sidewalk—where it would probably be squished flat by the crowd still gathered behind the crime tape. Because seriously, that was the kind of morning she was having.

Not only had she and Brandon almost been killed, but now it turned out her son was a werewolf. If Diego was to be believed. And for reasons she couldn't come close to explaining, she *did* believe him. Bree wasn't sure which one of them was crazier. Diego for claiming to be a werewolf or her for believing him.

Now, she and Brandon were going with Diego to the SWAT compound so they could supposedly meet up with even more werewolves. Nope, that wasn't crazy at all.

Her first instinct was to say *hell no*. Actually, her first instinct had been to grab Brandon and run for the hills. But something about Diego made her instinctively trust him. He barely knew them, and yet he seemed to genuinely care about her and her son. Her ex-husband had never looked at either of them that way, that was for sure. She was stunned at how good that made her feel.

"I need to tell my teammates where I'm going," Diego said as they started across the street.

The moment they reached the sidewalk, a man stepped in front of them, blocking their path. Average height with wavy blond hair, he wore a pair of dress pants and a short-sleeved shirt, both of which were slightly wrinkled, as well as glasses. The guy hadn't said a word yet, but Bree could tell from the way Diego's jaw tightened that he didn't like the guy. For some strange reason, Bree found herself not liking him, either.

"Officer Martinez, another day, another violent crime involving a suspect who doesn't fit the profile," the man drawled, the smile curving his mouth making her think he relished the idea of such violence. He held out a small recorder. "Can you confirm for the record that this morning's hostage situation was another case of a delirium overdose?"

Diego regarded the guy as though he would rather have stepped on him than answer the question. "Delirium? Are you serious?"

"Yeah. Everyone's calling it that now."

"You're the only one who's calling it that."

The man grinned. "Okay. You got me there. But it's catchy, isn't it?"

Diego scowled. "There's a reason we put up crime-scene tape, Hobbs. Because you're supposed to be on the other side of it. You know any official statement for the media involving an active case has to come through DPD public relations."

Since the guy was a reporter, Bree expected him to say something about the public's right to know. But Hobbs didn't bat an eye.

"No problem." Hobbs slanted a sly look at her and Brandon, gray eyes assessing behind his glasses, before he slipped the recorder in his pocket and turned his attention back to Diego. "I'm fine with a comment off the record. We both know there's something strange going on here. The people involved in this recent crime wave are ordinary, everyday people who wake up one morning and decide to do something out of character—like take a diner full of people hostage. The rumors are that there's a new drug on the street. I simply need a source to confirm it. I'll never mention you by name."

Diego snorted. "Good try, Hobbs. Not going to happen. Once more for the cheap seats, I have no comment on any active investigation, which includes this morning's events at the diner, or any other incidents of this so-called crime wave."

"So, you're confirming there's a crime wave?"

When Diego merely glared at him, Hobbs looked at her and Brandon, giving them what he probably thought was a charming smile. "Ernest Hobbs, *Dallas Daily Star*. I can only imagine the trauma you and your son experienced this morning. Care to talk about what happened in the diner?"

"Give it a rest, Hobbs," Diego practically snarled as he stepped between Bree and the man. "They've been through enough. Like I said, if you want a statement, you'll need to get it from public relations. Until then, get back behind the tape."

Hobbs looked like he was about to argue, but when Diego motioned toward a patrol officer near the diner, the reporter held up his hands in acquiescence.

"I'm going." Turning, he walked a few steps, then looked back at Diego. "The DPD can try to keep a lid on this, but that's not going to work much longer. There are frigging doctors and lawyers knocking off banks and jewelry stores. When this whole mess blows up in your faces, I'll be right there waiting to print every word of it, laughing my ass off the whole damn time."

Diego made a sound that was suspiciously close to a growl as he watched Hobbs head for the crime-scene tape at the end of the block.

"Is all that stuff he said about a drug out there making people do violent things true?" Brandon asked, eyes fixed on Diego. "Is that why the guy in the diner took all of us hostage, then shot himself?"

"We don't know," a deep voice said from behind them.

Bree turned to see three cops in heavy tactical gear approaching. Two of them must have come through the windows of the diner with the officer she'd seen earlier because their uniforms were torn in several places.

"But Hobbs is right about people doing stuff you wouldn't expect," the man continued. "If we're being totally honest, he might be right about the drugs. Something is causing them to act strangely, and drugs are about the only good explanation we can come up with."

It was obvious Brandon had a lot more questions about what happened in the diner, but he also seemed aware that now wasn't the right time for them.

"Bree, Brandon," Diego said, "these are three of my teammates—Trey Duncan, Hale Delaney, and Connor Malone."

All three of the men were built like Diego with muscles piled on top of muscles and attractive beyond all possible reason. Well, none of them were nearly as good looking as Diego, but pretty darn close. Were they all so well built because they were SWAT or because they were all werewolves?

Good heavens, she really had lost her mind. Now she was seeing werewolves everywhere.

Trey was the one with the deep voice. He had intense blue eyes to go with those tones, and Bree wondered why he was a cop instead of a movie star. Hale had dark-blond hair, blue eyes, and a nose that looked like it had been broken at some point. Connor had hair that couldn't seem to decide if it wanted to be blond or brown and a distinctly California surfer look that totally worked.

She was so busy gazing at all the hunky men around her that she hadn't realized Brandon was staring, too. Not until he asked the same thing she'd been wondering earlier.

"Are all of you like Diego?"

Connor looked at him in confusion. "You mean short?"

"Ugly?" Trey suggested helpfully.

"Misshapen?" offered Hale, arching a brow at the look Bree gave him. "What? He's practically as broad as he is tall."

Bree almost laughed at the exaggeration. Diego had broad shoulders, but he certainly wasn't short and misshapen, and definitely not ugly. Like she'd said, while these other three guys were attractive, they couldn't hold a candle to Diego. Chocolate-brown eyes she could get lost in. Silky dark hair she wanted to run her fingers through. And biceps she was sure she couldn't get her hand around. She had a real thing for well-muscled arms.

When Brandon still looked baffled, Diego apparently decided to take pity on him because he nodded. "Yeah, they're like me. Like us, actually. Though we both have a better sense of humor. It's not their fault. They're clueless when it comes to knowing what's funny and what isn't."

His friends all chuckled at that as Trey held out Bree's cell phone. "I think this is yours."

"It is! Thank you." She slid it in her purse with a smile. "I forgot all about it."

Which was crazy, considering she always had it with her. Then again, a lot had happened today.

"Could you tell Mike I'm bringing Bree and Brandon to the compound so we can talk to Gage?" Diego asked. "I'll probably need you to cover for me when Internal Affairs shows up, too."

Trey nodded. "Will do. I'll talk to Mike as soon as he's done with the chief. IA, too. But after listening to some of the statements from the people in the diner, I can't imagine Internal Affairs trying to jack you up over this. You did everything you could to talk that guy down."

From the expression on Diego's face, it didn't seem like he was buying that last part. He didn't say anything, though. Instead, he turned to her and Brandon. "You two ready to get out of here?"

Bree nodded. "Is it okay if we take my car? It's parked in the garage two blocks over."

"That's fine," Diego said, falling into step beside her and Brandon. "Better than trying to get through the crowds with one of the SWAT SUVs for sure."

A few people took Diego's picture as they moved through the crowd behind the crime-scene tape, and Bree knew she and Brandon would be in more than a few of them. Hopefully, they wouldn't show up on someone's Facebook or Instagram page. Or worse, one of the media outlets.

Bree was still imagining what her boss at the insurance company would say about one of his investigators being involved in a hostage situation, when she heard a voice that stopped her cold. Out the corner of her eye, she saw Brandon stiffen.

"Bree! Brandon! I'm so relieved you're okay!"

She turned to see her ex-husband pushing his way through the crowd to get to them. For a moment, Bree thought he was going to hug her, but the look on her face must have changed his mind because he stopped in front of them instead. Thank God. She really wasn't in a mood to deal with him and his games today.

"Dave, Officer Diego Martinez, Dallas SWAT," she said. "This is my ex-husband, Dave Cowell."

Dave's hazel eyes narrowed as he sized up Diego, and Bree braced herself. Saying he was possessive was an understatement. He'd always hated when other men looked her way, much less talked to her, and he didn't mind letting them know it. That's what had put him in prison.

But instead of going ballistic like usual, he extended his hand to Diego. "Officer."

While he hadn't gone into a jealous rage, there was no mistaking the disdain in Dave's tone. And from the way he was trying to crush Diego's hand as they shook, it was obvious there was some kind of testosterone-laden display going on. Diego didn't seem to notice.

"Mr. Cowell," he said.

With the pleasantries out of the way—if you could call them that—Dave turned his attention back to her. Even though he was as tall as Diego, he wasn't nearly as muscular. And while she'd fallen for those clean-cut good looks and that Ivy League charm when she was eighteen, they'd stopped doing anything for her a long time ago.

"What are you doing here, Dave?" She folded her arms. "And don't tell me you just happened to be in the area."

"No, I wasn't in the area." He regarded her thoughtfully, his expression impossible to read. "I heard on the radio there was a hostage situation at the diner and remembered we used to come here together when Brandon was little. And...I can't explain it, but I got a feeling you were both in danger. Something made me drive down here to make sure you were safe. Good thing I did because the first thing I saw when I got here was you and Brandon coming out of the diner and being taken to an ambulance."

Bree had to bite her tongue to keep from calling BS on that entire lame-ass explanation. Her ex had always been a vain, narcissistic man who assumed anything he said would be accepted without comment. The thought she wouldn't believe what he was saying likely never entered his mind.

Dave had always been erratic, but his stay in prison had made it worse. Since he'd gotten out, most of the time he didn't seem to remember he had an ex-wife or a son—which was perfectly fine with her. Other times, he'd show up and act like she and Brandon were precious to him. He never mentioned he'd been absent from their lives. He acted as though it had simply been a weekend business trip, not a five-year prison sentence. Bree didn't buy his act and knew Brandon didn't, either.

Currently, Dave worked in the downtown financial district near the Trinity River. If he was all the way over here in north Lochwood, it was more likely because he'd been stalking them than anything else. There was no way he could've gotten here this quickly otherwise.

"Thank you for worrying about us, but there was no

need," she said. "We have Officer Martinez to thank for saving our lives."

Dave's gaze went to Diego, his expression calculating. After a moment, his mouth curved into a duplicitous smile. "Then it looks like I owe you a huge debt of gratitude. Bree and my son are the most important people in the world to me. I don't know what I would have done if I'd lost them."

"I was just doing my job," Diego said. "The real credit should go to Bree and Brandon. They risked their lives to help two DPD officers. They were amazing."

Bree was stunned at how thrilled she got at Diego's words. It was silly, of course. She and Brandon had done nothing more than press some dish towels to the officers' wounds, desperate to stop the bleeding. They'd been successful more from luck than skill. Still, it made her stomach do funny little cartwheels to know Diego had seen their efforts and appreciated them.

"It's nice to know that someone else thinks as highly of Bree and Brandon as I do," Dave said with a nod, the fake smile disappearing. "They've been through a lot today, so if you'll excuse us, I'll take them home. Thanks again for your help."

Like hell he was taking them home, Bree thought as Brandon tensed beside her. Once again, Dave seemed to have forgotten they were divorced—and had been for years.

Diego must have picked up on the sudden tension, because before she could say anything, he stepped a little in front of her and Brandon like he'd done earlier, his big body forming a shield between them and her ex.

"That's not going to be an option at the moment, Mr. Cowell," he said firmly, and from where she stood, Bree knew his eyes were locked on Dave's. "Bree and Brandon both played a key role in the events that occurred in the diner. Getting their statements while their memories are still fresh is critical. We were on our way to the police station when you stopped us."

Diego's tone left no doubt in Bree's mind that she and Brandon would be leaving with him, regardless of what Dave thought about the subject. An all-too-familiar flash of anger entered her ex-husband's eyes and Bree held her breath, sure the idiot was actually going to try to fight Diego right there in the middle of a street filled with witnesses—and other cops.

Bree knew it was horrible, but she almost wished Dave would do something that stupid. She was certain Diego could deal with anything her jerk of an ex threw at him. She immediately chided herself, hating the thought of Brandon seeing something like that. There was no love lost between him and his father, but her son had been through enough because of Dave's anger-management issues.

To her surprise, Dave took a step back. She was even more stunned when the fury on his face disappeared to be replaced by curiosity.

"Why do you need their statements?" he asked in a tone that was way too calm and even for the man Bree knew. "I thought the gunman in the diner killed himself. Why would anyone care enough to bother with statements?"

"Who said anything about the gunman killing himself?" Diego asked from where he still stood in front of them.

Dave shrugged. "Everyone's talking about it."

Diego seemed to consider that a moment before he nodded. "You probably shouldn't believe everything you hear. Regardless, we still need their statements. Unless you have a problem with that?"

Her ex-husband regarded Diego for a moment before giving him a smile. "Of course not, Officer. I wouldn't dream of causing a problem." Leaning to the side to see around Diego better, he caught Bree's eye. "I'll call you later to make sure you got home okay, babe."

As Dave turned and walked away, a shiver of unease slid down Bree's spine. He continued to creep her out all these years after their divorce. He'd treated her like a piece of property when they'd been married and still did. The controlling jerk couldn't seem to get it through his thick head that she wanted nothing to do with him and hadn't for a long time.

Then Diego's big, warm hand was on her arm and the dread she felt immediately faded away. "You ready to get out of here?"

She glanced at Brandon, who eagerly nodded.

"Definitely," she said.

CHAPTER 3

After what the kid had gone through that morning, Diego expected Brandon to be quiet during the drive across town to the SWAT compound. Instead, he talked from the time they'd left the parking garage until Diego pulled Bree's SUV into the visitor parking lot across the street from the fenced-in facility. Brandon had asked a few general questions about being a werewolf, like if they turned every time there was a full moon—Hollywood was doing the werewolf community no favors with that crap—but mostly it had been a nonstop monologue on everything he'd experienced over the past month and a half since going through his change.

Brandon also admitted how scared he'd been during the hostage situation that his claws and fangs would come out and someone at the diner would see them. In his teenage mind, being called a freak would be the worst thing ever.

But as frightened as Brandon had been for himself, he'd been more concerned for Bree. The thought of the crowd turning on her for being the mother of a monster had terrified him. The words had brought tears to Bree's eyes and done a number on Diego as well. The thought of someone going after either of them made his inner wolf's fangs and claws come out.

He led Bree and Brandon through the gates of the compound and headed for the admin building, where the commander of the SWAT team and the alpha of their pack of alphas, Gage Dixon, was waiting for them. If anyone could help a werewolf still going through puberty, it'd be Gage. The man was a Jedi master when it came to dealing with bizarre crap like this.

They were barely halfway across the compound when Brandon paused, instinctively turning into the breeze, his nose twitching as he took in the many scents around him. Diego almost laughed both at the intense expression on the kid's face and the baffled one on Bree's.

"What's that I'm smelling?" Brandon asked, turning his nose this way and that curiously. "I smelled it earlier at the diner, but it's a lot stronger here."

Diego grinned when he caught Bree sniffing the air, trying to figure out what her son was smelling when he knew for a fact she couldn't smell anything.

"You're smelling the other werewolves in the compound," Diego told him. "There were only five of us at the diner this morning. This place serves as a second home for the eighteen alpha werewolves in my SWAT pack. Not to mention the other werewolves that frequently hang out here. It's not surprising you're picking up the scent even if you didn't have a clue what you were smelling yet."

"Alpha werewolves?" Brandon considered that. "Does that mean there are other kinds of werewolves? Am I an alpha, too?"

"Wait a minute," Bree said, holding up her hand. "Did you actually use the word 'pack' to describe you and the other members of the SWAT team? As in a pack of wolves? Is that how you see yourselves?"

"Will I be able to join your pack?" Brandon jumped in before Diego could answer, practically bouncing up and down in excitement. "Can I be on the SWAT team, too?"

Bree threw Diego a look of utter panic, her dark eyes silently begging him to say something to stop her kid from starting down this path. Diego opened his mouth to say something wise and insightful only to close it again when he realized he had absolutely no idea how to start. He considered himself above average when it came to giving advice, but right then, with Brandon desperately wanting answers to all his questions, he simply didn't know what to say.

Hopefully, Gage would.

"Let's put a hold on the really complicated questions until we get inside," Diego finally said, glancing over his shoulder to catch Bree's eye and give her a little nod of understanding. "There's someone I want you to meet who will be able to explain all of this to you better than I ever could."

Brandon looked like he didn't want to wait that long but nodded anyway.

When they got to the admin building, Diego held open the door for them. His gaze automatically locked on Bree's butt as she moved ahead of him. After the day she'd had, he felt bad about looking at her that way, but his inner wolf seemed to have a mind of its own and simply wouldn't be denied. And yeah, his inner wolf definitely liked what it saw. Bree might be wearing a simple pair of jeans and a T-shirt, but she made them look damn good. Snug enough to show off her feminine curves, making the view from behind spectacular.

At the sight of the tall, blond woman in Gage's office, he forced his mind off the image of Bree's incredible body and back to the subject of their new teenage werewolf. Diego had called Gage on the drive over to give him a heads-up about bringing in a young beta who was still going through his change. And Gage had called the one alpha werewolf they knew who had a whole pack of them.

That was some next-level thinking right there and one hell of a brilliant idea.

Jayna was the wife and soul mate of Diego's teammate, Eric Becker. She was also one of the only werewolves Diego had ever heard of who started out as a beta, then went through a second change to become an alpha to take over for the one who'd done a crappy job of protecting her pack. Jayna had taken over the pack, making it her own. Even though she and Becker were a couple, it was still her pack. Becker was essentially a co-alpha. Unique, for sure, but it seemed to work for them.

Diego led Bree and Brandon through the empty bullpen and into Gage's office. When he made the introductions, mentioning Gage and Jayna were also alphas, Bree and Brandon both nervously shook hands with them. That wasn't surprising. Tall and muscular with dark hair and intense dark eyes, Gage could sometimes be intimidating. As for Jayna, she had a presence about her that you only saw with female alphas.

"Let's sit," Gage suggested, giving them a smile and motioning toward the small conference table to one side of his office. "From what Diego told me on the phone, I get the feeling things have been pretty crazy for you two lately."

Bree laughed as she sat between Diego and Brandon. It was a beautiful sound that made Diego's inner wolf sit up and take notice.

"'Crazy' would be a bit of an understatement," she said, glancing at her son, a mix of worry and love on her face. "Like I told Diego, when these strange things started happening to Brandon after he'd been shot, I thought he was using drugs."

"Mom!" Brandon groaned, a hand coming up to cover his face in embarrassment, but not before Diego saw him flush. It would have been cute if the subject wasn't so scary. The thought of the kid getting shot made his stomach twist up in knots.

"Don't 'mom' me," Bree said, her lips curving into a smile. "All I knew was that something was going on with you. Something that was making you act different, and since you wouldn't talk to me about it, what else was I supposed to think? It makes sense it would be drugs." The smile faded and her eyes glistened with tears. "I was scared I was going to lose you, honey."

The pain in those words about ripped Diego's heart right out of his chest. Crap, he could barely breathe. He swallowed hard and fought through it. Why wasn't he maintaining his usual professional demeanor in this situation?

"But you weren't taking drugs," Bree said softly. "You were simply turning into a werewolf. I guess I had no reason to worry. Can't believe I didn't think of that myself," she added with a strangled laugh.

When Brandon looked chagrined at that, Diego assumed it was because he felt bad about hiding the werewolf stuff from his mother, but his gut told him there was more to it than that. He wanted to ask what the deal was, but bringing it up in front of everyone wouldn't be a good idea.

"I think most parents would have assumed the same," Jayna said gently. "The possibility that their son was becoming a werewolf isn't something most people would ever think to worry about."

Bree snorted, a sound halfway between a laugh and a sob. "Yet, here we are. Which I suppose begs the question—how did this happen? Diego told me Brandon's a werewolf, and since he showed us his claws and fangs, I guess that means he's one, too. He told us that the other members of his...pack...are alpha werewolves like the three of you. He made it sound so simple, but he never said how any of this is possible. I mean, if Brandon had been bitten by a werewolf, wouldn't I know? Even if he obviously tells me nothing about what's going on in his life, am I really that clueless about what's been happening to my son?"

Diego didn't know he'd reached out to take her hand until he felt the warm, soft skin under his fingers. He half expected her to pull her away. Instead she squeezed his hand tightly.

"Turning into a werewolf doesn't work the same way in real life that it does in the movies, Bree. A bite won't do it," Gage said from the other side of the table. "Some people are born with a little something extra in their DNA, and when they go through a traumatic event, the rush of adrenaline and cortisol flips the gene, turning them into a werewolf."

Bree's eyes went wide, her grip on Diego's hand tightening. "It happened when Brandon got shot, didn't it?"

"Yes," Gage said. "If he didn't have the gene, he probably would have died."

Bree's expression was thoughtful, and she looked like she might say something else, but Brandon spoke first.

"Did something like what happened to me happen to you guys and the other werewolves on the SWAT team?"

Jayna nodded. "My change was triggered when I got

assaulted. Gage was injured in combat, and Diego was shot in the line of duty."

Brandon leaned forward, his eyes suddenly lighting up. "I got shot like Diego. Does that mean I'm an alpha, too?"

Gage gave him a small smile. "What kind of werewolf you become depends on what you were doing when the traumatic event that turned you happened."

Meaning that if a person turned while they were risking their life for someone else, they became an alpha, like Diego. If not, then you turned into a beta, like Brandon.

"Okay," Brandon said. "So, what am I?"

"You're a beta," Gage answered.

"How do you know? I didn't tell you what I was doing or where I was when I got shot."

"We can tell what kind of a werewolf you are by your scent," Jayna said.

"Are you sure?" Brandon asked, disappointment clear on his face. "Maybe after I get older?"

"Nope," Jayna said. "You're definitely a beta."

"Is being a beta a bad thing?" Bree asked, a little of that earlier panic back in her voice. "Should I be worried?"

Jayna shook her head, lips curving into a smile. "No and no. Betas might not be as big or strong or as aggressive as alphas, but their true strength isn't in what they can physically do. It's in their ability to form tight pack bonds. Nothing ever comes between a beta and their pack. No werewolf—even an alpha—would try to take on a beta in a fight because that would mean going up against his or her entire pack."

Brandon considered that for a long time. "So, I'll be part of a pack that close?" he asked hopefully.

"Yup," Jayna said. "Once you meet the alpha you're

meant to be with, everything will fall into place like the pieces of a puzzle."

"How will I know when I meet him?" Brandon asked.

Jayna's gaze went from Brandon to Diego and back again. "You'll know."

Brandon nodded, but still looked a little unsure.

"Actually," Diego said, looking at Jayna, "I was thinking Brandon could meet your pack. Being around some other betas will be good for him."

Jayna nodded. "Everly's baby shower is this Saturday. Everyone will be there, and I can't imagine a better time for Brandon to get to know them."

Brandon looked at his mother expectantly. "Can we?"

"I don't know, honey. I wouldn't want to intrude."

Gage chuckled. "You never need to worry about that. You're part of our extended family now. Besides, there are going to be nearly fifty people there already. Everly and Cooper won't mind."

Brandon grinned. "Come on, Mom. You have to say yes."

She laughed. "Okay, okay. We'll go."

Diego relaxed back in his chair. Damn, he'd been as eager for Bree to agree as Brandon was.

"Excellent!" Jayna said, smiling at Brandon. "What do you say we go for a walk around the compound? I may be an alpha now, but I remember being a new beta werewolf and how confusing everything was. I could give you some pointers."

Brandon was half out of his chair before he remembered he should probably check with his mother. Bree let out another laugh.

"Go ahead."

No sooner were Brandon and Jayna out the door than

Gage announced he had some work to do in the training building, leaving Diego alone with Bree.

She chewed on her bottom lip thoughtfully before turning her head to gaze at him. Damn, she had beautiful eyes. "If beta werewolves bond as tightly as Gage said, will Brandon go off and live with his alpha when they find each other? Please be honest. Am I going to lose my son?"

The pain in Bree's voice tore at him, and yet Diego hesitated. That question was more complicated than it sounded. Jayna had been right when she'd talked about how tight betas became when they bonded with members of their pack. It was next-level stuff.

"When Brandon meets the werewolves he's supposed to bond with, they *will* be close, but their pack bond will never replace the love a child has for their mother," Diego said gently. "I've been a werewolf for eight years, and I see my mom at least once a week."

Bree visibly relaxed, a small smile curving the corners of her lips. "Your parents live in Dallas then?"

He nodded. "My brother and two sisters live in the area, too. We all get together at my mom and stepdad's a few times a month for dinner."

"That's awesome." Her smile broadened. "My sister, Beth, lives with us. She moved in after the divorce to help out with Brandon while I went to work. I couldn't imagine what I'd do if she ever moved back East where the rest of our family lives."

Diego gazed down at their clasped hands, not having realized he was still holding hers. She didn't seem interested in letting go, and neither did he.

"That guy at the diner—your ex," Diego said. He wanted

to tread carefully here, not sure if she'd want to talk about this or not. But when she didn't shut him down, he plowed ahead. "I sort of got the feeling you and Brandon weren't too comfortable around him."

She snorted. "You could say that." When he patiently waited for her to say more, she sighed. "I married Dave right after high school graduation. I was too young and foolish to realize what a controlling jerk he was until after Brandon was born. When Brandon was eleven, Dave went to prison for manslaughter and served five years, nearly six if you count the time served during the trial. Brandon didn't have the best relationship with his father before he went to jail. I didn't either, I guess. He got out a few months ago and... well, it isn't any better than it was before."

Five years didn't sound like a lot for manslaughter. "How is he out on parole already?"

Her slim shoulders lifted in a shrug. "Who knows? I was surprised he got released so soon. Then again, it wasn't like I kept tabs on him after he went to prison. We got divorced and I never looked back. We were married nearly ten years, have a child together, and I just walked away."

Diego opened his mouth to point out that she'd done the right thing, that if her instincts told her to run, she was smart to listen to them, but Gage chose that moment to walk in.

"We got a call," he said. "Silent alarm at Capital One Bank on Gaston. Looks like another barricaded suspect."

"I'll be right there." Diego muttered a curse, then looked at Bree. "I gotta go."

Bree nodded and pushed back her chair. "Don't worry about it. You have a job to do, and Brandon and I need to get home."

Outside, he was about to turn and tell her he'd check in with Brandon later when she put her hand on his arm.

"Can I see you again?" she asked. "Before the baby shower on Saturday, I mean."

Diego didn't know whether she was talking about going on a date or getting together so they could talk more werewolf stuff, but the mere idea of Bree wanting to see him again did some crazy things to his pulse.

"Yeah, of course," he said.

"Great!" She smiled. "What do you think about coming over for dinner? My way of saying thank you for saving our lives."

Diego had expected her to suggest grabbing a cup of coffee or something, but a home-cooked meal sounded even better. "I'd love to. I'll give you my number so we can nail down a day and time."

She gazed at him for a moment, then pulled her cell phone from her purse and held it out to him. "Tomorrow night works for me, if it's okay with you?"

He handed his cell to her, then quickly typed his name and number in her contacts. "It's a date."

Or maybe it wasn't a date. He still wasn't sure. But Bree didn't correct him, and he tried hard to keep the stupid grin off his face as she put her information in his phone. He was trying to think of something romantic to say when Brandon ran up to them.

"Are you leaving?" he asked. "Right now?"

"About two minutes ago, actually," Diego pointed out. "But yeah, I have to go."

Brandon frowned, clearly bummed. "You're going to be at the party Saturday when I meet Jayna's pack, right?"

Diego grinned. “I wouldn’t miss it.”

The kid smiled so big Diego was surprised he didn’t hurt himself. “Okay, I’ve got to get out of here. If you need to talk to me, I gave your mom my phone number. You can call or text me anytime—whatever you need. Okay?”

Brandon nodded.

Bree said something to him about being careful, but Diego was already running for the response SUV where Trey was waiting for him. He had to admit, having a woman concerned about him felt damn good.

CHAPTER 4

Bree and Brandon took the stairs up to their fourth-floor apartment rather than wait for the elevator. It wasn't because the elevator was slow, or they were in a hurry. It was because they still had bloodstains on their clothes, something Bree hadn't realized until they'd left the SWAT compound. The idea of being trapped in the confined space of an elevator with one of their neighbors was more than either of them wanted to deal with.

Thankfully, they made it to their apartment without running into anyone. Brandon held onto the bags of takeout from Keller's Drive-In as Bree fiddled with the key. She'd barely gotten it in the lock when her sister jerked the door open so fast Bree nearly fell face-first onto the tile floor of the entryway.

"Where the hell have you been?" Beth demanded. "I saw on the news that some psycho with a gun held up the diner and took everyone hostage. I've been calling and texting you nonstop, and when you didn't answer, I called the police and every hospital in the city. No one would tell me anything. I've been losing my mind for hours."

Brandon handed Bree two of the bags, gave her a look that said "Good luck!" then headed for his bedroom with his burgers.

"Wash your hands before you eat!" she called after him as he disappeared inside. "And remember to feed Finn!"

Finn was Brandon's ferret. The little guy was simply precious, but he could get fussy if they made him wait too long to eat.

Closing the door behind her, Bree placed the bags on the kitchen table, then walked down the short hallway to her own bedroom, her sister at her heels. She took one look in the full-length mirror on the inside of the closet door she'd left open and grimaced. She couldn't think of eating until she took off her bloodstained clothes. As she exchanged her jeans and top for a pair of shorts and a T-shirt, Beth leaned against the doorjamb with a frown.

"It didn't help that Brandon decided to leave his stupid phone in his room when you guys left," she grumbled. "Why didn't you answer any of my calls or texts? Didn't you think I might be worried?"

Bree sighed, ashamed to realize she hadn't considered her sister might have heard about what happened at the diner. Finding out her son was a werewolf on top of the two of them almost getting killed had kind of preoccupied her.

Ten years younger than Bree was, Beth had moved in with her and Brandon during Dave's trial. After the divorce, Bree had put the house they'd lived in with Dave on the market and gotten this three-bedroom apartment, wanting to put her ex and that part of their lives behind them. Moving back East to be near family probably would have been easier, but Brandon had already gone through so much crap with his dad that Bree hadn't wanted to take him out of a school he loved and away from friends he adored. But she wouldn't have been able to do any of it if her sister hadn't been there to help with Brandon while Bree worked full-time.

In a word, Beth was awesome.

Giving her dark-haired sister a small smile, Bree walked over to hug Beth. "I'm sorry. I had my phone in my purse on vibrate when we went into the diner, and after that, things got kind of crazy."

Beth nodded, but didn't say anything. Her gaze strayed to the clothes Bree had left on the floor, her face going a little pale. "Is that blood on your shirt?"

Bree looked down. The stains, which had been bright red originally, were now a dark rust-brown. The memory of how the blood had ended up there rushed back, and she swallowed hard. "Yes." She put an arm around her sister, gently turning her around and guiding her out of the room, eager to get them both away from the horror of what had happened at the diner. "Come on. There are two bags from Keller's in the kitchen with our names on them. Let's eat."

When they got to the eat-in kitchen, which was separated from the living room by a granite-topped peninsula, Beth took their food out of the bags and set it on the table. She grabbed a knife and fork while Bree poured two glasses of iced tea, grabbed mayo, mustard, and ketchup from the fridge, then sat down across from her sister.

"Were they right on the news about everything that happened at the diner?" Beth asked, opening the ketchup and squeezing some onto the wrapper beside her chicken club for her fries.

Bree nodded. Picking up her fork, she dug into her grilled-chicken Caesar salad and told her sister everything. Well…not everything. The whole werewolf thing needed to stay in the closet for now. But she did tell Beth about the gunman, the poor cops he'd shot, and how horrible it was to see the guy kill himself.

Beth shook her head as she nibbled on a fry. "I can't

imagine going through something like that. I'm so glad you and Brandon are okay."

"Thanks to Diego," Bree said, unable to keep the smile off her face as she said his name.

Her sister regarded her over the rim of her glass. "Who's Diego?"

"The gorgeous cop on the Dallas SWAT team who risked his life for Brandon and me today." Bree sighed. "You should have seen him, Beth. I couldn't believe how brave he was to walk into the diner without any weapons and try to talk that guy down. I mean, I know it's his job, but it was still so selfless. That kook could have shot him." She shuddered inwardly at the memory, not wanting to think about that part. "Then there was how great he was with Brandon. We were both kind of shaken up after what happened, and Diego went above and beyond to make sure we were okay. Brandon only met him a couple hours ago and already idolizes him."

"Brandon isn't the only one." On the other side of the table, Beth smiled. "I haven't heard you gush about a guy like this since you were in high school."

"I'm not gushing!"

Beth lifted a brow. "Trust me, you're gushing."

Bree speared a piece of chicken. "Okay, maybe I am gushing a little. But can you blame me? Brandon was so freaked out that Diego asked us to go back to the SWAT compound so they could talk about what had happened at the diner. It's hard not to like a guy who does something so awesome for your son."

"I won't argue with that." Her sister picked up her sandwich. "You should ask him out."

Bree grinned. "I already did."

Beth stopped chewing to stare at her. "Seriously?"

"Uh-huh." Bree pushed her salad around in the bowl, making sure every bit of seasoned chicken, crispy lettuce, crunchy croutons, and the juicy cherry tomatoes she'd asked them to add were covered in creamy dressing. She usually wasn't so picky when it came to her food, but right then, she wanted to avoid her sister's gaze. "Well, I didn't actually ask him out on a date. I simply asked him to come over for dinner as a way of saying thank you for what he did for Brandon."

Beth shrugged. "Sounds like a date to me."

"It's not like that," Bree insisted. "He risked his life for us. Making dinner is the least I can do for him."

"I agree. But since you've never invited a guy over before, Diego must be special."

Knowing she couldn't keep messing with her salad for the rest of the night, Bree took a bite to avoid answering right away. She wanted to tell her sister she was way off track, but if she was being honest, she'd have to admit Beth was right. There *was* something special about Diego—and it had nothing to do with him being a werewolf. She couldn't put her finger on what it was, though.

"Which is why I did something I never do and invited him over for dinner," Bree said. "I think it would be good to have someone like Diego in Brandon's life."

Beth's face took on a thoughtful look. "And what about having someone like him in yours? Wouldn't that be a good thing, too?"

Bree didn't say anything. Considering her track record with men, she wasn't sure she trusted herself when it came to the opposite sex. Since divorcing Dave—who turned out to be a real douche canoe—she hadn't been so great at picking men. Okay, maybe that wasn't entirely accurate. Granted, she could count the number of men she'd gone out with on one hand, but she'd genuinely hit it off with only a few of them. Unfortunately, none had been interested in having a relationship with a woman who had a kid. But she and Brandon were a package deal, and any guy who wanted to get serious with her needed to be okay with that. When it came to making decisions, her son came first.

Her sister sighed. "Look, I'm not saying you have to jump into anything, or make this out to be more than it is. All I'm suggesting is that you give it a chance and be open to where things go."

Bree couldn't deny there was something about Diego that made her want to take Beth's advice and see where things went. This crazy connection she was already feeling with him was wild for sure, but also thrilling. Why not just take it one *date* at a time and see what happened?

So, she nodded in agreement and focused on her Caesar salad, hoping Beth didn't dig any further into the dinner date she'd made with the big SWAT cop. Fortunately, with everything that had happened to her today, there was lots of stuff for her sister to focus on besides Diego. When she mentioned that Dave had been there, Beth forgot about everything else.

If there was anyone who disliked Dave as much as Bree did, it was Beth. Her sister despised the man with a passion.

Bree had talked to Beth for almost two hours after dinner before she decided she'd better catch up on some work. She stopped outside Brandon's room on the way to her home office, wanting to see how he was dealing with everything that had happened today. Not merely the whole werewolf thing, but also doing first aid on those two police officers, the trauma of being held at gunpoint for hours, then seeing that man kill himself. Bree knew that if she was still seeing all those horrible images flashing through her head every time she closed her eyes, Brandon almost certainly was, too. They hadn't discussed any of that stuff after leaving the SWAT compound.

But as she lifted her hand to knock on his door, she heard the familiar sounds of her son humming along with a song. She smiled and dropped her hand. She knew from experience that Brandon was lying in bed with Finn curled up at his side, headphones on, lost in thought.

Listening to music was Brandon's way of shutting out the world when he needed to be alone with his thoughts. It was a habit he'd started during his father's trial and something Bree never intruded upon. She wouldn't now, either, even after everything that had happened today.

Turning, she walked down the hallway a bit and into the office she and Beth shared. Her sister was a mortgage loan processor who worked from home all but a few days a month, so she used it way more than Bree. But since Bree had taken off today to hang out with Brandon, she should probably at least check her email.

She groaned when she saw an email full of attachments from her boss. Lots of pictures meant another case for her to work. That's what she got for being conscientious. Clicking on the message, she skimmed the email from her boss, then read through the file, randomly opening the attached photos as she did so. It didn't take long to figure out why her boss had given her a new case right on the heels of the one she'd gotten five days earlier. The two cases had similar MOs—if not an exact match—which meant whoever had done the first job had likely done the second one.

Lexington Mutual Group, the high-end insurance company where she worked as an investigator, did the normal stuff like writing policies for cars and homes, but the most profitable part of their business came from underwriting risky propositions other insurance companies wouldn't touch. Mansions built on the edge of a cliff, knees and ankles of college and pro football players, expensive jewelry, classic cars, paintings that were centuries old, rare stamp collections, even a collection of dinosaur bones. If it was valuable and someone was worried about losing it, LMG would insure it. For the right monthly premiums, of course.

When Bree had started working at the large company a little over a decade ago, it had been as an office assistant—something to occupy her time when Brandon had started kindergarten. When her son started first grade, she'd moved up into writing policies. It was mind-numbingly dull work, but it had gotten her out of the house and brought in a bit of extra money. Not that they'd needed it back then because Dave had been bringing in six-figure-plus commissions as an investment advisor.

But then he'd gone to prison and they'd gotten divorced and that six-figure-plus income had disappeared. Needing to make more money to support her family, Bree had begun doing claim investigations. That's when she realized her calling in life. Well, maybe that was a bit of an exaggeration. But she definitely loved doing it.

Essentially, Bree was a private investigator who worked exclusively for LMG, verifying claims to make sure the company wasn't being ripped off. The first year or so, she'd handled the small cases—restaurants that'd mysteriously burned down in the middle of the night, a newlywed couple who'd lost the bride's ten-carat engagement ring while snorkeling in the Gulf of Mexico—but as she got better at the job, the cases got bigger and bigger. She'd soon built a reputation for being tenacious and clever when it came to proving people were lying about a claim. She also became very adept at working with local and sometimes federal law enforcement, knowing the best way to keep LMG from having to pay off a claim when something actually had been stolen was to help the cops find the thief and recover the property.

Over the years, she'd become LMG's go-to investigator, especially when the company was looking at the possibility of a major payout.

Which was why they'd given her the Williamson case. Five nights ago, Garth Williamson, one of the company's richer clients, had come home from a late night at the country club to find his walk-in vault standing wide open and his wife's jewelry collection missing. A good amount of cash, bearer bonds, and other valuables had also been taken, but it was Vera Williamson's jewelry that mattered the most since it was covered by the LMG policy. At a tidy sum just shy of $2 million.

With a theft of this magnitude, Bree had been forced to stay in the background for the first few days, observing as the Dallas PD robbery unit did their thing. Even so, she'd learned enough to make her very suspicious.

Outwardly, it appeared to be a simple smash-and-grab job. The thieves had bashed in the french doors, scattering glass and wood all over the living room, then moved the large-screen TV and several pieces of high-tech electronic gear like they intended to steal it, but changed their minds after finding the safe and all the jewelry inside it. They'd ripped through the door and half of the wall hiding the vault with what looked like a crowbar and sledgehammer. They'd given the inside of the safe the caveman treatment, too, smashing the glass jewelry cases when they simply could have opened them and ripping shelves off the wall. Almost everything in the place screamed amateurs getting lucky.

Almost.

The inconsistencies were what bothered Bree. Like the fact that they hadn't tripped the home's security system when they'd broken in. Or that the exterior camera hadn't managed to catch a single glimpse of the burglars. Then there was the part where they'd opened the door of the safe without damaging it.

Maybe they hadn't set off the alarm because the sensor on the door had been faulty. As for the camera, it was possible the thieves had approached the house along a naturally existing blind spot. And the safe? She supposed Garth and Vera Williamson could have forgotten to lock it.

All of those explanations seemed like a stretch to her.

It was starting to look a hell of a lot like Garth or Vera—or both—had been involved.

Bree flipped through the file and photos of the newest case, quickly seeing the obvious similarities.

Claudette Montagne wasn't a new client with LMG, but she'd only recently moved to Dallas. She'd made her money in New York's fashion industry, then moved to Texas to expand her empire. Apparently, she'd pulled an all-nighter at her office, arriving back at her luxury loft on Blackburn Street at six o'clock in the morning to find that someone had stolen the two Jasper Johns paintings she had mounted on the wall of her bedroom. The cost to LMG was about $16 million if they had to pay out on the theft.

Like the Williamson job, the thieves had entered the loft with brute force. The photos the cops had taken showed that the front door had been kicked in forcefully enough to crack the frame around the lock. The other pictures showed pieces of furniture shoved aside, as if the thieves had been in a hurry to get through the apartment. Then there was the crude way they'd sliced the paintings out of their frames, as if the person doing it had no clue how valuable the two pieces were.

And also like the Williamson job, there were little things that didn't fit.

The sensors attached to the picture frames that should have picked up the movement of the painting being cut never sent any signal to the security company paid to monitor them. Then again, neither had the alarm on the door. The case file seemed to suggest Claudette had failed to turn the security system on...though the woman insisted she had.

When Bree opened the file from the Williamson case and compared it to the Montagne job, it was hard to ignore the resemblance. They had both been assigned to her because they were insured by the same company, but beyond that, they were both protected by security systems that seemed to have been circumvented, and both houses had physical damage, making it look to be the work of common criminals.

Bree couldn't help thinking this was another case of the client stealing their own property. Either that, or they had the same thief do it for them. She wondered whether Garth and Vera knew Claudette. Since they used the same insurance company, it wasn't crazy to assume they could have met there.

Bree sat back in her chair, considering the best way to approach the two cases. There'd been a lot of forensic evidence gathered at both scenes, but the thefts had occurred on opposite sides of Dallas within two different DPD divisions. That meant it was unlikely the cops had connected the cases.

Not that it would help her much if they did. There were thousands of burglaries reported in Dallas each year. Even high-profile cases like these would only garner a limited amount of attention. The cops would definitely work the cases diligently, but it would take time, especially if they needed to get the crime lab to go through the forensic evidence in order to come up with any suspects.

Unfortunately, policies written by LMG stipulated that first payments on loss claims had to go out within thirty days. Which meant Bree didn't have time for the cops to follow their normal process. She needed to do some digging on her own. Even if she only found enough to point the cops in the right direction, that could be enough to limit the damages her company had to pay out.

Taking a pen and notepad out of the drawer, she jotted down ideas on how she might establish a connection between the two cases as well as between Claudette and the Williamsons. It probably wouldn't hurt to dig into their known associates and see if any of them could be linked to someone who'd had a break-in like the ones in the photos. After that, she'd start working up a list of places that might be able to fence the jewelry and paintings that had been stolen. Off the top of her head, she could already think of a half-dozen different pawnshops she could check out tomorrow.

Speaking of all the stuff she had to do tomorrow, Bree couldn't stop the image of a certain hunky SWAT cop from popping into her mind. Dinner with Diego was definitely on the list of things she was looking forward to.

Bree knew she should focus on her job. Working two theft cases at the same time—both involving million-dollar claims—would be difficult enough without the gorgeous distraction that was Diego Martinez. Regardless of how much she'd insisted having dinner with Diego wasn't a big deal, putting the man out of her head was easier said than done. The mere thought of sitting across the table from the sexy cop in the privacy of her apartment made her so giddy with anticipation she felt like a teenager.

What should she make for dinner?

What kinds of things would they talk about?

Would this be the start of a relationship like Beth suggested or a one-time thing?

Bree glanced at her phone, wondering if it would be okay to call him. It was lame, but she wanted to hear his voice. She could always say she wanted to confirm their dinner plans.

Picking up her phone, she was scrolling through her

contacts for his name when it occurred to her that Diego might still be at that bank robbery. The memory of what he'd done at the diner came rushing back, and her chest tightened. Damn, she was on the verge of hyperventilating over the safety of a guy she'd just met and barely knew.

Bree fought to control her breathing, telling herself to calm down. The bank robbery Diego had gone on was long over. He was fine. In fact, he was probably already home watching TV. Or playing video games. Or reading. Or whatever he did when he wasn't on duty.

But just in case he was still at work, she decided to text instead of call him. Then forced herself not to check her phone every five minutes for a reply.

"Leave us the hell alone and go away!"

Diego jerked the phone away from his ear, wincing at the loud crash on the other end. Well, there went another one of the bank's landline phones, smashed to bits like all the previous ones when he'd tried to talk the bank robbers into giving themselves up or releasing some of the hostages or letting him send in food or any of the half-dozen offers he'd tried in an attempt to gain their trust.

These guys were more unbalanced than the man at the diner.

Biting back a growl, Diego set down the phone, then walked to the door of the SWAT RV and stepped outside. Keeping an eye on the front of the bank and the pieces of furniture the hostage takers had piled up in front of the entrance, he flipped through the handwritten notes he made earlier during his discussion with the regional manager of the bank, double-checking to see if there was another phone number he could try. But after going through five pages of scribbles, it wasn't looking good.

Diego smelled his two pack mates approaching before he heard them. He didn't need to turn around to know it was Trey and Hale. While Mike was talking to the on-scene commander a few feet away and Connor was on the rooftop across the street, using his scope to maintain a visual on the suspects in the bank, Trey and Hale had been scouting out the back of the building, making sure they had a clear path to the skylights that overlooked the bank's lobby. That was the way they'd go in if Diego wasn't able to talk the three gunmen out. Considering the standoff was approaching its fifth hour and they'd now lost their last phone line into the bank, a tactical breach was looking more and more likely. But with the way the hostage takers were starting to behave, Diego was concerned going in might push them over the edge.

"They still not talking?" Trey asked, stopping beside him.

Diego shook his head. "Oh, they're talking, but they're not giving me anything I can work with. The best I've been able to do is confirm that there are three armed men in there and that the bank guard and the other four hostages are alive. And while I doubt this is going to be big news to either of you, I've also confirmed we're looking at guys who are as whacked out as the other people we've been dealing with lately."

Trey and Hale did little more than shrug, like they'd already figured out that last part. Given the way the men in the bank frequently shoved the furniture aside so they could lean out one of the broken windows and shout things that made no sense to anyone but them, it *was* kind of obvious.

"You don't think there's any way you'll be able to convince them to come out of there?" Hale asked, his gaze going to the bank.

Diego let out a sigh. It might be quiet inside right now, but he had no illusions it would stay that way. "I wish I could say I see this all working out, but my gut tells me this is going to end exactly like the situation at the diner."

Hale frowned. "I know you blame yourself for that guy killing himself, but you know as well as I do, there was nothing you could have done to stop it."

Diego knew his friend was only trying to help—and on some level, he knew his pack mate was right, but still, a man had died by his own hand right in front of him. He might be focused on what was going on in that bank right now, but part of him was still back in that diner.

"With all the training I have at this kind of thing, shouldn't I have been able to do something?" he murmured.

"You did do something," Trey pointed out. "You saved two cops and more than a dozen civilians, including a beta and his mother. You controlled the situation and you did your job."

Diego hooked his thumbs in his tactical vest. "It's probably not a very healthy way to look at it—in fact, I know it's not—but I've always dwelled more on the ones I lost than the ones I've saved. And as crazy as that guy in the diner was, I can't help but feel like I lost him. In the end, he didn't want to die, but he pulled the trigger anyway."

Trey and Hale both looked like they wanted to argue, but then must have thought better of it. Because seriously, what the hell could they say?

"Guys, something's going on inside the bank," Connor announced suddenly over the radio, jarring Diego out of his introspection. "Two of the men have turned their attention to the hostages. They're swinging their weapons around and getting really worked up. I can't tell what they're saying, but from the expressions on the hostages' faces, it's freaking them out."

"What's the third guy doing?" Mike asked, his voice coming through Diego's earpiece calm and relaxed even as it seemed like the situation was starting to disintegrate.

Just as Diego feared it would.

"He's standing off to the side closer to the door, looking really out of it," Connor replied. "Truthfully, I'm as worried about him as the other two. Who knows what he'll do if he snaps out of his catatonic state?"

"Diego, any chance of reestablishing contact?" Mike asked.

"None," Diego said. "They smashed the last working phone in the bank and refused to answer any of the cell phones they took from the bank employees. To be honest, I don't think I ever had a chance of getting through to those guys in there. Not with the way they're acting."

Mike was silent for a moment, and Diego could practically hear the multiple scenarios running through his head.

"We can't risk waiting any longer," Mike finally said. "Connor, I want you back here. You'll be going in through the skylights with Trey and Hale. Diego, you're going to walk right in the front door. I want those men in the bank focused on you."

"Copy that," Diego said.

As Trey and Hale disappeared into the darkness, Diego

checked his gear, keeping an ear out for the slightest sound that something was going wrong inside the bank. He didn't bother to dump his tactical vest like he had at the diner. He'd need it if those men in there realized he was playing decoy. It was the same reason he slipped his SIG into his belt at the small of his back. He didn't want them to see him coming at them with a weapon, but he didn't want to go in there without one.

Diego was about to head toward the bank when Connor ran up, sniper rifle strapped across his back, a lithe black cat loping behind him like a four-legged shadow. Diego would like to say he was shocked to see the animal. But as bizarre as Kat the cat sometimes behaved, he wouldn't be surprised to learn she'd been up on the roof serving as Connor's spotter.

Kat had been hanging out with the SWAT team ever since December when they'd found her wandering around a warehouse being used to store drugs. The cat had taken one glance at Connor and promptly followed him back to the response vehicle and jumped in, then given them that look only a cat could pull off.

"I'm ready. We can leave now."

For reasons that absolutely no one could explain, Connor and Kat had developed a connection of sorts. In fact, they hung out together all the time. It would be hilarious if it wasn't so strange.

"Please tell me you're not going to let that cat follow you into the bank," Diego said, glancing at the green-eyed feline, who gazed up at him like she thought he was an idiot before jumping onto the hood of the response vehicle.

"No way. And don't call her *that cat*. She has a name." Connor quickly unloaded his sniper rifle and slipped it in the back of the vehicle. "I let her follow me up onto the roof because it's safe. We've already talked about the fact that she's not allowed to take part in any tactical entries. She'll stay here and guard the vehicle."

Diego nearly asked if Connor was flipping serious, then changed his mind. He almost assuredly was. The man was always talking to the cat. And the little beast was always staring back with those freakishly intelligent eyes and nodding like she was actually listening.

It was unsettling in a this-cat-is-trying-to-take-over-the-world kind of way.

Connor gave the cat a firm look, told her to stay put, then turned and jogged toward the perimeter of police cruisers parked in front of the bank, heading for the back of the building as Kat sat there calmly on the hood of the SUV, watching him. The moment Connor disappeared, she blinked and gave Diego a look suggesting that when she gained that aforementioned world domination, he'd be one of the first she did away with.

Yup, definitely unsettling.

Checking one more time to make sure his SIG was secure behind his gear belt, Diego headed for the front door of the bank, hearing the unmistakable sound of arguing coming from inside.

"Mike, it's getting hot in there," he murmured into his radio mic. "We may have to accelerate our timetable."

"Roger that," Mike confirmed. "Trey, let us know when you're in position."

"Wilco," Trey answered. "We'll be in place in less than two."

When he got to the door, Diego grabbed the handle and pulled it open. Not only hadn't the bad guys locked it, but they hadn't considered that piling crap up in front of doors that opened out didn't do much good. He shoved the stack of upholstered chairs aside, making an awful noise in the process. The hostages huddled near the counter let out a collective gasp at his unceremonious entrance, but Diego didn't so much as glance at them. The only people he focused on were the three gunmen.

Two of the men on the far side of the bank immediately lifted their weapons and started in his direction. But it was the red-haired guy in the T-shirt and jeans closest to him that concerned him the most—the one Connor had described as catatonic. Shit, the guy couldn't be more than twenty years old. The kid stood there, hazel eyes flat and lifeless, a smear of blood across his left temple and into his hairline. Diego had no idea where the blood had come from, but the moment the guy noticed him, his gaze went from empty to rage-filled.

Letting out a demented bellow, the guy lifted his weapon and started shooting, running at Diego like some sort of berserker. At the same time, the skylights in the center of the ceiling suddenly shattered, raining down glass and pieces of metal along with his teammates, but the guy coming at him wasn't fazed by their arrival. The frightened hostages, on the other hand, screamed in panic. Then a round sliced through the muscles of Diego's right shoulder while another slammed into the center of his tactical vest, and he had to stop worrying about everything but the madman coming at him.

Even though the ballistic plates in his vest stopped the second bullet, it still hurt like hell. The guy was almost on him, though, so Diego ignored the pain and lunged forward, avoiding taking another round to a part of his body that would hurt even worse as he slammed into the gunman. Even though Diego weighed over two hundred and thirty pounds and smashed into him viciously enough to rattle his own teeth, the guy didn't let out a grunt. Hell, he barely moved. Instead, he slammed right back into Diego.

Diego used the man's momentum, twisting and flipping the guy across his hip before taking him to the floor so hard he knocked the air out of the man with a grunt. But that didn't slow the rabid guy down, and he continued to try to point the automatic weapon toward Diego's face.

They struggled for control of the gun, and as strong as Diego was, it was still a near thing. Sure, he could have partially shifted and torn the guy apart, but he desperately wanted to take this guy in alive. After a few punches, an elbow to the face, and a head-butt, Diego finally got both hands on the gun. Then he twisted violently until he heard the bones in the man's wrists crack. When the guy released the weapon with a yelp of pain, Diego threw the thing across the room.

He thought for sure the fight would end there.

It didn't.

Still clearly out of his mind, the man continued to resist, punching and kicking until Diego yanked him up and tackled him again, slamming him into the floor with his shoulder. The guy finally stopped fighting, probably because Diego had managed to knock him out. Now that he wasn't on the attack, Diego took a good look at him. Sometime during the struggle, the blood smeared on the guy's temple had been wiped off, and lying there so quietly, looking more like he was asleep than unconscious, Diego was struck once again at how young and innocent his attacker looked. Probably because he was out cold.

Diego reached for the cuffs on his belt as Trey dropped to a knee to help. That was when Diego realized his pack mates had taken the other two gunmen alive as well. Hale stood guard over them as Connor herded the terrified hostages toward the door.

"Is it just my imagination, or are these people getting harder to deal with?" Trey asked as Diego handcuffed the unconscious suspect. "These three almost gave us more than we could handle—at least without shifting."

"I know," Diego agreed.

These guys had been a lot more violent than any of the other recent cases. Where the other offenders had seemed reluctant, these guys were willing to kill to get what they wanted.

As Diego flipped the guy over, his eyes fluttered open and he let out a groan. The expression on his face as he blinked up at Diego and Trey, then looked around the bank in confusion, was like nothing Diego had ever seen before.

"Where am I?" the kid asked, his voice rough from all the shouting he'd done, his youthful face full of alarm as he realized his hands were pinned behind his back. "What happened? Am I under arrest?"

Before Diego could say anything, two patrol officers stood the guy on his feet and guided him toward the door. Beside Diego, Trey looked as baffled as he was.

"Did he seriously have no idea where he was or how he got here?" Trey asked.

All Diego could do was shrug, wincing a little at the sharp stab of pain in his right shoulder, because he had no idea what to say. On the bright side, at least no one had died on this call. Unfortunately, they still had no explanation for what was happening to the people in this city.

The debriefing after the hostage situation at the bank took forever. Chief Leclair showed up again, once more disappointed to learn that this was likely another case of delirium—apparently that stupid word Ernest Hobbs had coined earlier had stuck. The jackass was probably on the other side of the crime-scene tape at that moment.

"I never thought I'd say this, but I'm praying all three of those men have rap sheets as long as my arm," the chief said. "It turns out the guy at the diner this morning was a high-profile investment advisor for one of the largest and most prestigious firms in the city. The press is having a field day with this."

Diego traded looks with his pack mates. "Something tells me those guys we took down in there aren't hardened criminals. They're practically kids."

Leclair muttered a curse. "I'd better go talk to the press before they print something they shouldn't. Then again, when has that ever stopped them?"

Giving them a nod, she left the RV, but not before giving Mike a long look. Those two were going to need to get a room soon, Diego thought.

Fifteen minutes later, they were headed back to the SWAT compound. Diego tried not to let it show, but he was beat. Not physically, of course. He was a werewolf, which meant it was damn near impossible to be tired in that way.

But mentally? He was drained. It had been one hell of a day, and something told him there were going to be a lot of days like it in the very near future.

The idea was almost enough to make him want to crawl into bed and sleep for a week straight.

He felt a vibration in his cargo pocket and reached in to pull out his cell phone, hoping it wasn't Gage saying there was another hostage situation. But if there was, his commander would have called, not texted. And this was definitely a text—from Bree.

> Just thinking about you and wanted to make sure you're okay. Text me when you get a chance.

A slow smile spread across Diego's face. Suddenly, he didn't feel nearly as tired.

CHAPTER 5

"If you don't calm down, you're going to hyperventilate," Beth said as she zipped up Bree's sleeveless dress. "You don't want Diego to show up for your first date and find you passed out on the floor."

Bree was tempted to tell her sister it wasn't a date but gave up. Who was she kidding? Of course, it was a date. The first real date she'd had in a very long time. That was why she was breathing like she'd run a half marathon. At least she wasn't sweating like she'd finished one.

She hoped.

Just in case, she threw a surreptitious glance in the full-length mirror attached to the back of her closet door, making sure her makeup was still perfect and that there wasn't any telltale glimmer to give away her near panic.

"Don't worry," Beth said softly. "You look amazing. Diego will melt into a puddle of goo the second he sees you."

Bree laughed at that image. She very much doubted Diego would melt at the sight of her, but it was nice to think he might, and that thought helped get her breathing back under control.

Beth glanced at her watch. "Get your shoes on. He's going to be here soon."

Bree took a quick peek at her own watch to see that her sister was right. *Crap.* She still had to check on dinner. Hurrying over to the closet, she slid her feet into the wedge sandals Beth suggested she wear, then turned to survey her reflection in the mirror. Her sister was right about that, too. The shoes did go perfectly with the little black dress she had on.

"You sure there's nothing else I can help you get ready before I leave for my date?" Beth asked as they walked into the kitchen. "Maybe toss the salad or butter the garlic bread?"

"I'm good, thanks." Bree bent down to pop open the oven and check the chicken parmesan she'd put in there to keep warm. It smelled delicious and looked even better. "You know, you and your boyfriend are more than welcome to join us for dinner. I'm sure Diego would love to meet you guys."

Beth laughed as she straightened the place settings on the table. "Oh, don't worry. I'm not leaving until he gets here. No way would I bail before getting a look at him. I have to make sure he's good enough for my sister, after all. But then I'm leaving so you can have your privacy. How do you expect anything good to happen unless you spend a little alone time with this guy?"

Bree would have pointed out that Brandon was probably going to be having dinner with them, but the doorbell rang before she could say anything. Her heart began thudding like someone was jumping around inside her chest with a pogo stick.

"That's Diego," she announced rather unnecessarily as she pointed a warning finger at her sister. "You behave!"

Beth gave her a look that made it seem like butter wouldn't melt in her mouth. *As if.*

Bree slowed her steps as she walked to the door, carefully smoothing her hands down the front of her dress, absently noting that her palms were a little moist. Why was she so nervous? It wasn't like she was some silly teenager who'd never been on a date. But as she reached for the knob, she realized that for all her talk, dinner with Diego was important to her. She might not know why, but she wanted it to go well.

Taking a deep breath, she pulled open the door with a smile and opened her mouth to give him a cheerful greeting.

The words got stuck in her throat.

Diego was dressed in casual slacks and an untucked button-down in a perfect blend of relaxed and dressy. The material of the shirt was tight enough in the shoulders to show off his muscles, and the couple buttons he'd left undone at the top revealed the start of some spectacular pecs. His hair was a bit disheveled, like he'd just crawled out of bed, and his jawline was perfectly scruffy.

The whole look—along with those soulful dark eyes of his—really worked for her. In fact, drooling wouldn't be inappropriate at this moment.

"Wow. You look absolutely beautiful," he said, his gaze slipping warmly over her body. "And I'm suddenly feeling way too underdressed."

She laughed. "Not at all. You look amazing."

He surprised her by flushing a little under his tan. Then, as if remembering he had something in his hands—which she didn't realize herself until he held them out—he flashed her a grin.

"These are for you."

Bree looked down to see him holding a bottle of red wine in one hand and a bouquet of flowers in the other. She suddenly wondered if this was the universe's way of making up for all the crappy things Dave had done. Because she couldn't imagine how Diego could get any better.

"You brought flowers," she said breathlessly, taking the beautiful arrangement of red, pink, yellow, and orange gerberas as she pointed out the obvious. "I won't say you shouldn't have because these are too gorgeous."

Abruptly realizing she was standing in the doorway, gazing at the colorful flowers like a complete loser, she quickly stepped back, trying to play it cool and praying she didn't start crying over the fact that a man had brought her flowers.

"Come on in," she said.

Closing the door behind him, she led the way into the living room, where Beth was waiting with a satisfied smile on her face.

"Diego Martinez, my sister, Beth," Bree announced as she headed for the kitchen with the bouquet.

As she trimmed the stems on the longer flowers and filled the crystal vase that had been collecting dust in the cabinet above her fridge, she listened to the conversation going on in the living room, praying her sister didn't say anything to embarrass her. Fortunately, it sounded as if Beth had taken the earlier warning to heart and was behaving herself.

Bree finished up with the flowers as Beth scurried in, a ridiculously big smile on her face.

"You said he was attractive," her sister whispered, leaning in close. "But you never mentioned he was a smokeshow. He's unreal!"

No, she hadn't. And yes, he was, Bree thought.

"Is that your way of saying you want to stay for dinner now?" she asked.

Beth shook her head with a laugh. "No, I'm going. But I expect a full recap of the date."

Diego wandered into the kitchen as her sister left, lifting his head a little as he sniffed the air. "If my nose isn't making things up, it smells like you're making chicken parmesan. If so, the wine should go perfectly with it."

She smiled as he set the bottle that she'd forgotten to grab from him earlier on the counter. It wasn't her fault. The flowers had rattled her. He was right, she thought as she glanced at the label. She couldn't have picked a better vintage if she tried.

"Does your nose ever trick you?" she asked, handing him a corkscrew.

He chuckled as he opened the bottle. Damn, he made something as simple as that sexy. "Not usually. I can smell a cream-filled doughnut a mile away."

Bree paused in the middle of grabbing two wineglasses from an upper cabinet, wondering if he was messing with her. Then again, Brandon could smell the other werewolves at the SWAT compound yesterday, so maybe not. She was about to ask as the apartment door opened and Brandon came in with a clatter only a teenage boy could make. When she heard him talking to another teen boy a moment later, she realized he wasn't alone.

Bree knew without looking it was Kevin Lawrence. Brandon and Kevin had been best friends since kindergarten, and he was one of the rocks in her son's life after her ex had gone postal and killed a man. While she'd been at her son's side through it all, there were some things boys never wanted to talk to their mother about. Discovering your dad was a murderer and would be in prison for years was one of those things. Kevin had been there for Brandon and supported him through it all.

But as good a friend as Kevin was, there was some stuff Bree didn't like about him. The biggest one being the fact that Kevin was the reason Brandon had been in that convenience store in the very worst part of Dallas the night he'd been shot. Brandon had insisted they'd only gone in to get some sodas, but she was sure they'd been there looking to buy drugs, and that Kevin had talked him into it.

She wanted to tell Brandon to stop hanging out with Kevin but couldn't. Her son could be both stubborn and independent—traits he'd no doubt gotten from her—and she was smart enough to know giving him an ultimatum would push him away. She only prayed Brandon had learned something from the entire horrible situation and wouldn't do anything that stupid again.

A moment later, Brandon stomped into the kitchen, shoes untied and a goofy smile on his face when he saw Diego. Beside her son, Kevin eyed him curiously. A little shorter than Brandon, he was wiry like her son but with blond hair and blue eyes.

He gave her a nod. "Hey, Ms. Harlow."

"Hey, Diego," Brandon said before she could greet either of them or introduce Diego. "Dinner smells great, Mom. Kevin and I are going to play *Fortnite*, so can we just take some plates of food to my room?"

Bree's first instinct was to say no and remind her son that they had a guest for dinner—a guest who'd saved his life and was planning to teach him how to be a werewolf—but she bit her tongue. With Kevin there, they couldn't very well talk about the werewolf thing over dinner, which meant there'd be nothing of interest to two teenage boys.

She set the glass on the counter, amazed at what she'd just said to herself.

Her son was a werewolf.

Diego was a werewolf.

If dinner tonight turned into something more between her and the hunky SWAT cop, she'd be dating a real-life werewolf.

It was like some crazy dream. But instead of freaking her out, it was as though the pieces that had left her confused for what seemed like the longest time were finally falling into place. All because she and Brandon and gone into that diner yesterday and Diego had walked into their lives.

"Of course, honey." She smiled at her son. "Grab one of the plates off the table while I get another for Kevin. Wash your hands while I take dinner out of the oven—both of you."

As her son and his friend moved over to the sink, Brandon introduced Kevin to Diego, saying he was the police officer who'd saved their lives at the diner yesterday. Bree smiled as she listened to the three of them talk. Diego got huge brownie points with both Brandon and Kevin when he got into a conversation with them about *Fortnite* while she piled their plates with food. Brandon could go on for hours about his favorite game, and after listening to them discuss the various levels and fastest way to get there, something told her Diego could, too.

The moment she was done with their plates, Brandon and Kevin disappeared into his bedroom, shoveling food into their mouths before they closed the door.

"I hope I made enough for dinner," she said as Diego helped her carry everything to the table. "I've seen how much Brandon has started eating lately, and figured you'd eat more, so I kind of went a little crazy."

"Don't worry," Diego said with a chuckle, setting the big bowl of linguine on the table next to the basket of garlic bread. "In my opinion, you can never have too many carbs."

"Spoken like a man who's never had to worry about fitting in his jeans," she muttered.

She placed three big pieces of breaded chicken covered in marinara sauce and gooey mozzarella on his plate, then put one on hers. She did the same with the pasta, serving him enough linguine for two people while giving herself a tiny bit. She'd make up for it with salad and the chocolate cake she'd made—which didn't count as a carb as far as she was concerned. In fact, cake was in its own special food group and therefore could be eaten in unlimited quantity. Like cabbage or broccoli, except it tasted better.

Across from her, Diego lifted his glass of wine in a toast. "To first dates...and whatever comes after."

Bree touched her glass to his with a smile. That was a sentiment she could definitely get behind. "To dinner. And whatever comes after."

The red wine was sweet with just a touch of a bite and went perfectly with the Italian dinner she'd made. She couldn't have picked anything better herself.

"I'm assuming Brandon's friend doesn't know he's a werewolf?" Diego asked as he cut into the chicken.

Even though Brandon's room was at the far end of the apartment, that didn't keep her from glancing in that direction anyway, afraid he and Kevin might overhear.

"I guess that answers that question." Diego chuckled. "Don't worry. They're both wearing headsets and buried in the game. They won't hear anything short of an elephant stampede."

Bree relaxed. Brandon could definitely get lost while playing his video games. Pretty much the same way he did when he was listening to music.

"We talked about it yesterday after leaving the compound and decided Kevin isn't someone we could share a secret like that with," she said, answering the question even if Diego already figured it out. "He's Brandon's best friend and has been forever, but even my son realizes Kevin could never keep a secret like this." She made a face. "I feel horrible about it, but we haven't told Beth, either. She's always tied to her convictions about how the world works. I don't want to think about how much she'd freak out if she found out werewolves exist."

"I know what you mean." He paused to take a big bite of chicken, chewing appreciatively. "My brother and sisters know about me, but not my mom or stepdad. They'd both pass out if they found out I have claws and fangs."

She almost laughed when he practically moaned after tasting the garlic bread and pasta. Even the salad seemed to really work for him.

"This is incredible," he said, spearing another piece of chicken with his fork. "I haven't eaten Italian food this good in a long time. I feel a little bad that you went to all this work for me, though. This has to take hours to make."

This time, she did laugh. "I'd like to take credit for going all out—you did save our lives, after all. But honestly, it's what I would have made for dinner tonight anyway. I simply made more. So, it wasn't a big deal."

He let out a deep chuckle. "Spoken like a woman who doesn't eat takeout from fast-food places most nights."

Bree paused with a forkful of salad halfway to her mouth to take in all those muscles on the other side of the table, finding it impossible to believe Diego got a body like that living on cheeseburgers and fries. "You're joking, right?"

"Nope." He twirled some pasta on his fork. "I eat a lot of junk food."

"Okay, let's say I believe that. How can you be so...fit?"

"I'm a werewolf. My metabolism works overtime."

She shook her head. "Well, that's just patently unfair."

The thought that he could look like that and practically live on junk food boggled the mind. She wanted to ask about other ways he was different from a regular person but decided that might be a little too personal to jump into right away. Instead, she changed the subject to something that had been in the back of her mind most of the day.

"I saw a news story from that reporter, Hobbs, today when I was scrolling on my phone," she said. "It was mostly about the guy who took us hostage in the diner and what happened, but he also mentioned the call you went on at a bank yesterday. He said there was a confrontation between three armed men and your SWAT team and that one of the cops was injured. Whoever it was, I hope he's okay."

She held her breath as she waited for him to answer. The thought of anyone on his team getting hurt worried her, but the idea of Diego in particular being in harm's way terrified her so much she could barely breathe. It was crazy since she barely knew him, but it was true all the same.

On the other side of the table, Diego stopped eating and picked up his wineglass, then took a slow sip.

"When we texted back and forth last night, you didn't

say anything about anyone getting hurt, so I was wondering if Hobbs got that part of the story wrong," she added.

Diego set down his glass, meeting her gaze. The look in his dark eyes made her heart beat out of control all of a sudden.

"I didn't say anything because I didn't want you to worry, but we did end up engaging with the suspects and one of us did get shot," he said.

"Oh God!" Her hand tightened on her fork. "Who?"

How could Diego sit there so calmly talking about this? She felt like her heart was racing at breakneck speed right now.

"It was me," he said, his voice so casual it was like he was confessing to eating the last chocolate chip cookie. He must have seen the look of alarm on her face because he quickly added, "But it was only a little nick on the shoulder. It barely bled at all."

Bree set down her fork on her plate with a clatter. "You got shot! Why are you sitting here and not in the hospital?"

Diego held up his hands in a placating gesture. "Bree, calm down. I'm fine. See?"

Unbuttoning two more buttons on his shirt, he pulled it to the side to expose his right shoulder. Bree gaped at the expanse of muscles on his upper chest and shoulder he treated her to, only to stare in disbelief the next second at the line of pink scar tissue there. Regardless of what he'd said about it being little more than a scratch, she was still surprised to see that the wound was closed up, like it was days—maybe even weeks—old.

"Werewolves heal faster than humans," he said, slipping his shirt back over his shoulder and buttoning it. "I didn't mention it to you last night because getting shot isn't a big deal for us and I didn't want you to freak out."

Like she had a few minutes ago. But he was nice enough not to remind her.

Her head still spun at the thought of him healing from a gunshot wound in the space of a few hours. She didn't know why she was having a hard time with this, especially since she'd bought the entire werewolf thing so easily. Then again, maybe all of the insanity was finally catching up to her.

Bree picked up her fork and absently pushed her pasta around on her plate. "I'm not sure I'll ever get used to this world I've suddenly found myself in. Alphas and betas, fangs and claws, wounds that heal overnight. It's a lot to take in." She looked at him. "Was it like that for you in the beginning?"

He picked up his own fork with a shrug. "If you want to know the truth, you and Brandon are handling all of this way better than I did. I thought I was going insane and that the people who kept insisting they knew what was happening were crazy, too."

"Were you already in SWAT when you turned into a werewolf?"

Diego ate a forkful of salad, considering her question. A vision of a werewolf à la Lon Chaney Jr. eating salad popped into her head, and she had a sudden urge to laugh. But didn't.

"No," he said, spearing a juicy cherry tomato. "Funny thing was, I talked to Hale about trying out for SWAT the night I got shot. He was already on the team, only I didn't know he was a werewolf back then. He and the rest of the Pack took me under their wing and taught me what it meant to be a werewolf."

She lifted a forkful of pasta to her mouth, and they both ate in silence for a while.

"What happened the night you were shot?" she asked softly, not sure it was something he wanted to talk about or even something she wanted to hear, but something told her it was important she did. "If you don't want to talk about it, I understand."

He took a bite of garlic bread and chewed slowly. Bree had no idea why she liked watching him eat, but she did. His mouth was mesmerizing.

"You know those books that always start out with 'It was a dark and stormy night?'" he said. "Well, that's exactly what it was like when I got a call for a disturbance at a club down on Harry Hines."

Diego paused, his beautiful eyes taking on a slightly distracted look as he pulled up the memories. Bree sat riveted, barely remembering to eat as he recounted the story about how he'd rescued a trio of women from some a-holes, getting shot three times and stabbed once. Tears stung her eyes as he told her how he felt like he'd failed the woman who'd been injured when he'd fallen to the floor and couldn't get back up. When he'd told her about how Hale had growled at him, telling him to keep fighting, a few of those tears rolled down her cheeks.

She wiped them away with her fingers. "Was the girl okay?"

Diego set down his knife and fork on his empty plate with a nod. "Yeah. She was in the hospital for a while, but she was okay. She stills sends me a Christmas card every year."

Bree's lips curved. "Did anyone ever figure out why those guys went after the girls to begin with?"

Diego shook his head. "No. One of the suspects died at the scene, and the other refused to talk. He ended up getting a sentence of twenty-five to life without ever offering up any explanation."

She frowned. "So, one man ended up dead, those women's lives got turned upside down, and you ended up becoming a werewolf and no one knows why those wackos did it?"

He shrugged. "Sometimes it happens that way. Things happen and we never know why. All we can do is pick ourselves up, keep going, and do the best we can not to let the experience color the way we look at the world."

She finished the last of her chicken, then set down her knife and fork. "Are you still talking about dealing with weirdos who do insane things, or have we drifted into a conversation about dealing with becoming a werewolf?"

"Maybe a little of both." He gave her a sheepish look. "Sorry, but I guess I get a little philosophical after a good meal."

She laughed. "If that's the case, I wonder how introspective you'll get after dessert because I made chocolate cake. Hope you're still hungry."

Diego flashed her a grin. "I never say no to chocolate or cake."

Pushing back her chair, she leaned over to pick up his empty plate, but he waved her off, taking hers out of her hand and picking up his own, along with the salad bowls.

"You don't have to do that," she protested.

"Maybe not, but I want to." He placed the plates and bowls on the counter, then opened the dishwasher. "You made a fantastic dinner. The least I can do is help clean up."

Bree watched out of the corner of her eye as he rinsed off the plates and put them in the dishwasher while she took the chocolate cake out of the fridge. A hunky guy like him helping out in the kitchen, and on the first date no less? Her mom would tell her to marry him immediately if not sooner.

Laughing to herself at that idea, she cut two slices of the moist chocolate cake with loads of creamy frosting, making sure to give Diego an extra big one.

"I thought we could have dessert in the living room," she said, nodding toward the couch. "More comfortable in there."

"Comfortable is good," he agreed, the sudden heat in his dark eyes unmistakable as he picked up their glasses of wine and gestured for her to lead the way.

CHAPTER 6

Diego tried not to stare at Bree's butt swaying gracefully in front of him as she walked into the living room, but it was impossible. Like everything else about her, it was simply captivating.

He picked up the bottle of wine and their two partially filled glasses on the way. As he did so, he couldn't help but admit that he'd been enthralled the moment he'd walked through the door. He'd smelled the Italian food cooking before he reached the fourth floor, but his interest in food had taken a back seat as soon as Bree's hypnotizing strawberry-vanilla scent hit him. It had nearly brought him to his knees. And when she'd opened the door and he'd seen her standing there in that little black dress that showed off her kissable shoulders, a hint of inviting décolletage, and a tantalizing glimpse of her long, toned legs, it had taken everything in him to keep from kissing her. Especially since he found himself immediately fantasizing about those parts of her body underneath her dress, his heart thumping and mouth watering at the image.

It had been great seeing Brandon again, as well as meeting Beth and Kevin, but it was sitting across from Bree during dinner that had been the amazing part of the evening. And yeah, the food was pretty damn incredible, too.

Diego refilled both their glasses before setting the bottle of wine on the coffee table and taking a seat on the sofa with her, making sure to leave some space between them even though his inner wolf begged him to sit closer.

Bree then leaned forward and picked up the plates, handing one to him with a smile. Diego eagerly lifted a forkful to his mouth and almost moaned. It was supremely moist and the ratio of chocolate frosting to cake was perfection. If the chicken parmesan and linguine had been amazing—and it was—then the dessert was world-changing.

He was still wrapped up in all that ooey-gooey chocolaty goodness when he realized Bree was sitting there with an amused expression on her face. He resisted the urge to look down at his shirt to make sure he hadn't dumped frosting on it.

"What?" he asked.

"Nothing." Her lips curved. "I like it when a man enjoys himself."

The words would have been rather innocent if not for the heat in her gaze and the subtle change in her scent making those strawberry and vanilla tones even sweeter. Forcing himself to focus on something other than Bree's scent, he took another bite of cake, then washed it down with some wine. Red wine and chocolate cake went together much better than he would have thought. Like he'd planned it.

"So," he asked, figuring he'd better change the subject before his inner wolf was over there humping her leg. "What kind of work do you do?"

When another smile tugged at the corner of her very kissable lips, her knew his attempt at casual conversation had failed dramatically.

"I'm an insurance investigator for Lexington Mutual Group," she said, taking a small bite of cake. "I look into high-price claims that have been filed and figure out if there's any kind of fraud going on. If the claim is legit and the insured property has actually been stolen, damaged, or destroyed, I try to help the cops track down the people responsible."

Huh. "So, it's kind of like being a private eye?"

"A little bit, I suppose," she said, shrugging those perfect tanned shoulders in the sexiest way he'd ever seen. "Except I don't have a fedora or a dimly lit office. Or a gun. The only camera I have is the one on my cell phone, and I never ever get into a physical confrontation with the bad guys. I find the evidence and turn it over to the cops, then stand back and let them take all the credit."

Diego was surprised by how much that last part had him breathing a sigh of relief. The thought of Bree out there doing something dangerous had him feeling all kinds of funny.

"You might not be cuffing the bad guys, but you still have one cool-ass job," he insisted. "How did you get into it?"

"I worked at LMG for years doing administrative work, but after the divorce from Dave, we needed money, so when my boss mentioned the investigator position, I jumped at it. The pay is great, and I ended up loving the work even though I hated the travel that comes with the job, especially when Brandon was little." She looked pensive as she took another nibble of cake. "I felt like I was deserting him. Every time I went on a two- or three-day trip to Houston or Austin, I'd spend half the nights crying in my hotel room."

The anguish in her voice was so painful, it was all he could do not to reach out and pull her into his arms. "When we lived in LA before we moved to Texas, my dad walked out on us," he said instead, his voice soft. "I was barely thirteen and my brother and sisters were all younger than me, and my mom had to work three jobs at one point to cover the bills. I'd hear her crying after she came home late at night because she couldn't be there in the morning when I got my brother and sisters up and ready for school. She hated being away from us so much, but we never held it against her. She was doing what she had to do to keep the family going. I'm sure it's the same way for Brandon."

Bree smiled gratefully at him, tears glistening in her eyes. "How old were you when your mom and stepdad got together?"

"Seventeen." He smiled at the memory as he used his fork to slice off another bite of cake. Though he'd since retired, his stepfather was a Dallas PD cop back then and one of the reasons Diego joined the force. "They met a little while after we moved here and probably would have gotten married sooner, but Mom wanted to make sure it was the real deal before she committed."

"I can understand that," Bree admitted. "Dating is complicated when kids are involved. As a woman, you want to go where your heart leads you, but as a mother, you know you have to keep your head and think about your children first. It makes finding that perfect someone so much harder."

Since he'd experienced all of that as the son of a mother who'd dealt with that same dilemma, Diego didn't see anything odd about what Bree had said, but from the chagrined look on her face, it was obvious she thought she'd said something wrong.

"I'm sorry," she said. "That sounded harsh, didn't it? I wasn't trying to scare you off or anything like that when I said I always have to put Brandon first. It's just—"

"It's okay," he said. "You don't ever have to apologize for

putting your son first. It's what makes you a good mother. I already knew that before you invited me over for dinner, and as you might have noticed, it didn't stop me from coming."

Bree opened her mouth, then closed it again. A moment later, she smiled. "I guess I'll just say thank you and leave it at that then."

Diego finished the last of the cake and set the plate on the table, then picked up his wineglass and took a sip before sitting back and looking at Bree.

"Speaking of the divorce, I get the feeling Dave isn't happy about it."

Bree stared at him, her fork halfway to her mouth, and Diego wanted to kick himself for circling around to her ex-husband again. But something about the guy made his werewolf side leery. Even if talking about Bree being with another man made his stomach clench.

Finishing her cake, Bree placed the empty plate on the table, then picked up her wine and sat back with a sigh, sliding off her shoes and curling her legs under her like a cat, revealing a breathtaking glimpse of thigh and making Diego's heart beat faster than ever.

"Talking about my ex," she murmured. "Not exactly what I had planned for tonight. But if you're going to be in our lives, I guess you should know what kind of jackass he is." She sipped her wine. "When I first met Dave, I was barely out of high school and thought it was true love. He's seven years older than I am, and at the time, I believed he was charming and mature. He'd already graduated from college with a degree in financial management and my family loved him, even when he took a job here in Dallas and we moved from back East only a few days after we got married.

"I got pregnant with Brandon a few weeks after we arrived here, and that's when Dave changed. He made snide little comments on how much time I spent with Brandon after he was born and didn't like when I decided to get a job. He didn't want me going out to lunch with my coworkers and hated when I spent time with my friends. By the time Brandon was halfway through elementary school, Dave was the poster child for anger management and extremely possessive when it came to me."

Diego bit back a growl. "Did he hurt you or Brandon?"

She shook her head. "No. Thankfully, he never got physical, but Brandon was still terrified of him. I tried to get Dave to go to counseling, but he wouldn't. That's when I went to see a divorce lawyer."

"What did Dave say when he found out?" Diego asked.

"Actually, he didn't know about it," Bree said, then quickly explained. "I was still working with the lawyer to make sure I'd get sole custody of Brandon and didn't want to say anything to Dave."

"That makes sense."

"I didn't want to make him suspicious, so when his firm had their annual Christmas party, I went with him." The hand holding the wineglass shook a little and Diego almost told her to stop, not wanting to upset her, but she was already continuing. "Dave was on the other side of the room with some people when he saw me talking to one of his coworkers. It set him off and he came over and told the poor guy to get away from me. All we were doing was talking and Dave lost his mind. The next thing I knew, he hit the guy over the head with a full champagne bottle right there in front of everyone. It cracked his skull and he died. It happened so fast nobody could do anything."

Diego did a double take. Okay, he hadn't seen that coming. "Damn."

She nodded. "I know. I couldn't believe it. Dave blew through every penny we had with lawyers, but still got twelve years in prison. Somehow, he got out in six. Apparently, he was extremely persuasive at his parole hearing."

Diego frowned. He'd have to look into that parole board hearing. The Texas judicial system was known for its leniency, but taking six years off a sentence for a vicious murder in front of witnesses wasn't the norm. "Has he been bothering you and Brandon since he got released?"

She took a slow sip of wine. "He's come around my office a few times and stopped by here. Once, he tried to talk to Brandon outside Kevin's house. It's always the same line about wanting us to get back together as a family. When he wants something, he has a hard time understanding why people won't give it to him."

Diego didn't like the sound of that. "How's Brandon taken his father going to jail for killing a man, then showing up like nothing ever happened?"

"Not well, as you can probably imagine." She ran a hand through her long hair. "The relationship Brandon had with his father before the trial would be described as complicated at best. He tried to get Dave's attention from the moment he learned how to talk, and my jerk of an ex pretty much ignored him. When Dave went to prison, Brandon tried to act like he didn't care, but I could see his world was falling apart. I tried to be there for him, hoping I could take Dave's place, but it didn't work. Things only went downhill when the other kids at school found out his father was in jail for murder. They became cruel in the way only children can be. All except for Kevin, of course. From then on, Brandon hung out exclusively with him."

"And you don't like Kevin," Diego surmised.

"I like him," she said quickly. "It's just that I don't always like the crowd he hangs out with."

Diego nodded. "I thought so."

"How did you know?"

"Just an educated guess," he admitted. "But when a kid comes in smelling like weed, it's not exactly going out on a limb assuming he hangs outs with the wrong crowd."

Her eyes went wide. "Kevin was smoking marijuana before he and Brandon came in?"

"He wasn't smoking it. But he was around other people who were."

That seemed to mollify Bree somewhat, but she still looked surprised. "You can tell all that simply from the way he smells?"

Diego grinned and tapped his nose with his finger. "I can smell what he had for breakfast yesterday. The great sense of smell and night vision are part of the package—along with the claws and fangs."

Bree returned his smile with a small one of her own but didn't say anything. Instead, she sat there looking thoughtful.

"You okay?" he asked.

"Yeah, it's just that..."

"Just what?" he prompted when her voice trailed off.

She bit her lip, as if unsure whether to continue. "The night Brandon got shot, he was supposed to be at the movies with Kevin, but instead they were at a convenience store all the way on the other side of town. When I asked him about it after he got out of the hospital, he told me they met one of Kevin's friends at the movies and went to the store to grab some sodas and junk food."

"But you don't believe that?"

Her brow furrowed. "I wanted to. But they drove past thirty fast-food places on the way to that convenience store, not to mention a dozen stores exactly like it. In addition to that, the officer I talked to at the hospital told me the store where Brandon got shot is a well-known location for drug dealing and that they suspected the shooting was between two gangs who both claim the store as part of their turf."

"Did the officer believe Brandon was the target of the shooting?"

"No," she said. "Not that it really matters. When I was sitting in the waiting room wondering if my son was going to live or not, it didn't help knowing he'd gotten shot by accident. Regardless of what Brandon says, he and Kevin almost certainly went there to buy drugs and he could have died because of it."

"Have you talked to him about it?" Diego asked.

She let out a weary sigh. "As much as any mother can have that conversation with their fifteen-year-old son. But he insists he and Kevin were there to buy soda and candy and that he had no idea the store was a gang hangout. He also swears up and down that he doesn't do drugs."

"Do you believe him?"

Bree considered that before answering. "I don't know. I want to, but I don't know if I can. And the thought that my own son is lying to me tears me apart inside."

The pain he knew she must be feeling right then seemed

to be a tangible thing, as though a steel band tightened around his chest, and breathing became almost impossible.

"I was already going to help him get his inner werewolf under control and come to grips with his nature, so I could talk to him about the drug stuff, too, if you want," he suggested softly.

Diego held his breath, worried he might be overstepping a bit with the offer. When he saw tears glisten in Bree's eyes, he was sure he had.

Dammit.

Before he realized what he was doing, he moved closer on the couch, his thigh touching hers as he leaned in to catch the first tear before it could slide down her cheek.

"Hey, I'm sorry. I didn't mean to upset you." he said gently. "If you don't want me talking to him about any of this, I won't."

Bree let out a little laugh. "It's not that." Her small, slim hand came up to wrap around his, her fingers curling around the one he'd used to wipe away the tears. "It's just that I can't believe how lucky I am to have met you."

He lifted a brow. "I'm not sure if I'd say our meeting was very lucky since you and Brandon were being held hostage at the time."

She laughed again, this time with an accompanying smile that had his stomach doing cartwheels and barrel rolls.

"Yeah, but if Brandon and I hadn't been taken hostage, we would never have met you," she said. "Which would have left my son still lost and confused, and me with no way to help him. You've come into our lives at the exact moment we needed you. That's why we're lucky."

Her words got to him in a way he'd never felt before. He had no idea what to say to her, so instead he wiped away a few more tears. Being this close to her—with her skin like velvet under his fingers, lips plump and perfect, scent so powerful he couldn't take a single breath without being overwhelmed—was intoxicating.

Diego didn't realize he'd leaned in to kiss her until he felt a light vibration in his chest and realized he was growling low and deep in his throat in a sound of pure pleasure.

A little voice in the back of his mind told him to stop kissing her, that this was moving too fast. But the much more vocal part of his consciousness—the part apparently in charge—insisted pulling away would be foolish beyond belief. The knowledge that Bree was kissing him back with a passion and heat that matched his own had a lot to do with deciding to continue.

So, he gave in, sliding one hand into her thick hair while gliding the other gently along her thigh and over her dress until he reached her hip. Then he tugged her closer, reveling in being with a woman who tasted better than anything this side of heaven. Kissing Bree felt like the most natural, instinctive thing Diego had ever done, and as his tongue teased its way a little farther into her mouth and his fingers tightened in her hair, he couldn't imagine ever wanting to stop.

It wasn't until he felt a tingling in his gums and fingertips that Diego realized he might be getting a little carried away. Popping fangs in the middle of a make-out session probably wasn't the way to encourage a repeat performance.

But if pulling away from Bree wasn't the hardest thing he'd ever done, he didn't know what was.

When he finally opened his eyes, it was difficult to look

at anything but those rosy-red lips. Then he caught sight of the heat in her gaze and found the urge to keep kissing this beautiful woman hard to resist.

Somehow, he got a grip and pulled back a little more, forcing himself to ignore the sexy whimper of complaint from Bree that had his fangs pushing harder against his gums and his pants tightening around his erection.

"Trust me when I tell you that kissing you for the rest of the night would be the highlight of the best date I've ever had," he said. "But my instincts are telling me this could be even better if we slow down."

She gazed at him for a long moment, her breathing and pulse slowly returning to normal, before a languid smile slid across those oh-so-kissable lips. "Your cop instincts…or the ones from your werewolf?"

He chuckled, taking her hand and urging her to her feet as he stood, hating the way the hem of her dress slid down to cover that delectable glimpse of thigh. "Which one would you trust more?"

Bree walked alongside him, one of her hands in his. "I think I'm good with either, since I'm pretty sure my son and I owe our lives to both. So, whatever they're telling you, I'll go along with."

When they got to the door, he turned to face her with a smile. "So, if I said my instincts are saying we should go out for dinner and a movie tomorrow night, what would you think?"

Stepping closer, she slipped her free hand behind his neck to tug him down for a kiss. "I'd think we should do dinner and a movie," she whispered against his mouth.

"Not that I don't love spending time alone with you, but

do you think Brandon would want to go with us?" he asked in between kisses.

This time it was Bree who pulled back. She gazed up at him with a brilliant smile. "Offering to include my son on our night out? If you keep this up, I'm going to start thinking you're too good to be true."

Chuckling, he bent his head and captured her lips again. His hands were starting to wander as his mouth traced down her slender neck, when he heard voices from Brandon's bedroom and remembered where he was.

He reluctantly broke the kiss and took a step back. "I'd better go, or we'll still be standing here kissing when the sun comes up."

"You're probably right," she groaned as he opened the door. "Although that doesn't sound too bad. Except for the part where I have to get up early for work."

Diego ducked back inside and grabbed another quick kiss, then backed down the hallway, his head spinning with how this beautiful woman had gotten to him. "I'll text you about Friday."

She leaned against the doorjamb, a smile curving her lips. "I can't wait."

The urge to go back for another kiss was almost irresistible, and he had a hell of a time turning to jog down the steps.

Crap, he was in so much trouble.

CHAPTER 7

"Earth to Bree. Come in, Bree."

Bree gave herself a shake and looked up from the file she was reading to see her assistant, Leslie Moore, standing there with a smile on her face and a big pile of folders in her hands.

"And she's back." Leslie walked into Bree's office with a laugh, her shoulder-length blond curls bouncing. About Bree's age, she was married with one child in kindergarten and another on the way. "You looked like you were a million miles away. Everything okay?"

Bree returned her smile. "Everything's fine. I didn't get a lot of sleep last night, so I'm a little fuzzy this morning."

Leslie nodded understandingly. "Have you tried chamomile tea? It does wonders for me whenever I can't sleep."

"I'll do that," Bree said, though she doubted there was any tea in the world that would have slowed her whirling mind after last night's date with Diego.

She took the stack of folders Leslie held out and set them on her desk, thanking her for the help. Leslie was definitely worth her weight in gold. She spent hours digging up background info on cases, then printing it out and putting it into some usable format. It would have added days to every case Bree handled if she had to do it herself.

But instead of opening one of the folders to see what Leslie had unearthed for her, she stared into space, her thoughts once again turning to last night and what was, without a doubt, the most amazing evening she'd ever had with a guy. In fact, the date had been absolutely perfect. There was simply no other way to describe it.

In her experience, first dates were awkward, sometimes painful, affairs, where two people with very little in common strained to fill long, uncomfortable stretches of silence with inane conversation. But last night had been nothing like that. Instead, the conversation had flowed nonstop for hours as they talked about things Bree would never have imagined discussing with a man on their eighth date, much less the first.

Whether the topic was Brandon, her jackass ex-husband, or the pain Diego had gone through when he'd become a werewolf, there didn't seem to be anything they couldn't talk about. Being open and honest with Diego seemed as natural as breathing. It was something she'd never experienced before—with anyone.

But as amazing as the conversation had been, it paled in comparison to that kiss. Okay, technically it wasn't simply a kiss. It had been a make-out session of the best kisses Bree had ever experienced in her life.

Sighing contentedly at the memory, she opened the top folder and flipped through a few pages, trying to focus on personal details of Garth and Vera Williamson's case, but it was difficult to think of anything other than Diego and how attracted she was to him.

Attracted?

Oh, hell. Who was she kidding? She was falling for the hunky SWAT cop big time.

The movie about the runaway bus and the guy and girl who end up mistaking the resulting adrenaline rush for something more abruptly flashed into her head. Part of her worried the same thing was going on with her and that she was merely feeling grateful for what he'd done for Brandon and her at the diner. But another part of her knew that wasn't it at all.

Truthfully, the intense connection she and Diego seemed to have was a little scary. If he hadn't tapped the brakes while they were making out on the couch, Bree knew there was a good chance she would have climbed onto his lap and… Well, from that point she had no idea how much further things would have gone because she'd never done anything like that with anyone before. Then again, she'd never been that into a guy before. That was why she hadn't gotten much sleep last night. She'd spent half the night thinking about what had happened…and the other half fantasizing about what could have happened.

Picking up her coffee, she took a sip, then rested her elbows on the desk, cupping the warm mug between her hands. While she was kind of bummed Diego had suggested taking things slowly, she knew he was right. Because this wasn't only about her. Brandon needed Diego in his life right now, both as a male role model with his head on straight *and* as a werewolf.

Brandon really liked Diego. Her son hadn't stopped talking about how awesome he was from the moment they'd met him at the diner. If she messed things up by pushing things too fast, she wouldn't only ruin her chances with a great guy, she'd likely also wreck the relationship between Diego and her son.

With another sigh—and a prayer this could work out for both her and Brandon—Bree forced herself to get back to work, turning her attention to the files before her, hoping she'd find some little detail that'd help with the cases. In addition to the Williamson and Montagne thefts, she'd picked up two additional cases—an elderly couple whose Ming vase had been stolen and a Texas oil baron who was missing a bowie knife that had belonged to Jim Bowie himself.

She was jotting down notes when she heard Leslie walk in. Bree looked up to give her assistant a smile, only to stiffen when she saw that her ex-husband was with Leslie.

What the hell is he doing here?

"I found this attractive guy in the lobby," Leslie practically sang, a big grin on her face. "He said he was looking for you, so I brought him straight here."

"Morning, Bree. I brought you coffee and a cheese Danish," Dave said, standing there in a four-thousand-dollar suit and two-thousand-dollar shoes, using that charming voice he only pulled out for special occasions while holding up a small white bag and a signature cardboard cup from Starbucks. "Thought you might want something to eat while we talked."

Leslie's smile broadened, her look one of pure approval. Only because Leslie didn't have a clue who the hell Dave was or what a jerk he could be.

Bree stood and circled her desk, taking the coffee and Danish out of his hand and promptly handing them to her assistant. "Toss these out, would you? Or feel free to enjoy the Danish, if you want. And the next time my ex-husband walks into the building, ignore him. That's what I always do."

Leslie glared at Dave, the smile disappearing from her face. Taking the coffee cup and bag from Bree, she turned on her heel and headed for the door, pausing to pointedly toss Dave's peace offering in the small trash can before leaving.

Dave grunted in displeasure, but Bree cut him off before he could say anything. "Did you forget the part of that conversation we had where I told you never to come to my office?"

"Come on, Bree," he protested as she moved back around her desk, putting it between them. "Why do you have to be like this? I just want to talk. I was worried about how you were doing after what happened at the diner. You never called or texted me."

"Why do I have to be like this?" She folded her arms, standing instead of sitting down so he couldn't tower over her. "Maybe because we're divorced and have been for over five years. Maybe because I've told you multiple times since you've gotten out of prison that I have zero interest in getting back together. Maybe because I've moved on and you can't seem to get that."

If Dave picked up on her anger, he didn't let it show. Instead, he stepped closer to her desk. "Come on," he said again, using that suave voice of his, the one he'd charmed her with when she was barely out of high school. "Let me take you to dinner tonight and we can talk about everything. You'll see this isn't anything we can't work out. If you give me a chance, you'll realize we're meant to be together. We always have been."

Dave spoke in the most rational tone of voice like he always did, making her concerns seem silly and unreasonable. It was a tactic that had worked on her for years. Well, no more. It had stopped being effective around the time she realized he wasn't merely narcissistic and unstable—which would have been bad enough—but a cold-blooded killer, too.

"Dinner? Just the two of us?" she asked, irritated he thought this line of crap would actually still work on her. "What about Brandon?"

He looked surprised for a moment, as if remembering he had a son. "Sure, bring him, too. I thought it could be the two of us at first, you know?"

Bree snorted. Dave had never treated Brandon as anything more than a bother. Certainly not as a son he loved.

"I'm not going out to dinner with you tonight or ever," she told him.

His hazel eyes glinted with annoyance; then his face went blank. Like someone had pulled down a shade over his emotions.

"You know," he said, eyeing her coldly, "sometimes I think about how nice it would be if you could make people do exactly what you wanted without going to the effort of trying to convince them."

Bree knew her ex was dangerous, but this was the first time she realized how crazy he truly was. Who said things like that? "There's something wrong with you, you know that?"

Dave slammed his hands down on the desk, a sneer curling his lip. "Why can't you see I'm perfect for you?" he demanded, anger beginning to bubble beneath the surface. "I have nice clothes and a great job. In fact, Garrett, Wallace, and Banks are going to make me a partner soon."

Bree had to fight the urge to call BS on that. Who would be stupid enough to put a murderer's name on the company letterhead? Then again, they *had* hired him in the first place, and Bree knew from experience that Dave was exceptionally good at getting people to invest damn near every penny they owned, so anything was possible. Not that she really cared.

"None of that means anything to me," she said. "It never did. But then again, I doubt you ever knew enough about me to realize that."

Anger verging on rage filled Dave's eyes, and Bree had to fight the urge to step back. She'd vowed a long time ago to never let him see how much he scared her. But that vow didn't keep her heart from thumping like crazy in her chest.

"You're sleeping with that asshole cop I saw you with the other day, aren't you?" he demanded, hands tightening into fists as he straightened up. "What the hell is so special about him anyway?"

Bree owed Dave absolutely no explanation for the choices she made in her life, but in this case, she had no problem answering. Just so he'd finally get it through his thick head that they were done.

"Not that it's any of your business, but it so happens Diego Martinez is everything you're not. He's a good, caring, compassionate man who risks his life every day for people he doesn't know, and I thank God he was in that diner or Brandon and I would probably be dead. Oh, and he's not a jackass with anger management issues, so that's a bonus."

That last part had been a stupid addition, and for a minute, she half expected Dave to move around her desk and come at her. He might have, too, if Leslie hadn't shown up with several of their larger male coworkers.

"You need to leave," Bree said, pinning Dave with a hard look. "Now."

Dave clenched his jaw so hard she thought he might shatter his teeth, and she braced herself in case he got violent. But to her surprise, he slowly backed away.

"Being a cop is a dangerous job," he murmured as he went, his face as cold and emotionless as Bree had ever seen it. "You might want to remember that."

She opened her mouth to ask what the hell that meant, but he was already out the door.

"You okay?" Leslie asked, hurrying over to her as their coworkers followed Dave. Probably to make sure he left. "Do you want me to call the police?"

Bree shook her head, sinking into her chair with a shudder, her heart beating fast and her hands beginning to shake. She clasped them together on top of her desk so Leslie wouldn't see.

"I'm fine," she said, hoping she sounded convincing. "He left. That's all that matters."

Leslie nodded. "I'm so sorry about letting him in. I didn't know."

"It's okay. Really," Bree murmured. "Thanks for getting help. I'm good now."

Leslie didn't look like she believed that but left.

Bree turned her attention to the folders on her desk, picking up where she'd left off reading. She was halfway down the page when she saw four little words buried there that made her stop and take notice.

Garrett, Wallace, and Banks.

Bree sat up straighter, reading that part again to make sure she didn't miss anything important. But after going through it twice, there was no doubt about it. Garth and Vera Williams used Dave's investment firm to manage their wealth. Some guy by the last name of Reed was their brokerage advisor.

Pushing the Williamson folder to the side, Bree reached for the other three files and started flipping. They'd all invested with Garrett, Wallace, and Banks as well. They also had the same advisor—Reed.

Bree told herself to stay calm and not read more into this than there was. It could be nothing. Rich people tended to all use the same investment firms. Word of mouth and all that.

But she couldn't deny this was the connection between the two thefts she'd been looking for. It wouldn't be unusual for an investment firm of the caliber of Garrett, Wallace, and Banks to maintain a list of all valuables their clients owned as well as details on how they were stored. They might have pass codes and combinations for the various security systems in place to protect the stuff.

While all of that was interesting—and definitely worth digging into—there was also the impossible-to-ignore issue of her ex-husband working at the same investment firm that represented two clients who'd recently been robbed. His name might not be listed as their advisor, but as an employee, Dave would have access to the same information as Reed.

Maybe it was wishful thinking on Bree's part, but wouldn't it be great if Dave turned out to be moronic enough to screw up and get himself sent back to prison?

She took a deep breath. As much as she wanted Dave to be involved, Bree would do this right and let the evidence lead her where it would. On the downside, digging into Dave's investment firm meant she'd probably end up running into him again.

As she began taking notes, Bree couldn't stop herself from replaying all the hateful, awful things Dave had said. Of all of them, it was his parting shot that scared her the most.

"Being a cop is a dangerous job. You might want to remember that."

Had that been a threat? Would Dave really try to hurt Diego?

Bree wanted to think it was nothing more than another example of her ex's lack of impulse control, but if that's all it was, why was she suddenly terrified?

"This is a complete waste of time," Connor groused as he yanked a file folder off the stack next to him and flipped through it. "What the hell does the chief expect us to find anyway?"

Diego looked up from his own stack of folders to glance at Hale and Trey, sitting across from him and Connor at the conference table in the training building, wondering if either of them wanted to answer their pack mate's question. Neither of them looked up, content to continue poring over their own folders. Even Kat the cat, sitting on the table by Connor, refused to glance up from the plate of tuna fish she was carefully nibbling on.

Everyone was ignoring Connor because this was the second time he'd asked the very same question. Then again, asking the same question over and over and expecting a different answer was a very Connor-like thing to do. Sort of like feeding a rescue cat tuna fish packed in sunflower oil because Kat was the only feline in existence that hated real cat food and refused to eat it.

Diego turned his attention back to the folder in front of him, going through every report the team had written over the past month, trying to find something they might have missed when it came to the bizarre incidents they'd been gone on recently. They'd been at it all morning and had nothing to show for it. But calling it quits wasn't an option now that half of Dallas was officially losing its collective mind after word had gotten out that the three men who'd taken those hostages at the bank the other night were kids from a local college on the dean's list who'd never so much as gotten a ticket for speeding. Pictures and tweets had been popping up all over social media ever since, friends and family swearing this wasn't normal behavior for the trio. With the twenty-four-hour news cycle pushing it, Ernest Hobbs's drug theory hadn't just taken off. It had exploded. And Chief Leclair and her office were feeling the heat.

Which was why Diego and his pack mates were trapped under piles of paper in the conference room, looking for a connection between these latest suspects and the previous ones. Or at least an idea about where they might have picked up this new drug. If such a drug existed. Unfortunately, though Diego knew how important it was to find something—anything—to give the chief and her detectives a place to start, he was having one hell of a time focusing on the piece of paper in front of him.

The only thing he seemed able to think about was Bree and kissing her last night. Part of him was still kicking himself for leaving when he had instead of seeing where those kisses might have led. Because damn, did she taste delicious.

"Diego, are you reading that file?" Trey asked, jerking him out of his daydreams.

Diego gave himself a shake to see his pack mate regarding him with an amused expression. "I'm reading it," he insisted as Connor and Hale—and even Kat—all lifted their heads to look his way. "Really."

"Right." Trey snorted. "That's why you haven't flipped a page in five minutes. It's obvious your head is a million miles away. So, why don't you tell us what's up? It's not like any of us are getting anything worthwhile accomplished right now anyway."

Hale sat back in his chair, a knowing look on his face. "And before you try to say nothing's up, I should probably point out that Bree's scent is all over you."

Diego had a hard time keeping the smile off his face. Even after the shower he took following physical training this morning, he still smelled like Bree. Not that he minded. He could have her scent on his skin all day, every day.

"Bree invited me over for dinner last night. It was"—his grin broadened—"amazing."

Actually, that was an understatement. His date with Bree had been beyond anything he'd ever experienced. If he wasn't so interested in maintaining his cool, calm alpha werewolf exterior in front of his pack mates, he'd be running around right now chest-thumping everyone in the greater Dallas metro area.

Around the table, his teammates were regarding him expectantly, obviously waiting for him to tell them about last night. Considering how many werewolves in the Pack had already found their soul mates, he'd think the rest would get tired of hearing about it, but from the eager expressions on his friends' faces, he guessed not.

"Do you think she's *The One* for you?"

The One. That one person supposedly out there that every werewolf was waiting to meet who would accept them for what they were. Up until a few years ago, they'd all thought it was a myth, an urban legend. Then Gage met his wife and they all started to believe that *The One* wasn't a folk tale at all, but the real deal—and that gave all of them hope. Especially when the rest of their pack mates began meeting *The One* they were meant to be with.

Diego would be lying if he didn't admit he'd spent a good portion of last night and most of this morning wondering if Bree was *The One* for him.

"Maybe it's wishful thinking, but when I was with Bree last night, I felt a connection like I've never experienced before," he said. "And when we kissed, it was unreal. My damn fangs and claws nearly slipped out the minute our lips touched."

"Premature fang eruption? Sounds like soul-mate confirmation to me," Connor said with a chuckle, exchanging a look with Kat as if he expected her to agree with him. Kat seemed more interested in her tuna than the conversation.

On the other side of the table, Hale grinned. "I knew it the second I saw you and Bree together. Congratulations! Though I have to admit, while I'm happy you've found the woman you're supposed to spend the rest of your life with, I'm a little pissed you met your soul mate before I even caught a whiff of mine. I've been a werewolf longer than you. Shouldn't seniority count for something?"

Connor snorted. "Catch a whiff? Your nose is complete crap. You could walk right past your soul mate and never know it. Hell, you might have met her already."

Hale scowled at that. His nose didn't work like the other werewolves in the Pack. He'd broken it severely years before going through his change, and it had never really healed. It was a sensitive subject for him, mostly because their pack mates ragged the hell out of him about it.

"Don't listen to Connor," Diego said as a panicked look filled his friend's eyes. "You'll know your soul mate when you see her. I'm sure of it."

Hale didn't look too sure about that. "So, you knew Bree was *The One* for you the second you met her? Even before going on a date with her?"

"Well...not really." He thought back to when he'd first seen Bree in the diner. He'd thought she was gorgeous, but they'd been in the middle of a hostage crisis, so he hadn't exactly been thinking about soul mates at the time. "Hell, if I'm being honest, I'm not sure if I'm sure of it now. I mean, it feels like she could be *The One*, but how am I supposed to know for certain? It's not like there are rules for this. Every time someone else in the Pack found their mate, things got crazy as hell. I could be reading everything wrong."

No one said anything, leaving Diego alone with his thoughts. While several of his pack mates had needed to be dragged kicking and screaming into relationships with their soul mates, fighting the connection for a variety of reasons that made sense to absolutely nobody, it wasn't like that for Diego. He wasn't sure why, but the idea of finding the woman he was meant to spend a lifetime with had never scared him. In fact, he'd been looking forward to it. Like discovering the woman you were quickly developing feelings for already had a fifteen-year-old son when you'd never given serious thought to what it would be like to have kids.

"Have you thought of talking to Bree about it?" Trey asked, his usual serious look back on his face.

Diego grimaced. If there was a chance Bree was experiencing the same emotions and feelings he was, it'd help to tell her about *The One*. But while he'd love to explain it, now wasn't the right time.

"We've known each other for barely more than forty-eight hours," he pointed out. "She just learned werewolves are real and that her teenage son is one. Now I'm supposed to tell her that fate has already determined who she's going to fall in love with after one date? And oh, by the way, it's me? I think we need to get to know each other a little better before I spring something like that on her."

"What are you going to do when her emotions start going all crazy like yours and she doesn't understand why?" Connor asked.

Diego shrugged. "I'll worry about that proverbial bridge when we come to it. Until then, I'm going to take it one date at a time and see how it goes."

"What are you guys doing on your next date?" Hale prodded. "I bet Gage can get you reservations at Chambre Français, if you want."

Chambre Français was a fancy French restaurant owned by a friend of Gage. He'd gotten some of the other members of the Pack in there when they'd wanted to impress their dates, and Diego knew his boss would get him in, too, but it wasn't exactly his kind of place.

"Bree and I have already made plans to go see a movie with Brandon."

"Crap," Trey muttered. "We've been so busy talking about her being your soul mate, I forgot she has a son who's a beta looking for an alpha to bond with. Any chance that alpha is you?"

Diego almost laughed. Helping Brandon learn how to control his inner wolf was way different from being his alpha.

"I don't think I'm qualified to be an alpha for a fifteen-year-old kid, especially not with all the crap Brandon is dealing with right now," he said. "Jayna would be a better fit for Brandon than I ever could. She already has experience dealing with betas, and if Brandon joined her pack, he'd be able to hang out with other werewolves like him all the time."

"While I'm more than ready to argue with you about your abilities to be an alpha for this kid, right now, I'm more interested in what kind of crap Brandon is dealing with," Trey said. "Assuming we're talking about more than the normal angst associated with a teenager finding out they're a werewolf."

Diego grabbed his bottle of water from the table and took a long drink, then told them about Dave, his possessive and controlling behavior, the manslaughter charge and divorce, and how hard it had all been on Brandon.

"Dave got out a few months ago, which has made things harder on the kid," Diego added. "Long story short, Brandon started hanging around with the wrong people. He was shot and turned because he was with a friend who might have been looking to buy drugs and walked right into the middle of a turf war between two gangs. Bree's worried she's losing her son to drugs and terrified about what Dave is going to do now that he's out of prison."

Connor frowned. "Is this Dave guy dangerous?"

Diego's inner wolf must have thought so, immediately

growling at the idea Dave was a threat that needed to be dealt with. But he kept that part of himself in check, focusing on the facts.

"He keeps showing up in places he's not wanted, including at the diner after the rescue," Diego told them. "But while it's obvious he's an asshole, I can't really say he's done anything yet to warrant being called dangerous."

"We could look into him, if you want," Hale offered. "Check in with his probation officer and see what he or she has to say about the guy. If anyone has an idea of what Dave is up to, it'd be his PO."

Diego nodded as he felt a twinge of remorse for going behind Bree's back and snooping around her ex. But every instinct Diego had insisted he do something, that Dave wasn't the kind of man to stand back and let someone else have what he considered his, not with his possessive personality.

He and his pack mates fell silent again as they went back to looking through files and taking notes about suspects, witnesses, and crime locations. Every so often, Diego glanced over at the stuff the other guys had written, but he couldn't for the life of him see a connection between these cases, other than the obvious—that none of the criminals involved met the typical definition of the *usual suspects.*

Connor was right. This was a waste of time.

When his phone dinged a few minutes later, Diego had never been so happy to get a text. "Our lunch order is ready for pickup. I'll go get it while you guys keep working."

"Make sure they included that small portion of meat for Kat that I ordered," Connor called out as Diego headed for the door.

Diego shook his head as he walked outside into the hot June Texas sun. The whole pack had tried to tell Connor that cats shouldn't eat spicy food, Mexican or otherwise, but he refused to listen. Or rather Kat refused to listen. And since it was obvious the cat was the one in charge, she was the one they'd have to convince before anything was going to change.

He moved across the compound's parking lot toward the front gate. He normally parked his Toyota Tacoma inside the fence line with his pack mates' vehicles, but the team's big RV had been sitting in the way this morning, getting loaded up for a call, so he'd parked his pickup across the street in the visitor lot.

As he walked, Diego replayed his earlier conversation with the guys, thinking seriously about what it would mean if Bree really was *The One* for him. Unlike his pack mates' significant others, Bree had a son to think about.

Diego had to get this right—with both Bree *and* her son.

He was so distracted by thoughts of Bree and Brandon as he reached his truck that he didn't notice the nondescript black van slowly approaching him until the passenger-side window rolled down. Diego half turned toward it, assuming the driver was going to ask for directions, when the barrel of an automatic rifle slid out the opening. Diego barely had time to leap to the side before a hail of bullets tore up the ground where he'd been standing.

He hit the pavement and rolled, not stopping until he ended up behind Trey's white Ford Bronco. He yanked his SIG out and stood in time to hear an engine revving followed by the loud crashing sound of metal on metal. He only realized it was the black van slamming into the other side of

Trey's truck when the Bronco slid sideways and slammed into him, sending him flying. He ended up flat on his back, air bursting from his lungs. Then all hell descended around him as automatic weapons fire tore apart Trey's vehicle.

His nose told him there were four men in the van. His ears filled in more details, alerting him that the men had split up, two coming around the back of the Bronco, the other two heading for the front, obviously planning to catch him in the cross fire and mow him down like a damn carnival game.

This was a flat-out ambush, plain and simple. They were here to kill him. Diego had no doubt his pack mates were already heading his way, but if he didn't do something to slow the four guys down, this would all be over before his teammates got there.

Diego was already shifting as he clambered to his feet and took off running with a low, deep growl. His claws extended so fast they hurt, and the feel of his fangs elongating was enough to distract him from the thought of how many times he was about to get hit with large-caliber rifle rounds and how painful it was going to be.

He didn't bother going around what was left of the Bronco, instead launching himself straight over the top, the muscles of his legs and back twisting violently as he flew through the air toward the two attackers moving around the front of the vehicle. Diego couldn't help but notice the emotionless expressions on the men's faces as he descended on them with fangs and claws extended, snarling and growling in his rage. Fearless, they stood their ground, turned their weapons his way, and lit him up.

Bullet after bullet ripped through his body—thighs,

stomach, upper chest. The pain was intense, but Diego ignored it as he landed on the first man while turning the SIG in his hand toward the second attacker and squeezing the trigger repeatedly.

Diego lost his grip on his handgun as he and the man he'd tackled tumbled to the ground of the parking lot, and he didn't have time to reach for it as he fought for control of the AR-15-style weapon the man was trying to wrestle in his direction.

Out of the corner of his eye, Diego saw the two attackers who'd been circling around the rear of Trey's truck loop back his way, weapons aimed straight at him. Diego reached out one hand and slashed his claws across the throat of the man he was wrestling with, then grabbed hold of the man's dark-blue shirt and flipped over with the body, wincing as multiple bullets tore into the corpse.

Shit. The man's buddies hadn't hesitated.

The sound of handgun fire erupted from his left, barely audible above the louder rifle noise. Diego instinctively knew it was his pack mates, and a second later, there were two thuds as bodies hit the ground.

The pain he'd been suppressing decided to make an appearance, and he clenched his jaw to keep from groaning as he lay there. Boots pounded the pavement, then someone was yanking away the corpse that was still draped over him. Diego looked up to see Trey, Hale, and Connor standing there looking down at him.

"Damn," Connor muttered. "I hope all that blood didn't come out of you."

Diego winced as Trey grabbed his hand and pulled him into a sitting position. "How bad is it?"

"I got hit at least three times," Diego told him, looking down and trying to figure out which blood on his uniform was his and which wasn't. "I'm pretty sure they're all still in me."

Trey cursed. "We need to get you inside so I can get those bullets out, and we need to do it fast before this place turns into a zoo."

Hale and Connor half carried, half dragged Diego across the street and through the compound into the admin building while Trey ran ahead. Diego gritted his teeth every step of the way. The bullets inside him wouldn't cause more damage, but a werewolf's body was well aware when there was foreign material in it and used the pain as motivation to make sure someone got it out. Having Trey do that wouldn't be fun, but it was a hell of a lot better than leaving the crap in there.

As they reached the door of the building, Diego heard the wail of approaching sirens. Trey wasn't going to be able to be leisurely about this, which was only going to make it more painful.

Shit.

Diego walked out of the admin building less than fifteen minutes later, Trey at his side, still complaining about his truck being totaled. They both stopped when they realized the SWAT compound had turned into that zoo Trey had mentioned.

There were at least twenty patrol units lining the road outside the fence line, while half a dozen ambulances were parked a little farther back. Beyond them were row after row of news vehicles as far as the eye could see.

The crime-scene techs were already processing the scene across the street in the parking lot, black tarps draped across the four men Diego and his teammates had killed. A slender woman with blond hair and a notepad kneeled beside one of the bodies, looking closely at the corpse. It was the guy whose throat Diego had ripped out, and the woman examining the injury so intently was Samantha Mills, one of the county's medical examiners.

As if sensing him and Trey standing there, the ME lifted her head and stared at them through the fence like she knew there was no way in hell those wounds had been created from a gunshot. The scariest part was that this was at least the third or fourth time she happened to be at a crime scene where he and his pack mates had used their fangs and claws.

"Do you think she knows something?" Trey murmured, gazing intently at the forensics expert across the compound. "She's looking at us like she knows exactly what we are."

"Maybe she has a thing for you," Diego suggested, forcing himself to stop looking in the direction of the ME—and the corpses.

Trey snorted. "I'm pretty sure that's not it."

Chief Leclair was near the training building, talking with Gage, Mike, Hale, and Connor. Catching sight of Diego and Trey, she motioned them over. Her eyes went wide when she saw the bloodstains on Diego's uniform. Damn, he wished he'd taken the time to change.

"Very little of this is mine," he said quickly.

Unfortunately, that didn't seem to provide as much relief as Diego had hoped. But at least she stopped looking at him like she expected him to pass out at any moment. Before she could reply, a uniformed officer hurried up to them and handed Leclair four plastic badges. The chief glanced at them with a frown before looking at Diego.

"Hale and Connor told me it seemed like those four men lying dead out there were going after you specifically. Do you think that was the case?"

Diego glanced at Hale to see him nod. "When we moved to engage them, they didn't bother to look our way. They were focused on you like a couple of bloodhounds."

Diego couldn't argue with that. "Hale's right. They rolled right up and started shooting at me and didn't seem to care if they hit their own in the attempt to take me out."

Leclair's frown deepened. "All four of the men were baggage handlers at DFW," she said, handing the ID cards to Gage while keeping her gaze fixed on Diego. "Please tell me you recognized them and know why they might have attacked you."

Diego shook his head. "I wish I knew."

Muttering under her breath, the chief said she'd be in touch, then headed across the street to where the crime-scene techs were working.

A familiar scent caught his attention, and Diego scanned the crowd of people beyond the police crime-scene tape to see Hobbs standing right up front, complete with his own photographer. Even at this distance, Diego could hear the guy's telephoto camera clicking away at a hundred miles an hour. He could only imagine what the headlines were going to say tomorrow.

Dallas PD—and SWAT—Powerless in the Face of This New Threat!

But then he remembered the blood and looked down at his torn and ruined uniform, forgetting about tomorrow's headlines. Instead, he prayed Bree didn't see these pictures. She would lose her mind, and he hated the idea of worrying her. It frigging bothered him more than getting shot to crap by four men intent on killing him for some reason he and his teammates might never know.

CHAPTER 8

"I CAN'T BELIEVE WE HAVE TO SEE A CARTOON," BRANDON complained with the cutest little beta growl as Diego followed him up the stairs toward the top row of seats in the movie theater. "I'm not a kid."

Diego bit his tongue to keep from laughing. Instead, he held the monster-sized bucket of popcorn in one hand while using the other to pull out his movie ticket, making sure they were heading toward the right seats. He'd never been to a theater where you actually picked out your seats when you bought the tickets, so he really had no idea what he was doing. It was obvious Brandon knew where to go since he headed straight to the three right-most seats in the back row. Probably because Bree had let him pick out the seats to make up for the fact that she had vetoed his selection, telling him there was absolutely zero chance of them seeing an action movie with stuff blowing up every five minutes. Using her executive authority, Bree had declared they'd be watching the new animated movie, and that was the end of the conversation.

While Brandon had let it be known he wasn't happy about the pick, Diego was secretly thrilled. It had been forever since he'd seen a cartoon, and it wasn't like he'd be able to see the movie with the guys from the Pack. Alpha werewolves did *not* go to see animated movies. Unless they could save face by blaming their significant others for making them see one.

As he and Brandon took their seats—leaving a space

in between for Bree—Diego glanced down at the entrance to see if she'd come in yet, but there was no sight of her. She'd gotten a call from work that she needed to take as they walked into the movie theater. Knowing what it was like being on call 24/7, Diego had understood, even when she said the call might take a while. They had plenty of time before the movie started. Besides, it would give him a chance to talk with Brandon.

They'd gone to Keller's Drive-In for burgers, fries, and shakes, sitting in his extended-cab pickup, laughing and talking. Diego had taken advantage of the privacy offered by his truck to give Brandon a few lessons on controlling his claws with some easy exercises to go along with the stuff they'd been talking about on the phone over the past couple days.

The kid had done really well, being able to extend and retract his claws half a dozen times in the hour-long session. Brandon had been thrilled and so had Bree. Diego had also been pretty jazzed, though he tried not to let it show too much. Seeing the kid already gaining some level of control over his abilities was satisfying as hell. It might be lame, but it made Diego feel good—even proud.

But a little while after dinner, Diego had picked up on a strange tension in the air. It took him a moment to realize it was coming from the kid. Brandon would go quiet every now and then, staring off into the distance, lost in thought. He was doing the same thing now.

Diego sat there in silence, wondering if Brandon might tell him what the problem was. But then he realized how stupid that was. Like any teenager was going to simply open up and talk about their problems.

"You want to tell me what's bothering you?" he finally asked, leaning over to offer Brandon some popcorn. "And don't try and say nothing. I'm a werewolf. I can tell when something's off."

Brandon opened his mouth, clearly ready to deny it, but then closed it again, his expression one of acceptance. "Are you going to be my alpha?" he asked quietly, staring down at the floor and clutching the arms of the seat in a death grip, his heart picking up speed. "And is that kind of like being my new dad?"

Since becoming a werewolf, Diego had been shot, hit by a car, felled by a pallet load of drugs dropped on him, and kicked by a Texas longhorn. All of those events had hurt like hell, but none of them had left him as stunned and speechless as Brandon's not-so-simple question. The alpha part was tough to answer, especially since he felt someone like Jayna would be a better choice for Brandon. But the second part about being his new dad? Holy crap, how was he supposed to reply to a question like that?

"Brandon, did something happen to make you ask that?"

The kid glanced at the bucket of popcorn Diego was still holding out to him, like he was wondering if he should grab a handful or not. "My father kind of ambushed Kevin and me outside the apartment complex today," he finally murmured, still not looking at Diego.

"Did he hurt you?" Diego asked, gums and fingertips suddenly tingling. "Threaten you in any way?"

Brandon shook his head. "No, it wasn't anything like that. He said he wanted to talk. I didn't really want to hear what he had to say, but I didn't know what else to do, so I hung around and listened."

"I'm guessing he said something that bothered you," Diego said, holding the bucket out until Brandon stuck a hand in and took some. "You don't have to tell me if you don't want to, but if you need to talk about it, I'll listen."

Brandon seemed to consider that, then shrugged. It was a simple gesture, but Diego could sense the sudden relaxation in the kid's lanky frame as he gave in to the need to talk to someone about what was bothering him.

"He said he wanted us to be a family again—like we used to be," Brandon said softly. "That he was a better person now. That prison had made him better. He wanted me to talk to Mom and tell her I wanted us to be a family again. He said she'd go along with the idea if she thought that's what I wanted."

Brandon's heart beat harder as he spoke, and his breath hitched several times, betraying how upset he was. But that was nothing compared to how pissed Diego was. *That lying, manipulative asshole.* Using a kid like that to get control over Bree, whom Diego knew wanted nothing to do with Dave anymore. It was messed up. It made him want to hunt the jerk down right now and thump the shit out of him.

But he took a deep breath and regained control over his inner werewolf, knowing he couldn't give in to his instincts. Bree wouldn't appreciate it, and it wouldn't help the situation, or Brandon.

"Is that what you want?" Diego asked softly. "To get back together with your dad and be a family again?"

He expected Brandon to think about it, so he was surprised when the kid quickly shook his head. "No! I wish he'd just go away. I don't need anyone like him in my life, and neither does Mom. We're better off on our own."

Maybe the kid hadn't intended to shut him out, but still, it was nearly impossible to describe the pain that lanced through Diego at those words. Yeah, he'd only just met Bree and Brandon, but there was a part of him that had been hoping to get closer to them both. But if Brandon didn't want that, Diego guessed he'd have to accept it.

"Is that the reason you asked about me becoming your alpha and whether that's like being a dad? Because you're worried I'm going to try and insert myself into your and your mom's life like your dad is trying to do?"

Brandon lifted his head to look at him, his expression part surprised, part thoughtful. "It's not like that," he said, looking down at the floor again. "Actually, I was hoping you'd want to be in our lives so my dad would finally go away."

The air left Diego's lungs once again—for a different reason this time. He'd apparently read the situation all wrong.

"I want to be in your life, Brandon. And your mom's, too. I care what happens to you both. It's why I made the offer to teach you what you need to know to be a werewolf and why I asked you guys to come to dinner and a movie tonight."

Brandon's brow furrowed. "So, you are going to be my alpha and take my dad's place?"

Diego took a deep breath. "None of this is that simple. I'm not an expert on this alpha-beta bond, but from what I understand, it's not like I have a lot of say in the matter. If we're right for each other, I'll end up as your alpha. If there's another alpha out there who's better for you, that's who you'll bond with. And as far as taking your dad's place, that's something I can never do."

Brandon looked up sharply, hurt and pain written on his face.

"I didn't mean I don't want to be there for you, however you need me," Diego quickly clarified. "But your dad is your dad. I can't be him. I can only be me. You'll have to figure out if that's enough. Until then, if you need someone to talk to, I'll always be there to listen."

Brandon considered that for a while before giving him a slight smile. "I'd like that. Sometimes, it's hard not to have someone to talk to. There's stuff I can't say to Mom—or Kevin."

Diego nodded. "I get it. Everybody needs someone they can spill to. Somebody that won't be upset, or take sides, or judge them. Someone who will listen."

Brandon looked at Diego like he was a Jedi master—or a mind reader. "Yeah. Someone like that."

He probably would have said more, but a couple with two small children came up the stairs. Diego immediately recognized the guy, even if he did look drastically different than he did at work.

"Diego Martinez. Long time, no see," the tall, wiry dark-skinned guy said with a laugh, waiting for his wife and kids to find their seats a few rows ahead of Diego and Brandon before continuing up the steps to shake Diego's hand. "Good to see you get a night off."

"Every once in a while." Diego chuckled, getting to his feet. "Nice to see they give you some time off every now and then yourself. Those two kids of yours are growing like weeds."

Dion Harbin was one of the best undercover narcotics cops Diego had ever worked with. The guy had spent the better part of the past four years buried inside the largest street gang in the city. Diego didn't know how his wife put up with it, especially with two little kids to take care of.

"Yeah, kids do have a habit of growing up fast." Dion glanced at Brandon. "Speaking of kids, who's this?"

"Dion, meet Brandon," Diego said as they shook hands. "Brandon, his mom, and I are doing dinner and a movie."

"Nice meeting you," Dion told Brandon, then nodded at Diego. "Well, I'd better get back to my family. I'll see you around."

"Is that guy a cop?" Brandon asked curiously as Dion rejoined his wife and pair of giggling kids.

"Do you think he's a cop?" Diego asked, scooping up a big handful of popcorn and dropping some in his mouth.

Brandon frowned as he thought about it. "I think he looks more like an accountant. Or maybe a librarian. Anything but a cop."

Diego chuckled. Dion looked like a different person when he wasn't undercover. That's one of the things that made him so good at the job. "Sometimes the people who don't look like cops make the best cops."

Brandon seemed to consider that for a while, gazing at Dion and his family in between eating bites of popcorn. Diego found the silence more comfortable than he'd thought it would be. Just him and the kid sitting together, eating popcorn covered in loads of gooey butter.

"So, you and my mom," Brandon said suddenly, turning to gaze at him questioningly. "If you aren't trying to take my dad's place with me, are you taking his place with her?"

Diego almost choked on his popcorn. He definitely hadn't seen that one coming, which was why he had no idea what to say. Luckily, Bree chose that moment to show up. And damn, did she look mighty fine walking up the steps in the long, flowing flower-print skirt she'd worn tonight.

"Sorry that took so long," she said when she sat down in between him and Brandon. "The company's managers are losing their minds over the possibility that they might have to pay out on these two claims I'm working. I had to brief three different levels of management."

Diego waved off her apology, thrilled she'd come and saved his ass when she did. If the amused expression on Brandon's face was any indication, he knew that, too.

"Don't worry about it," Diego said. "Your timing is perfect. The previews will start any minute."

Bree smiled and reached into the bucket for a small handful of popcorn. "What were you two talking about while I was on the phone?"

Diego exchanged looks with Brandon. "Just guy stuff. You know—football, cars, video games. Things like that."

"Not girls?" Bree asked, laughing.

He and Brandon exchanged looks again before they both shook their heads.

"Nope," Brandon confirmed, his face suggesting he already knew exactly how much Diego already liked his mother. "Just guy stuff."

"You know," Bree said, trying to hold in the laughter that threatened to have her rolling on the floor. "I don't think I've ever seen a person land on Boardwalk five times in a row. Are you doing it on purpose?"

Diego frowned as he counted up the last of his cash, then began totaling up the value of his few remaining properties. Even from where she sat on the floor across from him at the coffee table in the living room, she could see he didn't have enough.

"Of course, I'm doing this on purpose," he said. "Because it's so much fun giving all my money to a fifteen-year-old con artist who tricked me into playing Monopoly with a line about not having played in forever right before he proceeded to wipe me out in"—he glanced at his watch—"less than two hours. I think he set me up."

Bree couldn't keep from laughing this time. The indignant look on Diego's handsome face was impossible to ignore. Brandon started laughing, too, nearly spewing soda out his nose as he continued to count up all his winnings. She hadn't heard her son laugh so much in years. Seriously, not since he was five years old. Which just happened to be the last time her ex had bothered trying to act like a father who cared about his child.

Brandon had pulled out the Monopoly game within seconds of Diego bringing them home after the movie, asking if he wanted to stay for a while. Bree certainly wasn't ready for the date to end and had been happy to sit around on the living room floor playing a game that had only good memories for her. Diego eagerly agreed, saying he couldn't remember the last time he played Monopoly. Then, while Brandon disappeared into his room to grab his ferret, Diego whispered in her ear that if playing Monopoly meant getting to spend more time with her and Brandon, he was all for it.

"Mom, you ready to forfeit yet?" Brandon asked, looking her way as he leaned back on one elbow and ran his other hand over Finn's fur. The slinky ferret rubbed up against him lovingly. "Since I own pretty much the entire board anyway."

Bree handed over the embarrassingly small stack of funny money she had left to her son, who'd been performing the job of banker at the same time he'd been kicking their butts. "Okay, you win. Though I think Diego's right about you playing both of us."

Brandon laughed but didn't try to deny it as he started to clean up the board.

Bree motioned him away from the collection of game pieces, plastic hotels, and money. "Leave all that. It's been a while since we've played, but I still remember the rules. Losers clean up and put everything away."

Brandon had apparently forgotten that, but quickly jumped to his feet, grabbing his glass of soda and his ferret with the other. "Cool. I'm going to go to bed then. I'll probably listen to some music for a while, so I'll have my headphones on."

Bree didn't miss the pointed look he gave Diego as he headed down the hallway toward his room.

"What was that about?" she asked, eyeing Diego suspiciously.

Diego only shrugged his perfectly well-muscled shoulders and reached over to help clean up the game pieces. Bree studied his face, pretty sure there was something going on. He must be a really good poker player because his expression gave nothing away.

While Diego finished separating the money into the proper denominations, Bree went into the kitchen to get them some more wine. Then she joined Diego on the couch, lifting her long skirt a little so she could curl her legs underneath her. Diego's eyes flared yellow gold as he followed the movement, watching the flash of bare skin. It was crazy how her stomach fluttered a little at the realization he was practically hypnotized at the mere glimpse of her legs.

"Thanks for agreeing to play the game," she said, taking a slow sip of the wine Diego had brought on their first date. "I really appreciate it. It's been a long time since Brandon's had someone like you in his life willing to spend time with him."

Diego flashed her a smile. "Don't mention it. I had a good time tonight. In fact, I wouldn't have traded this evening for anything."

Bree returned his smile, realizing Diego wasn't merely saying those words to be nice. She'd seen the way Brandon had looked at him back in the movie theater when she'd walked up the steps. She had no idea what it was, but she was sure something significant had happened while she'd been busy on the phone. There was a bond forming between them, and she couldn't put into words how much she appreciated that.

She and Diego talked about the movie as they sipped their wine, laughing at how much Brandon had enjoyed it even though he was "too old to watch a cartoon." Once or twice Bree tried to wheedle out what the two of them had talked about while she was on the phone, but Diego simply smiled and insisted it was *just guy stuff*.

"There is one thing Brandon and I talked about tonight you should know," he said. "Something that involves your ex."

Bree's whole body went stiff. "What did that jerk do?"

Diego moved a little closer on the couch and took her hand, squeezing gently. "It's okay. Brandon isn't in any kind of danger. But he did tell me that Dave showed up outside the apartment wanting to talk about the three of you getting back together. It's obvious he was hoping to manipulate your son into putting pressure on you, saying it was what he wanted. Brandon's a sharp kid, though. He saw right through it, but I still thought it was something you should know about."

Bree couldn't even think right then. Everything was an angry blur of emotions. Fear that her ex could have tried to grab Brandon. Rage that the slimy bastard had come within a mile of her son. Worry that Brandon hadn't been comfortable telling her about it when he'd been okay telling Diego.

She didn't know if she wanted to scream, murder, or cry.

The conundrum was solved for her when Diego wrapped an arm around her shoulder and tugged her close. The warmth of his body enveloped her, and she rested her head against his shoulder, immediately calmer.

"I wish Brandon had told me," she finally said quietly. "I'm glad he has you to talk to, but that doesn't mean I don't worry."

"Like I said, there's nothing to worry about," Diego murmured, his words positively rumbling in that thick chest of his. "Brandon will tell you when he's ready. Just remember to act surprised so he won't know I ratted him out."

She snorted a little at that but didn't say anything. The fact that Dave was still trying to get back together with her was no surprise, but that he was apparently willing to use their son as bait was shocking. She liked to think there was at least some subbasement level he wouldn't sink to in his stupid game.

Obviously, she was wrong.

"Everything okay at work?" Diego asked her.

Bree lifted her head, worried that he'd been talking while she'd zoned out and she'd missed almost all of it. "What?"

"Work?" he repeated. "You were on the phone for a while at the movie."

She sighed, reluctantly sitting up and running her hand through her hair. "I'm working several big cases right now that seem to be connected, and if the company has to pay off the claims, it's going to cost millions. My boss had me on a conference call giving a status update to upper-level management in the New York office."

"What kind of cases are they?" Diego asked.

He sounded genuinely curious about her work, something none of the other men she'd dated had been. Most of them had tuned out the moment she mentioned anything about it, clearly bored.

"Four of our biggest clients had valuables stolen from their homes," she said, ready to bail on the conversation the moment his eyes glazed over. "A jewelry collection, two paintings, a vase from the Ming dynasty, and a knife that belonged to Jim Bowie."

"And you think there's a connection between the cases?" Diego prompted, one hand resting on her thigh, his big hand warm through the thin material of her skirt.

Loving that he was a cop, and therefore able to immediately pick up the subtle aspects of the situation, Bree eagerly told him about what she'd uncovered, particularly that it seemed like the work of amateurs but made her think it was an inside job.

"I think so." She could get used to brainstorming all her cases like this. Sitting so close to Diego they were touching was something she could definitely get used to. Even if it was a little distracting. "It turns out all four clients are represented by the same investment firm. No way can that be a coincidence, especially when you consider the firm might have access to information on their clients' security systems—maybe even passwords."

Diego seemed to consider that for all of a second before his eyes narrowed. "This investment firm isn't the same one Dave works at, is it?"

She hadn't necessarily planned on highlighting that particular fact, but she wouldn't lie about it, either. "Wow, with instincts like that, you should be a cop. Or a werewolf." She laughed. "But yeah, it is. And unfortunately, while I'd love to pin this all on my wonderful jackass of an ex, I can't. He's not the advisor to the LMG clients, and no matter how much I've tried, I can't connect him to the situation. Hopefully, I won't run into him when I'm over there sniffing around."

His jaw tightened. "Promise you'll be careful around him, all right? And if he makes trouble, I want you to let me know, okay?"

Bree smiled, once again surprised at the warm sensation that fluttered through her as Diego's protective side came out. "I will. I promise."

"And if there's any way I can help with the investigation, let me know," he added. "I've worked with a lot of the cops in robbery division. That might come in handy."

Bree was about to give him the standard *Thanks, I'll keep that in mind* comment, when she realized he might be able to help.

"Actually, there is something you could do for me," she said. "The head of security in the building where Garrett, Wallace, and Banks have their offices used to be in the DPD.

Any chance you could put in a good word with him for me and help me get through the front door?"

He nodded. "I can do that. How are you going to talk your way into Garrett, Wallace, and Banks once you're inside?"

She grinned. "I'll have you know I can be very persuasive when I want to be. And that I have a talent for poking my nose where it doesn't belong. But enough about me. What have you been working on lately? Anything new on the guy in the diner or the ones in the bank? Have they figured out if this delirium thing is being caused by a drug?"

"Not really," he said. "My teammates and I aren't very involved in investigations. We get paid to kick in doors and take down bad guys, so we don't get to talk to the forensic techs or interview witnesses. And with this case being as high profile as it is, the detectives running the show are keeping everything close to the vest. They probably wouldn't tell us anything even if we asked."

"I get that, I guess. But if it were me, and I wanted to know what was going on, I'd go sniffing around on my own and talk to the medical examiner, maybe even some witnesses."

Diego's mouth quirked. "Are you telling me Bree Harlow is a rule breaker who does whatever she wants whenever she feels like it?"

Bree laughed, leaning in a little closer. They might have been talking about work, but that didn't mean they couldn't get a little playful. Especially considering the direction their conversation had taken.

"I'm not sure I'd go as far as calling myself a rule breaker." She ran one hand up along his shoulder until her fingers weaved into his short hair, toying and tugging there. "Maybe it would be better to say that sometimes I can be a bit naughty?"

Diego's gaze locked with hers, going from warm to smoldering. "Naughty isn't so bad." Leaning forward, he traced his lips along the side of her neck, making the skin there tingle as he moved toward an earlobe that was practically begging for attention. "Actually, naughty can be good. Very, very good."

Bree turned her face to his, forcing his lips to follow until they were exactly where she wanted them. She moaned softly as his tongue slipped in, amazed any man could taste this good. There was a hint of the wine there, and under that the savory flavor of the buttered popcorn from the movie. But more than any of that, there was the taste that was uniquely him. Impossible to describe, it was tantalizing all the same. Addicting almost.

One of Diego's hands found its way into her hair, taking a firm grip and moving her this way and that as his mouth devoured hers. The pure masculinity of the move, along with the sounds of pleasure he was making sent heat pooling between her legs.

Bree couldn't remember ever being this aroused, and something told her Diego was just as turned on. As crazy as it sounded, all she wanted to do was get his T-shirt and jeans off and make love to him right there on the couch. She would have done it, regardless of the fact that she'd known Diego for less than a damn week, if they were anywhere other than her living room with her son right down the hall.

She pulled back, her breath coming in rapid gasps, her heart beating like mad. She gazed into Diego's eyes, seeing the heat in the golden glow filling them. He studied her, like he could read her mind, and slowly, his fingers slipped from her hair.

"Too fast?" he murmured.

She hated the fact that she had to nod, the same as she hated that he'd taken his fingers from her hair and hated that her lips had left his. "As much as I want to have my way with you right now, I can't. Not with Brandon in his room. And if we try and slink off to my bedroom, he'll know what we're doing. I can't—not yet."

Bree silently prayed Diego would understand, terrified he wouldn't. But then he smiled and leaned forward to kiss her gently and all her worries disappeared.

"I understand," he said, mouth brushing hers again. "And when we *are* alone some night, I can't wait for you to have your way with me."

The words sent a delicious little shiver rushing through her. "Me too."

CHAPTER 9

Diego pulled the SWAT team's SUV into a parking space beside Hale and Connor along the back side of the building that housed the Dallas medical examiner's office on North Stemmons Freeway. Mostly glass with some brick tossed in for good measure, it looked more like a modern art museum. He'd teased Bree last night about suggesting he and his teammates stick their noses where they didn't belong, and now, this morning, they were going to do just that.

There'd been another delirium incident right before sunrise, this one even stranger than the others. Six members of a highway construction crew had shown up at their job site near the financial district, ready to fill in potholes, but instead decided they wanted to make a career change and tried to take down an armored truck packed with freshly printed money from the Federal Reserve Bank on Pearl Street.

The men protecting the armored vehicle had been heavily armed, and the botched robbery attempt had ended with two of the construction workers dead while the rest barricaded themselves in a nearby coffee shop. Diego and his teammates had dealt with the standoff without anyone else dying, but it had been a lot harder than it should have been. The four men had been nearly uncontrollable, even with nearly half a SWAT team full of werewolves on the scene. Of course, when it had gotten out that the suspects were once again a bunch of everyday guys, a good portion of the city had lost it, including more than a few members of the DPD.

It had only been four hours since the attempted robbery on the armored truck, but since then Diego and his pack mates had been going nonstop to keep up with calls coming in from random patrol officers worried their next domestic disturbance was going to turn into a full-scale riot. It didn't help that Hobbs was out there hyping up his drug theory, telling people to be on the lookout for suspicious-looking characters. People were reporting every stranger they saw walking down the street.

When the SWAT team had finally been able to take a breather, instead of spending the downtime reliving the fantastic time he had with Bree and Brandon last night, Diego had talked to Gage, telling him they needed to get ahead of this situation before the Pack was simply overwhelmed. And if Leclair wasn't going to make them part of the process and let them help figure out what was going on, then they needed to do this themselves. Gage had reluctantly agreed, though he told the Pack to keep it low-key. He didn't want anything getting back to the chief.

Which was why Diego, Trey, Hale, and Connor were currently sitting in the parking lot of the ME's office.

"How are we going to play this?" Connor asked as they headed for the entrance to the county's Southwest Institute of Forensic Sciences—the place where all the magic happened. At least as far as crime-scene techie stuff went. "You know they're not going to tell us everything they know about the case simply because we ask, right?"

Diego didn't say anything right away. Bree had talked about being persuasive and poking her nose where it didn't belong. But she'd been gazing at him with those beautiful, brown eyes at the time, so it was possible he might have missed some important details on how exactly to get what you wanted. Yeah, maybe he and the guys should have come up with a plan on the way over here.

"We'll be our naturally charming selves and see how far that gets us," he finally said, realizing as soon as the words were out of his mouth that it was probably the dumbest plan in the world.

"That leaves Trey out." Hale chuckled, giving Trey a good-natured shove. "He might be good at pulling bullets out of werewolves, but he was obviously absent when they were handing out charm."

Trey snorted but didn't deny it. He wasn't a talker, and everyone knew it.

Their SWAT uniforms and badges got them through the security checkpoint and past the main reception desk. After that, they followed the signs to the medical examiner's. Not pausing to consider whether this was a good idea or not, Diego stopped outside Samantha Mills's office. He only hoped she didn't bring up how those guys who'd tried to kill him at the SWAT compound had died. He'd made up some crap about a bullet ricocheting and slicing through the neck of the guy he'd raked his claws across, but no ME worth their degree would buy that.

Taking a deep breath, Diego knocked on the door.

Here goes nothing.

"Come in."

Samantha Mills was at her desk, white lab coat on, blond hair up in a messy bun, face intense as she wrote something on a notepad. With its light-gray color scheme, the room was sleek and modern like the rest of the building. Shelves with medical journals lined one wall, while another showcased antique medical devices and… Holy crap, was that really a human skull?

Diego was about to clear his throat when she abruptly looked up to regard them with curious blue eyes. Even though he was the one standing directly in front of her, it was Trey who seemed to capture her attention. Her gaze locked on him for a good five seconds. Beside him, Trey's heart sped up a little.

No surprise there. Trey'd had a thing for the doctor ever since he'd first laid eyes on her.

"Can I help you?" she said, turning her attention to Diego and acting as if Trey wasn't there at all.

"Chief Leclair sent us over for an update on the delirium case," he said casually, as if this was something he did all the time.

Dr. Mills lifted a brow, then leaned back in her chair and folded her arms. "I really doubt that, since I gave the chief and the delirium task force a status briefing an hour ago. Interestingly enough, none of you were there."

Crap.

Even though he had no idea what to say to that, Diego opened his mouth, praying something intelligent would come out, but Trey spoke first.

"Chief Leclair has no idea we're here and would probably be pissed if she knew."

Okay. Full disclosure. That wasn't how Diego thought they were going to play this.

"But we didn't have a choice," Trey continued. "We're the ones on the front line with this delirium thing day in and day out, and it's getting worse. Those men who came to the SWAT compound were there to kill Officer Martinez, and we don't have a clue why. We have to find a way to stop all of this, but to do that, we need to understand what we're up against and you're the only one who can help us." He stepped closer to her desk. "Please, Dr. Mills."

Trey's voice was a low rumble full of anguish. Out of the corner of his eye, Diego caught sight of Conner's jaw dropping. On the other side of him, Hale's eyes went a little wide. Diego was as stunned as they were. He hadn't heard Trey string together this many deeply profound words since he'd known him. From the expression on the ME's face, Trey's plea definitely had the intended effect. Besides the fact that her heart was racing, her eyes were full of emotion, and her lips were slightly parted. Like she wanted to kiss Trey right there in front of all of them.

Apparently, Trey had better game than any of his teammates had realized. And all it had taken to bring it out was a woman who handled dead bodies for a living. But far be it from Diego to judge his friend for that.

"He's telling the truth," Diego said when the silence continued to stretch to the point of being uncomfortable. "Those men I faced at the SWAT compound were like robots. They were completely focused on seeing me dead and unconcerned if they ended up getting killed in the process. If there's anything you can tell us that will help—anything at all—we'd really appreciate it."

Her gaze went from Trey to Diego and back to his pack mate. "Okay, I'll tell you everything I know, though it probably isn't as much as you'd like. But I'm not going to do it for free."

Diego glanced at his teammates to see that they seemed as confused as he was. "What do you want in return for the information? It can't be money since you probably make more than the four of us combined."

Her lips curved. "I don't want money. I want a favor."

Well, he hadn't expected that.

"While we might be able to help you with a speeding ticket or parking fine, it's not like we can kill someone for you. Or dispose of a body, either," Trey said. "You know that, right?"

Dr. Mills tilted her head to the side, eyeing Trey with what looked like amusement on her face. "I'm a medical examiner. If I wanted someone dead or a body dissolved down to the consistency of soft Jell-O, I could do it myself."

Diego wasn't sure whether to be relieved at that announcement or not.

"Don't worry," she added. "I promise I won't ask any of you to do anything illegal. Well, not any sketchier than the stuff you already do. And before you even try and deny it, I've been the ME on at least two dozen SWAT crime scenes. I know you guys play fast and loose with the truth when it suits you."

Hale and Connor looked as worried by that admission as he was. Trey, on the other hand, was gazing at the pretty blond doctor with an expression of pure adoration. Yup. Werewolf puppy love, for sure.

"One favor," Trey agreed. "But from me, not anyone else on the SWAT team. That way, if it *is* something illegal, I'm the only one on the hook."

Samantha Mills didn't even have to think about it before she nodded. "The task force has statements from the suspects your team managed to capture alive. They all remembered exactly what they were doing right before the crimes down to the last little detail. They were out doing normal, everyday stuff up until the moment they decided to go on a crime spree."

Diego couldn't help wondering how much of that was due to lawyers whispering in their ears, trying to create a defense for their clients by confusing the issue.

"It's after they committed the crimes that things get interesting," Dr. Mills continued. "The detectives working the case said none of the suspects remember how they got to the scenes where they committed those crimes, what they did there, or why they did it. A few of them said it was as if they were watching themselves do what they did from a distance, while the rest said everything was a complete blank. Like an alcoholic blackout."

"Do you think that's even possible?" Connor asked. "Blacking out in the middle of committing a crime, I mean."

"I've never heard of it before, but it could be possible," she admitted. "According to the detectives who talked to the suspects, they were terrified out of their minds when they realized they'd committed horrible crimes they have no memory of doing that were going to put them in prison for years."

"Do you think the delirium theory is right and some kind of drug is making these people behave this way?" Diego asked.

"You'd think so, but I've done a full tox screen on the blood from the dead suspect at the diner and the three men currently in jail from the bank holdup, as well as preliminary bloodwork from the four baggage handlers who attacked you at the SWAT compound the other day, and still haven't gotten a single hit for any known street or prescription drug. At least no drugs in the traditional sense."

Diego frowned. "What do you mean, traditional sense?"

She let out a sigh. "Every one of the blood samples we've tested so far displayed an extremely high level of cortisol and adrenaline."

"What could cause something like that?"

"Typically, cortisol and adrenaline are the by-products of extreme stress. You know, the whole fight-or-flight thing. But in those cases, the amount of chemicals released into the bloodstream is relatively minuscule and is usually burned off relatively fast. I can't imagine what a person would have to go through to produce the amounts we found in these samples."

"Would cortisol and adrenaline make people do what they did in these delirium cases?" Hale asked. "Could they have purposely taken them?"

Dr. Mills shrugged. "As far as taking them on purpose, it's possible. They both have dozens of legitimate medical uses. Just not in the levels we're seeing in these people. Regardless, all they do is raise your blood pressure, provide a burst of energy, and deaden pain to a degree. They don't change your moral behavior and certainly don't make you lose track of time."

"So, that's a dead end," Diego said.

"Not necessarily," she said. "I think the cortisol and adrenaline we're finding are actually a secondary outcome of being exposed to something we haven't found yet that's causing these suspects to behave the way they did and creating the memory loss."

"Any ideas what this *something* might be?" Diego asked.

"Not yet." Leaning forward, she flipped open a folder and took out a map of downtown Dallas, spinning it around so they could see. There were little numbered yellow dots all over the place. "These markers are where the people claimed to be right before their memories went fuzzy."

"They're all near the financial district," Diego remarked.

"Exactly," she agreed. "The task force is focusing its attention on the known drug dealers who work that area."

"Maybe we should check some of these locations and see if we can find anything the task force might have missed," Trey suggested.

"Good idea." Diego glanced at Hale and Connor. "Trey and I will take Uptown Plaza and see if we can find out anything on those college kids who tried to rob the bank. You guys head over to the construction company and ask around about the workers who hit the armored truck."

"Sounds good," Hale said.

Trey looked at the doctor. "If we find anything, will you tell us if it means something?"

She nodded. "I'll look."

A slow smile curved Trey's mouth. "Thanks. We appreciate the help."

Samantha Mills returned his smile with a flirtatious one of her own. "I'm not doing this for your appreciation. It's all about that favor you're going to owe me. And when it's time for you to pay up, I'll make sure to come looking for you."

"I can't thank you enough for helping me out, Detective Collins," Bree said as the former DPD robbery cop escorted her up the lesser-used service elevators to the ninth floor, which was occupied by the offices of Garrett,

Wallace, and Banks. "I would never have gotten up here without your help."

The big man with the slight belly and the walrus mustache laughed, the sound echoing in the elevator and bouncing off the stainless-steel walls. "First off, I haven't been a detective for almost five years, so you can call me Ryan. And as for getting you onto the ninth floor, if you can find a way to stick it to one of those stuck-up pricks up there, I'll consider the favor more than repaid. Those snobs are one of nearly forty businesses in this building, but they act like they're the only ones who matter. They treat everyone in this building—especially my security people—like crap."

Bree could kiss Diego right now. Reaching out to Ryan Collins, the head of security for the building, had been a lifesaver. If not for that, she probably would have been escorted from the building already. Garrett, Wallace, and Banks weren't the easiest people to approach without an invitation. Unless you were a multimillionaire looking to invest, of course. And since she hadn't learned anything she didn't already know after talking to each of the victims of the thefts, snooping around the investment firm could be pivotal to her investigation.

When the elevator came to a stop, Ryan reached out and hit the button to hold the doors closed. "Okay, before we go in there, let's go over the plan again."

"You're going to hook me up with Jerri Sherwood, who's dating one of your fellow security guards. She'll lead me around under the guise of interviewing for an admin position with the company."

The cover was another reason she owed Diego big. Even if she'd been able to get onto the ninth floor, without somebody like Jerri Sherwood to walk her around, she would have stood out like a sore thumb.

"Remember to stay away from the front reception area. They'll know you're not there for an interview since they book all of those," Ryan said. "Just act like you belong up there and no one will be the wiser. If you run into any problems, text me and I'll do my best to get you out of there in one piece."

Bree nodded. This wouldn't be the first time she'd waltzed into a place she didn't belong. She could definitely pull it off. As long as she didn't run into Dave, she'd be fine.

Ryan took his hand away from the button, and the doors opened onto a service corridor. A tall, blond woman was waiting for them. Ryan quickly introduced Bree to Jerri, then took the elevator back downstairs.

"You look great. No one will suspect you aren't here for an interview," Jerri said, giving Bree's silk blouse and trousers a nod of approval. "Just try and sound dumber than you are if we talk to any of the guys."

Bree stared, incredulous. "Excuse me?"

"The place is filled with men who think the world revolves around their wallets or their dicks," Jerri said as they started down the hall. "The idea of an intelligent woman terrifies them to the point of impotency. If we run into men dressed in suits worth more than your car, smile and nod at whatever they say like you're a mindless simpleton. They'll eat it up like gravy over biscuits."

Crap. Jerri had just described Dave—and most of the men he'd worked with at his previous investment firm, now that Bree thought about it—to perfection. It was embarrassing to think how her eighteen-year-old self had swooned over him.

The hallway led to a huge cubicle farm with a battalion of office workers focused on their computer monitors. Several people glanced their way, then went back to what they were doing. The perimeter of the room was lined with individual offices, some with glass walls, some more private.

Jerri played her part convincingly, introducing her to people, explaining the layout of the floor, pointing out how the runners, researchers, number crunchers, and assistants occupied the central area, while the more senior investment advisors occupied the coveted offices. The bigger the office, the more money that particular broker had brought into the company.

Bree listened as Jerri mentioned each broker by name, waiting for her to point out Ken Reed's office, but after making it nearly all the way around three walls of offices, they still hadn't gotten to it. Maybe he was a partner in the firm?

She did a double take when Jerri pointed out the big corner office closest to the front as Dave's. *Damn.* Apparently, he'd been telling the truth. Since the door was closed, hopefully he was in a meeting or out of the building.

"How did Dave Cowell get a corner office so fast?" she whispered.

Jerri glanced at her as they kept walking. "Do you know him?"

"You could say that," Bree muttered, but didn't offer any more information.

Jerri looked curious but didn't push for details. "Dave had the partners eating out of his hand from day one. From what I heard, he told them that if they hired him and gave him a corner office, he'd come in the next morning with four million-dollar investors."

"And?" Bree prompted.

"He came in with five," Jerri said dryly. "Since then, he's made GW&B a serious buttload of money. The partners want him up front so bad they can taste it."

As they continued along the outside of the cubicles, Bree was about to ask Jerri about Reed when they passed by a table along the wall with flowers and framed photos of the man who'd taken them hostage at the diner a few days ago. She stopped in her tracks.

"Do you know who this is?"

Jerri nodded. "That's Ken Reed. He's one of our senior investment advisors. Or at least he was until he decided to take a diner full of people hostage and kill himself. Of all the brokers who work here, he was the nicest by far." She shook her head. "We're all still in shock. I have no idea what made him snap like that."

Bree stared at the photos, her head spinning. The investment broker she was looking for was the same guy who'd held her and Brandon at gunpoint the other day? What were the odds of that?

Her gaze went from the picture of him in a suit and tie to one beside it where he was dressed more casually. His hair was longer in the second photo and he had a mustache. She leaned down to take a closer look at it, abruptly realizing she recognized him.

Ken Reed had worked with Dave six years ago. In fact, he'd tried to drag her ex off the man Dave had beaten to death. She couldn't believe she hadn't recognized him at the diner. Then again, she'd pretty much blocked everything out from that night.

Next to that photo was another. In it, Dave and Ken

were standing side by side, arms draped over each other's shoulders like they were the best of buds. What the…?

"Are you okay?" Jerri asked. "You look like you saw a ghost."

Bree straightened up. "Were Ken and Dave friends?"

"Yeah. Ken got Dave an interview with the senior partners."

The idea of Ken helping Dave get a job was ludicrous after what had happened at their previous place of employment. But Dave could be very manipulative, so anything was possible.

Bree looked at the photos again, focusing on why she was at Garrett, Wallace, and Banks in the first place. And it wasn't to figure out why Ken and Dave had been so chummy. Ken had been the investment advisor for four people who'd been robbed, and then he'd ended up dead under the most bizarre of circumstances. Had he been involved in the robberies, then become so racked with guilt that he'd gone into that diner intending to commit suicide? But that didn't make sense. If he regretted stealing that stuff, wouldn't he have mentioned it while he'd been ranting and raving like a madman?

She was still trying to wrap her head around it when saw someone approach them out of the corner of her eye. She turned, cursing silently when she saw Dave standing there.

"Bree," he said, giving her a smile. "What a nice surprise! I was just thinking about you. Let's go into my office where we can talk."

Taking her arm, he quickly hustled her the half-dozen feet to his office before she could pull away, closing the door behind them.

"Since you're here, I guess that means you reconsidered my offer to have lunch." He walked around his sleek, modern desk to pick up the phone. "Let me have my assistant reschedule my afternoon meetings. I'll just be a minute."

Bree fought the urge to roll her eyes. She'd come to the conclusion a long time ago that her ex was dense, but this attitude of his took the cake.

"I'm not here for lunch," she snapped.

Dave's eyes narrowed. "Then why are you here?"

It took her a second to come up with an excuse, but when it popped into her head, it wasn't actually an excuse at all. "I'm here to tell you to stay away from Brandon. And before you deny it, I know for a fact you showed up at the apartment to harass him. Brandon is finally in a good place after all the crap thrown his way, and I don't need you trying to weasel your way back into his life, confusing the hell out of him."

Dave's expression darkened, and it suddenly struck her that provoking a man who'd once beaten someone to death in a fit of anger wasn't the best idea in the world. But she couldn't back down, not when it came to protecting her son.

Her ex didn't explode like she thought. Instead, he simply stood there, the emotions on his face changing so rapidly it was impossible to keep up with them. Anger was quickly followed by frustration, then confusion, and maybe even a little acceptance, strangely enough.

"Brandon is my son, too, you know," he finally said.

She wasn't surprised he went there. And if he was even the slightest bit sincere, she would have felt bad about wanting him to stay the hell away from Brandon. But everything with Dave came down to what he possessed, be it money, clothes, a fancy car, a big house, or his wife and kid. It was all the same to him.

"You were never interested in Brandon, even before you went to prison," she pointed out. "Now you're using him because you think it'll help you win me back. Not that you actually want me, either. It's the win that's important to you, and always has been."

His lip curled in a sneer. "That damn cop is putting you up to this, isn't he? He's trying to take my place as Brandon's father and your husband. But Brandon is mine and so are you!"

"I don't belong to anyone and neither does Brandon," she told him. "Certainly not to you, that's for damn sure."

Dave paced back and forth behind his desk for a minute before grabbing a ceramic paperweight the size of a baseball. Bree braced herself, ready to duck, sure he was going to toss it at her, but instead, he smashed it down on the top of his desk with a curse, shattering it into pieces and cutting his hand.

"I see you still haven't worked through your anger-management issues," she said with a wry snort.

Dave gazed at his hand for a moment before looking at her with a strange expression on his face. Before she realized what he was doing, he came around the desk toward her, holding out his bloody hand like some kind of bizarre offering.

"I need a Band-Aid," he said, his voice low and seriously creepy as he moved closer.

Bree backed away, not liking the look in her ex-husband's eyes. "Get your own damn Band-Aid," she said, turning for the door.

But Dave was in front of her, cutting off her path.

Her heart beat faster as she realized she was trapped. She was opening her mouth to scream when the fire alarm suddenly went off, distracting Dave enough for Bree to make a mad dash for the door.

She slammed it behind her, both stunned and relieved to see Ryan standing there. He wrapped a protective arm around her shoulder, hurriedly guiding her toward the crowd of people heading for the nearest stairwell.

"Jerri texted and said you might need an assist," Ryan said loud enough to be heard above the alarm and the commotion. "You okay?"

She nodded. "Yeah, I'm fine."

As they blended in with the crowd, Bree ignored the urge to glance over her shoulder to see if Dave was following them. She didn't think it was possible, but her ex was even more psychotic now than he'd been before. And maybe even more dangerous.

"You're really going to help me get into the police academy, right?" the mall cop asked nervously, his gaze going from the bank of security monitors to Diego, then Trey.

He and Trey had gotten to Uptown Plaza about thirty minutes ago, but after wasting a bunch of time wandering around, they realized the only way they were going to get any answer was if they could see the mall's security footage from the time frame those three college kids had supposedly been there. And that wasn't going to happen unless they could get one of the security guards to show it to them.

That was where Rich Newell came in. Dark-haired with a youthful face and wire-rimmed glasses, he was a twenty-five-year-old mall cop who wanted to go to the police academy. Diego and Trey offered to help him get in.

"You have three years of military service, an honorable discharge, and a clean driving record," Trey told him. "Plus, you have some college credits on top of that. The truth is, you don't need our help to get into the academy, but if you want a letter of recommendation, we'll give you one."

Rich nodded, his face still unsure. "In return for showing you the security footage from several days ago?"

Diego leaned forward, resting his elbows on his thighs. "Rich, we're not trying to use you. We're trying to figure out why three college kids did something as crazy as trying to rob a bank. If this is going to get you into trouble or if you feel like you have to give up your integrity for this, don't do it."

Rich's gaze went back to the monitor, clicking through various folders that carried no recognizable pattern Diego could see. "I want to. I'm helping you guys stop this delirium thing. Nobody is gonna fire me for that, right?"

Diego wasn't too sure of that but didn't say anything.

It seemed to take forever to find the right date and time frame for the video footage they were looking for. Diego tuned out as Rich began explaining about the hundreds of cameras positioned around the mall, how they were all constantly downloading to a centralized server, and how difficult it would be to find a particular group of people when you didn't know which entrance they'd come in or which stores they visited.

After what felt like a lifetime of scanning through footage, they finally picked up the three men Diego recognized from the bank robbery coming in one of the mall's side doors.

"That's them," he told Rich.

They were forced to jump from view to view and monitor to monitor, following the trio all over the place when it was clear they had no real destination in mind. The guys looked nothing like the three he and his pack mates had gone up against in the bank. They were laughing and joking, obviously having a good time. Nothing like the nearly catatonic men they'd been only a short time later.

"If you guys could tell me what you're looking for, I might be able to help," Rich said, glancing over his shoulder at Diego.

"Unfortunately, we're not sure," Diego admitted. "We're hoping watching them in the hours and minutes right before they tried to rob the bank might help us understand why they did it."

The three college kids stopped by a bakery to get some muffins and coffee, then sat at a table for almost an hour talking. When they were done eating, they tossed their trash, then disappeared down a long hallway.

"What's down there?" Trey asked, sitting up in his seat.

"The restrooms," Rich said. "We don't have any cameras in that hallway."

Diego cursed silently.

The clock on the bottom of the video continued to run until even Rich frowned.

"They've been in there a long time," he said.

"Tell me about it," Diego muttered.

When the three guys finally emerged from the hallway, what Diego saw on the screen sent a shiver down his back.

The demeanor of the men had changed. Instead of being relaxed and chill, talking and laughing like before, they walked through the mall like robots, devoid of expression. Like the life had been sucked out of them.

"Is there anything else down that hallway?" Diego asked, looking from one monitor to the next as the three college kids headed for the nearest exit. The time stamp on the video showed that they'd left the mall twenty minutes before the bank job.

Rich shook his head. "Just the restrooms. Do you think they were taking that delirium drug in there? Is that why they looked so spaced out?"

Diego exchanged looks with Trey and knew his pack mate was wondering the same thing. "I don't know."

He looked at the monitor that covered the entrance to the restrooms again, wishing they'd been able to see what those three guys had been up to, when he caught a glimpse of a man who'd just walked out of the hallway.

"Rewind the video of the restroom area," he said, then waiting impatiently while Rich did as he asked. "Stop there."

Diego stared at the image of the tall man in a dark suit. Unlike the three college kids who'd walked out of the hallway a few moments before him, the guy was grinning like he'd won the lottery.

Son of a bitch.

Beside him, Trey leaned forward in his chair. "Is that Bree's ex-husband?"

"Yeah."

Diego's inner wolf stirred, telling him something seriously weird was going on and that Dave was involved. He just wasn't quite sure how yet.

He looked at Rich. "Can we get a copy of the video footage from the time those guys walked down that hallway until this guy came out?"

"Sure."

Opening a drawer, Rich grabbed a CD, then copied the footage. Promising they'd write letters of recommendation to the police academy, Diego thanked the kid, then he and Trey were out the door.

"Do you think Dave put those guys up to robbing the bank?" Trey asked as they headed toward their SUV.

"I don't know. He might be prone to violence, but this seems totally out of his wheelhouse. Bree told me he already has money, so why have a bunch of amateurs rob a bank for him? And how does the delirium drug fit in? Is he a dealer?"

Diego was starting the engine of the SUV when his phone rang. He dug it out of his pocket and immediately put it on speaker when he saw Hale's name on the screen.

"You guys find anything worthwhile?" Diego asked.

"Maybe," Hale said. "Talking to anyone at the construction company was a waste, so we decided to check the traffic cams in the area where those guys were working. You'll never guess what we found."

"You're right," Trey said. "So tell us."

"Footage of those four construction workers standing on the sidewalk having coffee when a BMW pulls up and a guy in a nice suit gets out and gives them a box of doughnuts, shakes their hands, then leaves."

"That's it?" Diego asked, confused. "A good Samaritan handing out doughnuts?"

"That Good Samaritan was your girlfriend's ex," Connor said. "And less than a minute after he left, those guys dropped everything—including the doughnuts—then got in their work truck like a bunch of frigging zombies and took off."

Diego exchanged looks with Trey. If Dave had simply shown up at the mall, that was one thing, but interacting with the construction workers before they tried to jack that armored truck was too much of a coincidence.

"What about you guys?" Hale asked. "Did you get anything?"

Diego told them what he and Trey had learned, saying Dave had been at the mall and mentioning the way those three college kids had acted after coming into contact with him.

"What's our next move?" Connor asked.

Diego didn't even have to think about it. "We figure out what the hell Dave is up to. Something tells me he's a whole lot more than an investment advisor."

CHAPTER 10

"I thought everyone on the team had the day off for the baby shower. Unless they have to go on a call, I mean," Bree said as Diego led her and Brandon through the SWAT compound toward the huge, open-sided tent set off to one side and filled with people. "Are they doing training or something?"

Diego followed her gaze to where a group of people were rappelling off a tall structure that looked like a building but without windows or doors.

"They aren't training," he said with a laugh. "Rappelling is something we do for fun at parties."

She caught sight of movement at the top of the wall, watching with dread as Trey and a teenage boy moved to the edge and began to bounce down the wall like it was the most natural thing in the world. Her stomach plummeted right along with them. And she wasn't even the one up there!

She quickly looked away as Trey and the boy covered the last ten feet in a single big leap that made her think they were both going to smash themselves into the ground up to their necks. "You and your friends have a strange idea of what fun is."

Diego chuckled again, guiding Bree and Brandon to the tent, nodding and smiling at people and stopping in between so they could pet the adorable dogs milling around wagging their tails before leading them over to a tall, muscular man who simply had to be another alpha and a pretty, dark-haired, pregnant woman, introducing them as Landry and Everly Cooper. Everly smiled and warmly hugged Bree like they were longtime friends, then eagerly opened the gifts she'd brought—a gift card to a store that sold everything you could ever need for babies and a big plush wolf.

After another round of hugs and a promise to swing by to talk more later, Diego introduced Bree and Brandon to the rest of the SWAT team and their significant others, as well as everyone else who'd come to help Everly and Cooper celebrate. Her head was spinning with names and faces by the time they came to a tall, blond woman and an even taller man with dark hair. Bree could tell right away that they were werewolves simply from the way they carried themselves.

"Bree, Brandon, this is Rachel Bennett and her mate, Knox Lawson," Diego said. "Rachel is on the SWAT team, and Knox runs his own private security company. Believe it or not, they met right here on the SWAT compound."

Bree smiled and was reaching out to shake Rachel's hand when Diego made a funny strangled sound, pointing at his teammate's left hand. More specifically, the diamond ring sitting there.

"When the hell did that happen?" he asked, his voice revealing his astonishment even more than his question. "And why didn't I know about it?"

"It happened last night," Rachel said with a smile, giving her fiancé an adoring look. "Today is all about Everly and Cooper, which means our announcement can wait, so try and keep your voice down, huh?"

Diego snorted. "Good luck keeping that rock under

wraps." Stepping forward, he hugged Rachel, then did the man-hug thing with Knox. "I knew you guys were perfect for each other the moment I saw you together."

Rachel seemed a little dubious about that. "Really? Because I tend to remember you hating the idea of Knox and me working together. You didn't trust him to watch my back. You flat out called him a player. And when you thought he was a hunter, you kicked in the door of my apartment and threatened to shoot him."

"Well...yeah," Diego admitted. "But other than that, I thought you two were perfect for each other."

Bree couldn't help but think that was the lamest thing she'd ever heard. From the look on Rachel's face, it was obvious she thought the same thing. Something told Bree the two of them would get along perfectly.

While Diego ran off to grab something to drink for her and Brandon, Bree congratulated Rachel and Knox as her son watched people rappel on the far side of the compound.

"Diego said you and Knox met here," Bree said. "Were you working on the same case or something?"

Rachel laughed as if the idea was the funniest thing she'd ever heard. Knox, on the other hand, looked rather sheepish. "Not even close. Knox was hanging out with some seriously bad dudes who were here trying to kill us because they didn't like werewolves."

Bree thought for a moment that Rachel was kidding. Then she realized the other woman wasn't laughing.

"But don't worry," Rachel added. "He made up for it later by saving my life twice—first from his buddies, then from a psychotic killer clown."

Sure Rachel was definitely messing with them, Bree

glanced at her son to see Brandon staring at the couple with eyes as wide as saucers.

"Um…you're making up that stuff about the killer clown, right?" she asked, suddenly not so sure.

Both Rachel and Knox shook their heads.

"I wish she was making it up," Knox said. "Unfortunately, it's all true. There really was a clown. He really was psychotic. And he really tried to kill us. Then again, I'm not sure the thing could be called a clown since it wasn't even human."

Bree wasn't sure what to say to that.

"You'll get used to all the weird stuff that goes on around here," Rachel said, giving her a smile. "I promise."

Diego came back with their drinks then, bottles of iced tea for him and Bree and soda for Brandon. The conversation went from how Rachel and Knox had met to how their teammates had met their significant others. Except for Gage and a few of the other guys, everyone else had met their mates—as Diego called them—in some kind of crazy situation. Not unlike how she and Diego had met, she supposed.

While Bree was having a great time laughing and talking about how people stumbled their way into relationships, one glance at her son told her he was bored out of his mind as he gazed longingly at a group of teens and young adults standing by the rappelling wall. Even though Brandon would much rather hang out with people closer to his age, she knew he wouldn't simply walk over there and introduce himself. Her son hadn't been shy and reserved like that when he was little, but after Dave and everything that had happened, he'd changed.

Diego must have picked up on that, too, because he

motioned toward the teens. "How about I take you over there and introduce you to the beta pack, Brandon? I know they've been waiting to meet you."

Bree could have kissed Diego. But from the way Brandon stood there indecisively, it was probably going to take a little more urging than that.

"And after I introduce you, I can take you up on the wall and teach you to rappel, if you want," Diego added.

Brandon's eyes filled with excitement at that. She, however, had to admit she was terrified at the thought of her son so high in the air, held up by nothing but a thin rope. But when Brandon looked her way with an eager expression on his face, Bree didn't have the heart to say he couldn't do it.

She looked at Diego. "You're sure it's safe?"

"I'll be right there beside him the whole time," Diego promised. "He'll be fine."

She was still nervous, but nodded. Grinning, Diego leaned over to give her a quick kiss, then asked Knox if he wanted to do some rappelling, too, before he and Brandon took off. Knox kissed Rachel, then followed, leaving Bree and the female werewolf alone.

"Brandon fits right in with them," Rachel said as they watched him chatting with the group of young people Diego and Knox introduced him to. "That's the way it works with betas. Five minutes from now, they'll all be friends for life."

Bree silently agreed. Within moments, Brandon was smiling and laughing, a sure sign he was comfortable with them.

She let out a sigh of relief. "I know Diego said your pack would accept Brandon right away, but I was a little nervous anyway."

"You're part of the Pack now, too, by the way," Rachel said. "Both because you're Brandon's mom and because of your connection to Diego."

Bree opened her mouth to say she and Diego hadn't been dating long enough to have a connection yet, but then closed it again. Regardless of the fact that they'd just met, there was definitely something between her and Diego, even if she didn't quite know what it was yet.

"You like him a lot, don't you?" Rachel asked, her dark eyes thoughtful, like she was reading Bree's mind. "Diego, I mean. You haven't taken your eyes off him since you two arrived."

Bree smiled and sipped her iced tea, unable to resist glancing at him. "Yeah, I guess I do. Even if things are happening crazy fast."

Rachel's lips curved. "I wouldn't worry too much about how fast it's happening. Diego is worth the rush."

"You and Diego seem like good friends," Bree said, running her hand down the back of the pit-bull mix named Tuffie who'd come over to visit. "Have you known each other long?"

"Since I moved here and joined the Pack in December. He's been like an older brother to me since the day we met." Rachel lifted her bottle of beer and took a sip. "I was having a hard time dealing with my change when I first got here. Diego helped me through it by being there for me to talk to, but also by looking out for me. He's very protective of everyone."

"I kind of got that impression," Bree said, thinking about the three women he'd saved the night he'd gone through his own change.

Rachel looked out across the compound. "Now that y'all are together, there's nothing he won't do for you and Brandon."

Hand still caressing Tuffie's fur, Bree followed Rachel's gaze to see that Diego and Brandon were already at the top of the rappelling tower. Her heart nearly seized in her chest as they slowly worked their way over the edge, leaning out with their backs to the ground until there seemed no way they couldn't fall. But as high up in the air as they were, no matter how incredibly dangerous it seemed, Brandon was more relaxed than she'd ever seen. He completely trusted Diego. That was when Bree abruptly realized she trusted him, too. It was difficult to describe how amazing it felt to be able to believe in a man again.

Bree dragged her gaze away from Diego and Brandon. Watching them slowly move down the wall was making her dizzy. She didn't want to imagine what it would be like looking down from that high.

"How long were you and Knox together before you knew it was real?" she asked Rachel. "I've only been in one relationship in my life, and it was a total disaster. I don't want to move too fast with this one and mess it up."

Rachel smiled at she looked over at Knox, who'd already rappelled down the wall and was at the bottom, talking to one of Diego's teammates. The big werewolf lifted his head and gazed at her as though he could feel his fiancée's eyes on him. After a long, heated glance, he went back to the conversation he'd been having.

"I met Knox in February and now we're engaged, if that tells you anything," Rachel said. "So, if you're afraid of things moving fast, don't be. Trust me when I tell you that what you have with Diego is real."

Bree frowned a little as she considered that. "I thought it was real with my ex, and look how that turned out."

"This is different," Rachel said. "Diego is not your ex, far from it. Just trust your instincts."

Bree gave her a wry smile. "You may not have noticed, but I'm not a werewolf like you. I don't have your instincts."

Rachel grinned. "You have them. You simply have to learn to trust them and accept that Diego is an amazing guy. All you need to do is let him know you're open to the idea of being with him, and things will take care of themselves."

Bree let her gaze go to the rappelling wall again, pushing her hair back behind her ear. Diego and Brandon had made it safely to the bottom, and while she couldn't hear what they were saying, it was obvious from the way they were laughing they'd both had fun. Seeing Diego bonding in a way Brandon never did with his own father almost brought tears to her eyes. Rachel was right. Diego truly was amazing. In addition to being attractive as sin, sexy as hell, and more caring than any guy she'd ever met, he was incredible with Brandon.

Why was she hesitating to take the next step when everything about being with Diego felt so right? Had her travesty of a marriage to Dave wrecked her confidence so completely? But then Diego glanced her way and flashed her a grin that made her warm all over, and those instincts Rachel mentioned told her if she didn't take a chance with him, she'd regret it for the rest of her life.

Maybe she needed to stop thinking so much and follow them.

Diego and Brandon moved down the wall much faster the second time, each of them kicking away from the wooden vertical surface in front of them in time with each other, the rappelling rope singing as it slid through their gloved hands while they flew through the air. When they hit the ground at the exact same time, Brandon let out a shout of excitement. Diego was pretty stoked, too. The kid was a natural at this.

"One more time," Brandon begged, running the last of the rappelling rope through his carabiner. "Maybe Australian style?"

Diego shook his head with a chuckle. He could only imagine Bree's reaction to that. "Your mom about vapor-locked when you went down backward. She'd absolutely lose it if she saw you go down face-first. How about we save Australian rappelling for another day?"

Instead of being disappointed, Brandon looked at him like he'd just announced Disney was opening a new park right outside Dallas with unlimited FastPasses for everyone.

"We can do it again sometime?" he asked excitedly. "Really?"

"We can do it anytime you want. At least when I'm not working," Diego promised. "And if I am working, you can rappel with anyone from the Pack, if you want. They'd all jump at the chance to hang out with you."

Brandon shook his head as he began to loosen the straps on the rappelling harness. "Nah. I'll wait until you have time to do it with me."

Diego couldn't explain the warm sensation that crept into his chest at that announcement. But he liked it—whatever the hell it was. He moved away from the base of the tower to make room for the next group getting ready to come down the wall, motioning for Brandon to do the same. "Works for me."

"Cool." Brandon watched as Connor came down the wall with Kat balanced on his chest. "By the way, I wanted to say thanks for spending so much time with my mom. I haven't seen her smile this much in a long time. I think she really likes you."

Damn if hearing that didn't make his heart do a backflip in his chest. "I like your mom, too."

Brandon seemed to consider that for a moment before turning to look curiously at him. "Do you *like* my mom or do you *really* like my mom?"

Diego almost laughed. Was he actually getting grilled by a teenager? If the serious expression on Brandon's face was anything to go by, the answer to that was yes. Talk about a role reversal. Next, the kid would be asking him what his intentions were with his mother.

"Would you be okay with that?" he asked. "If I *really* liked your mom, I mean."

"Definitely!" Brandon grinned. "I think it'd be really cool if you two got together. I know she's given up a lot for me, and she deserves something good in her life."

Whoa. That had to be the sweetest, most selfless thing he'd ever heard any kid say.

He was about to tell Brandon that very same thing when Moe Jenkins, a tall, muscular beta from Jayna's pack, jogged up to them.

"Burgers and steaks just went on the grill, Brandon. Want to grab some food and head inside to play some video games with us?"

Brandon glanced at Diego. "Mind if I hang out with Moe and the other betas for a while?"

"Go ahead," Diego said. "I'll let your mom know where you are."

Diego was still standing there watching Brandon and Moe head toward the training building, laughing and talking about video games, when Jayna appeared at his side, wanting to know what the goofy grin on his face was all about.

"It's good to see Brandon fitting in with your pack," he said. "I knew getting him to spend time with them would be good for him. You're going to be a great alpha for him."

Jayna stared at him for a moment, then laughed. "I'm not Brandon's alpha. You are."

"Wait." Diego did a double take. "What?"

"You're his alpha."

Diego felt his heart beating faster. "I can't be his alpha."

"Why not?"

"Because I don't know how to be an alpha for a fifteen-year-old kid." Diego's head was spinning. "He needs someone who knows what they're doing."

A smile curved Jayna's lips. "You guys got here two hours ago, and he hasn't looked my way once. He doesn't care that I already have a pack or lots of experience with betas. As far as his inner wolf is concerned, you're the alpha he's comfortable with, the one he believes will take care of him. It was probably already a done deal the moment you and Brandon met. It was simply a matter of both of you coming to realize it. And after watching you two come down that wall together, I can see he's already made his decision. The rest is up to you."

He was so ill-equipped to take care of Brandon it wasn't funny. Accepting the idea Bree was *The One* for him had been simple. But being Brandon's alpha? "Jayna, I don't know what I'm doing when it comes to being an alpha for another werewolf. What if I'm not ready? What if I screw it up?"

The thought was almost enough to make him hyperventilate.

"You won't know what you're doing in the beginning," Jayna said gently. "You probably aren't ready, and you'll almost certainly screw things up a few times."

He scowled. "If that's your idea of making me feel better about this whole alpha thing, you suck at it."

Jayna gave him a small smile. "What I'm trying to say is that it's okay to make mistakes. Trust me, I made a lot of them. As long as you make decisions based on what's best for Brandon, you'll do fine."

Diego wasn't so sure of that, especially since it had the sound of a well-worn cliché that never works out in reality.

He blew out a breath. "Okay, so where do I start?"

Her smile broadened. "Why don't you start with getting Bree something to eat while Brandon hangs out with my betas? After that, follow your instincts."

That was something he'd been doing since getting a handle on his werewolf side all those years ago, so maybe he should do it now and stop worrying so damn much. Because while he was nervous as hell about being Brandon's alpha, his inner wolf was surprisingly chill about it.

Deciding to take Jayna's advice, he dropped the rappelling gear off, then stopped by the grills for a few cheeseburgers. After adding some baked beans and potato salad, he picked up two more bottles of iced tea and sat down beside Bree where she was hanging out at a picnic table with Rachel and Knox under the tent.

Bree leaned over and kissed him on the cheek, thanking him for the food, making his heart immediately speed up. On the other side of the table, Rachel and Knox both grinned.

"Thanks for teaching Brandon how to rappel," Bree said, picking up the bottle of ketchup he'd brought and squeezing some onto her cheeseburger. "He looked like he was having a great time. You guys have really bonded."

"Yeah, I guess we have." Diego grinned. "He's a great kid. I like hanging out with him."

As the four of them sat there chatting, it occurred to Diego that Bree and Rachel were laughing and talking like they'd known each other for years. The idea of the Pack welcoming her was more comforting than he could have ever imagined.

Damn, you have it so bad for this woman.

Bree looked at him as she sipped her iced tea. "You mind if we drop Brandon off at Kevin's house later?"

"Sure," he said. "You want to catch a movie or something after?"

But Bree didn't say anything as she took another bite of cheeseburger and slowly chewed. When she was done, she gave him a sexy smile. "Actually, I thought we could hang out."

He told himself the simple reason Bree licked her lips was because of the juicy burger she was eating, but when he heard her heart drum a little faster, he thought there might be another reason.

"Works for me," he said, feeling his inner wolf stir as he gazed into Bree's warm eyes.

"Good," she said. "I was thinking maybe we could go to your place and you could show me around."

Diego ignored the knowing grins from Rachel and Knox on the other side of the table, as well as his own suddenly rapidly beating pulse, focusing all his attention on Bree. "I'd love that."

CHAPTER 11

If Bree had to guess what she thought Diego's place would look like, she'd have said an apartment with a great view of the city or maybe a condo. A ranch-style home a few minutes outside the city surrounded by a veritable forest of lush trees definitely wasn't it. But it was absolutely beautiful.

"Is this a werewolf thing?" she asked as they stepped up onto the wraparound porch. "Living in the woods like this, I mean."

Diego glanced at her over his shoulder as he unlocked the back door. "In a way, yeah. When I first went through my change, my sense of hearing was out of control. I couldn't sleep at night from all the traffic noise in the city, so I moved out here where it was quieter."

When Diego led her inside and flipped on the lights, she was as wowed by the interior as the exterior. With high ceilings and no walls separating the kitchen, dining area, and living room, the space was open and airy. Sleek, stainless-steel appliances were the perfect complement to the granite countertops and central island, and the big, cushy sectional across from the gigantic wall-mounted television above the fireplace was—as Brandon loved to say—dope.

"You want something to drink?" Diego asked.

"Sure," she said. "Whatever you have is fine."

Bree wandered into the living room to check out the dozens of framed photos on the wall above the couch. Soft spotlights illuminated the collection, giving them a gallery feel. There were more framed photographs on almost every surface, from tables to built-in bookcases, some with fantastic digitally enhanced effects that made them seem almost otherworldly. But while the landscapes and wildlife pictures were stunning, it was the photographs of the people that caught her attention. She immediately recognized his SWAT pack mates, but the other faces she didn't recognize were what pulled her closer.

"Are these photos of your family?" she asked, looking closely at a photo of two women and a man, individually and as a group, who had Diego's eyes and smile. Around them were pictures of an older couple in which the woman bore a striking resemblance to the man Bree was quickly falling for.

Diego came over to stand beside her, two glasses of white wine in his hands and a sentimental expression on his handsome face. Bree could feel the heat coming off his body and sidled closer so she could feel more of that warmth.

"Yeah," he said, handing her one of the glasses. "That's my brother, Alejandro, and my sisters, Alicia and Karolina. And these are my parents, Sofia and Dominic. Well, technically, he's my stepfather, but I think of him as my real dad all the same."

She sipped her wine, taking in the rest of the photos. There were pictures of all the iconic places people think of when they imagine the Dallas-Fort Worth area, as well as all the natural wonders surrounding them.

"Did you take all these yourself?" she asked.

He nodded. "I got into photography when I was in high school. It was right after my real dad bailed on us and I needed something to focus on to keep from thinking about how he'd abandoned us. I fell in love with it and kept doing it. As you can see from all the photos, it's a full-time hobby. Or obsession, I guess."

She smiled. "I think they're beautiful."

"Thanks." He grinned. "Wanna see the rest of the house?"

Bree nodded eagerly.

As they wandered from room to room, he talked about some of the renovations he'd made when he'd bought the house, as well as explaining the effort he had to go through to get some of the wildlife photos he'd taken.

"You wouldn't believe how hard it is to sneak up on a wild animal when you smell like a wolf," Diego said with a chuckle as she admired a close-up of a tiny gopher staring at the camera with a confused look in his eyes.

One of the bedrooms in the house was set up for guests, while Diego had turned another into a photography studio, complete with a fancy computer, multiple monitors, and a printer that looked more expensive than Bree's car. But it was the third bedroom Diego showed her that she was most interested in because it was his.

His king-size bed wasn't obscenely huge, but it was definitely more than big enough for two. The forest-green comforter and cream-colored sheets looked perfectly cozy, and the pillows seemed fluffy enough for a person to lose themselves in. The rest of the master suite was equally inviting, full of warm, earthy tones and beautiful furniture, but Bree was too focused on the bed and wondering what it would be like to sleep there to notice.

Although, since talking with Rachel at the party, Bree had to admit being in a bed with Diego and not sleeping was something she'd rather do more.

"So, do you want to watch something on Netflix?" Diego asked.

She turned her gaze away from the bed to smile up at him. "Or we could skip Netflix and chill instead."

Bree thought she saw gold flare in Diego's eyes, but it disappeared too quickly for her to be sure. There was no mistaking the hunger she saw in their depths, though, and her pulse quickened.

Taking her glass from her hand, Diego placed it on top of the high dresser along with his, then stepped closer. The heat of his body enveloped her, making hers tingle in anticipation. He slid one hand gently into her hair, but didn't move to kiss her. Instead, he gazed down at her as he teased the base of her scalp with his fingers. His touch was enough to make her feel warm all over.

When he finally did take that last step to close the scant distance between them, her heart was already pounding before his lips touched hers. She reveled in how perfect he tasted, sighing as his tongue slid in and tangled with hers, drawing a moan from them both. She would never get enough of him.

Bree slipped her fingers into his belt, the back of her fingers grazing the skin there as he tugged her closer until she was pressed against the hard-on in his jeans. Even through all their clothes, it felt amazing.

Dragging his mouth away from hers, Diego trailed kisses along her jaw, so he could nibble her neck. The feel of his extremely sharp teeth on her skin made her head spin. When had her neck become so sensitive?

She let her head fall back, giving Diego better access. He made use of it, moving his mouth down to the part of her collarbone left exposed by the straps on her dress. There was no way she could consider holding back the whimper that escaped as her body hummed. This was so insane.

And glorious.

Lifting his head, Diego gazed at her for a moment, then swung her up in his arms and, in two quick strides, set her down on the bed. Grabbing the back of his T-shirt, he yanked it over his head, then reached down to unbuckle his belt.

Bree stared, transfixed, unable to move. She'd fully intended to get undressed, but one look at that muscular upper body of his and she was frozen solid to the bed. She'd already known he was built from how good he looked in his uniform, but seeing those broad shoulders, mouthwatering pecs, and luscious abs made her wonder why he wore clothes at all. It was a crime against humanity to deprive the world of such a sight.

Well...to deprive her of the view, at the very least.

As he kicked off his boots, Bree pushed herself up on her elbows, noting the incredibly detailed tattoo of a wolf's head on his chest with the letters SWAT underneath it moving and snarling as his pecs rippled. Even though it was a true work of art, she couldn't miss the scars accompanying it.

There was the one she'd already seen on his right shoulder, now barely visible as more than a faint line a touch lighter than the rest of his skin. Other ones even older were scattered here and there. But there were fresher scars, too—one to the upper chest and another to his stomach—that looked like they couldn't be more than a day or two old. Had something happened to Diego that he hadn't told her about?

But now wasn't the time to ask.

Instead, she watched as the rest of his clothes came off and he stood there naked. Even with the additional scar on one of his thighs, the total package was so stunning she decided that any talk about where the scars had come from could wait until much, much later. Right now, she was more focused on the fact that Diego was completely naked, while she was still fully clothed. That was definitely a first for her.

The sight of his muscular legs made her stomach flutter like there were butterflies in it. She'd always been a leg woman, truly appreciating a well-muscled pair that looked like they could run all day. Diego had that part covered. But they also looked powerful enough to kick a car over at the end of that run.

As for the thick erection between those legs? All she could say was that perfection was a clichéd and overused word, but even that was clearly unsuitable in this case.

Beyond perfection?

More perfect?

More perfecter?

Nope, none of those came close, either.

Moving closer to the bed, Diego reached out to slowly pull off one sandal, then the other. He tossed them casually aside, then slipped his fingers under the straps of her dress. She had half a second to reach behind her and unzip it before he dragged it off. He was so strong, he probably could have gotten her dress off whether she'd gotten to the zipper in time or not. For some crazy reason, that was a really hot thought.

She was busy wiggling out of her bra when she felt hands at her waist. Two big, strong, warm hands. Then her panties were coming down, the slight tearing sound they made as he hastily worked them over her hips impossible to miss.

Then Diego was staring down at her naked body with a hunger and intensity that would have been scary if it wasn't so arousing. As his gaze wandered over her skin with little flickers of yellow gold in his eyes, she realized no one had ever made her feel so desired simply by looking at her.

"You're beautiful," he breathed.

The compliment made her blush and she smiled. "You're pretty beautiful yourself."

Bree started to move, planning to roll over and scramble up with every intention of throwing her arms around Diego and kissing him until they were both dizzy. But when he cupped her butt in his big hands and slid her toward him until she was right on the edge of the mattress, she realized he had his own plans.

Spreading her legs, he ran his fingers along her calf and down her thigh to trace them along her folds. Her breath caught as he swiped lightly across her clit, and all she could think at the moment was that he possessed the most wonderful fingers ever.

"Do you like that?" he asked huskily, his eyes piercing, words coming out in a sexy rumble that Bree was sure she could feel in her chest. Before she could answer, he moved closer, leaning over her, his strong, naked body pushing her legs back until her knees were pressed tightly to her breasts. He was so big compared to her. "When I touch you like this," he added, his face above hers, eyes glinting with that flash of color, his warm breath caressing the sensitive skin of her lips. "When I tease you."

He dipped a finger deep inside her as he said that last

part, finding that most sensitive place there like he had a road map and drawing a gasp out of her that answered all of his questions. But from the patient expression he wore, he seemed to be waiting for her to answer his question the old-fashioned way—even as he continued to caress her G-spot at the same time the pad of his thumb made little circles on top of her clit.

Expecting her to form intelligent words when he was touching her like that was patently unfair. Bree could barely think, much less talk. But worried Diego might stop what he was doing if she didn't speak, she somehow found her voice.

"I love when you touch me like that," she practically shouted, realizing now how wonderful it was that his house was out in the middle of nowhere. "Please don't stop."

He lowered his head until his mouth was mere inches above hers, a wicked smile on his face. "Oh, you don't ever have to worry about me stopping. I've just started."

Then he was kissing her, a second finger slipping inside with the first, the movements faster and far more intense, his thumb grinding deliciously on her clit while he made love to her mouth.

She wrapped one leg around his back and spread herself wider as the fingers moving inside her became more insistent. It was hard to kiss him when she was gasping for breath and moaning at the same time, but she sure as hell tried.

When her climax exploded through her, Bree yanked her mouth away from Diego's, arching back on the bed and screaming long and loud. Even after she was sure her body couldn't take anymore, he kept working her with those amazing fingers, backing off her sensitive clit but continuing to caress her G-spot until she thought she'd pass out.

By the time Diego was done with her, Bree was so wrung out that she collapsed back on the bed like a limp noodle the second he moved away. As she rolled over on her side and reached her hand between her legs, wanting to calm the tremors still rippling through her, a small part of her semi-coherent mind wondered where he was going. She heard some soft rustling sounds, then the bed dipped as Diego joined her. Pushing herself up, she rolled over to meet him, her heart beating faster when she saw the foil condom packet in his hand.

"Let me help with that," Bree said, reaching out to take the packet from him and nudging him onto his back.

After the mind-numbing orgasm she'd had, a part of her was a little surprised she was so ready for more, but the idea of having him inside her had her body trembling with need. She wondered if it was because she hadn't been with a man in a long time. But she knew it wasn't that. It was Diego, pure and simple. There was something about him that made her want to wrap herself around him and stay there forever.

Bree got the condom package opened and reached for Diego. But the moment she wrapped her hand around his shaft, instinct took over and she leaned over to take him in her mouth. The desire to get her lips around him had nothing to do with wanting to make sure he was hard enough to put the condom on. This was purely about wanting to taste him.

She moaned at the first touch of his flavor on her tongue, swirling it around the head before taking him as deep as she could. She almost laughed at the groan of pleasure Diego made, but her mouth was full, so she couldn't.

It was easy to get lost in the rhythm of going down on

Diego's cock, her hand moving in perfect counterpoint to her mouth and tongue. What had started as an urge to get a taste quickly turned into a desire to have him calling out her name as he came in her mouth.

Diego took the decision away from her, weaving his fingers in her hair and tugging her up and away from his throbbing cock with a growl that went right through her core.

"Not that I'm not enjoying the hell out of that," he murmured, reaching for the condom she'd somehow remembered to hang onto. "But if I'm not inside you in the next five seconds, I'm not going to be responsible when I lose it and start sprouting fangs and claws."

Bree slapped his grabby hand away and kept the condom for herself. "I think I might like to see that."

Grinning, she quickly rolled the latex sheath over him. The second it was in place, she swung her leg across his hip. Diego grabbed her hips and eased her down slowly. The feel of him inside her was exquisite and she closed her eyes, dropping her head back. It might have been a long time, but it had never felt this good.

"Yes," she sighed as he settled in nice and deep, holding her there. "Just like that. Stay right there."

Bree had the urge to simply sit there astride Diego's hips, his cock deep inside her, undulating slowly side to side as she drifted her fingers down to touch herself.

But Diego didn't give her the chance.

Instead, he used his grip on her hips to lift her until the tip of his shaft was still inside her, then he simply dropped her. The impact of his hard length filling her so fast drove the air out of her lungs and started a tingling in her tummy that suggested it wouldn't be long before he made her come again.

Diego used the grip on her hips to set the pace, but once she had it, he let those hands drift up until they were cupping her breasts, thumbs and forefingers pinching and teasing her nipples as she rode him. The combination of sensations, from the electric sparks radiating out from her nipples to the lightning bolts shooting through her every time she came down on him and he discovered places that had never been touched in her life, was nearly overwhelming and she never wanted the sensations to end.

Bree leaned forward a little, both to push her breasts harder into Diego's big, strong hands and to allow her clit to grind against him perfectly. Then he started thrusting, the motion making pleasure ripple deep in her core, and she knew this one was going to be huge.

"Harder," she demanded. "Don't stop. I'm close."

Diego definitely didn't stop. Grasping her hips, he pounded into her so hard and fast Bree swore there were sparks flying off their bodies with every thrust. She collapsed onto his chest, burying her face in the curve of his neck and shoulder, and screamed as her vision went white behind her clenched eyelids. Her thighs tightened around his hips, and she held on for dear life as he yanked her down on him over and over, her clit grinding against him as spasm after spasm ripped through her. She wasn't sure how it happened—or why—but her teeth somehow found their way into the muscles of his shoulder as she continued to ride out the best orgasm in the history of humanity.

Diego let out a deep growl, and she was flying through the air. She didn't have a chance to catch her breath before her back hit the bed and he was thrusting again.

She came again. Or maybe she hadn't stopped coming

from the first one and this was simply the second drop on the roller coaster.

Either way, she arched her back and spread her legs wider, giving Diego all the room he needed to pound her into oblivion. When he slammed in deep and grunted out a long, deep groan, she could barely keep her eyes open. But she was glad she did because she got to see him gazing down at her with eyes that were completely yellow gold, the tips of his fangs just visible over his lower lip.

It probably should have been terrifying to be so vividly reminded she was making love with a werewolf, but at that moment, she couldn't imagine a sexier sight in the world. Reaching up, she curled her hand around the back of his neck, dragging him down until his full weight was pressing her into the bed. Then she wrapped her legs around him and squeezed tightly, never wanting to let him go.

Diego moved enough to get rid of the condom, then they spooned together, his body keeping her warm as they both slowly came down from their orgasms. She had no idea if it had been the same for him, but she knew he'd ruined her for every other man out there. She couldn't imagine wanting to be with anyone else. The mere thought of not being with Diego made her stomach twist into knots.

Bree pushed that notion away, wondering why she was thinking it anyway, and immediately felt better. She relaxed, sinking back against Diego, wrapping her hand around the arm he had over her and holding tight. She was half a second from drifting off into sleep when she realized she couldn't do that. One glance at the clock on the bedside table confirmed her worst fear.

Forcing herself up, she rolled over to face Diego, wishing

she didn't have to wake him. "I'm sorry to ask, but could you take me home now?"

His eyes snapped open immediately, concern and what looked like hurt there. "You can stay, if you want. You know that, right?"

Bree leaned in and kissed him. "Of course, I know, and I'd really love to stay. But I can't. Brandon has no clue where I am, and he's going to be home in less than an hour. I know this is horrible timing, but I don't like the idea of not being there when he gets home. Not when I haven't talked about our relationship with him yet."

She braced herself, worried Diego would complain, get upset, or try to cajole her into staying for the night. That was her experience with other guys, and while she wanted to think he wouldn't act like that, she wasn't sure.

But instead, Diego kissed her long and slow on the mouth. "Don't worry about it." He twirled her hair around his finger, absently playing with it. "We shouldn't have you sleep over until Brandon is on board with the two of us. It's a package deal. I respect that."

Her heart stuttered in her chest a few times, hoping against hope she hadn't screwed something up. "Are you sure that you're okay with this? I know it's something we should have talked about before jumping into bed..."

He gently pressed a finger to her lips, shushing her. "Yes, I'm sure. Yes, I'm okay with it. And no, it's not anything we needed to talk about before jumping into bed. Because I understand. I hope you don't regret what happened."

It was impossible to miss the tension in Diego's body as he spoke, and once again, Bree was sure she'd ruined everything.

She moved closer, until her forehead was resting against his. "I could never regret making love with you. It was the most perfect moment I could ever wish for. Please don't think that my needing to go means anything other than what I said. I simply want to be there for Brandon when he gets home. It's important to me."

Diego gazed at her for a long moment, then nodded and smiled. "And you two are important to me. So, come on. Let's get you home."

The bands that had been tightening around her chest suddenly disappeared and she could breathe again. Cupping his face, she gave him a tender kiss. "Thank you for understanding."

CHAPTER 12

"Do you think they forgot we're in here?" Hale asked.

Diego, Trey, and Hale sat at a table in the small room the guards at Coffield Unit used as a break area. They'd made the hour and a half drive down here on the off chance a guard or another prisoner might be able to give them some information on Dave. Since coming to the conclusion Bree's ex was somehow involved in this whole delirium thing, they'd learned absolutely nothing about the guy, and Coffield might be their best bet.

"They didn't forget we're in here," Diego said, though they'd been waiting for nearly fifteen minutes. "It could take a while to find anyone who knows Dave well, especially since he's been out for months."

At least Diego hoped that was the case. There was always the possibility the shift supervisor they'd talked to when they'd first gotten there had gone straight to the warden, who was at that very moment talking to Chief Leclair, wanting to know why three SWAT cops were sniffing around asking about a released convict.

"You and Bree finally slept together, huh?" Trey said.

Diego had been wondering when his teammates were going to mention it. Even after showering this morning, Bree's scent was all over him. Not that he minded. Being surrounded by her pheromones 24/7 was fine with him. Besides, it wasn't like he was hiding anything from his pack mates.

"So, did you?" Hale asked, needing a verbal response since it wasn't like his crappy nose was going to tell him anything.

Diego had never been the kind to kiss and tell, but he knew if he didn't answer, Trey would.

"Yeah." He grinned. "Brandon went to a friend's house to play video games, so Bree and I went back to my place."

And it had been perfect.

Understatement there.

He couldn't begin to describe how devastated he'd been when she'd announced she had to go home. Irrational as it was, his inner wolf had been afraid his mate was rejecting him and howled in agony. When she'd told him it was so she could be there when Brandon got home, he felt worse, but this time for an entirely different reason. He hadn't thought about Brandon, and he was supposed to be his alpha. This whole idea of having a pack of his own was new to him, so he should probably cut himself some slack, but still. Luckily, Bree had been doing this parent thing longer, so he was going to have to follow her lead.

"Have you and Bree talked about *The One* yet?" Trey asked. "Now that you're sleeping together, she must have picked up on the fact that there's a connection between the two of you."

Diego winced. "I...um...haven't gotten around to that."

Hale did a double take. "Seriously?"

"I know I should have, but it's not exactly an easy topic to bring up, you know. Especially after sleeping together."

"I don't see what's so complicated about it," Hale said. "Just tell her she's your soul mate and that you're destined to be together. Easy peasy."

Diego opened his mouth to tell Hale he was an idiot, but Trey cut him off.

"Don't listen to him. He hasn't been in a serious relationship since he was sixteen years old, and that ended with him getting his face punched in. Go as fast as your instincts tell you to go, and everything will work out fine."

Diego wasn't so sure of that, but before he could say anything, the sounds of heavy footsteps heading down the hallway outside the break room caught his attention. There'd been hundreds of different sounds coming from various parts of the prison the whole time they'd been there, from the clank of cell doors slamming closed to the shouts of angry inmates, but right now, he was only interested in whoever was finally coming to talk to them.

Three uniformed correctional officers walked in. Two of them were men whose name tags read Beasley and Garcia. The other was an older woman with graying hair and a stern expression wearing the rank of sergeant and carrying a black backpack over one shoulder. Her name tag read Clark.

"The shift supervisor said something about you wanting to talk to anybody who knew an ex-con named Dave Cowell," the sergeant said, eyeing them curiously as she set the backpack on the floor beside her. "Let me guess. You think that piece of crap has done something that's gonna get his ass shipped back here, don't you?"

"Sounds like you wouldn't be surprised if that happened," Diego said.

Garcia snorted. "Cowell showed up here with an impulse-control problem for the record books and left a cold-blooded manipulative killer. To say we expect him back would be putting it mildly."

Diego threw a glance at Trey and Hale to see they were almost certainly thinking the same thing he was—that they'd come to the right place.

"We did a little digging in Cowell's prison file." Trey leaned forward to rest his forearms on the table. "But other than some minor comments about run-ins with other prisoners and a lot of time in solitary, there wasn't much there."

"Official records are like that. Nothing but the facts," Beasley said in a deep voice. "Of course, they rarely tell the real story about a person like Cowell."

"What *is* the real story about him?" Diego prompted. "The one that's not in the official records."

"First, you tell us what he did," Clark shot back. "Must be something good if they've sent SWAT down here to talk to us."

Diego didn't answer right away. This could get tricky if the wrong thing got back to the wrong people. But if he wanted the prison guards to talk to them about stuff that was off the record, there'd have to be an exchange of trust. That's the way the system worked.

"We don't know anything for sure. That's why we're here." He glanced at Trey and Hale, who both nodded. "Officially, we're not supposed to be messing around in this case, but we think there's a good chance Dave Cowell is involved in the delirium attacks."

That announcement should have provoked at least some kind of response, but the three corrections officers barely raised their eyebrows.

"Cowell came in thinking he was a tough guy," Clark said. "He probably figured beating a man to death would give him some kind of street cred in here. But Coffield is full of guys who make him look like a Boy Scout, and most of them took an instant dislike to his attitude."

"That's where all those scuffles you saw in the records came from," Garcia added. "He'd mouth off to someone and a fight would start. He spent a good part of his first four years or so in solitary or restricted to his cell, usually for his own protection."

Interesting.

"His first four years?" Trey said, catching the significance of that the same way Diego had. "Did something change?"

"Yeah, it did," Clark murmured. "In the form of a new cellmate named Will Bremen. And a more unlikely prisoner you'd never meet. The man had been some kind of scientist—a biologist or chemist, I think—before receiving a four-year sentence for possession with intent. Police in Houston found him passed out naked in a hotel room surrounded by a couple kilos of heroin. Swore it was for personal use, but with an amount like that, no one believed him."

Diego caught the looks Trey and Hale gave him at the mention of Bremen's college background. They had to be thinking what he was—that delirium was a drug and Dave had shared a cell with a man who was either a biologist or a chemist. No way that was a coincidence.

"Are you saying Bremen started protecting his cellmate?" Hale asked.

The three correction officers exchanged looks and frowned.

"None of us ever really figured it out," Clark admitted. "It seemed that when Bremen was around, no one bothered Cowell."

Diego tried to sort through that. Did Bremen pay off a

few of the prison's top dogs to keep Dave safe? That had to be it, right? He seriously doubted a guy who was a scientist would be intimidating enough in the physical sense to make the other inmates back off.

"Can we talk to Bremen?" Diego asked. "See what he's willing to tell us now that his cellmate has been released."

Clark shook her head. "I wouldn't have a problem with it, but unfortunately, Bremen was killed about six months after he got here. His body was found in the laundry area when he missed a head count. Strangled to death, though there were also multiple lacerations, including some that looked like bite marks."

Damn. They could really have used whatever the guy knew about Dave.

"Was Dave involved?" Trey asked.

"There were rumors there'd been arguments in their cell in the days before Bremen's death, but nothing we could ever use," Clark admitted. "The case remains open and is likely to stay that way."

"What happened to Dave after that?" Diego asked.

Clark sighed. "That's where things get strange." Unzipping the backpack she'd brought with her, she pulled out a laptop, then set it on the table and booted it up.

"There was a huge fight in the cafeteria two days after Bremen died," Beasley said as the sergeant clicked through folders on the desktop. "Everybody knew it was a move against Cowell, someone probably planning to shank him or something. But that's not what happened."

Clark spun the laptop around so Diego, Trey, and Hale could see the screen. On it was a video showing the cafeteria crowded with tables, chairs, and prisoners. It wasn't difficult to find Dave, even in the dull-white, shapeless uniforms all the men wore.

"See the big guy with the bald head walking across the room toward Cowell?" Clark said from the other side of the table, as if she'd watched the footage a hundred times. "Keep an eye on him. He's the one with the shiv."

Diego didn't watch the man as the sergeant suggested. Instead, he kept his eyes on Dave. Two large men were seated on either side of him, and Diego would bet money they were working with the one with the homemade knife. Probably there to make sure he didn't jump aside at the last second.

Even though Dave was looking down at the food on his tray, the set of his shoulders and the way his gaze drifted left and right to the men hemming him in suggested he knew something was coming. Of course, none of that explained why the man was grinning like an idiot.

The bald guy dived forward then, arm coming down to drive a slender piece of metal deep into Dave's exposed back. But right before the weapon hit its mark, the big guy to Dave's left jumped up and slammed his serving tray into the attacker's throat. A split second later, the man to Dave's right stood and punched the inmate on the other side of him as the guy got to his feet.

Things got crazy then as the entire cafeteria full of inmates began punching and kicking each other, food and serving trays flying everywhere. Prison guards in heavy riot gear quickly moved in to start separating the major combatants.

Dave remained in his seat through the entire event, eating his food and smiling at the scene around him.

"The guy with the shiv ended up dead with a crushed

larynx," Clark added as the footage came to an end. "The man who killed him insisted he didn't do it even when we showed him the video. He swears it couldn't have been him and that he didn't remember any of it. The other big guy—the one who started the brawl—told us the last thing he remembered was walking into the cafeteria. After that fight, no one ever bothered Cowell again."

"Tell them about the parole board meeting," Beasley said, leaning forward. "That was even crazier than the riot."

Diego looked at Clark to see her shrug. "I'm not sure if I'd describe it as crazy, but I was in the room as the board members were prepping for Cowell's parole hearing. Based on the number of physical altercations Cowell had been involved in, not to mention the fight in the cafeteria, they had no intention of supporting any kind of early release. Fifteen minutes later, I come back to find out two of the more influential members of the board had flipped their positions and pushed for his immediate release with no probation. When I asked later why they'd done it, it was like they didn't know what I was talking about."

"I think I understand now why you weren't surprised when I mentioned Dave might be involved in the delirium attacks," Diego said. "The riot in the cafeteria and the parole-board hearing have delirium written all over them. Which is crazy, because this stuff you told us about happened months before the earliest known episode in Dallas. I can't believe no one has ever made the connection."

"Not from lack of trying on our part," Clark said, closing the laptop. "We've sent copies of our reports and the video of the cafeteria fight to the task force and called them a few times, but I guess they have no interest in running down tips from a bunch of correction officers. Hell, the only person who's ever showed any interest is that damn irritating reporter from the *Dallas Daily Star*."

Diego did a double take at the paper's name. No way could Clark possibly be talking about that one particular pain in the ass. A lot of reporters were irritating.

"You talking about Ernest Hobbs?" Trey asked.

"Yeah." Clark looked at them in surprise. "You know him?"

"You could say that," Diego muttered.

"Hobbs showed up here a couple weeks after Cowell got out, sniffing for a story about the guy's early release," Clark continued. "While I normally wouldn't talk to any reporter, Hobbs was different. He seemed to actually care about what we had to say and the work we do here. I showed him the same video I showed you. He asked to see any other footage we might have on Cowell. It wasn't like he could take anything with him, so I turned him over to one of our support staff. Hobbs spent days in the archive room watching security footage from all over the prison, getting insight about Cowell's day-to-day life here."

"He must have found something interesting among all that video footage, because he hauled ass out of here like his tail was on fire," Beasley said. "Not long after that, all the insanity in Dallas started and Hobbs was writing stories about delirium."

Diego shared a look with Trey and Hale before turning back to Clark. "Can we see the same video footage Hobbs looked at? Something tells me Hobbs found the piece of the puzzle that makes sense of all of this."

Eight hours later, he, Trey, and Hale were pulling into the parking lot of the SWAT compound. They'd spent all afternoon and into the evening watching miles of video footage from the prison's security cameras, but as boring as the exercise had been, they'd actually picked up a few valuable nuggets of information.

First off, everything had changed for Dave after his cellmate had been killed. One day, the man had been a literal punching bag. The next, he was running the cell block with no fewer than two heavily muscled inmates protecting him at all times.

Then there was the missing security footage. It had taken a while to notice it, but after digging for a bit, they'd realized the video all around the prison's laundry area from the day Bremen had been killed was gone. Shocking to no one at all, the staff support person who'd helped Hobbs with his story had quit.

"So, let me get this straight," Trey said as Diego parked the SUV and cut the engine. "We think Bremen created a drug that not only makes people do crazy crap like robbing a bank, but it also leaves them susceptible to certain suggestions from people like Dave. And that Dave killed Bremen to get the drug, used it to help get released from prison with no probation, and is now using it to make people steal for him. And if that isn't far enough out there, we're going to also tell Gage that Hobbs has been aware of this information for some time and has been sitting on it so he can, what, sell more newspapers?"

"Wow," Hale murmured from the back seat. "When you put it that way, it sounds ridiculous, doesn't it?"

Diego sighed. "Look, I know it sounds crazy, but we have to tell him what we learned. But maybe after we talk to Samantha Mills to see if a drug could do any of this stuff."

Beside him, Trey looked thoughtful. "I could swing by the ME's office tomorrow and talk to her, tell her about Bremen and see what she thinks."

They were halfway across the parking lot, with Diego trying to organize his thoughts on everything they'd learned, when his cell phone rang. He pulled it out and glanced at the screen. He didn't recognize the number but answered anyway. Lots of people had his contact info.

"Diego, it's Dion Harbin," a soft voice said, like he was worried someone would overhear him. "I don't have time to go into detail, but I'm at the Blacklight Club on Harry Hines. That boy I saw you with at the movies is here with another kid and they're hanging out with some gang-bangers, smoking weed and trying to act older than they really are. The joint narcotics/gang task force is about to raid the place, and if the kid is here when they do, he's going to jail. I can't break my cover to save him. You need to get your ass here, ASAP."

Shit.

"I'm on the way." Diego looked at his pack mates. "Tell Gage there's a situation with Brandon. I'll be back as soon as I can."

"You need help?" Trey asked.

"Thanks, but I have to do this on my own," he yelled over his shoulder as he ran for his SUV. "I got this!"

Hopefully.

CHAPTER 13

Diego couldn't remember a time in his life when he'd been so scared. He'd been shot, stabbed, blown up, clawed, run over by cars, and watched as his pack mates had nearly lost their lives. But as crazy as it seemed, all of that paled in comparison to the thought of something happening to Brandon. The idea that his beta could get arrested and dragged off to jail had him nearly shifting behind the wheel of his truck.

Probably not a safe way to drive.

Then again, he was stripping out of his cop gear at the same time he was weaving through traffic, pulling on a plain blue T-shirt he had in the back seat, so that likely wasn't very safe, either.

Regardless, he drove across town like a madman, flashers blinking as if that would help him get through the evening traffic. More likely he'd cross paths with a patrol unit and get pulled over for speeding. That was all he frigging needed.

But his luck held, and ten minutes later, he pulled into the far end of the parking lot of the Blacklight Club, relieved to see the place wasn't surrounded by a platoon of cop cars and paddy wagons yet. At least he'd gotten here before the raid started.

He only prayed he got Brandon out of there before the real party started. Oh, yeah. And Kevin, too. Because he had no doubt Kevin was the other kid Dion had seen.

Diego climbed out of his SUV and strode toward the

club, fingertips and gums tingling at the urge to move faster. His first instinct had been to squeal to a stop right in front of the door, so he wouldn't have to waste any more time, but then he realized how stupid that'd be. He needed to get Brandon and Kevin out of there. Not draw attention to himself while he did it.

His inner wolf took in the surrounding area as he walked, absently noting the vehicles in the lot and people hanging around. The name of the club had changed, but it wasn't much different than it had been eight years ago when his life had changed so drastically. The irony of it being the same place wasn't lost on him.

Diego pushed the memory away and focused on the present.

Blacklight sat squarely in the no-man's-land that existed between two rival gangs—the Locos and the Hillside Riders. This meant the place was largely left alone, making it one of the few clubs in this part of town that wasn't overrun with drugs. Then again, if Dion and his task force were planning to raid the place, something must have changed and the club had fallen under the control of one of the two gangs, if not some outsider trying to muscle their way into a new territory.

He bit back a growl at the thought of Brandon and Kevin getting involved with a gang. From what Bree had told him about the night Brandon had gotten shot, that wasn't outside the realm of possibility.

Diego focused on keeping it casual as he headed for the door and the crowd of people near it. He didn't stare, but he didn't miss the two or three people showing off the neck tattoos he recognized as belonging to the Hillside Riders.

Guess that answered his earlier question. The Riders had obviously made their move.

A few of them glanced his way as he opened the door, but other than that, no one paid him any attention. It had been a smart call to change out of his SWAT uniform T-shirt.

As he walked into the loud, packed club with its flashing strobes and strategically placed blacklights illuminating the fluorescent paint on various surfaces as well as some of the patrons, his nose was immediately assaulted by the smell of a few hundred people, along with the typical scents he'd expect in a place like this—booze, sweat, drugs, and sex. He made his way toward the chaos of the dance floor when he caught sight of another man with a Rider tat adorning the left side of his neck. The scruffy-looking guy was leaning against the wall, his attention fixed entirely on his cell phone, appearing unconcerned about Diego walking by or the chest thumping club beat coming from the sound system.

But as Diego moved past him, the guy surreptitiously lifted his hand, fingers spread, and silently mouthed the words, *five minutes*. Then the man he barely recognized as Dion Harbin pushed away from the wall and disappeared into the crowd.

Damn, Dion was good. If it wasn't for the man's familiar scent, Diego wouldn't ever know he was the same cop he'd run into at the movie theater.

Off to the left of the dance floor was the bar area with a dozen or so high-boy tables. To the right were booths, separated by arched doorways that led off to other parts of the club—bathrooms, offices, storerooms, and probably a kitchen, based on the clanking and clatter coming from the nearest opening. The stench of drugs came from that direction. Mostly heroin and fentanyl.

Diego drifted onto the dance floor, ignoring the bodies swaying around him as he casually lifted his nose into the air and started separating out the various scents. Even through the mishmash of competing smells swirling around the place, he was still able to pick up on Brandon's anxiety and fear. The kid was nervous as hell for some reason. Suddenly, Diego's fangs extended, and his muscles began to spasm with the instinctive need to shift and find his beta. To get Brandon out of there no matter how many people he had to rip apart to do it.

He was halfway across the crowded dance floor, a low rumbling growl slipping from deep in his chest, when he finally caught sight of Brandon standing with Kevin and two other people by one of the hallways. One was a kid maybe a year or two older than Brandon. The other was a guy in his midtwenties with a Hillside Riders tat inked across his neck. Kevin was gazing at the strobing lights on the opposite side of the dance floor with the glassy-eyed look of someone high as a kite while Brandon talked to the gangbanger. The older kid nodded his head eagerly at whatever they were saying.

Diego headed that way, fighting for control over his shift and his anger as he let his nose tell him everything he needed to know about the gangbanger and the situation. There was a bag of weed in the guy's left coat pocket, some kind of opioid in his pants pocket, and a gun tucked away under his coat.

What the hell was Brandon doing hanging out with the same kind of people who had gotten him shot not too long ago? After spending time with the kid and introducing him to the beta pack, Diego had been sure Brandon would leave these kinds of mistakes behind.

Apparently, he'd been wrong.

Brandon must have smelled him approaching because his head snapped up, his eyes scanning the crowd until they locked on his. For a second, Diego saw what he thought might be relief there before the anxious expression returned. Then Brandon's gaze flicked back and forth between the gangbanger and Diego, making him wonder what was going through the kid's head. Was he embarrassed Diego was there...or relieved?

Diego would have liked to deal with this carefully, but unfortunately, there wasn't time to be subtle. Factoring in how long it had taken to find the kid, it was likely they only had another two or three minutes before this place was locked down.

The moment he reached Brandon's side, he wrapped a hand around his arm. "We need to leave—now."

The gangbanger eyed him with a mix of amusement and contempt. "Who's this? Your daddy?"

Diego ignored the question, giving Brandon's arm a tug. They didn't get more than two steps before the gangbanger was in Diego's face, pushing his hand away from Brandon's arm, then putting a palm on Diego's chest and trying to shove him back. It didn't work, but it was still irritating as hell.

Diego wouldn't normally worry about making a scene, but he'd been hoping to avoid it in this case. Unfortunately, he didn't have time to play nice.

The gangbanger reached for the gun in his waistband, but Diego was faster. Getting a grip on the front of the guy's coat, he picked him up and slammed him back against the wall hard enough to make the guy's head bounce. Dropping him to the floor, Diego turned to grab Brandon, only to spin back around at a warning from his inner wolf. A big, burly guy with a gang tattoo came at him fast, right hand scrambling at his waist for a gun.

Diego closed the distance between him and the man, latching a hand around the guy's wrist before he could pull the gun. Diego squeezed, feeling bones crack beneath his grip as he wrapped his other hand around the gangbanger's thick neck and slammed him to the floor.

The sound of the impact was loud enough to be heard over the music, and from the corner of his eye, Diego saw that other people in the club had definitely noticed the scuffle. Diego ignored them and reached out for Brandon, who was staring at the two unconscious gang members like he'd never seen anything like it.

"If we're not out of here in the next thirty seconds, your life as you know it is over," Diego growled. "So, move!"

He nudged Brandon toward the exit with one hand, practically having to carry Kevin with the other. Thankfully, neither kid fought him as they pushed their way through the crowd staring at them curiously. The older kid they'd been with simply stood there and watched them go.

Dion was nowhere to be seen, and there wasn't a barricade of DPD patrol units outside when they shoved their way through the doors. Diego didn't slow down but kept urging Brandon to move fast until they reached his truck.

"Get in!" he ordered Brandon as he shoved a fumbling, mumbling Kevin in the back seat and strapped the seat belt on him.

Diego had just pulled out of the parking lot onto Harry Hines when cop cars started pouring in. He had no doubt his fellow police officers had the back exit of the club blocked before the cavalry got there. Eyes wide, Brandon turned and looked out the back window, probably figuring out exactly what he'd avoided.

Brandon didn't say anything as they drove across town. Neither did Diego. He didn't trust himself to speak without growling yet, so he clenched his jaw and stayed quiet. Kevin passed out and started snoring a few blocks later.

"Did he only smoke weed or was it something else?" Diego asked brusquely. "Did he snort anything? Take any pills? Do I need to worry about him having something in his system that will kill him?"

Brandon flinched at his tone, and for a second, Diego thought the kid wouldn't answer. Finally, he shook his head, lowering his gaze to stare at the floorboards. "Just weed... like me. I don't think it was that much since I'm not feeling it at all."

Diego breathed a sigh of relief. At least he didn't have to worry about Kevin overdosing. The kid had probably smoked marijuana with a high THC percentage. Well, higher than he was used to dealing with. Not that Diego was any happier knowing there'd been weed involved.

"Werewolves can't get high from most drugs," he said, trying to keep his voice as calm as he could. "So, while you weren't getting anything out of the experience, your best friend was getting blitzed to the point of passing out."

"Oh," Brandon said quietly.

Diego's chest tightened until it was tough to breathe, and it took every bit of his control to keep from reaching over and dragging his beta in for a hug and telling him it was all okay now. But he couldn't do that. Brandon had screwed up, and Diego needed to find a way to get through to the kid so it wouldn't happen again. As bad as tonight was, it could have been much worse.

"Where does your mother think you are right now?" he asked, figuring it would be best to come at this slowly.

Brandon opened and closed his mouth a few times before answering. "The movies," he finally said, his voice barely above a whisper.

"The movies." Diego snorted. "Well, I guess if the lie worked before, why bother coming up with another one? You mom is so desperate to trust you, I can see why she'd buy it again."

Brandon cringed. "Kevin and I really were going to see a movie, but then we ran into Wyatt and...well...he talked us into going with him. We ended up at the club."

Diego decided to skip over the question of how anyone had gotten two kids as young as Brandon and Kevin into a club like Blacklight in the first place. That wasn't important at the moment. "I'm assuming Wyatt was the other guy with you. The one who seemed so friendly with the gangbanger."

Brandon's head snapped up. "How did you know he was a gangbanger?"

"The neck tattoo," he said. "It's hard to miss someone affiliated with the Hillside Riders. Their tattoos are very distinctive."

Brandon seemed to consider that a moment. "Kevin and I didn't know he was taking us there to meet with someone from a gang. If we had, we wouldn't have gone with him."

"Then why did you go with him?"

Brandon let out a heavy sigh, slumping in the seat. "Wyatt just graduated from my school. He's so popular that girls practically climb over each other to get near him. We figured if people thought we were friends with him, they'd want to be friends with Kevin and me, too."

It didn't make Diego feel any better to discover high school hadn't changed much since his day. Kids would still do insanely stupid stuff to be with the in crowd. "And how exactly did Wyatt become so popular with the girls? Anything to do with the fact that he's in with the Riders?"

Brandon didn't say anything for a while. "Yeah. I guess he sort of has a reputation for being dangerous. In school, everyone knew if you were looking to score drugs, Wyatt was the person to talk to."

Diego shook his head. "And this is the guy you thought would help you get girls?"

"Not just girls!" Brandon protested, throwing a quick glance over his shoulder at Kevin still asleep in the back seat when his voice came out louder than he probably intended. "Any friends at all. Since it got out that my dad is a murderer, people have avoided me like internet malware. I might have friends in Jayna's beta pack now, but Kevin is still screwed. He stuck with me from the beginning, even when it cost him all his friends. When Wyatt started talking to the two of us, we went with it. I want Kevin to find friends like I've made."

If Diego hadn't been driving, he would have smacked his hand to his forehead and held it there until the desire to groan went away. Only a teenager could think that getting close to the local gangbanger wannabe was a good idea.

"Did you ever think of introducing Kevin to the betas in Jayna's pack instead?"

Brandon flushed. "No."

"Is Wyatt the same guy who took you to that convenience store where you ended up getting shot?"

"Yeah," Brandon mumbled. "We were supposed to go to somewhere cool, but then Elliott stopped at the store. He said he had to meet someone."

"Which is a nice way of saying he was stopping to buy drugs," Diego muttered, checking the rearview mirror to make sure Kevin was still sleeping.

"We didn't know he was buying drugs," Brandon explained, looking contrite. "We thought it was cool that a guy going to college in the fall was letting us hang out with him. Then the shooting started and he bailed, even when he saw that I'd been shot."

"Not much of a friend," Diego pointed out. "And yet he showed up at the movie theater tonight and you took off with him again."

Brandon stared down at the floor again. "He said he was sorry for bailing on us and that he wanted to make up for it by introducing us to a guy he knew."

Diego already knew how this part ended. He thought it possible he was developing a migraine, though werewolves didn't get headaches. "The guy from the Hillside Riders. Why would he want you and Kevin to meet a guy like that?"

The silence was much longer this time. When Brandon finally answered, his voice was so soft even Diego's werewolf-enhanced hearing had a hard time picking it up.

"At first the guy was really cool. He gave us some weed to smoke for free. But then he told us that Wyatt said we'd be willing to sell drugs at school. Since Wyatt graduated, they need someone new and they wanted Kevin and me."

Diego's fangs made an appearance then, as a surge of anger—and fear—rushed through him. Shit, this was worse than he'd feared. Brandon had been a hop, skip, and a jump from being a damn drug dealer for an effing gang.

"We wouldn't have done it," Brandon added quickly. "Kevin and I would never do something like that. I swear."

Thankfully, Diego could tell the kid was telling the truth. But while that definitely counted for something, it still wasn't enough. He had to make sure Brandon understood how stupid he'd been.

"The Hillside Riders are using the back offices and kitchen of the Blacklight as a place to make and package drugs," he said. "There were almost twenty gang members in there tonight, all of them armed and ready to kill to protect their drug trade. Do you have any idea what could have happened if a rival gang made an appearance tonight? Or if one of those gangbangers started shooting when the police raided the place?"

Brandon swallowed hard. "I could have been shot again," he said, the words barely distinguishable over the sound of the road rushing under the truck tires.

"Yeah, you could have." Diego didn't want to keep piling on, but he knew he had to. "And while you're a werewolf—and therefore hard to damage—you aren't indestructible. A bullet through the head or the heart and you're as dead as anyone else. That would suck for you, but how do you think your mom would handle that, huh? Think she'd be okay with losing her son because he was hoping to hang out with some people who'd make him popular?"

Brandon didn't say anything, and in the dim light, Diego could see tears starting to run down the kid's face. Diego wanted more than anything to pull over and yank the kid in for a hug. But he couldn't. Not yet.

"And what about Kevin?" he demanded. "You know, the best friend who stuck with you when everyone else bailed? What if he'd gotten shot the first time in the convenience store? What if I hadn't gotten there tonight in time to get you out before the raid and he'd gotten shot in the club trying to cover your ass again? You survived getting shot, but Kevin might not. How would his family feel if that happened? How would you feel?"

Brandon dropped his face into his hands and started to sob uncontrollably.

That was it. Diego couldn't take any more of this tough-love stuff. He was this close to breaking down in tears himself at seeing his beta hurting like this.

Easing over to the shoulder, Diego put the SUV in park, then undid both his seat belt and Brandon's and pulled him in for a hug.

"I'm so sorry," Brandon mumbled against Diego's shirt. "I don't mean to be such a fuckup."

"Shh. It's okay," Diego said, making calming sounds as he rubbed Brandon's back. Tears stung his eyes and he blinked them back. "You're not a fuckup. You're a teenager. You made mistakes and you're almost certainly going to make more in the future. But some mistakes you don't get a chance to come back from. I want you to really think about what you're doing before you make one of those mistakes and regret it for the rest of your life."

They sat there on the side of the road there for a while, talking about how overrated it was to be popular, how Wyatt was likely looking at a police record, which would probably get him kicked out of college, and how Brandon was going to do things differently when he and Kevin went back to school in the fall.

"No more worrying about being with the cool kids, right?" Brandon said, his tears finally dried and his face clear.

"Right," Diego said. "How about you worry about finding people who accept you and Kevin for who you are and make friends with them instead?"

Brandon nodded.

"Good," Diego said. "How about we get you home?"

Brandon was quiet as they drove toward the apartment, staring out the side window, lost in thought. After a few minutes, he looked at Diego. "You're going to tell my mom about all of this, aren't you?"

"No, I'm not," Diego said after a moment to think about it. "You are. I'll be right there with you while you do it, but part of doing what's right from now on starts with you stepping up and telling your mother everything."

Brandon didn't look happy but nodded in resignation.

CHAPTER 14

Bree figured she and Diego would go straight home after having dinner at the fancy French restaurant they went to, but instead he surprised her by taking her to a club with a full parking lot and Latin music drifting out of an upstairs balcony already packed with customers sitting at small tables.

"We're going dancing?" she asked, embarrassed when her voice almost came out in a squeak. "I love to dance! I haven't been in forever. I think the last time I danced was when I was in high school. You-know-who didn't like it. Said it made him look uncool."

She doubted looking uncool would ever be a problem for Diego. Something told her he was a very good dancer.

Diego chuckled as he opened her door. "Then I'm glad I took a chance and decided to come here. I kinda thought you might like it."

Once inside the beautiful entryway with its colorful walls, hardwood floors, and whirling ceiling fans, Bree started to get a little nervous. She hadn't been exaggerating when she said it had been a long time since she'd gone dancing.

The smiling, dark-haired hostess showed them to a table off to one side of the dance floor. While it was close enough to give them a great view, it was far enough away that she and Diego could talk without having to shout. As the server took their drink orders, Bree watched the couples on the dance floor moving and twirling to a hip-swirling beat that was already making her tap her toes. She recognized the dance, but wasn't sure she could replicate the smooth, confident steps.

"I've never salsa danced," she admitted when the server left. "I don't think I'll be able to move like them."

Diego smiled and reached across the table to take her hand, not bothering to glance at the couples dancing. Instead, he had eyes only for her. "Don't worry about it. I can teach you the steps. Just relax and let the rhythm take over."

Bree wasn't so sure about that, but she was willing to give it a shot. No way was she passing up the opportunity to dance with Diego.

Their drinks came as Diego was pointing out the basic steps, highlighting the foot placement and the sway of the dancers' hips. The more Bree watched, the more she was sure that an embarrassing face-plant was coming her way in the near future. Even though she loved to dance, she wasn't all that graceful at it.

"How's Brandon handling being grounded for the rest of the summer?" Diego asked, sipping his Jack and Coke, his attention once more focused on her.

She picked up her strawberry daiquiri and took a careful sip. The perfect balance between rum and fruit, it was cool and refreshing. She didn't often drink anything but wine and had no desire to make herself look any more foolish on the dance floor. "Better than I thought he would."

Bree had been shocked when Diego had walked into the apartment the night before with Brandon and Kevin trailing behind him a whole hour before she was supposed to pick them up at the movie theater. Then she'd almost lost her mind as Diego gave her a brief synopsis of the evening's events.

To say it had been a very long night was putting it mildly. Kevin's parents had come over and listened as Brandon and Kevin spilled every single detail of their involvement with Elliott Gillespie and his Hillside Rider gang contact. Diego hadn't said much, letting her son and his best friend answer all the questions. Bree was horrified—not to mention terrified—that Brandon had put himself in a position like that again. But there was some part of her that was proud he was standing up to all of it now.

She had no doubt Diego had played a huge part in that.

She and Diego, along with Kevin's parents, had sent the kids to Brandon's bedroom so they could talk in private. Diego filled them in on the details Brandon and Kevin hadn't known anything about, specifically the part about an undercover officer getting a call to him just in time. After that, they'd all talked about the best way to handle what the kids had done. Deciding it wouldn't do either Brandon or Kevin any good to forbid them to hang out since they were each other's only friends, they settled on grounding both kids until school started.

When Kevin and his parents had left, she and Diego had told Brandon he was grounded for the rest of the summer. He and Kevin could hang out at the apartment or at Kevin's home and play video games, but would only be allowed to go other places if she, Diego, or Kevin's mother or father were with them. Brandon must have realized he was getting off easy because he didn't try to argue.

"I think it helped that we presented a united front last night," she said, giving thanks for what had to be the fiftieth time she had Diego to help her with Brandon. "There's no doubt in my mind that the maturity he's displaying right now has a lot to do with you being in our lives. He knows how important you are to me. And I think you're just as important to him."

It was impossible to miss the effect her words had on Diego as his eyes blazed vivid yellow-gold and his fingers moved across the table to intertwine with hers. For a moment, she thought dancing might be off the agenda for the night, although she certainly wouldn't have minded if he wanted to go home and spend some quality time in bed. Or anywhere else, for that matter.

Diego took a deep breath, the glow fading from his eyes as he visibly fought to get himself under control. She'd be lying if she said she wasn't a little disappointed.

"So," he said slowly, and Bree felt a moment of glee knowing her words had discombobulated him so badly. Big bad SWAT werewolf tripped up by a little romance. "How's your investigation going? Any progress in figuring out how Dave's investment firm is involved in those robberies?"

She didn't think about keeping the newer details of her case from him. As soon as she had the complete picture of Ken's involvement in the case, it would all be getting turned over to the cops anyway. She wouldn't mention her little meeting in Dave's office, though. She had no doubt Diego would be upset if he found out she'd been alone with her psychotic ex-husband. The part about Dave taking his anger out on an innocent paperweight and dripping blood would have Diego sprouting fangs and claws right here in the middle of the club.

"I did find the link between the robberies and Dave's investment firm, though I'm not quite sure what it means yet," she said. "It turns out the connection is Ken Reed."

Diego frowned. "As in the Ken Reed from the diner who took you hostage, then shot himself?"

She shrugged. "Yeah, that one. Don't ask for the details because I don't have them yet. All I know for sure is that he was the investment advisor for every one of the victims in my robbery cases, along with some that aren't mine."

"What do you mean, some that aren't yours?"

"Until today, I'd been working on the assumption there were four robberies and that the victims were all LMG clients." Thank goodness for Jerri at Garrett, Wallace, and Banks. Bree wouldn't have learned anything if it wasn't for the other woman. "But on a hunch, I got someone at the firm to give me the full list of Ken's clients. I showed that around to some other insurance investigators I know, and it turns out there've been three other robberies with very similar MOs. That means in the past month or so, there have been seven high-end home burglaries with a total insured value of over forty million dollars."

Diego let out a low whistle. "Have there been any robberies since Ken shot himself?"

"None that I know of," she said. "Which reinforces the idea he was working alone, as difficult as that is to believe. I'm hoping once I do some more digging, I might be able to figure out where he hid the stuff he stole. If not, there's going to be a lot of insurance money getting paid out."

Bree didn't mention that doing more digging involved getting into Ken's apartment to look around. Diego might frown on that, especially if she had to pick the lock to get in.

"Speaking of cases, have you figured out anything new about delirium yet?" she asked. "Did you ever get a chance to do any poking around?"

Diego sipped his drink. "Yeah. I followed your advice and did a little digging myself. But we're not quite sure what to make of what we discovered."

"Maybe I can help."

He leaned forward, resting his forearms on the table. "It looks like this delirium thing started in Coffield Unit state prison with a scientist type who was an inmate there. It gets confusing after that, but the bottom line is that Ernest Hobbs might be involved as well."

"The reporter?"

Diego nodded. "He was at the prison looking into another inmate around the time the delirium attacks started in Dallas."

Bree blinked. This was big. "I'd like to say I'm stunned a reporter would sit on information like this, but even though I've only met Hobbs once, I think I can safely say this seems right on track for him."

"No kidding." Diego snorted. "He probably saw this story as a way to make himself famous and decided to sit on the information until the right time. Trey and I spent a good portion of the day trying to track him down with no luck."

Bree was more than ready to talk some more about Diego's case and help him come up with a plan to find Hobbs sooner rather than later, but he shook his head with a laugh, then took her hand and gently tugged her up from her chair.

"I know exactly what you're doing," he said, leading her onto the dance floor. "You think if we keep talking about Hobbs, delirium, and people stealing stuff, I'll forget we came here to dance and you can avoid getting out there and embarrassing yourself."

Bree laughed. Honestly, she had been delaying this part for as long as possible. "Okay, okay. But let's go slow or I won't be held responsible for stepping on your toes."

In the end, it wasn't nearly as bad as she'd thought it would be. They kept to the side of the dance floor at first, Diego walking her through the steps and keeping it simple until she found the rhythm of the moves. The basic salsa was a lot like other four-step dances she vaguely remembered, and within minutes, Diego had her out on the main part of the floor with everyone else, swinging and twirling without thinking about it.

It was easy to lose herself in the dance, her hands on Diego, their bodies occasionally coming together to slide against each other, his mouth finding hers at the perfect moments. She thought it would take all her attention to stay in step, but she quickly found she barely thought about the pattern of the dance at all.

She was definitely thinking about Diego, though. Like how warm his skin was where they touched. The taste of his lips when they kissed. The heat swirling deep inside her as she thought about where the evening might end.

Bree was so entranced with the way his eyes were glowing she didn't realize something was wrong until Diego stiffened and suddenly pulled her to one side so quickly she nearly yelped in surprise. Just as she opened her mouth to ask what was wrong, a large body went flying past them, fist swinging in Diego's direction. The attacker missed by a mile and went stumbling across the floor, aided by a well-placed shove from Diego. People scrambled and yelled in complaint as the man flipped over several times and came to a hard stop up against a set of speakers as tall as she was.

Bree knew it was her ex before the idiot got himself pushed upright and back on his feet. Stupid could be identified from any angle.

Dave spun around after getting his feet under him. The fall had busted open his lip, and he stood there glowering at her and Diego as he wiped the blood off with his hand. Standing there with blood running down his chin, eyes wide, skin flushed, and breath coming in ragged gasps, he seemed unhinged.

"What the hell are you doing with him?" Dave demanded, pinning her with a glare.

The music was still playing, but no one was dancing. Instead, everyone had moved to give them space, all the while staring at her nutjob of an ex looking to start a fight he couldn't win.

"I'm dancing with him," Bree said as calmly as she could. "That's what people do at a club. They don't attack people like a psycho."

Dave's eyes narrowed. "He stole you and Brandon from me."

She opened her mouth to set him straight about that, but Dave was already rushing them, bloody hand reaching for Diego, madness in his eyes. He'd had that same look the night he beat that man to death all those years ago.

Diego moved to intercept Dave and got a hand on Dave's outstretched arm, spinning her ex around and tossing him across the dance floor until he thudded to a stop against the speakers again.

The music ground to a stop as Dave once more scrambled to his feet, face suffused with so much anger Bree thought he might explode. Then again, he'd just gotten tossed around like a dog's chew toy and gotten embarrassed in front of all these people. Dave's pride was one of his biggest faults.

"You should probably stop," Diego said, the hint of a growl in his deep voice. "There's no version of reality that exists where you'll get your hands on Bree, Brandon, or me ever again."

Bree held her breath, waiting for Dave to try anyway, right there in front of everyone. For a moment, it looked like he was about to, but then a dark-haired man in a dress shirt and slacks hurried onto the dance floor.

"I called the cops," he warned, looking first at Diego, then at Dave. "They're already on their way."

Dave looked at the man for a moment, then stared daggers at Diego. "I will fucking destroy you for this."

Turning, he strode toward the door and stormed out of the club.

Diego started to move after him, but Bree caught his arm. "Let him go. I want him out of our lives."

She could tell from the set of Diego's jaw that he didn't agree with her, and part of her wondered if it would be better to let the cops arrest Dave and send him to prison again. But she hadn't been kidding. She wanted the drama to end. And it never would if she kept pulling Dave back into her life.

"I didn't actually call the cops," the guy from the club said to them. "But I will now if you want me to. I have video footage of everything that happened and have no problem turning it over to them."

Diego looked at her questioningly, but Bree shook her head. Sighing, he turned to the guy, pulling his badge from his pocket and flashing it. "No, don't call them. But if you could hold onto that video footage for a while, I'd appreciate it."

The man nodded. "You got it."

The music started up again and people slowly moved back out onto the floor, though Bree doubted the energy level in the club would be the same as it had been. Not for a while.

"You want to dance some more?" Diego asked.

From the way he said it, she could tell his heart really wasn't in it, but she knew he'd stay and dance if that was what she wanted. It wasn't.

"No, let's go home," she said, taking his hand. "Brandon will be at Kevin's house for a few more hours, and I don't want the date to end yet."

"You know you should get a restraining order against him," Diego said as they walked into her apartment. "At the very least."

Bree leaned in far enough to see the kitchen counter and the dining room table. Nothing was lying on either one, which meant neither Brandon nor Beth were home yet. They both constantly left their stuff around on the first available flat surface they found. She was glad they weren't there. She didn't want either of them hearing this conversation about Dave. If Bree had her way, neither of them would ever have to hear that man's name again, much less see him.

"I know." Dropping her purse on the couch, she flopped down on the soft cushions with a sigh. "Any chance you know the right people I need to talk to? Maybe I can go see them tomorrow in between working my case."

"Yeah, I know some people at the courthouse," he said as he joined her on the couch. "I can call them and get them a copy of that video from tonight, too. That, along with describing his behavior over the past week or so should be all you need."

Bree hoped it was as simple as he made it sound. She didn't want to waste any more of her life on her asshole of an ex than she had to. "Would you like something to drink?"

"I'm not really thirsty," he murmured, gently pulling her on his lap and kissing her. "At least not for a drink anyway."

Bree laughed, lifting her hand to run her fingers through his hair. "I loved dancing with you tonight," she said softly as he tipped her head back and traced warm, tingling kisses down her exposed throat. "I hope we can go again sometime."

"Anytime you want."

His teeth grazed against the skin right at the junction of her neck and shoulder. She wasn't sure, but it seemed possible his fangs were a bit extended, judging from how sharp they felt. The sensation sent a tingle of excitement through her core, warming her up all over. *Wow*. When did she start liking the whole biting thing?

They continued making out like a couple of teenagers until Bree remembered Brandon would be home soon. For all she knew, Beth could walk in any second. She'd rather neither of them see her sitting on Diego's lap. Brandon would probably blush so hard he'd pass out, and Beth would rag her for the rest of her life.

Best to avoid the whole thing and move this session somewhere else.

Breaking the kiss, she slowly slid off Diego's lap and stood, reaching out for his hand. "Would it be okay if we take this to the bedroom?"

"I'd love to take this to the bedroom, but…" he said slowly as he stood to join her, hand in hers. "Brandon will be home soon."

"I know." She stepped closer, resting her other hand on his chest as she gazed up at him. "Brandon understands we're together. In fact, this morning he asked why he doesn't see you around here more often. If you're comfortable with it, I'd like you to spend the night. That way, we can all have breakfast together."

Bree held her breath as he thought about it, praying he said yes. She had no idea why it was so important to her, but something inside her told her Diego was the man she was supposed to be with. The thought of going slowly and taking her time made her feel like she might burst into flames.

He brushed her hair back from her face. "Are you sure about this? I don't want you jumping into this because of what happened tonight with Dave. If you're worried he'll chase me away, you don't need to be. I can promise you, I'm not going anywhere."

For some crazy reason, tears stung her eyes and she wrapped her arms around Diego, pressing her cheek to his chest so he wouldn't see.

"Thank you for saying that, but Dave has nothing to do with my decision to ask you to stay," she said softly, pulling back to look at him. "When I met Dave, there was a part of me that knew I wasn't in love with him, but for some reason, I sat back and let it all happen anyway. The marriage, moving out here to Texas, having a kid so young. I can't honestly regret the things that brought Brandon into my life, but I do regret not making my own decisions. With you it's different," she added when it was obvious he had no idea where this was going. "With you, I know everything is real. I don't have to be afraid it's some crazy situation I have no control over. You're what I want—in my life and in my bed. Now, it's a matter of whether you want that, too."

Diego didn't say a word. Instead, he took her hand, leading her down the hallway toward her bedroom. Nothing she'd ever done had felt so right.

CHAPTER 15

"DID I HEAR YOU TALKING TO SOMEONE ON THE PHONE about a restraining order?" Hale asked as he reached around Diego and Trey to push the button for the sixth floor of the *Dallas Daily Star* building.

Diego threw a look over his shoulder at his pack mate. "Yeah. I was talking to an ADA I know at the courthouse to see if she could help push through the paperwork. Bree and I went to a club last night, and that asshole ex of hers attacked us on the dance floor. He was deranged, ranting and raving about how I'd stolen Bree and Brandon away from him. I wanted the idiot arrested, but a restraining order was the most Bree would agree to."

"Is Bree okay?" Trey asked as the elevator started up. "You could have stayed home with her instead of coming with us on the next leg of the Ernest Hobbs wild-goose chase. You know that, right?"

Diego nodded. A part of him had wanted to do exactly that. Not because Bree was traumatized or anything, but simply so he could spend the day with her and Brandon in case Dave showed up. "She's fine. I stayed at her place last night, and we talked for a long time. As much as he hates me, she doesn't think Dave will try to hurt her or Brandon. I'm not sure I agree, but she insisted on going to work. Her sister is working from home today so she's with Brandon."

The elevator came to a stop, and the doors opened onto the *Dallas Daily Star*'s bullpen, a bunch of cubicles that reminded him of a rat's maze, with people running everywhere and the noise level only slightly below bedlam. They'd been here twice yesterday to talk to Hobbs, but he'd been out of the office. Gage's wife, Mackenzie, who was also a reporter for the *Star* had called them that morning and said Hobbs was in today, though she had no idea how long he'd be hanging around.

Mackenzie must have been waiting for them because she met them the moment they stepped off the elevator. Tall and slender with long, dark hair and blue eyes, she tried to look casual as she filled them in on where Hobbs's desk was.

"Hobbs was still at his desk a few minutes ago, and I haven't seen him leave, so let's hope he didn't take off."

Diego thanked her as she headed off in the opposite direction, reading something on the cell phone in her hand.

"You and Bree spent the night together?" Hale asked, picking up their earlier conversation where they'd left off.

Diego sighed in frustration. Out of everything he'd told his pack mates, the part about spending the night was the only thing Hale had picked up on?

"Sounds like things are going well with the relationship," Trey remarked, sounding like a talk-show host halfway between Doctor Phil and Jerry Springer. "Dinner and a movie, then a hit-it-and-quit-it booty call, now a stay-over."

Diego didn't know if he'd describe the first time he and Bree made love as a hit-it-and-quit-it booty call, but he didn't correct his pack mate because he was too busy picking up Hobbs's scent to see if the man was still there. He was.

A few people looked their way curiously as he and his teammates headed around the outside of the cubicles, but no one paid much attention since they seemed to know where they were going.

"Things are going well," Diego admitted, glancing at Trey. "And for the record, don't use slang like that in front of me. You sound like my stepfather trying to be cool. It's creepy."

Hale chuckled before peeling off and heading down a center aisle through the maze so he could cut off Hobbs if the reporter tried to make a run for it. Hale's nose might be crap, but he made up for it with his other senses.

Trey ignored the jab about sounding like an uncool old man. "Since things are going well, that means you talked to her about *The One*, right?"

Damn, the guy was like a broken record.

"No, we haven't talked about her being *The One* for me," Diego ground out, his nose telling him to take a left and almost running Trey into a cubicle wall.

"Why not?" Trey asked, waving an apology to the cubicle gopher who popped his head up at the noise. "Is it because you don't think she's *The One* for you?"

Diego shook his head. "She's definitely *The One*, I'm sure of it."

Trey frowned, eyeing Diego like he'd grown two heads and a beak. "You're not making any sense. If she's *The One*, talking about it should be easy."

"Unfortunately, it isn't easy because Bree has this thing about free will."

Trey looked more baffled. "Okay, now I'm really confused."

"Bree married Dave right out of high school," Diego explained. "Or more precisely, she let him and her family talk her into marrying him. Then she let him talk her into moving away from family and having a kid before she was ready. Other than Brandon—which is the one thing she wouldn't go back and change—she has a whole laundry list of regrets and has vowed to be the one in charge of her life from this point forward."

"Okay. I suppose I understand," Trey said, though he looked like he was still perplexed as hell. "Actually, no I don't. What the hell do her previous bad choices about Dave have to do with her being *The One* for you?"

Diego let out a heavy sigh as two women poked their heads around the edges of their cubicles with blatant curiosity. It was difficult to keep from growling at them.

"How do you think Bree will see the soul-mate connection?" he asked Trey, moving farther along the line of cubicles and away from the nosy people. "Will she think it's this wonderful confirmation of what she already knows or as the hand of fate stepping in and making decisions for her?"

A light came on in Trey's eyes as understanding filled them. "Well, crap. That complicates things more than a little. What the hell are you going to do?"

Diego shrugged, sniffing the air and determining Hobbs's scent was still stuck in the same place. "I'm going to keep seeing her as if we're two normal people with no special bond to worry about or discuss. I fall in love with her and she falls in love with me. No big deal."

Trey seemed to think about that for a second or two before shaking his head. "I got to tell you, that has to be the dumbest plan I've ever heard of. I mean, that's in the category of jumping off a building with an umbrella because you think Mary Poppins can really fly."

Diego ignored him and homed in on the scent of the man they'd come here to find.

"Seriously, Big D," Trey continued, trailing behind him. "You have to know this is going to blow up in your face. Someone in the Pack is going to end up mentioning the legend. Hell, all anyone ever seems to talk about is catching bad guys and finding *The One*. Bree is going to be pissed when she finds out you've been keeping this from her. Worse, she might end up thinking you don't believe she's your soul mate. That would be bad. As in bad... bad...bad."

Diego didn't want to entertain the possibility of that happening. Neither did his inner wolf, who was nervously pacing back and forth. "Don't you think I know that? But until I come up with something better, that's the plan I'm going with."

They were close enough to Hobbs's scent by then to hear him slip out of his cubbyhole. The fact that his head was barely visible over the walls could only mean he was moving around in a crouch. Obviously, he'd heard them coming.

Trey peeled off to the left while Diego continued to follow Hobbs's track as he scurried away. It was almost fun following him, even if the chase didn't last very long.

The thud as Hobbs bounced off one of his pack mates up ahead was loud enough for Diego to hear, and he rounded a few more cubicles to find Hobbs getting to his feet while he glared up at Hale and Trey.

"Hobbs." Diego smiled. "Just the man we've been looking for. You have a minute to talk?"

The reporter turned that glower on him. "Afraid not. I have a story I need to track down."

"Funny how that works," Trey murmured. "We have a

story to track down, too. About a *Dallas Daily Star* reporter actively involved in the delirium attacks and covering up information so he can get a good story."

That must have gotten Hobbs's attention because his entire demeanor changed. He drew himself up, running his hand nervously down the front of his loosened tie and looking around. "Not here. Let's go to the conference room."

Hobbs led the way to a corner room, walking in front of them like he was heading to his own execution. Once inside the room, he immediately shut the door and closed all the blinds, then gestured to the rectangular conference table.

"How'd you figure it out?" Hobbs asked as he sat down at the head of the table. "And why are you guys here and not cops from the delirium task force?"

"We went down to Coffield and talked to a few people," Diego said, willing to answer the first question. "They remember you going down there because you were very interested in Dave Cowell. You spent hours watching security footage and left with some of that footage in your possession. Footage you got from an IT support-staff guy without the warden's knowledge."

Hobbs didn't say anything, his heart beating fast as he tried to figure out how badly he was screwed. Diego didn't let him wait long to find out.

"We're ready to assume you're sitting on certain facts hoping to break a big story. The alternative is that you're working with Cowell, helping him rob banks and jewelry stores and pocketing your share." Diego shrugged. "You get to decide which way this goes from here."

Ernest looked around the table, regarding each of them. "I'm not involved in any of this, but I'm willing to tell you everything I know. In return, I want exclusive rights to this story when everything hits the fan."

Diego snorted. Hobbs was definitely living down to the very low opinion he had of the man. The guy would sell his mother for a story. "If we decide you did nothing worthy of putting you in jail—and we get first edit on your article—we don't have a problem with letting you write the story. But if you lie to us—"

"Deal," Hobbs said, obviously not needing to hear the rest of the threat. "But I have to tell you up front, there's a part of what I'm about to tell you that might be difficult to believe. It's a little out there."

"Try us," Hale said. "We do okay with weird."

Hobbs sat there a moment looking down at the table, like he was trying to collect his thoughts. "I'd heard around the courthouse that a guy convicted of manslaughter with a shitty prison record had walked out of Coffield a free man halfway into his sentence. My gut told me there was a story there, so I did some digging."

"The security video footage was from the laundry area where Dave's cellmate died," Diego interrupted, not interested in the long version of this story. "What was on it?"

"I saw Cowell lead Bremen into an alcove, like he knew the camera wouldn't be able to get a clear shot of him, then there was a struggle."

"If you couldn't see them, how did you know there was a struggle?" Trey prompted from beside Diego.

"I could just make out Bremen's feet peeking out from the alcove. They were bouncing and jerking like someone was beating on him. Thirty seconds later, Cowell walked out. He had blood running down his chin, and he was chewing on something."

Diego exchanged looks with his pack mates to see they seemed as confused as he was. He turned back to Hobbs. "What do you think Dave was eating?"

Hobbs made a face. "Isn't it obvious? Cowell was eating a chunk of his cellmate."

Diego did a double take. From the corner of his eye, he caught Trey and Hale looking at each other in surprise. One of the correctional officers from Coffield had mentioned something about bite marks on Bremen's body, but seriously?

"You're telling us Dave Cowell ate human flesh so he could corner the market on the delirium drug Bremen created?" Diego asked.

Crap, he couldn't believe he was saying this out loud.

Hobbs stared at him, like Diego had caught him off guard. After a moment, he shrugged. "I told you it was bizarre. It gets even stranger."

"We're listening," Hale said.

Hobbs sat back in his seat. "Delirium isn't a drug at all."

Diego's eyes narrowed. Another of his assumptions kicked to the curb. "What is it then?"

"I don't know what it is," Hobbs said. "But after seeing the video, I started following Cowell. I saw him walk up to a guy standing beside his BMW, talking on his phone. Cowell bit his own finger hard enough to make it bleed, then wiped the blood on the guy's arm. One second, the guy is on his phone, the next he's handing Cowell his wallet, Rolex, and car keys. He freaking stood there and watched Cowell drive away in his BMW."

Hale frowned. "Did he call the cops?"

Hobbs shook his head. "Nope. He stood there on the curb for an hour, staring into space."

Diego would have called BS if his inner werewolf wasn't so sure Hobbs was telling the absolute truth. Now that he thought about it, this explained why those college kids and the construction workers had acted differently after encountering Dave. It seemed too impossible to be real, but it made some kind of weird sense.

"I watched Cowell do the same thing multiple times over the next few days. He'd wipe his blood on them, then take control of them." Hobbs shook his head, as if he couldn't believe it himself. "But then I was stupid enough to get too close so I could hear what he was saying to one of his victims and he caught me. I thought he was going to murder me on the spot, but instead he said he'd let me go if I came up with a story for the paper so people wouldn't figure out the truth. That's when I came up with the delirium drug thing."

"All he wanted out of you was a cover story?" Trey asked. "Why didn't you go to the cops the moment he let you go?"

"Because he said he'd make me throw myself off the top of the Bank of America Plaza and I believed him," Hobbs said. "Besides, the story is giving me the best exposure I've had in my whole career. He lets me know when some of the robberies are going down so I can make sure to be on the scene before anyone else. Why would I kill the Golden Goose?"

Diego would have pointed out that people dying was a pretty good reason to tell the cops, but he knew that fact would probably mean little to a man like Hobbs.

"I'm still getting an exclusive out of this when you guys catch Cowell, right?" Hobbs asked, looking at each of them in turn.

Diego resisted the urge to bare his fangs in a snarl. "We already said you would."

That must have been good enough for Hobbs because he leaned forward, forearms on the table, face eager. "I'm not sure of the details, but Cowell mentioned a huge job he was doing that would set him up for life. We're talking millions."

"Did he say what it was?" Trey asked.

"No. And I had to be careful about pressing him too much. The guy's kind of a loose cannon."

Tell me about it, Diego thought.

He was still wondering where the hell a person could steal millions of dollars when Hobbs looked at him, a serious expression on his face.

"There's one other thing you should probably know. Cowell is obsessed with getting his wife and kid back. It's all the whack job ever talks about. Whenever he gets these millions he says he's going to steal, he plans to leave the country with both of them."

Bree glanced over her shoulder one more time before carefully pulling the crime-scene tape off the door, then turning her attention to the expensive-looking lock by slipping in a tension wrench and a medium-sized hook pick. As she felt her way through the tumblers, she wondered what Diego would think of this particular skill set she possessed. Something told her he wouldn't approve, which was why it wasn't a talent she'd be sharing with him anytime soon.

It wasn't like Bree was a master lock-picker, but she wasn't shabby at it, either, and a few seconds later, the door of Ken Reed's apartment swung open. She quickly ducked inside so she wasn't exposed in the hallway any longer than necessary, then repositioned the crime tape and quietly closed the door.

The first thought that entered her mind when she turned around was that investment advising obviously paid very well. The next was that Ken would probably have gladly given all this up to have his life back.

Leather, granite, and stainless steel were prevalent throughout the spacious and modern penthouse apartment. But it was also somewhat cold and impersonal, the walls decorated with pieces of art that had almost certainly been picked out by someone paid to accomplish the task. There wasn't a single family photo that Bree could see from where she stood, and that seemed kind of sad.

Shaking off those depressing thoughts, she ignored the huge living room and chef's kitchen, making her way toward the back of the apartment where she assumed Ken's bedroom was.

The master bedroom was the first door on the left. It was obvious from the moment she stepped inside that the police had spent a good amount of time searching this room. The California king mattress was slightly askew, the silky comforter bunched up, drawers of the nightstands and dressers left ajar, and clothes hanging haphazardly in the walk-in closet.

Bree walked over to the closest nightstand and opened the drawer. She expected to find the usual stuff—mainly porn, condoms, and lube—but instead it was filled with notebooks.

O-kay.

She skimmed through each notebook and saw that they were filled with potential investment opportunities Ken had interest in. Apparently, he liked to write everything down before going to sleep. Either that or he woke up in the middle of the night from his dreams of making millions and couldn't go back to sleep until he wrote them down.

Despite the fact that she was essentially trespassing on a crime scene, Bree found her mind wandering until it ended up right back in her own bedroom that morning. Waking up beside Diego had been incredible.

When she was with Diego and wrapped in his arms, it was like everything was perfect in her world. Which was obviously insane because right now, her world was actually a complicated mess complete with unsolved cases, a psychotic ex-husband, and a teenage son who'd recently turned into a werewolf and was hanging out with gangbangers. Still, with Diego at her side, it seemed like none of those obstacles were too much to overcome. They had instinctively presented a united front when grounding Brandon the other night, becoming a team where each of them made the other stronger. She wasn't sure when or how it had happened, but she *felt* the connection between them, and she could work with that.

Brandon and Beth had both been having breakfast by the time she and Diego finally made it out to the kitchen. She'd expected it to be a little awkward since it was the first time Diego had slept over, but her sister had acted like it wasn't a big deal at all, and Brandon had been thrilled to see him there.

It was all enough to make Bree start thinking about how great it would be when Diego was in her bed every night and eating every breakfast as a family became a permanent thing. And yeah, thinking about them all as a family made her heart do a cartwheel.

Still smiling, she searched the other nightstand, dressers, and walk-in closet, but didn't find anything interesting. She wondered if the police would have noticed any evidence concerning Ken's involvement in the burglaries even if they'd stumbled across it. She doubted it. The cops had almost certainly been there looking for evidence connecting Ken to the delirium drug. Or at least something that would explain why he'd targeted those officers in the diner, then shot himself. Maybe a suicide note. If they saw something about rich people and high-end valuables, they most likely wouldn't pay attention to it.

Bree assumed the room across the hall was a guest bedroom and held out little hope of finding anything there, but when she opened the door and saw the sleek desk and shelves lining the walls, she realized Ken had turned the space into an office. Maybe she might find something after all.

The computer to one side of her desk caught her attention right away, but when she booted it up, the first thing she saw was the blinking cursor waiting for a password. Not that she hadn't expected to see it. Everybody had their computers password protected these days. But it was still a pain.

Bree started searching through the desk, keeping an eye out for a password list at the same time she looked for anything else that might be interesting. Mostly, it was more of the same stuff she'd seen in the bedroom nightstands: notepads and individual pages covered with investment strategies for different clients, potential foreign investments, hedge-fund options, tax-saving schemes. She was starting to think that not only was Ken anal retentive when it came to writing everything down, but he'd lived and breathed for his job and his clients. Which made it hard to understand why he'd suddenly start stealing from them.

She was seconds away from giving up hope of finding anything to connect him to the thefts when she found the spiral notebook buried among the stuff filling the inbox atop the right side of the desk. Picking it up, she flipped through it. Most of the pages were empty, but when she got to one with a list of Ken's clients, she stopped cold. Four names were circled in red and three others in blue, and there were dates beside each name. Holy crud, these were the seven people who'd been robbed. This was Ken's hit list, his plan on who he was going to rob and when.

Bingo!

She flipped to the next page and saw detailed descriptions of the valuables belonging to each person and exactly what had been stolen. There were comments on the various security systems in place at each residence and how difficult it would be to circumvent them, along with notes that a thief would need to have certain passwords and combinations to get through some of the systems.

Thank God Ken had an obsessive habit of writing everything down. This was as good as a confession. Not that the man would ever end up in jail, but she had no doubt she'd find details on where he'd hidden the fortunes he'd stolen. Because a man like Ken would definitely write it down.

But the words on the next page of the notebook stopped her celebration. The page was almost entirely blank, except for one urgently written sentence he'd underlined.

SOMEONE IS SETTING ME UP!!!

She stared at the words for a long time before slowly flipping to the next page. It was a list of people who had complete and open access to Ken's client list, including the private information that would have been protected. The list was relatively short—the three partners within the firm, two people from the firm's IT department, one from the legal branch that handled documentation to the government, three people from the admin section, and all alone at the bottom of the page, another name Bree was intimately familiar with.

DAVE COWELL.

Circled and underlined.

She flipped back to the beginning of the notebook, reading it again with fresh eyes. It hadn't been apparent the first time through, but now she saw it. It was all in the word choice, the way events had been laid out in factual past tense. Ken hadn't been writing down the details of the clients he planned to steal from. It was the details of his clients who'd already been robbed. Ken wasn't confessing. He was investigating. Just like she was. Except he was investigating because he was sure someone was trying to make it look like he'd done the crimes.

And Bree's instincts were telling her his investigation had ended with him walking into a diner during rush hour and ultimately shooting himself in the head.

She frowned as she read the part where Ken came to the painful conclusion that Dave was behind the thefts. When the firm hired Dave, Ken had shown him his list of clients so Dave could quickly get up to speed on how things worked at Garrett, Wallace, and Banks. Ken had tried to help him, and Dave had used him. Her ex-husband had stolen millions in jewelry, art, and collectibles, knowing the cops would track it back to the person managing those clients.

She flipped the pages faster and faster as Ken outlined how he'd started following Dave every time he'd left the office. Ken listed every place Dave went, including dates and times, with comments on who he talked to and what happened. Ken wrote that he assumed one of these outings would lead him to wherever Dave was hiding the stolen goods, or maybe the buyer he was planning to sell the stuff to. Instead, Ken noted a bizarre meeting with a man who willingly gave Dave his car and another in an alley where a woman gave Dave a backpack full of jewelry. Ken was sure they were the items stolen from Garth and Vera Williamson.

But it was Ken's description of the nights Dave spent sitting in his car outside her apartment building that made her cringe. Dave had been stalking her for weeks. Thank God she'd gotten the restraining-order paperwork done before coming here.

With a shudder, she read through several more pages of agonizing details relating to what Dave ate for lunch and who he slept with before finding a whole page dedicated to a meeting Ken was sure would be with either a fence or an accomplice. But instead of sitting down to talk with someone who fit the criminal stereotype, Dave had met with someone with a very familiar face—Ernest Hobbs.

Sure she'd read wrong, Bree backed up and started again, only to figure out she'd been right the first time. Dave had met with the reporter from the *Dallas Daily Star* to talk about stealing stuff. This wasn't a guess on Ken's part, either. He'd actually been brave enough to move closer and overheard Hobbs giving advice about which bank Dave should hit next.

Bree's head was spinning by the time she read the last

page of notes, as Ken described following the reporter across town to a self-storage unit near the farmers market before coming home to finish writing up all his notes about what he'd seen. The man's last line in the book said he'd planned to take everything he'd collected to the police the next morning. Based on the date Ken had written at the top of the page, that next morning was the same day he'd taken her, Brandon, and everyone else hostage at the diner, then committed suicide.

Getting to her feet, Bree left the room and headed for the door, taking the notebook with her. This was so much bigger than she'd thought. Dave and this damn reporter weren't merely involved in robberies. She didn't know how, but something told her they were responsible for Ken's death, too.

She dug her phone out of her purse, fumbling to enter her pass code as she reached for the doorknob. She needed to tell Diego about this. Now.

Bree was so focused on her phone she didn't see someone standing on the other side of the crime-scene tape until she bumped into them hard enough to bounce off. She opened her mouth to lie about what she'd been doing inside Ken's apartment only to gasp.

"Oh crap," was all she had time to say before a hand reached out and grabbed her.

CHAPTER 16

"SHE'S STILL NOT ANSWERING HER DAMN PHONE," DIEGO growled as Hale took a sharp right turn, sliding the SWAT SUV into the parking lot of Bree's apartment building and slamming on the brake in time to keep them from running up onto the sidewalk in front of the building.

The truck barely came to a stop before Diego jumped out and ran for the entrance. The drive over had taken forever, even with lights flashing and siren blaring. Or at least it had seemed that way as he'd desperately tried to reach his soul mate on the phone. But the call to her office got him a secretary who said Bree was out on an investigation and every call to her apartment and cell went straight to message.

While he'd sat there panicking, Trey had been talking to first Gage, then Samantha Mills, telling them everything Hobbs had said. The ME had handled the news that Dave's blood was to blame for the delirium effect surprisingly well for a medical professional, asking intelligent questions without coming out and saying they were lunatics. Diego couldn't blame her. He was a frigging werewolf who'd fought vampires not too long ago, and he was still having a hard time accepting Dave could turn people into puppets simply by wiping his blood on them.

"Diego, you need to stay cool!" Hale shouted at him as he charged up the stairs ahead of his pack mates, taking the steps three and four at a time. "We don't have a clue what we're walking into."

Easy for you to say, Diego thought as he fought to keep

his fangs and claws from extending. *It's not your soul mate and beta at risk.*

The mere notion of Bree or Brandon being hurt was almost enough to send his inner wolf spiraling out of control.

He reached the fourth floor and raced for Bree's apartment. He could pick up her scent, even out here in the hallway, but because she lived in the building, it was hard to tell yet whether it was an older scent or if she was currently in her apartment.

Diego slowed to let Trey and Hale catch up, then took a step back, ready to kick the door of her apartment right out of the frame. That was when he realized it was already slightly ajar. His heart dropped into his stomach. He threw a quick look at his pack mates before slowly pushing the door open, his fangs extending as he picked up a trace scent of blood. The only thing that kept him from losing it was the knowledge that the blood didn't belong to Bree or Brandon. He only prayed it wasn't Beth's, either.

He cautiously moved into the living room, SIG drawn and ready as he surveyed the apartment. His nose confirmed neither Bree nor Brandon were there when someone hurtled out of the hallway from the direction of the bedrooms. There was a flash of silver that could have been a weapon and an angry screech; then the person was on him.

He cursed, this close to squeezing the trigger before he realized it was Bree's sister. He barely got his arm up in time to protect himself, relieved despite the pain when the butcher knife plunged into his right forearm instead of his neck. Knocking the blade out of her hand, he dropped his weapon and focused on trying to keep Beth from hurting him without hurting her in return.

Beth continued to fight, scratching and biting at him as Diego pinned her arms to her sides and held them there. Hale jumped in to help while out of the corner of his eye, Diego saw Trey continue through the apartment, weapon drawn, undoubtedly looking for other threats.

"How the hell do we stop her?" Hale asked, trying to get a grip on her legs. "It's like she's on a bad LSD trip."

"I don't know," Diego said. "Just keep her from hurting herself."

Hale let out a grunt as Beth twisted around and sank her teeth into his forearm. "Who's going to keep her from hurting us?"

Diego didn't have an answer for that, mostly because he was busy avoiding a swinging fist as Beth got an arm loose and attempted to smash him in his face. He'd finally managed to get her arm restrained when Trey hurried back from the bedroom.

"There's some kid in one of the rooms playing a video game like a frigging zombie," he said as he came over to help with Beth. "He won't stop playing that stupid game no matter what I do."

Diego had no doubt it was Kevin. The fact that the kid wouldn't stop playing threw him for a loop though.

He was prying Beth away from Hale's arm when he picked up a strong whiff of the same blood he'd smelled when he pushed the door open. Shit, it was Dave's blood. It had the same tangy, slightly acrid odor he'd smelled at the salsa club when the jackass had busted his lip. And at the bank when those college kids had tried to rob the place. There'd been blood on the temple of the guy he'd fought. The moment it had rubbed off on Diego's uniform, whatever hold Dave had on him disappeared.

As Beth continued to twist and turn in her effort to get away, he caught sight of something red on her neck directly below her ear.

Blood.

And it was still wet.

"Get a towel," Diego ordered. "Dave's blood is on her neck, and we need to wipe it off."

Hale looked like he wasn't sure about the logic of leaving him and Trey alone to deal with Beth, but then released his grip on her flailing legs and jumped up. That earned him a kick to the crotch before he could get clear, but he kept going, limping slightly as he ran for the kitchen. He came back a moment later, dropping down beside Diego.

"Don't let the blood get on you," Diego warned, holding Beth's head still so Hale could wipe it off.

It was startling watching how fast the change happened. One second Beth was snarling and snapping, the next she relaxed, her body going limp. The moment she saw Diego and his pack mates, her eyes widened, a look of pure terror on her face.

"Brandon," she murmured, trying to sit up. "Where's Brandon? He's here for Brandon!"

"He isn't here." Diego put his hand on her shoulder, gently keeping her where she was. "Calm down and tell us what happened."

Beth looked confused for a moment, frowning like she was trying to remember something. If she was like most of the other people Dave had gotten his blood on, she might not remember anything but a few phantom images that didn't seem real…if they were lucky.

"It's all so blurry," she said, putting a hand to her head as Diego helped her sit up.

Beside them, Trey got to his feet, murmuring something about going to check Kevin for Dave's blood.

Diego nodded, then waited as patiently as he could while Beth shook her head repeatedly, like she was trying to jar loose a memory. A few moments later, Trey came out of the bedroom guiding Kevin to the couch. The kid seemed out of it, kind of like he had after smoking weed.

"Dave showed up at the door," Beth finally said, wincing like it hurt to say the words. "I told him Bree wasn't home, but he pushed his way in. He said he already had Bree and that he was here for Brandon."

Diego's heart seized in his chest, fear shooting through him as he fought the urge to jump up and run after Dave right then. He couldn't do that, though, because he had no idea where that asshole psycho had taken them.

Tears filled Beth's eyes and rolled down her face. Diego's sympathetic side wanted to tell her to stop if it hurt too much to talk about, but he couldn't do that until he knew what had happened to Bree and Brandon.

"It gets so fuzzy from there," Beth said, reaching up to wipe the tears from her cheek as more slid down her face. "He grabbed Brandon and I couldn't do anything to stop him." She gave them a pained look. "Why couldn't I stop him?"

Diego put his hand on her shoulders again, giving them a gentle, reassuring squeeze. "Beth, I need you to focus on what else you heard. Did Dave say where he was going? Where he was taking Bree and Brandon?"

Beth gazed at him as if she had no idea what he was

saying. Then an almost vacant look came across her features and he thought she might pass out.

"Dave said he was going to be rich and that he was going to leave the country and take Bree and Brandon with him," she said softly, the words coming out as if she wasn't sure they were right. "I tried to stand in his way, but he pushed me aside, saying he needed to hurry."

"Why did he need to hurry?" Diego asked urgently, having visions of Dave hustling Beth and Brandon on a plane at that very moment. "Are they leaving right now?"

Beth looked confused again as she shook her head. "I don't think so. He said he needs to get money first."

"Where's he getting the money from?" Trey asked, moving closer. "Did he say anything that would give us a clue? Or where Bree and Brandon would be while he got the money?"

Fresh tears rolled down Beth's face. "I don't know. I'm sorry."

Diego patted her on the shoulder, telling her it would be okay though he knew it wouldn't. His inner wolf wanted to rip Dave apart.

"He said he had to be there when it went down," Kevin suddenly said from where he still sat on the couch. "That he couldn't control so many people unless he was close enough to them."

Diego opened his mouth to ask Kevin if he remembered anything else, but Trey's phone rang, interrupting him.

Trey took out his cell, putting it to his ear as he walked into the kitchen. Diego was still trying to get Kevin to piece together what he remembered when his pack mate came back in.

"That was Gage. Someone is trying to rob the Federal Reserve. He wants us there ASAP."

Hale looked at Diego. "What's bigger than the Federal Reserve Bank?"

"And if Dave needs to be close to control whoever he has doing the job for him, that means he'll be somewhere nearby."

"Along with Bree and Brandon," Diego said. Picking up his gun from where he'd dropped it earlier, he shoved it in his holster, then got to his feet. "Let's go."

The building across the street was a mismatched collection of glass and white stone structures of different heights that definitely shouldn't have worked together, but somehow did. If Bree were the kind of person who was into architecture, she might say the place was beautiful. But she wasn't, and she sure as heck wouldn't have been gazing at the place right now if she wasn't tied to an office chair with nowhere else to look than out the long row of plate-glass windows directly in front of her.

Bree looked around to either side of her, trying to figure out where she was. It didn't help much since the only things she could see from her vantage point were a few empty desks, a dusty floor lamp, and another chair similar to the one she was tied to. From what she could piece together, she was in an empty office space, probably on the third or fourth floor based on the view she had out the window.

She yanked at the clear packing tape wrapped tightly around each wrist, twisting until she thought the stuff was going to cut off the blood flow. It was useless. She'd never break the stuff in a million years. She would have screamed for help, but there was a cloth gag in her mouth. No matter how hard she tried to yell, the sound came out muffled.

The worst part was she couldn't really remember how she'd ended up bound and gagged, any more than she could remember ending up in this room. She had a few vague images bouncing around her head of being hustled into a car, then sitting there for a long time while it sped along the highway. But all of it seemed fuzzy, like maybe she'd dreamed it.

The only thing she remembered for sure was running into her ex-husband outside Ken's apartment. After that, everything was a blur. The mere thought of Dave had her heart pounding in fear. She was certain he was responsible for her being here, though she didn't know how.

Why couldn't she remember anything?

Turning back to the window, Bree studied the building across the street again, hoping it would help her figure out where she was. The structure was vaguely familiar, and it felt like she should know what it was. It probably would have helped if she could see more of the front of it, but from where she sat, all she could see was a parking lot to the left and a bit of green space surrounded by a security wall in the middle. The only interesting things were the roll-up doors along the back of the building and one serious-looking gate that guarded the closest opening in the security wall. Whatever was in that building, Bree figured it must be valuable.

That's when it hit her. It was the Federal Reserve building, which meant the road below her had to be North Pearl

Street. Now she knew where she was. That still didn't explain how the hell she'd gotten here.

Noise from behind her made her jump, and she jerked her head around in an attempt to see what was going on. Her pulse beat faster at the hope maybe someone had found her. For a moment, she let herself believe it was Diego. That his werewolf nose and instincts had led him right to her.

Her heart plummeted when she saw Dave come into the room, leading an unresisting Brandon by the arm. Panic surged through her when she saw the blood smeared across her son's forehead, little beads of it running down the bridge of his nose and one temple.

She fought against the tape holding her to the chair, struggled harder than she ever had, screaming into the gag the whole time, twisting and jerking in a crazy attempt to flip the chair over and reach her injured son.

"Cut it out," Dave said in a casual tone as he pushed Brandon down into the other office chair and started strapping each wrist down to the arms of it with packaging tape. "There's nothing wrong with him. Do you really think I'd hurt my own son?"

Bree replied to that inane question into the rag in her mouth, screaming so hard it felt like her throat was tearing. But Dave ignored her as he put all his attention into binding Brandon to the chair, wrapping extra loops around his ankles as if he was going to get up and run away, which was crazy considering the condition her son was in right then. From the blood on his head, the blank-eyed expression, and the zombie-like way his body went wherever Dave pushed it, it was obvious Brandon was dealing with a concussion—at the very minimum.

That was why she was so stunned to see the change that came over her son the moment Dave wiped the blood off his forehead. Brandon's eyes cleared as he looked around the empty office in confusion, his whole body going rigid when he saw Bree. He shook his head violently, like he was trying to shake off a dream. Then he started to fight against the tape holding him to the chair, desperation clear in his eyes as he tried to shout something through the gag in his mouth.

"You can stop struggling, Brandon," Dave said, moving the chair a little so he was partially facing her. "Neither of you will get loose until I cut you loose, and all the fighting will do is make it harder on you both. So, just stop."

Bree would have kicked her ex in the balls right then if she could have gotten one of her legs free. Instead, she settled for staring at him, imagining all the different ways he could have suffered right then. She had a vision of a piano falling on him, which suggested that she might be losing her mind.

Dave ignored her death stare and moved over to a section of the window, leaning his head against the glass and staring down at the building across the street intently, like he was expecting something to happen. Bree finally paused for a moment to take a good look at the man who'd lost his mind and decided to kidnap them. He looked like crap.

As he stood there staring out the window, she noticed his hands and his forearms were covered in bandages and almost every finger had gauze wrapped around it. Even though the material was heavily layered, spots of blood had seeped through most of them. What the hell had he been doing to himself?

It was hard to miss how pale and sallow his skin was. There were purple smudges under his eyes, like he hadn't slept in a week. He was sweating, too, and she briefly wondered if he was sick. Both mentally and physically. When he started mumbling to himself about it being hard to control so many people, Bree was sure she'd been right about the mental illness part at least.

It must have been a full five minutes before Dave turned away from the window and walked over to regard her with an expression that made her stomach twist and roll so much, she thought she might be sick.

"I've gotten everything started over there, so that should give us time to talk," he announced.

She flinched back in the chair as far as she could when he reached for her, which wasn't very far. Dave snorted a little, stepping closer to untie the gag from behind her head. She heard Brandon grunt in anger. Knowing he was as scared of what Dave was going to do as she was made Bree more terrified.

"What the hell do you think you're doing?" she shouted as soon as the gag was out of her mouth. "I have a restraining order against you. You can't kidnap us like this. You aren't supposed to be within two hundred feet of Brandon or me."

It probably wasn't the most intelligent way to start the conversation, considering she'd already decided her ex-husband had lost his grip on reality. But surprisingly, Dave remained rather calm in the face of her rant.

"Now, why would you go and get a restraining order?" he asked, looking almost hurt as he crossed his arms over his chest. "How are we ever going to work through our issues if we can't be in the same room?"

Bree stared, not sure how to deal with this rational, yet delusional version of her ex. She took a deep breath and let it out slowly. "Dave, we aren't getting back together—ever. Even if we ignore the fact that I divorced you and that you kidnapped us, there's still the part where you've been stalking me. Not to mention the way you attacked Diego the other night."

Dave's lip curled at the mention of Diego, and she charged on before he could become fixated on the wrong part of this.

"Worse, I found out you've not only been stealing, but that people are dying because of you. After all that, how could you think getting back together was a possibility?"

Bree expected him to blow up at her, or at least deny everything she'd said. Instead, he looked like a kid caught with his hand in the cookie jar.

"Actually, *I've* never stolen anything. I got other people to do it for me. So, if anyone died, it was their fault. Not mine."

Bree thought Dave was trying to play with her head and confuse her again, but when his expression never changed, she realized he was telling the truth. Or at least thought he was.

"What do you mean, you got other people to do it for you?" she asked slowly, trying to work through that while keeping in mind she was likely dealing with someone who was mentally unstable. "Did you hire people to steal for you?"

"No, I didn't hire them." He was silent, as if considering whether he should explain what he meant by that. Finally, he shrugged. "I wasn't planning to tell you this, but if we're going to get back together, I guess I should. My ability will be important to both of our futures, so there's no reason not to tell you."

Bree barely kept from rolling her eyes at the way her ex made it sound like he'd gained a comic-book superpower. It was enough to keep her from pointing out once again there was no way in hell they were ever going to be together again.

"What kind of ability?" she prodded. "Are you talking about something you learned in prison?"

"Yeah," he said. "My cellmate, Will, had it and I got it from him. When we first met, he told me that he could control people and make them do what he wanted. I thought he was full of shit at first, but then I saw him do it. He'd get other inmates to give us cigarettes or junk food, have the guards leave our lights on for an extra ten minutes so we could read at night. Sometimes he'd use it to keep the other inmates from messing with me."

Bree almost laughed. So, Dave's cellmate was a charmer who was able to talk people into being nice and giving them things. It sounded like a great skill to possess, especially in prison, but not exactly a superpower.

"I told him he was wasting his gift," Dave said pacing back and forth. "He could have run the prison and been the most powerful man in there. Instead, he used it to bum smokes and candy bars. He claimed it was a talent that shouldn't be abused and refused to go along with anything I suggested."

Dave stopped in front of her, an ugly gleam in his eyes that reminded her of the one she'd seen there the night he beat that poor guy to death all those years ago.

"What did you do?" Bree whispered, afraid she already knew the answer.

"I took it from him," he said, as if that should have been

obvious. "He rambled on all the time about how he'd been on some kind of DNA research team that got genetic material that had been frozen in the ice somewhere for thousands of years. He'd got some of it into his system, is the way he put it. I wasn't exactly sure what that meant, and I have to admit I wasn't paying a lot of attention when he talked about that part. But I was smart enough to figure out how I could get some of his DNA into my system."

Bree felt her stomach turn as her mouth went dry. "Dave, what did you do? Tell me you didn't..."

"I got him alone in the laundry area, and then I choked him to death and took a big bite out of him." He turned back to look out the window, frown lines appearing across his forehead as if something across the street was bothering him. "I wasn't sure if drinking his blood alone would do it, so I took a little extra, you know? Eating human flesh isn't fun, but it was definitely worth it."

Bree gaped at him. If she'd had any doubts before, they were erased now. Holy crud, he'd eaten another person because he had delusions that would give him superpowers. Her ex-husband was a damn cannibal. She'd always known he was a little off, but she never imagined he could go as far as something like that.

A few feet away, Brandon was staring at his father like... well, like his father had just confessed to eating his prison cellmate.

"I was right," Dave continued as if he hadn't admitted to be the biggest whackadoodle on the planet. In fact, from the self-satisfied smirk on his face, he seemed to think his little act of cannibalism had been the brightest thing anyone had ever done. "Once I had the ability, I was able to make people do anything I wanted. I had a crew of muscle covering my back 24/7, and getting the parole board to go along with my early release was a piece of cake. The two people I marked with my blood fell all over themselves to get me released without probation. Once I got out, having people rob banks and jewelry stores for me only made sense. A little bit of blood and it was ridiculously easy to get those people to steal for me. The best part was, they couldn't remember doing it afterward."

Pieces began to fit into place then. Oh. My. God. Diego said the delirium drug had likely originated in Coffield. It turned out he was half right. Delirium had started at the prison. But it wasn't a drug. It was Dave and his blood. She guessed that explained all the bandages and gauze on his hands and arms. She wasn't sure how such a thing was possible, but apparently, it was.

"I have to admit," Dave said, still looking out the window, his face paler than before, "it took a while to learn how to control more than a couple people at a time, and when the numbers get too high, maintaining control can be a bit challenging. Actually, it can be kind of painful. It gives me really bad headaches, like my brain is on fire."

She wanted to ask if that was why he was sweating and pale at the moment, because he was trying to control too many people, but before she could get the words out, Dave continued.

"I did all of this for us," he said, spinning away from the window to look at her. "So we could have the money we need to leave here and start fresh. We'll get it right this time. Just the three of us. And the people I've been stealing from have so much effing money, they aren't going to miss it."

Bree's head spun as she tried to keep up with her ex's

view of reality. Then again, he'd eaten someone, so she supposed it was a given that his perception was screwed up.

"Dave," she said, keeping her voice soft and even. Right now, her ex-husband had suddenly become someone she didn't want to set off. "I suppose I can understand what you mean about you and Hobbs stealing from the banks and maybe the jewelry stores, but you were stealing from your own company's clients, too. Priceless works of art, family heirlooms, collections that took some of these people a lifetime to put together. Of course, that stuff is going to be missed."

It was Dave's turn to stare. Or, more precisely, to look at her like she was stupid. "My own company's clients? What are you talking about? I wouldn't know a Rembrandt from a paint-by-number, and I'd never steal from my own company's clients."

After everything he'd already confessed to, she was supposed to believe he'd grown a conscience and decided ripping off his employer's clients was more than he was willing to cop to? "I found Ken Reed's notes. He knew you were breaking into his clients' homes and stealing from them. He knew it was you. That's why you killed him."

Dave stared at her, managing to actually look stunned. "I never stole anything from Ken's clients. I wouldn't do that to the best friend I ever had. And I certainly didn't kill him. I've never killed anyone." He must have realized the obvious fallacy in that last part because he shrugged. "Okay, sure there was that guy I killed to get myself locked up in the first place, and then my cellmate, and those baggage handlers from the airport I sent on a suicide mission to kill your cop boyfriend. But that's it. I had nothing to do with Ken's death."

Bree wanted to point out how incredibly coincidental

it was that Ken had ended up dead the day after figuring out Dave and Ernest Hobbs were involved in stealing half of Dallas blind, but something else Dave had said registered, stabbing into her like a sharp knife.

"What do you mean you sent people to kill Diego?" she demanded. "He never said anything about that."

"It doesn't matter," Dave said, wiping the back of his hand across his sweat-soaked forehead. "None of this stuff you're talking about matters. Not now. The three of us are together, and after the guards from the Federal Reserve I'm controlling drive those trucks out of there, we'll have enough money to go somewhere far away from here. Somewhere we can rekindle the love you've let us lose."

She might have been distracted by the thought that baggage handlers had tried to kill Diego and he hadn't told her, but Dave's words got her attention.

"Dave, I'm not in love with you," she said. "I haven't been in love with you for a very long time and I'm never going to be in love with you in the future, so you can drop any plans you have for rekindling anything. I'm not going anywhere with you and neither is Brandon."

She expected an angry outburst from her ex this time for sure, but that wasn't what she got.

"Oh, you and Brandon will be going with me," he said flatly, his expression ice cold. "And we'll rekindle anything I damn well want whether you do your part voluntarily or not. I'd prefer not to mark you with my blood and control you, but I will if I have to. At least until you decide it's better to love me of your own free will. And trust me, you'll want to decide that quickly. You don't want to know what I could make Brandon do while you watch."

Bree was too stunned by his threat to reply. From the corner of her eye, she saw Brandon was just as terrified. The thought that he could make her son do anything he wanted scared the hell out of her.

Before Bree could come up with something to say to calm Dave down, the sound of squealing tires and sirens filled the air outside. She glanced out the window and saw half a dozen cop cars and two black SUVs with SWAT decals on the side come sliding to a stop in front of the gate to the Federal Reserve that had opened at some point when she hadn't been paying attention. Two armored trucks exited the building through the roll-up doors and were now trapped inside the walled compound. Several guards in uniform ran out those same doors and began to shoot at the police. More gunfire came from slots in the sides of the armored vehicles.

Dave's reaction was immediate and violent. "Dammit, no!" he shouted, slamming the palm of one hand against the window glass hard enough to leave bloody fingerprints. "How the fuck did they get here so fast. This was all planned out."

As Bree watched, another black SWAT SUV slid to a stop a few yards away from the others. Three big SWAT cops jumped out, rifles in hand. One of them was Diego.

He and his pack mates immediately headed toward the gate and the shooting going on there. Bree's heart jumped into her throat as bullets hit the concrete all around them. But before he'd gotten more than a few feet, Diego skidded to a stop, his nose lifting into the air. A moment later, his head snapped around until he was staring straight at her and Brandon through the window. Bree swore she could see him mouth their names, then he was running toward them, yelling something over his shoulder to his teammates.

Oh, God.

Diego was coming to rescue them. The knowledge both thrilled and terrified her.

"Dave, you should leave," Bree said.

She didn't want Diego to get in a fight with her ex. It wasn't because she cared what happened to Dave, but she didn't like the idea of what would happen if Dave got his blood on Diego. He had no way of knowing how dangerous her ex truly was.

"If you're still here when Diego gets up here, he's going to kill you," she added, praying it would be enough to scare Dave.

But instead of running, her ex walked over and stuffed the gag back in her mouth. "We'll see about that."

Giving her a smug smile, Dave turned and walked away. Bree craned her neck trying to see where he went, but the room was empty.

Where the hell was he?

CHAPTER 17

Diego's heart was beating out of control the entire drive to the Federal Reserve, the thumping so loud in his ears he'd barely been able to follow the chatter on the radio and the phone conversation Trey had with Gage and Samantha Mills. He vaguely remembered Trey passing along the tip about how wiping off the blood seemed to stop the delirium effect, but for the most part, Diego ignored them. Instead, he stared out the rear passenger windows as Hale drove the team's SUV toward Pearl Street.

He knew it was horrible to say it, but right now he didn't care that much about the delirium crap. He just wanted to find Bree and Brandon. His worst fear was that the robbery at the Federal Reserve was a big distraction and that Dave had already taken the two people he loved out of the country while he wasted time on this damn bank job. Nobody tried to rob the Federal Reserve Bank. It was too well protected.

It was at that moment, as he prayed they weren't making a horrible mistake, that Diego realized how much he loved both Bree and her son. The thought of them being hurt or gone out of his life was enough to make him think a man—even one who was a werewolf—could truly die from fear and anguish alone.

"We're about a minute out," Hale said from the front seat. "It looks like Dave has gotten control of a good portion of the Reserve's security guards. There's an all-out war going on at the main gate. Gage and the rest of the Pack are trying to keep them from getting out with two armored truckloads full of cash."

"Has anyone seen Dave yet?" Diego asked softly. "Or Bree and Brandon?"

Hale met his gaze in the rearview mirror. "No one has said anything, but they only now got on scene and the shooting is intense."

The next sixty seconds was the longest minute of Diego's life, and he fingered the pistol grip on his M4 nervously as he silently urged Hale to go faster.

When their vehicle slid to a stop behind half a dozen other cop cars, Diego was out before the tires stopped squawking, flipping his weapon off safe and heading toward the sound of gunfire. But he made it barely more than a few strides before a tingling along the back of his neck made him spin around to look behind him.

He had no idea what made him look up at the windows on the building across the street. It wasn't like he could smell anything inside, and there was nothing to hear but shouting, sirens, and gunfire. But something made him stare at a section of windows along the fourth floor of the building.

The glass there was heavily tinted and impossible to see through despite his werewolf vision. Even if there were people up there, they were almost certainly gawkers taking in the police drama going on right in front of them. Still, his inner wolf insisted that what he wanted was behind those windows. That if he waited, something horrible would happen.

Diego was running before he'd actually made the conscious decision to follow his instincts, shouting over his shoulder that he was going after Bree and Brandon. Trey shouted something back, but Diego was running too fast to hear what his pack mate said.

He picked up Bree's and Brandon's scent the moment he entered the street that ran between the building that had attracted his attention and the one to the southeast of it. Dave's scent was heavy on the air, too, and Diego let out a deep-throated growl. For a moment, he was torn between letting his nose drag him farther down the street toward a white van parked there. He forced the urge aside as he realized that was probably the vehicle Dave had driven to bring Bree and Brandon here.

Focusing, he followed his nose to one of the building's side doors. He jerked it open to find a set of stairs. All three scents mingled there and Diego raced up the steps, letting his nose lead him. All he could think about was reaching his mate and his beta in time. Thinking about anything else was impossible.

His fangs and claws were out before he reached the second floor. By the third, his body was starting to lean forward in an attempt to facilitate a full shift into his four-legged form. He fought the urge with everything he had. While he certainly wouldn't have minded finding Dave and sinking his fangs into the guy's throat and ripping his entire head off, he knew that wasn't a good idea. Besides the whole issue with the man's blood, there was the practical issue of not being able to open doorknobs in his wolf form.

He pulled himself back from the edge and made it to the fourth floor, yanking the door open so fast the metal handle bent in his hands.

Bree's and Brandon's scents hit him full force as he entered the wide hallway leading to what looked like office spaces. It didn't smell like anyone had used these rooms in a while, which was probably why Dave had come up here. But all of that rational stuff disappeared as Diego realized how close he was to the two most important people in his life.

His nose led him to the second room on the right and he listened for a moment before cautiously opening the door. He wasn't sure what he'd find, but when he saw Bree and Brandon bound and gagged, he lost it. A growl ripping from his throat, he rushed forward and slid to his knees in front of Bree. His M4 fell to the carpeted floor, but he didn't care. The only thing he could focus on were his soul mate's panic-filled eyes as she violently shook her head back and forth.

Diego forced his fangs and claws to retract, afraid he was scaring her with them. He was reaching for the gag in her mouth when his inner wolf shouted at him to move.

Dave.

Berating himself for his stupidity, Diego threw himself to the side, coming up on a knee, his SIG in his hand.

Something wet and warm splattered against his face as Dave approached him. The asshole had been lying in wait for him the whole time. Not that it mattered because Diego was going to make the man sorry he'd ever been born.

He surged to his feet, aiming the sights of his handgun in the center of Dave's chest, praying the man gave him an excuse to pull the trigger. But as his finger tightened around it, he couldn't see the sights of his weapon anymore.

He couldn't see the weapon at all.

Panic gripped him as he realized his hand and arm wouldn't obey the commands his head was sending. Shit, he wasn't on his feet like he'd thought, but on his knees in the same position he'd been when he rolled away from Bree.

Just before that wet, warm sensation had hit him in the face.

Diego fought against the invisible restraints holding him in place, his heart rate accelerating like mad as every muscle attempted to move at once. He could feel his stomach twisting as more and more adrenaline dumped into his system, trying to force the slightest twitch of anything that would confirm he was still in charge of his own body. But absolutely nothing worked.

That wasn't true. At least two parts of his body seemed to remain under his control—his eyes and ears. The sights and sounds of Bree and Brandon as they attempted to fight to get free of their bonds so they could help him were as terrifying as the paralysis itself.

Diego had no idea how long he fought that silent battle before Dave dropped to a knee in front of him. Hair lank, sweat rolled down his pale face and his nose dripped bright-red blood.

"What was that you said to me the last time we met?" Dave asked in a taunting voice that didn't seem to go with how exhausted he looked. "Something about me never laying a hand on you, wasn't it? Well, as you can see, it turns out I don't have to touch you to get what I want. A little bit of my blood on your skin, and I can have anything I want. Even if what I want is you dead." He let out a harsh laugh. "Actually, that's exactly what I want. So, why don't you lift that gun you're holding in your hand right now, press it against your temple, and pull the trigger?"

The words might have been posed as a question—or maybe a suggestion. Regardless, Diego obeyed all the same, his hand coming up to rest the heavy weight of the SIG's barrel against the side of his head.

Bree's and Brandon's screams were muffled by the gags as they twisted in an effort to get free of the tape, but all of that faded away as Diego felt his finger tighten on the trigger of his weapon. He fought against the order with everything in his soul, his whole body straining as he tried to move the barrel away from his head. His inner wolf joined the struggle, growling and flinging itself against the walls of the mental prison holding it hostage.

Diego felt his fangs extend, the taste of blood in his mouth giving him a boost as he realized at least one tiny corner of his mind—the one belonging to his werewolf—retained some level of control.

He fought harder, trying to get his fangs to come out more and struggling to extend his claws. He couldn't tell if it was working, but he noticed Dave was getting agitated as hell, his face twisting in rage as Diego continued to fight him.

"Dammit," he shouted, fresh blood running down his face as his nose started to bleed more. A vessel in his right eye burst, a red stain quickly filling the white. "What the fuck are you doing? Pull the trigger! Do it! Do it now!"

Face filled with rage, Dave smacked him hard, knocking Diego sideways so he was looking straight at Bree and Brandon. Despite the fangs in his mouth and the claws pushing their way out, Dave's direct and specific order had his hand tightening on the gun. Diego could hear the trigger bar inside the weapon grate backward, and he knew it was a fraction of a second from releasing the hammer and firing the gun.

Bree's eyes locked with his, tears streaming down her face as she yanked so hard on the tape holding her to the chair she was practically bleeding. A few feet away, Brandon was frozen solid in his chair, his eyes vivid yellow-gold, small fangs extending over his lower lip.

"Why won't you fucking shoot yourself?" Dave shouted. "Do it, damn you!"

Diego barely heard him as he saw his beta shift, the muscles of Brandon's forearms twisting as the thick layers of tape around them shredded.

Dave was so focused on Diego that he didn't see Brandon leap at him until his son slammed into him, driving him to the floor. The attack caught Dave off guard, and in that second, Diego felt the chains holding his mind in check start to weaken. The gun fell to the floor, and his claws and fangs shot out to their full length. Diego spun around, ready to end this himself only to see Dave shove Brandon away from him, his blood all over the boy's face.

"Get off me, you freak," Dave yelled, both eyes riddled with burst vessels now. More blood streamed from his nose and his ears as he scrambled backward. With a wail of agony, Dave lifted one hand to his head, pounding his temple as he flicked his attention from Diego to Brandon, then back again.

"Why won't you two fucking die?" he shouted.

The words dropped Brandon on the spot and sent a spike of pain through Diego's chest so intense it felt like a hand had reached in and crushed his heart. But for all the agony, the only thing Diego could think about right then was how scared Brandon must be.

That thought gave him all the strength he needed, and Diego fought off the mental shackles holding him down and leaped over his beta, landing squarely in front of Dave.

One shove sent the asshole flying backward through the air, slamming him into the wall hard enough to crunch halfway through the Sheetrock.

Diego advanced on Dave, ready to rip the son of a bitch's throat out if necessary, but Dave's eyes rolled back into his head and he slumped limply to the carpet, unconscious.

Within seconds, the sound of shooting outside faded away.

Diego heard gasping from behind him and turned to see Brandon lying on the floor, looking like he was going through a full-blown panic attack.

He was at his beta's side in a heartbeat, dropping to his knee and putting a calming hand on Brandon's chest. Brandon's claws and fangs were still out, his eyes were as yellow-gold as ever, and his heart was thumping out of control exactly as it had in the diner not too long ago. Like that day, Brandon was stuck in his shifted form, too freaked out to get himself under control.

Not surprising. Between the kidnapping, being trussed up to a chair, and having his father try to kill him, Brandon had been through one hell of a day.

Diego paused long enough to reach out and slice through the tape binding Bree to the chair, then he ripped a piece off the bottom of his uniform T-shirt and used it to wipe Dave's blood off Brandon's face, making calming sounds the whole time.

"I'm here, Brandon," he said softly, rubbing gently on the kid's chest with his hand and forcing him to breathe. "Your alpha is here and you're going to be okay. I promise."

Diego repeated the words over and over until Brandon finally calmed down enough for his fangs and claws to retract. A moment later, his eyes stopped glowing and returned to their normal brown color.

"You're really my alpha?" Brandon asked softly, looking up at him in awe from where he lay on the floor. "You didn't say that to get me to calm down?"

"No. I'm your alpha and you're my beta." Diego smiled. "I'm pretty sure you already knew that. It took a while for me to catch up to the idea."

Brandon threw his arms around Diego and hugged him so hard it almost hurt. Then Bree's arms were around both of them, and Diego couldn't possibly ever put into words how right it felt for all of them to be together like this.

"I love you so much," she said softly. "I can't explain it, but I know with all my heart that if I looked for the rest of my life, I'd never find anyone more amazing and more perfect than you. Not just for Brandon, but for me. I love you."

Diego turned his head a little and pulled her in closer, kissing her until he could almost forget where they were and what the hell had almost happened to them. But then he heard the thump of heavy boots running up the stairs and knew he didn't have much time before they were interrupted by his concerned pack mates.

He pulled back to look at her as Brandon sat there with a knowing look on his happy face. "You don't ever have to explain. I fell in love with you before our first date was over and have been waiting for the right time to tell you. I didn't think it would be a time like this," he added, glancing at Dave's unconscious body. "But the time and place don't matter as much as the fact that I love you."

Bree leaned in for another hug when Trey, Hale, and Connor ran into the room with weapons drawn. They all slid to a stop at the sight of him locked in a group hug with Bree and Brandon while Dave lay sprawled out on the floor by the wall.

"I guess that explains why the Reserve's security guards stopped shooting all of a sudden," Trey said, glancing at Dave. Diego wasn't surprised his pack mates didn't walk over to check to see if Dave was alive because, like him, they surely heard the man's heart beating. "What'd you do to him, pound his head against the wall until he passed out?"

Diego shook his head. "I'm not sure what happened. He was trying to control both Brandon and me, and I gave him a shove. Next thing I know, he passed out."

"I think it was because Dave overextended himself," Bree said, sitting back on her heels. "Before you got here, he was already complaining about how much it hurt to control so many people. Controlling you and Brandon at the same time as you were shifting must have burned him out, I guess. It's like it was too much for him."

Beside Diego, Brandon shuddered. Diego quickly helped Bree and Brandon to their feet, then looked at his pack mates. "Let's go into the hallway."

No one argued with that suggestion, and a few minutes later, they were all standing outside the room. Hale stood closest to the doorway so he could keep an eye on Dave.

"What do we do with Dave?" his pack mate asked. "We can't risk all that blood getting on innocent people."

"Maybe get the paramedics to treat it like a biohazard situation?" Connor suggested. "We can tell them Dave OD'ed on delirium and any contact with his blood will spread the drug."

Diego considered that for a moment. "That could work."

At least it was the best they could come up with right now. Connor took off to get the paramedics, leaving Diego time to catch Trey and Hale up on what they'd missed while they told him about the fighting across the street.

"The two armored trucks were each carrying a pallet of cash, one hundred million in each," Hale said. "If Dave's crazy mind-control scheme had worked, he'd be set for life and then some. Luckily, we kept them from escaping without having to kill anyone."

Standing beside Diego, her arm around her son, Bree did a double take. "You guys already knew about what Dave could do with his blood before you got here?"

Diego nodded. "Yeah. We cornered Ernest Hobbs and he told us everything. Turns out, Dave threatened our intrepid reporter into creating the delirium drug story as a cover for his crime spree. I hate to say it, but without Hobbs's information, we never would have figured out what was going on. Fortunately, it's all over now."

Bree let out a sigh. "Actually, it isn't."

"What do you mean?" Trey asked.

"I've been investigating several robberies connected to Dave's investment firm," Bree explained. "I thought the guy who took us hostage at the diner was behind it, but it turns out Ken Reed was investigating the thefts and realized he was being set up. I found a journal of sorts that Ken was keeping about the robberies. He suspected Dave right away, so he started following him. Not only did Ken see the people Dave turned into puppets deliver the jewelry and stuff they stole to him, but he saw him meet with his partner in crime, which turned out to be Hobbs."

Hale did a double take. "Are you sure about that?"

She nodded. "Ken overheard Dave and Hobbs talking about which banks and jewelry stores my ex should hit."

Diego got a sinking feeling in his stomach. "Dammit. Hobbs played us like a freaking violin. Why didn't any of us pick on the fact that he was lying? We're freaking werewolves."

"We must have mistaken his rapid heartbeat for nerves when we talked to him earlier," Hale said.

Diego cursed silently. His pack mate was right. Still didn't make him any less pissed.

"I'll call Gage and tell him we need to get a BOLO out on Hobbs," Trey said.

"While the cops are out looking for him, we might be able to recover all the stuff he and Dave stole," Bree said with a grin. "I think I know where they stashed it."

"This doesn't really seem like the kind of place a criminal would store millions and millions of dollars' worth of money, jewelry, art, and collectibles," Trey said from the front passenger seat as Hale pulled the SWAT SUV into a parking space of the self-storage facility.

Studying the clean and neat facade of the building, Bree had to agree. But this was the address from Ken's notes.

Diego sat in the back seat beside her, clearly still annoyed she'd blackmailed him into letting her come with them. While the moment they'd shared, where they'd confessed how much they loved each other, had been amazing, it didn't change the fact that Diego hadn't wanted to bring her along. They'd argued for a few minutes, until she finally pointed out she wouldn't give him the address for Dave and Hobbs's cache of stolen goods unless they took her with them. She agreed with him that Brandon should go back to the SWAT compound with Connor and that cute cat that always followed him around, but since she'd figured out Hobbs and her ex had been working together, she deserved to be there when they recovered all the stuff they'd stolen.

"This is as much my investigation as it is yours," she'd insisted.

Diego scowled at her, but she could tell there was no way he could refute that logic. "Okay," he finally said. "But only because we're going to a self-storage place and I don't think it'll be dangerous."

That was good enough for her.

Since it was within normal business hours, the front gate was open, giving them access to the storage units. If it had been a few hours later, the facility would have been locked up and the only way in would have been to enter with a pass code they didn't have. Diego told her they then would have had to get a warrant.

They were halfway down the hallway toward Hobbs's storage unit when Diego and Trey stiffened and pulled their weapons. Hale quickly followed suit.

"Hobbs has been here," Diego muttered, motioning for her to stay behind them. "Recently."

The place was a maze of twists and turns, but Diego and his pack mates didn't slow as they hurried past the endless line of individual storage units, and Bree had no choice but to run so she could keep up.

The metal roll-up door on the unit Hobbs had rented was open, and when Bree finally caught up and got a peek inside, she was relieved to see the space was filled with what had to be at least twenty sealed cardboard boxes, some discarded pieces of bubble wrap, and a few rolls of packing tape.

The mere sight of the tape was enough to draw a shudder from her body. Being strapped down to that chair while Diego and Brandon had been struggling with Dave had been the worst moment of her life.

She, Diego, and Trey walked inside while Hale stayed near the door, half of his attention on the hallway. Holstering his gun, Trey took out a pocketknife and sliced open one of the larger boxes, while Diego did the same with another.

"This one has some kind of paintings," Trey said, pulling back several layers of bubble wrap to reveal a piece of color-splashed canvas.

"Jewels and a vase of some kind over here," Diego announced as he peeked in the top of an opened box.

It only took Bree a few seconds to confirm what she already knew. "This is all the stuff stolen from Ken's clients. If everything is here, you're easily talking fifty or sixty million dollars' worth of stuff."

When they opened the other boxes, Bree was relieved to see they held the rest of the stuff that had been stolen. She was getting everything back—every single piece—which meant she'd saved her bosses millions. She felt like doing a happy dance.

"Okay, two questions," Trey said, looking around at all the boxes they'd opened. "One, if this is all stuff from Ken's clients, where's the crap they stole from the jewelry stores and banks? And two, where's Hobbs? It's obvious this stuff is packed up and ready to go."

"Maybe the stuff from the other jobs is stored in a different unit?" Hale mused, but Diego and Trey motioned him to silence, drawing their weapons and aiming them at the entrance to the unit.

A few seconds later, Bree heard a rhythmic squeak that could only belong to rolling wheels. She held her breath as Trey moved closer to the entrance, taking up position across from Hale in time for both of them to point their weapons at Hobbs as he walked in, shoving a trolley cart in front of him.

The reporter froze at the sight of them…and all the open boxes in the storage unit. Bree could practically see the calculations rolling around in the guy's head. He was almost certainly trying to figure out how good his chances were of turning around and making a run for it.

He must have decided the odds were against him because his shoulders slumped and he let out a heavy sigh. "How did you find me? I thought you'd be busy with Dave and his mad scheme for the rest of the night. I wouldn't have called in that anonymous tip to the police about the Federal Reserve if I'd known you'd be done this fast."

Bree felt her jaw drop. "I thought you and Dave were working together on these thefts. That's what Ken Reed's notes said."

Hobbs's gaze moved to her as Hale approached him, gun holstered and cuffs out. "So that jackass kept notes? I'll be damned. I knew I should have questioned him more before telling him to take that diner hostage, then kill himself."

Wait. What?

Bree opened her mouth to shout a warning right along with Diego when Hobbs lifted his hand to his mouth in one smooth, practiced motion and bit into his index finger. Before she could get the words out, he brought his hand up, wiping the blood on Hale's cheek.

Diego's pack mate never saw it coming.

"Kill them," Hobbs said softly before running out the door.

Bree felt Diego's arms around her seconds before he took her to the floor and the shooting started. It took half a second to realize Hale was shooting at them instead of the escaping Hobbs.

Hobbs could control people like Dave could. How had she missed that?

In the tight confines of the metal-shrouded space, the shooting sounded loud enough to pierce her eardrums and seemed to last forever. But when it was over, Bree knew it had probably only been a few seconds. That's when she realized Diego was no longer on top of her, shielding her with his body. The realization terrified her, and she shoved herself up to peek over the cardboard boxes that had gotten flipped over and knocked about.

Both Trey and Diego were on top of Hale, holding him down as he punched and kicked, growling and snarling, fighting them at the same time he tried to reach for his gun lying a few inches away.

If Hale got hold of the gun, there was no telling what he'd do.

Knowing Diego wouldn't like it, Bree took a deep breath and scrambled to her feet, then moved closer to them—and the gun. She got to it in time to see Diego wiping the last of the blood off Hale's face with a piece of bubble wrap. Hale stopped resisting immediately, his gaze looking lost and confused, exactly like Brandon had earlier.

Blood stained Diego's and Trey's uniforms as they climbed to their feet, and she immediately ran over to them.

"I'm okay," Diego said. "Stay with Hale. And for God's sake, don't follow us."

Before Bree could think to ask what that meant, Diego and Trey raced out of the storage unit, leaving her alone with a barely coherent Hale, worrying about what was going to happen to the man she loved like crazy and wondering how he expected her to follow an order like that.

It was easy for Diego and Trey to follow Hobbs's trail through the storage facility and out a back door. The second they emerged into the late-day heat, the roar of a fast-approaching vehicle had them jumping back into the building just in time to avoid getting run down. The crash as the white SUV slammed into the building was horrendous, tires squealing and metal tearing. Diego thought Hobbs would back up and try to run them down a second time, but instead he kept going, the engine roaring louder as he raced for the gate that enclosed the back of the storage facility.

Diego ignored the slight twinge of pain in his hip from the gunshot wound Hale had given him and took off running after the SUV, Trey right behind him. He'd hoped Hobbs would be forced to slow down at the gate, but that didn't seem to be the reporter's plan because he kept going full speed. Diego unloaded a full magazine into the area around the left rear tire, while Trey aimed at the right one. Then Hobbs was smashing through the gate, parts of the vehicle flying everywhere as he kept right on going.

"I hit the tire on my side," Diego shouted to Trey as they raced after the SUV, which was smoking pretty good as it turned the next corner and disappeared. As he ran, he dropped the spent magazine and reloaded before holstering his weapon. He didn't want people on the street freaking out when they saw him and Trey with their weapons out.

"I hit the one on my side, too," Trey told him, doing the same with his SIG as they sprinted hard along the side of the storage facility. Thankfully, there was no one to see them running faster than they should have been able to. "Then I put a couple in your side because I know you negotiators like to talk more than shoot."

"Jackass," Diego snorted as they made it up to the corner and turned onto Canton. Between the smoke filling the air and people gawking, it was incredibly easy to follow Hobbs from that point.

Thirty seconds later, they found the white SUV where it had crashed against the side of a building on Chavez Boulevard, both back tires shredded and the smashed-up engine streaming antifreeze everywhere. Hobbs was nowhere in sight. He and Trey picked up Hobbs's scent quickly, though. They were only a few seconds behind him.

Diego let out a growl of frustration when the trail took a right on Taylor. "Crap, he's heading toward the farmers market."

"A lot of people are going to be there at this time of day," Trey said.

They both started running faster, less concerned about being seen than with having to face a horde of people the reporter might have taken control of.

"How the hell did Hobbs get the same ability Dave and

Bremen had?" Trey asked as they streaked toward the crowd ahead of them at the end of the block. "What, did Dave let him take a bite out of him?"

"I don't know," Diego said. "It doesn't really matter at this point. We need to figure out a way to take him down without giving him a chance to gain control of us."

Trey didn't have anything to say to that. Diego couldn't blame him. This was the strangest situation he'd ever dealt with. Even if Hobbs was unarmed, he was still an extreme threat. How did you deal with a man you couldn't get close to? Short of shooting the guy. And neither of them was going to shoot an unarmed man.

As they reached the farmers market, the air filled with the scent of fresh produce and the murmur of casual conversation. A few people looked their way curiously, but most didn't seem interested. Still, it was possible to see the faint ripple through the crowd indicating where someone had passed through in a hurry. It looked like Hobbs had run right down the middle of the main covered concourse, past hundreds of people.

Diego got a sick feeling in the pit of his stomach. This was Texas, which meant that probably twenty-five or thirty percent of the people in this crowd were armed. This could go bad so many ways.

They were halfway through the main section of the market, Hobbs's scent still strong and clear, when a huge guy in a cowboy hat and jeans suddenly lumbered out of the crowd and threw himself at Trey. People shouted in surprise and quickly backed away. Diego cursed, smelling the blood before he saw a trace of it on the back of the guy's neck.

Trey had already sensed the big guy coming and ducked

out of his way, but the man didn't seem to care, turning to lunge at him again. Trey put a hand in the middle of the man's chest and shoved, flipping him off his feet and slamming him down on his back.

Diego didn't have a chance to do more than yell out where he'd seen the blood on the guy as two more men hurtled out of the crowd—one going low, the other high—slamming Diego to the ground. A split second later, a gunshot rang out somewhere in the crowd, then more people jumped on him, punching and kicking.

He'd never been in a fight like this, with people doing their best to kill him when he felt so restrained he didn't want to pull his Taser. Things got even crazier when several people from the crowd joined in, tackling two of his attackers and dragging them off him. Diego would have thanked them, but then he realized they had Hobbs's blood on them, too. With the first attackers out of the way, the two he'd mistaken for Good Samaritans immediately launched themselves at Diego, rage on their faces.

Trey yanked him out of the pile of violent humanity, shoving the people Hobbs was controlling far enough back to let them catch their breaths.

"We can't keep doing this," Diego yelled, shoving another person back before disarming a second, though he had no idea if the man was there to help him or kill him. "Hobbs could have taken control of dozens of people for all we know."

"Go after him," Trey called back, almost taking a knife through the chest from a woman with blank, glassy eyes. "I'll slow them down."

Diego didn't pause, turning to take off running through

the panicked crowd at full speed. He doubted anyone would pay attention to someone running as fast as he was when the entire place was going mad.

He didn't have to go far to find Hobbs's trail, following it at a dead sprint for two blocks until he smelled the man somewhere directly ahead of him. Apparently, the reporter had been sure his ambush would take care of him and Trey because he wasn't moving very fast now.

Hobbs saw him just as Diego caught up to him, and dodged into an Italian café. The place was already in turmoil when Diego pushed through the door, people shouting and scrambling for the exits as the reporter backed away, brandishing a knife he must have grabbed from behind the counter.

"Everyone out!" Diego shouted, drawing his weapon and moving forward.

Unfortunately, he wasn't fast enough to keep Hobbs from getting a hostage, a young girl who couldn't have been much older than eighteen or nineteen. She struggled with the reporter for a few seconds until he swiped his bloody finger across her neck. The slim girl immediately stopped moving and stared straight ahead. That didn't keep Hobbs from wrapping an arm around her and dragging her closer, or placing the knife against her throat, careful to make sure it was on the opposite side of where he'd left his own blood.

"Don't do anything stupid, Hobbs," Diego warned, moving into a position that gave him a clear shot at the man's face, no matter how much he tried to hide behind the girl.

"Oh, I won't have to do anything stupid," Hobbs said in an incredibly casual voice as he traced the edge of the blade against her skin, enough to bring a line of blood to the surface. She didn't react. "Because you're going to step aside and let me walk right out that door."

"You know I can't do that," Diego said, taking a bead on the center of Hobbs's forehead. He would have pulled the trigger—he knew he could make the shot—but all it would take was one little twitch as the reporter fell and the knife would slice right through the girl's neck.

"Then I'll have to kill the girl," Hobbs sneered, moving the knife a little harder, drawing more blood.

Diego shook his head. "I doubt you're that dumb. You kill the girl, and I kill you before she hits the floor. I'll feel horrible about not saving her, but you won't feel anything at all. Ever again."

Before Hobbs could reply, the door behind Diego opened and then Trey was there, looking somewhat worse for wear, his tactical vest slashed in several places and a laceration across his left cheek. But his handgun was dead steady as he moved to the side and took a bead on Hobbs from that direction.

Tension filled the air as the sound of sirens drifted closer. The area outside this café was about to get very crowded.

Hobbs must have picked up on that, too. His knuckles whitened where he gripped the knife, dragging the blade a little deeper into the girl's skin. The way she didn't squirm or make a sound was creepy and more than a little disconcerting.

"So, how'd you get Dave to share his ability?" Diego asked. He needed to get Hobbs focused on something other than the impending arrival of the cavalry. "Surely he didn't simply offer it to you. Dave doesn't strike me as the sharing kind of guy."

Hobbs gave him an appraising look. "Whatever happened to Dave? You kill him?"

Diego shook his head. "Trying to take down the Federal Reserve was a little too much for him. He's sleeping it off."

Something flickered in Hobbs's eyes, like he'd heard something he'd been waiting for. "Everything I told you at the newspaper this morning was true," he said, relaxing a bit while still keeping the girl in front of him. "I merely left out the part about the bargain I made with him. Turns out Dave wasn't very clever or much of a strategic thinker, and he knew it. In exchange for a little blood and some skin, I became his personal advisor, helping him with his scheme to get rich and reclaim his ex-wife. Almost sad how easy it was to manipulate the guy. He didn't wonder why I was interested in those client files Reed let him borrow. He actually believed me when I said I was interested in getting into the stock market."

Diego would be the first to admit he'd been a little distracted by the whole blood-and-skin thing, really hating the visual that put in his head, but he hadn't missed the part about Ken's client list. Hobbs played everybody. Especially Dave.

"You got Dave fixated on the big targets, the banks and jewelry stores, while you went behind his back and cherry-picked the good stuff from Ken's client list, knowing it would all lead back to Dave in the end anyway," Diego said. "That way the cops would spend months trying to figure out where Dave hid the stuff, not thinking to look anywhere else."

Hobbs didn't say anything, but the smirk that crossed his face told Diego everything he needed to know. He saw the man's eyes dart toward the windows, likely watching the cop cars pull up outside.

"But for that part to work, you'd need Dave dead, right?" Diego continued, trying to draw Hobbs's attention back to him. "Let me guess...the Federal Reserve job. That was your idea, wasn't it? You pushed him toward a target so big—so impossible—it was bound to backfire and get him killed. You sent the tips to the cops, saying exactly when the job was going down to make sure DPD would be there to clean up this one last loose end."

"Worked with Reed, didn't it?" Hobbs said with a smile. "The only thing I didn't plan for was you. Well, and getting trapped in here."

"You have to know this is over, Hobbs. There's no getting out of here unless you give up."

Diego was afraid the guy would decide to go down in a blaze of glory instead of getting arrested. Which wouldn't have been a big deal, if it wasn't for the girl in his arms.

But suddenly Hobbs pushed the girl away and dropped the knife, turning toward the windows of the café instead of toward Diego and Trey.

"I give up. Take me in," he said, putting his hands behind his back. "But you know that no jury in the world is ever going to believe I made Reed kill himself or that I had anything to do with those bank jobs. There's no connection between me and any of the people Dave had do those jobs."

Trey grabbed the girl and used a big towel to wipe Hobbs's blood off her neck, then quickly wrapped the towel around the man's bleeding hand while Diego cuffed him.

"But we still caught you with all the stuff from Reed's client list," Diego pointed out. "That should get you fifteen to twenty in Coffield. You know where that is, right? I know you've been there."

Hobbs laughed as cops flooded into the place, Hale right up front. "Oh yeah, I know where it is. Though I can't imagine I'll be staying there too long once I *speak* to the right people."

Diego glanced at the patrol cops who walked over to lead Hobbs outside.

"Consider him a biohazard," Diego called out to them. "Spit guard over his head and zero contact with his blood."

The officers nodded their head in understanding, but that didn't wipe the smile off Hobbs's face as they led him out.

Diego watched as the officers put Hobbs in the back of a patrol car. "We can't let that guy into the normal system. He'll be a ghost within hours."

"Maybe this is something we need to call the feds about," Trey said. "STAT seems to have the only people who can handle someone like Hobbs."

Yeah, this was definitely right up their alley.

"You know, I think that'd be a good idea," Diego said as they headed outside, pausing to take in the chaos there. He immediately caught sight of Bree standing out on the street near the SWAT SUV and he smiled. "I don't know about you guys, but it's been one hell of a long day, and I'm ready to think about something else besides bank robbers, blood, and mind control."

"You mean like finally telling Bree she's *The One* for you?" Trey asked with a snort and a poke to the shoulder.

"Maybe not that. Not yet," he said. "But I'm definitely ready to go home with her...and my beta."

CHAPTER 18

"Damn, I really love that guy," Bree said, letting out a dreamy sigh as she watched Diego's biceps flex as he served the volleyball. He, Brandon, Kevin, Knox, Hale, and Connor were playing against a team made up of his pack mates and some beta werewolves, and right now the game was tied. "I mean, I never thought I could love a man this much, but I do."

Beside her, Rachel laughed. They'd been sitting at one of the empty picnic tables for the past fifteen minutes, watching the game along with most of the other people at the SWAT compound there for what Bree learned were their famous weekly cookouts. Trey had put the burgers, steaks, hot dogs, and chicken on the grill—much to the delight of the Pack's pet pooches—and the aroma was already filling the air. She might not have the keen nose of Diego and her son, but she could definitely smell all that delicious food.

"That's because Diego is *The One* for you," Rachel said, reaching out to grab a handful of Doritos from the bowl between them.

Bree smiled, sipping her iced tea as she considered the notion. "I never thought of it like that, but I guess he is."

Over in the volleyball pit, Brandon and Diego high-fived each other after her son scored a point for their team. In the two weeks since Dave had kidnapped them, Diego had been more of a dad to her son than her ex had ever been. And Brandon absolutely loved Diego like a father. She'd never seen her son so happy.

"Diego still hasn't told you, has he?" Rachel asked, grabbing some more chips. "I talked to him the other day about this, and he said he was going to tell you."

Bree picked up a Dorito and nibbled on it, glancing at her. "Told me what?"

Rachel hesitated, as if debating whether to say any more.

"Told me what?" Bree prompted again, a little nervous now.

"Diego should really be filling you in on this, but since he obviously won't, I guess I'll have to." Rachel sighed. "When you fall in love with a werewolf, you're more than soul mates. Diego didn't happen to walk into that diner when you needed him. Fate—or a higher power, I guess you could say, and maybe a little werewolf magic if such a thing exists—put him there. We have a few negotiators on the team, and any of them could have gone on that call, but Diego was the negotiator who did. You two are meant to be together. You're the one woman who's perfect for him and can accept him for being a werewolf. He's the one man you've been looking for your whole life though you didn't even know it."

Bree looked over at Diego again, watching as Brandon volleyed the ball to him and he spiked it over the net. What Rachel said was like something out of a romance book, but the connection she'd described was exactly what she'd been feeling for Diego.

"Why didn't Diego tell me any of this?" she asked.

Rachel made a face. "Because he's a guy and that means he's stupid when it comes to this stuff. He had this idea in his head that you'd be upset if you thought there was some outside force that brought the two of you together."

"What?" Bree frowned. "That's ridiculous."

"That's what I said."

Bree finished her Dorito and reached for another, trying to puzzle out why Diego thought she'd be upset by fate putting them together. She'd already told him on their first date how lucky she and Brandon were to have met him when they both needed him.

She was still thinking about that when Diego and Knox came over to the table with Hale and Connor, plates of food in their hands. She hadn't realized they'd finished their game. Diego's tall, blond pack mate had a small plate for Kat with her own cheeseburger, something the cat appreciated, if the way she jumped up on the table to sit near him was any indication.

"Who won?" she asked as Diego set a plate with a cheeseburger, potato salad, and baked beans in front of her, then sat beside her. His plate had two of everything on it, along with gigantic helpings of sides.

He leaned in to kiss her. "We did. That kid of yours is a damn good volleyball player. I think I actually managed to talk him into trying out for the team at school."

Bree did a double take. Her son had never participated in any extracurricular activities in school, though she'd talked herself blue in the face trying to convince him. Tears stung her eyes, and she gave a Diego a kiss as she blinked them away. "If I didn't already love you so much, I'd fall in love with you for doing that. Thank you."

Diego surprised her by blushing a little, and he quickly took a bite of his cheeseburger.

"Where is Brandon anyway?" she asked, glancing around as she picked up her own burger.

"He and Kevin are eating with the betas and some of the other teens."

Bree followed the direction of Diego's gaze to see Brandon and Kevin sitting at a nearby table, plates of food in front of them. While the food was delicious, the two boys had eyes only for the two teenage girls across from them, who were clearly as interested in Brandon and Kevin. She smiled, unable to help it.

"Something tells me we're going to have to deal with Brandon dating soon," she said to Diego.

"Not if we ground him until he's eighteen," Diego joked.

Bree laughed and bit into her burger. It was juicy and perfectly cooked, the cheese on top gooey and melted over the sides. She almost pinched herself more than once the past two weeks to make sure she wasn't dreaming. But she knew better. No dream she'd ever had could be this wonderful.

After Diego had finished all the paperwork that came with taking Dave and Hobbs into custody—and she'd finished up her own stack of paperwork that came with recovering the stolen property—they'd met up at her apartment to have dinner with Brandon as a family. It would probably still be a while before her son wasn't haunted by seeing Dave try to kill Diego, and he was seeing a psychologist Diego said had helped Rachel through a rough patch, but with each passing day, the memory got more and more distant.

It helped that STAT, the federal agency Diego told her about that handled supernatural threats, took custody of Dave and Hobbs, locking them up someplace where neither of them could ever hurt anyone else. She and Brandon would never have to worry about Dave getting released and inserting himself into their lives again. Luckily, all the people he and Hobbs forced to commit crimes for them wouldn't be going to jail. As far as the world knew, Dave and Hobbs had given their victims a drug known as delirium, and when Diego and his teammates took them down, they destroyed the drug at the same time.

That same night, over dinner, Diego had asked if she and Brandon would like to move in with him. Bree was over the moon at the idea and was thrilled to know Brandon was excited about it, too. He'd been a little nervous he'd have to go to a different high school if they moved, but as it turned out, Diego's house was in the same school district. They'd moved in with Diego the next day. Bree thought that living in the country would take some getting used to, but it was perfect. And while her sister would never say it out loud, she knew Beth was excited to have the apartment to herself. Now, she didn't have to feel guilty about abandoning them to move in with her boyfriend.

Bree was silently marveling at how Diego could have possibly finished his burger and steak and was halfway through his hot dog when Trey came over to join them, grabbing a bite to eat in between manning the grills. His cell phone rang, and he dug it out of his cargo shorts to answer it as he sat down. He mostly listened to whoever it was on the other end before saying something too softly for Bree to hear, then hanging up.

"That was Samantha Mills," he said, cutting into his steak.

"Has she learned what was in Dave's and Hobbs's blood?" Diego asked.

Even though STAT had moved in quickly to whisk Dave and Hobbs away to keep anyone from coming into contact with their blood, Trey had given the medical examiner the piece of material Diego had used to wipe the blood off Brandon and the bubble wrap that had Hobbs's blood on it. While SWAT had a good relationship with STAT, they weren't confident the feds would tell them what was in the blood that turned Dave and Hobbs into puppet masters.

"Nothing beyond what she already told us about there being something in it she can't identify," Trey said.

"Then why did she call?" Hale asked. "Or did she just want to hear your voice?"

"Funny." Trey scowled. "While she doesn't know what's in their blood, she learned Will Bremen was part of an international research team studying a Paleolithic man they found frozen in the ice in Antarctica. She thinks the man they found had this same stuff in his DNA."

"Kind of like we have something in ours that makes us werewolves," Diego mused, digging into his potato salad.

Trey nodded. "A few days after thawing this guy, there was a fire at the research station that supposedly destroyed everything, including their big find. Bremen was the only one who survived."

"That's convenient," Connor muttered. "It sucks not knowing what really happened up there."

"Dave told me Bremen said he got some of the guy's DNA in his system, but he didn't know how," Bree offered.

"Let's hope Bremen was the only one on that research team who did, or who knows how many people might be out there right now with the same capability," Diego said.

That was a scary thought.

On the other side of the table, Hale scooped up a forkful of baked beans. "So, you ever going to stop playing games and ask Samantha out or what?"

Trey flushed, mumbled something about going to put some more burgers on to cook, then got up from the table and made a beeline for the grills.

"What was that about?" Bree asked.

Diego chuckled. "Trey has it bad for the good doctor but won't admit it."

"Ah," she said.

As they finished eating, Diego and his pack mates placed bets on if and when Trey and Samantha Mills ever got together, and if so, which one would ask the other out first.

On the other side of her, Rachel set her knife and fork on her empty plate. "Who's ready for another game of volleyball?"

When everyone collected their empty plates and tossed them in the trash except Diego, Rachel lifted a brow in his direction.

"You guys go ahead," he said. "I'm going to hang out with Bree."

Rachel gave him a knowing grin, then hurried over to catch up with her pack mates already heading for the volleyball sand pit, Kat trotting alongside Connor.

Beside Bree, Diego leaned in close, his warm breath tickling her ear. "Brandon told me he's staying over at Kevin's house tonight."

"Uh-huh," she said. "That means we have that big house all to ourselves, so you'll be able to tell me about *The One*."

Diego jerked back, doing a double take. "Who told you about that?"

"Rachel."

He scowled. "I should have known."

Bree lifted her hand to cup his scruff-covered jaw. "Did you really think I'd be upset we're destined to be together?"

Diego shrugged, giving her a sheepish look. "I wasn't sure and I didn't want to mess things up."

"You could never mess things up," she said, kissing him. "I've known I was going to fall in love with you since our first date. Knowing we're soul mates makes what we have that much more special. And when we get home, I'm going to show you how much."

He rested his forehead against hers. "Home. I like the sound of that."

Don't miss Paige Tyler's all-new, pulse-pounding SWAT spin-off series. Keep reading for an excerpt of the first book in STAT: Special Threat Assessment Team

WOLF UNDER FIRE

Available now from Sourcebooks Casablanca

London

Jestina Ridley moved through the dark, dirty alley, careful to avoid the broken glass and occasional uncapped syringe, praying something useful would come out of this little visit to the seedier side of Stockwell. But after sidestepping one especially wet and smelly patch of asphalt, she rephrased that thought, deciding this particular part of southwest London was pretty much all seedy. Definitely not the kind of place tourists flocked to after midnight.

Good thing I'm not a tourist.

"I've got nothing," Jaime Wilkerson grumbled through the tiny radio bud wedged in her ear. "I told you this was going to be a waste of time. That guy we talked to doesn't know squat about this kidnapping."

"In all fairness, he never said the kidnappers were holding the girl here," Neal Goodwin, the other member of their

Special Threat Assessment Team, pointed out, his gravelly voice rough over the radio. "He said the people who grabbed the kid used one of these abandoned buildings to stage their equipment and plan the job. He didn't say they'd still be here."

Jes stifled a groan. Neal was right, but she'd hoped they'd get lucky all the same. She and the other two members of her STAT team had been in London for three days checking out a kidnapping with clear supernatural indicators, and so far, they'd come up with nothing.

A week ago, someone had snatched fourteen-year-old Olivia Phillips out of her bedroom on the eighth floor of her apartment building. Her father was a high-level official in MI5, the British Security Service, which meant the place where they lived had better security than most, including watchdog monitors on all the elevators and doors, as well as cameras along every corridor and a handful of roving guards.

None of it had mattered. Olivia had gone missing in the middle of the night and whoever kidnapped her had left the two men guarding the building dead, their throats torn out. The way the men had been killed—along with the mystery of how the kidnappers had gotten into the apartment—had immediately put the crime on STAT's radar, since it looked like the handiwork of supernatural creatures.

After seeing autopsy photos of the guards' bodies, Jes had no doubt some kind of paranormal was involved in the kidnapping, but that didn't make it any easier to track down the thing. Especially since Olivia's parents had stopped cooperating with law enforcement within twenty-four hours of the girl's disappearance, claiming they were doing it on the advice of legal counsel. Jes thought it was more likely because the kidnappers had contacted them to negotiate a ransom and warned them not to involve the cops. Considering the father worked for MI5, it was also possible he was freezing out the locals and letting the British version of the FBI handle the investigation.

Not that it mattered who was running the case for the Brits. Jes and her team were here for one reason—to determine if there were supernatural elements at play and deal with them accordingly. Because that's what STAT did: figured out what scary thing they were dealing with and made it go away.

"All right, let's call it a night. Wrap up whatever you're doing and meet back at the car." She sighed. "We'll come back tomorrow and check out the area again, this time in the daylight. I doubt we'll find anything, but maybe we'll get lucky and someone might remember seeing something."

Jaime and Neal agreed, sounding as frustrated as she felt. Both of the guys had been with STAT for over a year and knew how bad it could be in the real world when things that went bump in the night targeted their prey. Olivia had been missing for so long, even one more night could mean the difference between getting the girl back alive or not.

Jes continued along the alley, checking out the rear entrances to a series of low-cost government housing buildings that looked like they hadn't seen a legitimate tenant in years. The doors were nailed shut, the windows boarded up, and there wasn't a single light to be seen inside or out. If there was a place in this neighborhood where a supernatural creature might hang out, it'd be here. But when she stopped every so often and peeked through the cracks between the wooden slats over the windows, shining her small flashlight inside, she didn't see anyone.

She was heading toward the grassy side of the apartment building to meet up with the rest of her team when she heard a low, menacing growl over her earpiece that chilled her to the core. It was immediately followed by gunshots, then shouting.

Jaime and Neal.

Crap!

Pulse pounding, Jes pulled her Sig 9mm with her free hand, clicking off the safety with her thumb as she raced across the scrubby grass in the direction of the sound. She rounded the corner of the building to find herself face-to-face with construction equipment, trash-filled dumpsters, and a handful of big, metal storage pods. As she weaved her way through the maze, she realized the growls and gunfire had ceased and all that was left was an eerie silence. She fervently prayed that meant Jaime and Neal had taken down whatever the hell they'd come across.

But if they had, why hadn't they called out *all clear* over the radio?

"Jaime? Neal? Do you copy?"

No answer.

Double crap!

Jes smelled the blood before she saw the two bodies lying motionless on the ground near one of the dumpsters. She ran toward them, her heart in her throat. If she could pick up the odor of blood, there had to be a bucketload of it.

There was.

Dark red pools of it that looked black even in the glow of her flashlight.

Damn, she hated being right.

Knowing her teammates were almost assuredly dead but needing to check all the same, she crouched beside Jaime when movement near one of the storage containers caught her attention. She jerked her head up to see something big and hulking in the darkness less than fifteen feet away. That same low growl she'd heard before rumbled from its chest as it gazed at her with glowing yellow eyes, and a chill ran along her spine.

Jes brought up her weapon, resting it on the hand that held the flashlight, and pulled the trigger in quick succession, knowing there was no way she could miss at this distance. But the creature disappeared before the bullets could find their mark. One moment, it was there, and the next, it was gone. Before she'd even gotten a good look at it.

As fast as the thing moved, it could easily come at her from a dozen different directions, but she couldn't worry about that. One or both of her teammates might be alive. All that mattered was helping them.

But when she turned her flashlight on Jaime and Neal, she realized it was too late. Whatever had killed them had savagely torn out their throats. They had been dead before they'd hit the ground.

She swallowed hard and pulled out her phone, thumbing the speed-dial button for the STAT emergency operation center in Washington, DC as she scanned the area around her for the creature that had killed her teammates.

"This is Agent Ridley," she said. "Two agents are down and I need a cleanup team out here ASAP. Tell McKay we have confirmed supernatural involvement. I'm going to need backup."

Washington, DC

Jake Huang cursed silently as he strode down yet another hallway on the fourth floor of the J. Edgar Hoover building. How the hell was he going to find the conference room where he was supposed to meet with his new boss in this damn maze? He supposed he could ask one of the other FBI agents who zipped past him in their perfect professional clothes with their perfectly styled hair and perfectly shined shoes, but ultimately, he couldn't bring himself to admit he didn't know his way around the place yet. He was a federal agent now. Shouldn't he know this kind of stuff?

Then again, maybe he should cut himself a break. He'd only been in DC for less than a week and had spent most of that time trying to find a place for him and the twins to live. His boss, Nathan McKay, had given him a quick whirlwind tour of the huge FBI headquarters, then told him to focus on getting settled before worrying about the job. Of course, that was before McKay had called this morning telling him he had thirty minutes to be at the office.

So much for getting settled in.

If it were just him, Jake would have grabbed the first apartment he could find close to work and called it a day, but he had other people in his life now, namely Zoe and Chloe Haynes, the eighteen-year-old beta werewolves he'd rescued from a vampire coven and recently become responsible for. Bringing teenage werewolves who'd gone through their first change barely two months ago to a city as big as Washington, DC was crazy to say the least, but that's what it meant when an alpha stumbled across betas who needed him. They became a pack and a huge part of each other's lives.

When McKay had offered him a position on the joint FBI/CIA Special Threat Assessment Team—aka STAT—the first thing he'd done was ask Zoe and Chloe what they thought. If they'd been against the idea, he would have walked away from the once-in-a-lifetime opportunity. Even though it meant uprooting the life they'd just started in Dallas, the twins had urged him to take the job. The girls were thrilled at the idea of living in the nation's capital, while he was excited to have a job that would let him openly reveal his werewolf nature and use the abilities that came with it.

Jake turned down another long hallway, sure he'd covered every square foot of the floor he was on, when he picked up a familiar scent—werewolves. One female alpha. One male omega. Doubting there could be many people like him wandering around the building, he let his nose lead him in the right direction.

He chided himself for not thinking of using his keen sense of smell before this. Then again, he'd only recently started embracing his werewolf side. Ever since he'd first turned four years ago, he'd done his best to forget what he'd become.

He half closed his eyes, letting his sense of smell take over and guide him in the right direction. That not only let him shut out a lot of the external distractions so he could focus on the two scents, instead of everything going on around him, but it also kept anyone from freaking out if they noticed his dark eyes were now bright golden yellow. Having someone see him walking the halls like he was stoned wasn't ideal, but it wasn't as bad as them realizing his eyes were glowing like some sort of creature on Halloween.

Fortunately, nobody seemed to notice one way or the other.

A few moments later, he walked into a small conference room to find Harley Grant and Caleb Lynch waiting for him. McKay, thankfully, was nowhere in sight. At least Jake wasn't late.

"Either of you have any idea what McKay wants to see us about?" Jake asked as he sat down across the table from the two werewolves he was somehow supposed to form a pack with even though they'd just met a few days ago.

As if all it took was shoving the three of them in a small room together and waiting for magic to happen.

Jake wasn't an expert on the subject, but from what he'd heard, werewolves were normally drawn together naturally, finding each other without having to work at it. Kind of like him with Zoe and Chloe. But McKay had hired him and the other two werewolves with the expectation that they'd form a pack. Probably because McKay had recently worked with another pack of werewolves—namely the Dallas PD SWAT Team—and seen how impressive the results could be when people like them worked together.

"No clue." Caleb leaned back in his chair, casually propping the sole of his boot on the edge of the table. Tall, with dark eyes and a perpetual smirk, his shaggy, dark blond hair looked like it hadn't seen a brush in a week. "McKay said it was something urgent, but it's been an hour since he brought us in here, so I guess it can't be that urgent."

Jake winced. "That's probably my fault. He called me forty-five minutes ago, but it took me a while to get here. All I know is that he's got a mission for us."

Caleb looked like he couldn't care less about Jake's

excuse or the mission. Actually, he didn't look like he gave a damn about anything.

That was par for the course with omega werewolves. And Caleb was a prototypical omega. Big, strong, and as fast as any alpha, he was barely able to keep his inherent werewolf nature under control, not to mention he was nearly incapable of caring about anybody but himself. Loners by choice, omegas rarely formed pack bonds. Jake could only imagine how much fun it was going to be trying to get the man integrated into the team.

To make matters worse, Caleb was a convicted criminal. The only reason he wasn't in jail right now was because he'd agreed to work for STAT. One screwup and the man would go straight back to prison. Jake didn't know exactly what the other werewolf had done to get him tossed in a cell or why the commander of the Dallas SWAT Team had vouched for him, but he had, and now, Caleb was Jake's problem.

Jake glanced at the third member of their dysfunctional pack to see if she had anything to add to the discussion. From the disinterested look on the pretty blond werewolf's face, Harley didn't seem to care any more than Caleb did about the meeting.

He wished he could say he was surprised, but he wasn't. While he'd only talked to the female alpha for a while the first day they'd met, Jake could already tell gaining her trust wasn't going to be easy. From the little she'd said about her werewolf abilities, he got the feeling she'd yet to accept her inner wolf. He couldn't shake the sensation that Harley didn't like what she was. It made him wonder what the hell McKay had said to get her to agree to the job.

Jake opened his mouth to ask if either Caleb or Harley

had found a place to live yet—because the silence was starting to get uncomfortable and it seemed like a safe thing to talk about—when the door to the conference room opened and their boss walked in. Brown hair sporting a touch of gray at the temples, McKay appeared every inch the federal agent, right down to the black suit and wire-rimmed glasses.

Harley sat up a little straighter.

Caleb didn't even have the good sense to take his foot off the table—nice to confirm he did indeed have the social graces of a sea slug.

Two other agents were with McKay, a man and woman, both of whom were probably in their mid- to late-twenties. Six feet tall with dark hair, a square jaw, and blue eyes that looked like they didn't miss a thing, the guy looked like someone central casting would give you if you asked for a standard-issue FBI agent, dark suit and red power tie included.

The woman, on the other hand, was different. In fact, the only thing "standard issue" about the petite agent was the navy-blue pantsuit she wore. And while Jake wasn't an expert on the FBI or CIA, he was pretty sure her vivid purple hair wasn't the norm. But that wasn't the only thing unique about her. Nope. Her eyes were purple, too. Lavender, actually. At first, he thought she was wearing contacts but then realized the color was real.

Considering STAT had recently recruited werewolves, it wasn't surprising to think they hired other supernaturals. Maybe the unique-looking woman was more different than she appeared.

"Sorry I'm late," McKay apologized.

He closed the door, then flipped a switch on the control panel beside it. A moment later, a high-pitched hum filled the room, making Jake wince. On the other side of the table, Harley and Caleb mirrored his reaction. Shrill noises and keen hearing didn't mix, but the meeting must be seriously classified if McKay was going with a frequency jammer to keep anyone else from picking up their conversation.

"Jake Huang, Harley Grant, Caleb Lynch, meet two more members of the team—Forrest Albright and Mistal Swanson." McKay pulled out the rolling chair at the head of the table and took a seat. "Forrest was FBI for almost five years before joining STAT a year and a half ago. Misty has been with the organization a little less than that."

While McKay fiddled with the keyboard on the table in front of him, trying to boot up the computer connected to the huge screen on the front wall, Misty sat down in the empty chair next to Jake. Forrest sat beside her.

"What about you, Misty?" Caleb said, casually eyeing the woman across from him. "McKay didn't say where you worked before joining STAT."

Mistal flipped her long, colorful hair over her shoulder and turned her gaze on the omega. "McKay recruited me after I graduated from college because of my unique abilities."

That was cryptic, Jake thought. Harley seemed just as curious. "What abilities are those?"

At the far end of the table, McKay finished tapping on the keyboard as the STAT organization's logo filled the screen, along with several warnings about protecting classified information and sensitive sources.

"Misty is a technopath," their new boss said, as if that explained everything. When Jake and his fellow werewolves continued to stare at him, McKay added, "She's similar to a telepath, only she reads electronic equipment, not people."

Jake had no idea what the hell McKay was talking about. At least Harley and Caleb seemed equally confused.

"Okay," Jake said. "But that doesn't really answer my question."

McKay looked at Misty. "Want to give them a demonstration?"

Lips curving, Misty held her hand out to Jake. "Give me your cell phone."

He'd just upgraded his phone before moving there, so he didn't want Misty blowing it up or anything. But he had to admit he was curious, so he dug it out of his pocket and handed it to her. Before his eyes, Misty's lavender irises went completely white, making her seem even more supernatural.

"Your pass code is 1-2-3-4? Seriously?" She laughed. "Not that there's much in here to protect. A contact list with a dozen names and a handful of photos, all of them with the same two kids—twin girls. You're in some of them. And you're smiling." Misty's eyes returned to their normal lavender as she handed the phone back to him. "You should smile more often. It's a good look on you."

Jake stared at her, not sure what to say to that. Hell, he didn't even understand what he'd heard.

"I can access any electronic device I touch," she explained. "And since the Internet connects everything and everyone, that means I can get into pretty much anywhere and anything if I want to."

"So you're basically a hacker?" Caleb's voice was casual as usual, but Jake got the feeling he was impressed.

Misty gave him a smile. "Yes. Although I prefer the word technopath."

"How is that even possible?" Harley asked, a stunned expression on her face.

Misty opened her mouth to answer, but McKay interrupted.

"I understand you all have questions, and any other time, I'd have the whole team get to know each other, but unfortunately, that's not an option right now. We have a situation in London. Two STAT agents are dead. I need to get your team up to speed and on a plane ASAP."

Jake sat up straighter.

Shit just got real.

Fast.

And they were going to have to learn how to be a team and work together—fast.

He shoved his phone in his pocket. "What do we have?"

McKay pushed a button on the keyboard. The moment a photo of a red-haired teen girl with freckles appeared on the screen, their boss went into briefing mode, telling them fourteen-year-old Olivia Phillips had recently been kidnapped and that the security guards for her apartment building had their throats ripped out.

"At approximately 0200 this morning London time, our STAT team was attacked by an unknown supernatural." McKay flipped to another slide, this one of two men lying on the ground with their throats torn out, blood soaking their ragged clothes.

He moved to the next slide, a photo of a beautiful woman with full, pouty lips, long dark hair, and even darker eyes. Jake was so locked on the picture he barely heard what McKay was saying until he realized the woman was the third member of the team in London. Which meant she was soon going to be *his* teammate. His heart suddenly hammered in his chest at the thought.

What the hell?

"Senior field agent Jestina Ridley didn't get a good look at the creature but took several shots at it. The thing is so fast it disappeared in a blur before she could even hit it."

Jake frowned, dragging his gaze away from the photo, getting his head back in the game and wondering if that was an exaggeration on Agent Ridley's part. The creature couldn't actually be that fast. Then again, she could also have been so rattled by the brutal death of her teammates, she'd been confused about what had happened afterward. It wouldn't be the first time he'd seen someone do that in a stressful situation.

McKay must have seen the doubt on Jake's face because he gave him a pointed look. "Don't downplay Jes's observations. She's got more field experience with supernaturals than any other agent in STAT. If she says the creature was so fast it was a blur, then it was a blur. You're the lead agent for the team—that was part of the deal when we recruited you. And while you have a load of tactical expertise, Jes has been dealing with supernatural creatures for a long time. Make good use of her experience with them."

"Understood," Jake said.

He didn't have a problem working with someone more experienced in the field. He might have been a Navy SEAL and a cop in his former life, but this agent thing was new. Although he couldn't imagine she'd be thrilled to work for someone so lacking in seniority as far as time in STAT was concerned. Hopefully, it wouldn't be an issue.

"For reasons we haven't fully worked out yet, Olivia's

parents are no longer cooperating with the police, which makes it difficult to determine exactly what the current situation is and how these supernaturals are involved," McKay continued. "It could be a vampire, a werewolf, or something completely different."

While Jake wasn't thrilled at the idea of facing more vampires—he'd had his fill of them weeks ago out in Los Angeles—the possibility of going up against other werewolves sucked even worse, and he hoped the supernaturals who'd kidnapped Olivia and butchered those four men were anything other than his own kind.

Across from him, Harley and Caleb looked like they were thinking the same thing.

"When you get to London, you'll hook up with Jes at the American Embassy, confirm what kind of creatures we're dealing with, and figure out how to stop them." McKay looked at each of them in turn. "This goes without saying, but don't let anyone else know what you're in the UK for or what you're doing. The world isn't supposed to know supernaturals exist, much less that we have some working for the U.S. intelligence community."

McKay didn't have to worry about Jake saying anything to anyone. Like most werewolves, he was good at hiding what he was. His gut told him Harley and Caleb were no different.

Jake's gaze went to the computer screen at the front of the room and the photo of Jestina Ridley again. While his human side was already focused on the importance of the mission, his inner wolf was eager to get to London for a completely different reason—the gorgeous STAT agent he'd be working with.

ACKNOWLEDGMENTS

I hope you had as much fun reading Bree and Diego's story as I had writing it! If you read the previous book in the SWAT: Special Wolf Alpha Team Series (*Wolf Rebel*) then you remember we hinted at *The One* for Diego. What we didn't tell you is that his mate would have a teenage son who is a newly turned beta werewolf!

This whole series wouldn't be possible without some very incredible people. In addition to another big thank-you to my hubby for all his help with the action scenes and military and tactical jargon, thanks to my fantastic agent, Courtney Miller-Callihan, and editors at Sourcebooks (who are always a phone call, text, or email away whenever I need something), and all the other amazing people at Sourcebooks, including my fantastic publicist and the crazy-talented art department. The covers they make for me are seriously droolworthy!

Because I could never leave out my readers, a huge thank-you to everyone who reads my books and Snoopy Danced right along with me with every new release. That includes the fantastic people on my amazing Review Team, as well my assistant, Janet. You rock!

I also want to give a big thank-you to the men, women, and working dogs who protect and serve in police departments everywhere, as well as their families.

And a very special shout-out to our favorite restaurant, P.F. Chang's, where hubby and I bat story lines back and forth and come up with all of our best ideas, as well as a thank-you to our fantastic waiter-turned-manager, Andrew, who makes sure our order is ready the moment we walk in the door!

Hope you enjoy the next book in the SWAT: Special Wolf Alpha Team series coming soon from Sourcebooks, and look forward to reading the rest of the series as much as I look forward to sharing it with you. Also, don't forget to look for my new series from Sourcebooks, STAT: Special Threat Assessment Team, a spin-off from SWAT!

If you love a man in uniform as much as I do, make sure you check out X-OPS, my other action-packed paranormal/romantic-suspense series from Sourcebooks.

Happy Reading!

ABOUT THE AUTHOR

Paige Tyler is a *New York Times* and *USA Today* bestselling author of sexy, romantic suspense and paranormal romance. She and her very own military hero (also known as her husband) live on the beautiful Florida coast with their adorable fur baby (also known as their dog). Paige graduated with a degree in education, but decided to pursue her passion and write books about hunky alpha males and the kick-butt heroines who fall in love with them.

Visit Paige at her website at paigetylertheauthor.com.

She's also on Facebook, Twitter, Tumblr, Instagram, Tsu, Wattpad, and Pinterest.

X-OPS EXPOSED

More thrilling action and sizzling romance from *New York Times* bestselling author Paige Tyler

Lion hybrid and former Army Ranger Tanner Howland retreats into the forests of Washington State to be alone. He's too dangerous to be around people—including his love, Dr. Zarina Sokolov. Little does he know, she's following him.

Zarina is determined to save Tanner with the anti-serum she hopes will turn him human again. But a vicious ring pitting hybrids against each other for sport lies in wait. Can Tanner save his fellow hybrids and Zarina—or will he lose control again?

"Everything that fans [have] been patiently waiting for and more."

—*RT Book Reviews*, ★★★★

"Does it get any better than this? Tyler...is an absolute master!"

—*Fresh Fiction*

For more Paige Tyler, visit:

sourcebooks.com

NIGHT OF THE BILLIONAIRE WOLF

USA Today bestselling author Terry Spear brings you a shifter world like no other

Lexi Summerfield built her business from the ground up. But with great wealth comes great responsibility, and some drawbacks she could never have anticipated. Lexi never knows who she can trust… And for good reason—the paparazzi are dogging her, and so is someone else with evil intent.

When Lexi meets bodyguard and gray wolf shifter Ryder Gallagher on the hiking trails, she breaks her own rules about getting involved. But secrets have a way of surfacing. And with the danger around Lexi escalating, Ryder will do whatever it takes to stay by her side…

"Entertaining and suspenseful, an amazing read."

—*Night Owl Reviews* for *Billionaire in Wolf's Clothing*

For more info about Sourcebooks's books and authors, visit:

sourcebooks.com

WICKED COWBOY WOLF

Cowboys by day, wolf shifters by night—don't
miss the thrilling Seven Range Shifters series
from acclaimed author Kait Ballenger

Years ago, Grey Wolf Jared Black was cast from the pack for a crime he didn't commit. Now, he's the mysterious criminal wolf known only as the Rogue, a name his former packmates won't soon forget. But when a vampire threat endangers the lives of their entire species, Jared must confront his former packmates again, even if that means betraying the only woman he's ever loved...

"This story has it all—a heroine with grit and a hero who backs up his tough talk with action."

—*Fresh Fiction* for *Cowboy Wolf Trouble*

For more info about Sourcebooks's
books and authors, visit:
sourcebooks.com

BEARS BEHAVING BADLY

An extraordinary new series from bestselling author MaryJanice Davidson featuring a foster care system for orphaned shifter kids (and kits, and cubs)

Annette Garsea is the fiercest bear shifter the interspecies foster care system has ever seen. She fights hard for the safety and happiness of the at-risk shifter teens and babies in her charge—and you do not want to get on the wrong side of a mama werebear.

Handsome, growly bear shifter PI David Auberon has secretly been in love with Annette since forever but he's too shy to make a move. All he can do is offer her an unlimited supply of Skittles and hope she'll notice him. She's noticed the appealingly scruffy PI (and his sugar fixation), all right, but the man's barely ever said more than five words to her... Until they encounter an unexpected threat from within and put everything aside to fight for their vulnerable charges. Dodging unidentified enemies puts them in a tight spot. Very tight. Together. Tonight...

"Davidson is in peak form in this hilarious, sexy, and heartfelt paranormal romance."

—*Booklist* Starred Review

For more info about Sourcebooks's books and authors, visit:
sourcebooks.com

Also by Paige Tyler

STAT: Special Threat Assessment Team

Wolf Under Fire

SWAT: Special Wolf Alpha Team

Hungry Like the Wolf

Wolf Trouble

In the Company of Wolves

To Love a Wolf

Wolf Unleashed

Wolf Hunt

Wolf Hunger

Wolf Rising

Wolf Instinct

Wolf Rebel

X-Ops

Her Perfect Mate

Her Lone Wolf

Her Secret Agent (novella)

Her Wild Hero

Her Fierce Warrior

Her Rogue Alpha

Her True Match

Her Dark Half

X-Ops Exposed